# MURDEROUS OPPORTUNITIES

## BOOK 5 OF THE WILBARGER COUNTY SERIES

## DIANNE SMITHWICK-BRADEN

D S B
Mysteries

First printing

Paperback ISBN: 978-1-7324735-6-0

ebook ISBN: 978-1-7324735-7-7

Published By DSB Mysteries
www.diannesmithwick-braden.com

Cover design by Dave King   kingsizecreations.com

Printed in the United States of America
Suggested retail price $15.95

*For Mama*

# MURDEROUS OPPORTUNITES

# CHAPTER ONE

ANDREW CLIFTON COULD HEAR the hum of a large fan turned on high. He thought he heard strange music as well. *What is Maddie doing?*

He opened his eyes and quickly closed them again. He didn't know where that bright light was coming from, but he wanted it to disappear.

"Maddie, will you turn that thing off?"

There was no response.

"Maddie! Turn that damn thing off! It's the middle of the night!"

Still no answer.

He covered his eyes with his hand and peered through the space between his fingers. He looked around the room.

*This isn't my bedroom!*

Drew tried to sit up but fell back onto the bed with his eyes closed. It felt like his brain was trying to pound its way out of his skull. The room spiraled and twisted like he was looking through a kaleidoscope.

He waited until the room stopped spinning to look around

again. He was lying on a twin bed covered with a navy-blue quilt. An identical bed was across the room. Matching curtains hung on the windows. Dallas Cowboy and Denver Bronco posters adorned the walls.

He slowly sat up. The hammering in his head intensified with every movement. He rested his elbows on his knees and held his head in his hands, waiting for the waves of nausea to subside.

*Where am I? When did I get here? How did I get here?*

He searched his pants pockets. His cell phone, wallet, and keys were missing.

*Oh, this isn't good! Think, Drew, think! Where did you go? What did you do?*

He held his head in his hands again and tried to focus. He remembered arguing with Maddie. He remembered leaving the house. He remembered driving.

*I went to a bar. I ordered a couple of drinks. I talked with a woman. We had a few drinks together…*

Drew lifted his head, and his eyes opened wide.

*No! No, I couldn't have! Maddie will never forgive me if I…*

He got to his feet and staggered toward the bedroom door. He stumbled into a hallway and shouted.

"Hello! Is anybody here?"

No one answered.

A door was ajar a few feet from where he stood. The bright light, music, and fan noise came from inside the room.

He teetered toward the door and shouted over the noise, "Hello! I'm sorry to bother you, but I need to get home."

When there was no response, he pushed the door open. His eyes, unaccustomed to the bright light, began to water. He shielded them with his hands and shouted again. The music and fan were too loud for anyone to hear.

When his eyes began to adjust, he peered inside. There was someone in the tanning bed. Stepping into the room, he saw clothing lying on a nearby chair. Realizing the tanner was nude, he covered his eyes with one hand and knocked on the top of the tanning bed with the other.

"Hello! Can you help me!"

There was still no answer.

He raised the top of the tanning bed enough to get the tanner's attention and kept his eyes directed toward the face.

"I'm so sorry to bother you, but…."

Drew screamed in horror. Bile rose in his throat. He tore from the room and ran through the house. In his flight, he toppled over an ottoman and knocked a lamp off an end table.

At last, he reached an exit. He jerked the door open and stumbled off the porch, falling to his knees. The contents of his stomach spewed onto the lawn.

He heard heavy footsteps coming toward him. Looking up, he saw a dark form framed in the glow of the porchlight.

"Looks like you've had one hell of a night," said a gruff male voice.

Large hands picked Drew up and roughly dusted him off.

Drew tried to tell the man what he'd seen, but the words stuck in his throat. He pointed toward the house and tried to break free.

"Had a few too many," said the voice. "I'll get you home."

Again, Drew tried to explain. He struggled to show the stranger what had happened when the words wouldn't come. He gestured wildly and stammered. "In the there…somebody…in there."

The man led Drew to his car and pushed him into the passenger seat. Drew struggled to get out. The man punched him in the face and closed the door.

The stranger got into the driver's seat and fastened his seatbelt.

"Tryin' to tell me somethin'?" the man chuckled. "Guess it can wait."

He started the engine and drove away with Drew unconscious in the passenger seat.

* * *

The morning sun streamed through the bedroom window and woke Sheriff Wade Adams from a sound sleep. He rolled over and looked at the clock.

"Lizzie! We've overslept!" he shouted and bolted out of bed. "I should be on my way to work by now!"

Lizzie jumped up and hurried toward the kitchen. "I'll find something for your breakfast while you get dressed."

"I don't have time," Wade called after her. "I'll get coffee at the office."

"Aren't you hungry?" Lizzie asked with concern and turned toward him.

"I'll send somebody for donuts," he answered while he dressed. " Or I'll have a big lunch."

Wade put on his cowboy boots and stood. He took his bride of thirteen months in his arms and kissed her.

Lizzie snuggled into his arms. "I wish you didn't have to go in today."

"Me too. Do you have a full schedule?"

"Not too bad," Lizzie answered. "I have four client meetings.

The couple walked arm in arm to Wade's truck.

"I'd rather stay here with you, but I'd better get going," Wade said.

"We'll be all alone this weekend," Lizzie reminded him. "We should take advantage of every minute."

"I like the sound of that," Wade said with a mischievous grin and kissed her goodbye. "I'll see you tonight."

"Have a good day," Lizzie said and watched him drive away.

The newlyweds lived at the Paradise Creek Inn. It was located on the Fletcher farm in western Wilbarger County, Texas. The Fletchers owned and operated the family business.

Lizzie was the managing partner. She had lived at the inn since she returned from Chicago six years earlier. It was her education and experience that made the venture a success.

Arson forced the business to close for more than a year. It had been a struggle to recover the family's primary source of income.

Business at the inn had been steady since the newlyweds returned from their March honeymoon. Lizzie had been booking events and guests every day. The upcoming holiday season looked promising.

The couple decided it was best to begin their life together at the inn. Lizzie needed to be on-site for overnight guests. She often worked late during scheduled events. Wade didn't work late unless it was crucial.

Wade drove into town thinking about how his life had changed since marrying Lizzie. They'd taken a short weekend trip to celebrate their first anniversary. Since then, there had been little time to call their own. He and Lizzie were both looking forward to the weekend.

Running the inn was more demanding than he realized. Before they married, he stayed at his place when the Fletchers were busy with guests or events.

Now, there was nowhere else to go. The house he once leased had a new occupant. Deputy Brandon Lodge allowed him to use the guest room when needed. But it wasn't the same.

Wade parked in his space at the Wilbarger County Sheriff's department and went inside. Lost in his thoughts, he was startled when a deputy greeted him.

"Morning, Sheriff."

Wade tried to mask his surprise and said, "Good morning, Wagner. You're here late. Was it a busy shift?"

"No, it was another slow one," answered Drake Wagner. "I was waiting for someone else to come in before leaving. Maddie called and said she'd be late. Something about her son."

"I'll hold down the fort," Wade said. "Go home and relax."

"Thanks, I'll see you tomorrow," said Drake and left Wade alone.

Wade strode into his office, put his hat on the shelf, and sat down. He drummed his fingers on the desk. Wade didn't like Drake Wagner. His feelings made attempts at casual conversation awkward. He would have stayed to chat if his other deputies had been there.

When the Wilbarger County Commission approved the funds to hire two new deputies last year, he'd been excited at the prospect of being fully staffed. His excitement waned when Maddie presented him with Drake Wagner's application.

He'd thought it best to leave the decision to the rest of the team. In the end, they chose Wagner and Sherri Logsdon.

Both were a good fit for the department. The only things against Wager were his lack of experience and the fact that he was Lizzie's ex.

Wade would have preferred to remain shorthanded, but that wouldn't have been fair. The team had worked overtime and extra shifts far too long. He promised his team that he'd put his personal feelings aside and make the best of the situation.

He could ignore his animosity for Drake when they were busy. Unfortunately, it appeared that the criminals of Wilbarger County had collectively decided to take a break.

The low criminal activity was good for the county. But it made for long, dull days at the Sheriff's department. Wade knew from experience that the lull wouldn't last long.

A light tap on his door interrupted his thoughts.

"Hi, Maddie. How are the party plans going?"

Maddie gave him a weak smile and wiped a tear from her cheek. "Do you have a minute?"

Wade looked at his deputy and realized something was seriously wrong. Maddie seldom cried, especially at work. He stood up and walked toward her.

"Of course, sit down. Do you want some coffee?"

"No, thanks. I'll get some later," Maddie replied.

Wade closed his office door and sat down in a chair beside her.

"Are you all right?"

"Not really. I'm sorry I was late this morning. I had to take Brody to daycare and check on something."

"I thought Drew took him to daycare every morning."

"He does, but…he couldn't today."

"Maddie, what's wrong?" Wade coaxed and took her hand.

"I…I…can't find Drew," she said and broke down.

Wade got up, took a box of tissues from a shelf, and handed it to Maddie. He returned to his seat and waited until she was ready to talk.

Maddie sniffed and said, "I haven't heard from him since last night."

"Tell me what happened."

"We had a big fight, and he stormed…out…out of the house. I don't know…if he even realizes that…that today is Brody's birthday," Maddie said between sobs.

"I see," Wade replied. He didn't know what else to say.

"I've called his cell at least every thirty minutes," Maddie continued after she'd regained control. "It rang at first, but now it goes to voicemail. I started texting him, but he hasn't answered."

"You've had arguments in the past and managed to work it out, haven't you? I'm sure you'll be able to work this out too. He might have gone to his folks' or a friend's house."

Maddie blew her nose and shook her head. "His family and friends haven't heard from him. I went by the bank after I dropped Brody off. He didn't show up for work this morning."

"Drew probably needed some time to clear his head," Wade said, trying to reassure her. "I'm sure you'll hear from him soon."

"Wade, you don't understand," Maddie said and swallowed hard, trying to find the right words. "Drew hasn't been himself lately. It's…it's hard…to talk about."

"Maddie, you know I'm here for you," Wade began. "And what

you tell me won't go any further. But wouldn't you be more comfortable talking with someone else, a minister or professional counselor?"

Maddie shook her head and wiped a tear from her cheek. "I know I can trust you, and you're the one person who might understand."

"All right, I'm listening."

"First, I have a personal question to ask, if you don't mind."

"You can ask me anything. I'll tell you if it's too personal."

Maddie looked down at the tissue in her hands for a moment, summoning her courage.

"Do you ever have nightmares about the day Craig was killed?"

Stunned, Wade took a moment to answer. He'd been expecting a relationship question.

"Yes...I...had them all the time...at first," he admitted reluctantly. "I don't have them as often now. Are you having nightmares?"

"No, not me," she said and looked at Wade. "It's Drew."

Wade could see the tears brimming in Maddie's eyes again. "What's been happening?"

"He's been having nightmares on and off for the past four years," she began. "They were terrible right after the murders in Rayland. I used to find him standing in the barn in the middle of the night, running his fingers over the bullet holes."

"That was a horrible experience," Wade said with compassion as he recalled the details of the case.

Maddie nodded. "The nightmares eventually stopped, but the anniversary of Paul Randolph's death triggers them again. The dreams have started in October for the past two years and lasted a month or two."

She paused and took a deep breath. "This year has been different. For the past six weeks, Drew's been waking up screaming almost every night. There have been times that I woke up in the middle of the night, and he'd be gone. He always answered when I called or texted. Nothing that I've done for him has helped. I don't know what else to do."

Wade gently squeezed her hand. "People handle terrible experiences in different ways. I struggle with Craig's loss every day. I had to have help to deal with it."

"What kind of help?"

"A counselor from the hospital helped me through the initial part. I came out of the coma to learn that Craig was dead, and I survived. His funeral was over, and his body was already buried. The rest of you were further along in the grieving process. I had no one else to talk to about it."

"I didn't realize that," Maddie said. "I don't think any of us did. I'm sorry we weren't there for you."

"You did the best you could. I was the only one there that day. No one else could understand how I felt...how I still feel about it."

Maddie could see the anguish in Wade's eyes. "I'm sorry to dredge up painful memories. I didn't know where else to turn."

"What was the fight about?" Wade began, "If you don't mind telling me."

Maddie's eyes filled with tears again when she said, "It was my fault. Drew came home and plopped in his chair. Brody wanted to talk to him about his birthday party. Drew acted like he couldn't see or hear him. Brody climbed on his lap and put his hands on either side of his dad's face. He said, 'Daddy, can you hear me?'"

She cried at the memory for a few minutes before she could continue. "Drew pushed Brody to the floor and started yelling at him. You should have seen Brody's little face. He was crushed."

"I can imagine," Wade replied and shook his head at the thought.

"That's when I lost it," Maddie continued. "I told Drew that he needed to get help before he destroyed our lives. We argued for over an hour. Then he just walked out."

Wade reached across his desk and picked up a notepad and a pen. He wrote a few lines, tore off the page, and handed it to Maddie. "This is my counselor's name and number. He's been a tremendous help to me."

"Thank you," Maddie said and wiped her eyes. "I don't know if Drew will talk to me about it. He sits in his chair, staring into space. It's like we aren't there. When he does interact, he's impatient with Brody and short with me. The argument last night was the worst we've ever had."

"Why don't you go home and see if Drew's there.," Wade suggested. "Maybe the two of you can talk it out."

"And if he isn't?"

"We can file a missing persons report. It will be easier to find Drew with all of us on the case."

"Thanks for listening, Wade. I'll go home at lunch and see if he's there. I'll let you know if I'll be late getting back."

Maddie left the office at noon and drove home. Her mind was so full of thoughts about Drew that the fifteen-minute drive to Rayland was over before she realized it.

Drew's SUV wasn't in the garage. She went inside and searched the house. There was no indication that he'd been there since she left that morning.

She took out her cell phone and called the Sheriff's department. She asked to speak to Wade when Lodge answered the phone.

"Drew isn't here," she said when Wade answered. "I think it's time to file that report."

"I'll get it started," Wade replied. "You can fill in the missing details when you get back."

The call ended, and Maddie went to the refrigerator. Opening the door, she stared inside. Her mind wasn't on food. She was thinking of Drew.

*Why hasn't he called? Where did he spend the night? Why didn't he go to work? Is he hurt? Could he be in the hospital somewhere?*

She closed the refrigerator and wandered around the house, wiping tears from her face.

*I can't let my imagination run wild. Drew's probably safe. He's taking some time to get himself together.*

She went to the bathroom and splashed cold water on her face. She stared at the bottle of Polo Black cologne on the counter.

"Drew, where are you?"

# CHAPTER TWO

"No! PAUL, LOOK OUT!" he shouted. "He's coming! He's got a gun. Run! Run! AAHHHHH!"

Andrew Clifton woke up screaming. He gripped the sides of the bed, trying to control his trembling body. His head throbbed, and his stomach churned. He took a deep breath and slowly opened his eyes.

He found himself again in an unfamiliar room. This time, he wasn't alone. He could hear someone whistling nearby.

He swung his legs off the bed and managed to stand. He stumbled to the bedroom door and slowly opened it. Following the whistle, he entered what once must have been a bright, cheerful room. It was now dull and depressing with age and wear.

The small kitchen's appliances were outdated, as was the decor. The walls were faded canary yellow, and the worn linoleum floor still showed traces of avocado green. The yellow and green color scheme continued in the curtains and tablecloth.

A short, round man with thinning hair and wrinkled clothes greeted him. He reminded Drew of a private detective on television. All that was missing was a trench coat.

"Hell of a nightmare," the stranger said and went to the refrigerator. He took an ice pack from the freezer and handed it to Drew. "For your eye."

Drew picked up the compress and winced when he applied it to his tender face. "Who are you?"

"Good Samaritan."

"I don't understand."

"Saved your ass!" the man said, filling two shot glasses with a brown liquid. He set the bottle on the counter and handed a glass to Drew.

"Drink up," he ordered.

"What is it?" Drew asked, eyeing the contents of the glass.

"Jack," the man said, emptying his glass in one gulp. "Hair of the dog."

"Where are we?"

"My place. Used to be my mom's."

"Where is she?" Drew asked, dreading the answer.

"Passed on," the man said, filling his glass again.

Drew stared at the man before he said, "I need to call my wife."

The man shook his head and said, "Last thing you want to do."

"Why?" asked Drew with suspicion.

The man walked to the kitchen table and sat down. He swallowed the entire contents of his glass. "Have a seat," he said, pointing to an empty chair.

Drew reluctantly placed his glass on the table. He pulled the chair out and sat down.

"Remember anything about last night?" asked the stranger.

Drew shook his head. "Not much. Who are you?"

The man scratched his head and stared at Drew.

"Well?" Drew asked, impatient.

"Name's David Foust."

"Mr. Foust, I'm Andrew Clifton. I need to get in touch with my wife. Do you have a phone that I could use?"

"Bad idea," Foust said and pointed at Drew's glass. "Drink up."

Drew pushed the glass away in defiance. "Why is that a bad idea?"

"Cops lookin' for you," Foust said. "Or will be."

"Why would they be looking for me?" Drew asked warily.

Foust leaned forward and crossed his arms on the table. He searched Drew's face, then looked him in the eye.

"You're in serious trouble," Foust said.

"Why am I in trouble? I haven't done anything wrong," Drew answered, afraid.

"Dead body in that house where I found you," Foust said and sat back, waiting for Drew's reaction.

The ice pack fell to the floor. Drew's jaw dropped, and his eyes opened wide. He shook his head and covered his face with his hands.

"I thought that was a dream," he said at last. "One of my nightmares."

"Nope," Foust assured him, leaning back.

"What happened?" Drew asked, dropping his hands back to the table.

"Don't know for sure," Foust said. "Looks like you killed somebody."

"I didn't kill anyone!" Drew protested. "I woke up in that house and found... I didn't even know who it was!

"Maybe, maybe not," Foust said and looked at Drew's bruised face. "Sorry 'bout your eye. Took some...persuasion to get you in the car."

Drew frowned and picked up the ice pack. He put it back on his sore face and asked, "What happens now?"

"Stay here and lay low."

"I can't stay here!" Drew exclaimed. "I have a family and a job."

"Not much choice unless you want to turn yourself in," said Foust.

"What are you going to do?"

"Try to find out what the cops know," Foust replied.

"Why are you doing this?" asked Drew, astonished.

"When I see the opportunity to make a buck, I jump on it."

"How could you make money from this?"

"Bound to be a reward for the capture of a killer," Foust began. "Willing to pay to keep my mouth shut?"

Drew clenched his jaw and glared at Foust. "I didn't kill anyone. There's no need to pay you."

Foust stood and pushed his chair under the table. "No matter. Somebody'll pay."

Drew didn't respond. He tried to process what was happening.

"Be back in a day or two," Foust continued. "Food in the fridge. Should last three or four days." He nodded at the bottle on the kitchen counter. "That's all the whisky. Security bars keep people from breakin' in and vandalizin' the place. I'll lock 'em when I leave."

"But I won't be able to get out!" Drew shouted.

An evil smirk spread across Foust's face. He nodded and said," Catchin' on, are ya?"

Drew jumped to his feet and started toward his captor.

"Uh, uh, uh," Foust said, jerking a Glock from his jacket pocket. He pointed it at Drew's heart.

"Where are you going?" Drew demanded.

"Got work to do," Foust said with a smirk. "No point in screamin' for help. Nobody close enough to hear."

Foust backed out of the house, still holding the gun on Drew. He locked the security bars over the door before returning the gun to his pocket.

Drew ran to the door and pounded on the frame. "You can't do this! Let me out!"

He shouted and banged on the door. He watched Foust get into his car and drive away. He stood there until Foust's car was out of sight.

Dejected and scared, he walked to the counter and picked up

the bottle of Jack Daniels. He carried it to the kitchen table and swallowed the contents of the glass he'd left there.

He sat down and poured himself another drink. The whisky burned his throat when he gulped it down.

Tears welled in his eyes. He crossed his arms on the table, laid his head on them, and moaned. This time the pain wasn't coming from his head.

"Maddie, I'm so sorry. Brody, I hope you can forgive me for missing your big day," he said and sobbed himself to sleep.

* * *

Wade had begun the missing persons report when Maddie returned to the office. They completed the paperwork and called the team to the conference room.

"We have a case to discuss," Wade began. "We'll record this meeting so that Deputies Gonzalez, Wagner, and the rest of the night shift will have the information."

"What sort of case?" asked Deputy Calvin Baker.

Wade started the recording before answering, "This is Friday, October 13, 2017. We have a missing person. I'll let Deputy Clifton take it from here."

Maddie stood and looked at the faces of her coworkers. Although they were her friends, explaining the situation would be embarrassing and painful. She gathered her courage, held her head high, and squared her shoulders.

"My husband, Andrew, is missing. We argued last night, and he left, angry. I'm not sure of the time. It was near sundown because it was getting dark. He didn't come home, and I haven't been able to get in touch with him. The main reason for my concern is that Drew has had episodes of unusual behavior for several weeks.

The second reason is that today is Brody's fourth birthday. Drew has always made it a point to make our son feel special on his big day. He would never intentionally disappear and disappoint our son."

Maddie couldn't continue. Her eyes filled with tears, and she turned to Wade. The Sheriff stood and completed the briefing.

"Maddie has called and texted Drew many times without a response. Family members, friends, and his place of employment haven't heard from him. Do you have any questions?"

"What behavioral issues does your husband have?" asked Deputy Sherri Logsdon.

"I can only guess," Maddie answered. "He's refused to see a doctor about his symptoms."

"What do you suspect?" Deputy Clint Odom asked.

Maddie wiped her eyes and tried to control the tears before answering. "His behavior could be the result of depression or substance abuse. I haven't found any drugs in the house. I haven't seen him drinking at home, but I've smelled alcohol on his breath several times in the past few weeks.

"I don't know Drew as well as some of you," Odom said. "But, this seems completely out of character."

"It is," Wade replied. "That's why we're getting started right away. With any luck, we'll find him in time for Brody's party. Maddie will run the office while we search."

"I'll send the report to nearby police and sheriff's departments," Baker said. "I may be able to locate his phone or find where he's used a credit card with computer searches."

"Good idea. Maddie will provide a list of family and known associates. Logsdon and Lodge will interview those people," Wade directed. "Odom and I will canvas the area. Baker will keep us updated if he finds anything. You may want to reschedule any appointments you have before getting started. It could be a long day.

The meeting ended, and Wade went to his office. He took out his cell phone and dialed Lizzie's number.

"Hi, Husband," she answered.

"Hi, Wife," Wade said with a grin. "I'll be late getting home. Don't make dinner for me, and don't wait up."

"It sounds serious."

"It could be," Wade told her. "The circumstances are unusual. We need all the manpower we have on this one. Reed won't be back until Monday."

"It sounds like we won't have our weekend alone after all," Lizzie said with disappointment.

"I'm sorry, Honey."

"It's not your fault," Lizzie replied. "What happened?"

"Drew Clifton is missing. We hope to find him quickly, but we don't know where to start."

"Oh no! Maddie must be beside herself!"

"That's putting it mildly," Wade said.

"I hope you find him tonight," Lizzie said. "I don't know what I'd do if you were missing."

"I remember how it felt when you went missing last year," Wade told her. "Not knowing where you were, if you were hurt, or worse. I almost lost my mind."

"Find him soon, for Maddie's sake," Lizzie urged. "I love you."

"I love you too," Wade said and ended the call.

He took his cowboy hat from the shelf and put it on his head. He went into the outer office and waited for Odom to finish his call.

"We'll take my truck," Wade said. "Let's start searching the roads while we still have daylight. His vehicle could have broken down somewhere."

"Yes, Sir," Odom said. "Which direction do you think he was likely to go?"

"Your guess is as good as mine," Wade admitted.

The two men climbed into Wade's Ford F-150 Super Crew and discussed where to begin their search. They decided to start at the Cliftons' home and work toward Vernon.

Sheriff Adams and Deputy Odom had found no sign of Andrew Clifton or his SUV by the time they reached Vernon. They stopped for a short dinner break and discussed where to look next.

"Could he have gone toward Crowell?' Odom asked and took a bite of his burger.

"It's possible," Wade admitted and picked up a french fry. "He could have gone any direction. Even out of state."

"But, that's not what you believe," Odom observed.

"People are creatures of habit. I think Drew is somewhere in this area. It concerns me that his phone goes straight to voice mail, and no one has heard from him.

"Could he have planned it this way?"

"I can't imagine he'd intentionally miss his son's birthday."

Deputies Lodge and Logsdon walked into the restaurant. Wade indicated that the pair should join them. The two deputies ordered their food and sat down with Wade and Odom.

"Have you had any luck?' Wade asked.

Lodge shook his head. "No one has seen or spoken to Drew since yesterday."

"And they didn't have any ideas where to look for him either," added Logsdon.

"Have you talked with everyone?' asked Wade.

"There are still a few people we haven't contacted," Lodge said. "We thought we'd talk with those folks after we eat."

"I take it you haven't learned anything either," said Logsdon.

The conversation stopped when a voice echoed from the counter, "Number two fifteen, your order is ready."

"Don't say anything else 'til I get back," Lodge begged.

He returned a minute later with Logsdon's order and his own.

"Thanks, Lodge," she said with a smile.

Lodge beamed at her and winked.

Wade raised an eyebrow at Lodge and shook his head.

"We didn't find anything either," Wade said. "We were discussing where to look next when you got here."

The four law officers discussed ideas and options while they ate. They finished their meals before returning to the office to update Maddie and the rest of the team.

Maddie rushed to greet them when they entered the office. Hope and exhaustion showed on her face.

"Anything?" she asked.

Wade shook his head and said, "I'm sorry."

She hung her head and said, "I wish I could stay and help. But I have to think about Brody. I don't know what I'm going to tell him."

"Are you going ahead with the party?" asked Wade.

Maddie nodded. "It's too late to cancel now. He's been looking forward to this for weeks. He'd be devastated if we didn't go ahead with it."

She went to her desk, gathered her things, and started toward the door. She stopped and looked at Wade.

"Promise me that you'll call no matter when no matter what."

"I will," Wade assured her. "Is there anywhere you can think of that Drew might go?"

Maddie shook her head. "I've been wracking my brain all afternoon."

"All right. Let us know if you think of anything," Wade told her. "I'll take your shift this weekend."

"But it's your weekend off!"

"You need to be with Brody."

Maddie nodded and made her way outside with tears streaming down her face.

Deputies Drake Wagner and Marina Gonzalez entered the office and reported for duty.

"What's wrong with Maddie?" asked Gonzalez.

Wade explained the situation to the deputies on the night shift.

"What can we do to help?" asked Wagner.

Baker may need help with the computer searches. Odom and I plan to continue our search for Drew's vehicle. Logsdon and Lodge still have a few people to interview.

"I haven't found anything yet," Baker said. "Clifton hasn't used any of his cards since last weekend. The last call made from his cell phone was yesterday afternoon."

"Any news from other agencies?"

"Not yet, and Clifton isn't at any of the nearby hospitals or morgues. He hasn't been at any of the local hotels either."

Wade sighed and asked, " Does anyone have any suggestions?"

"I might," offered Gonzalez. "About a month ago, Antonio and I were at a casino in Devol, Oklahoma. I saw Drew there."

"Was Maddie with him?" asked Baker.

"I don't think so. He was sitting alone at the bar. Antonio won a jackpot, and we celebrated. Drew was gone when I looked for him afterward."

"Which casino?' asked Wade.

"The Kiowa," Gonzalez replied.

"Odom, how do you feel about visiting the casinos?" asked Wade.

"It beats driving around in the dark," Odom joked.

"I suggest we complete our current tasks and call it a night," Wade said. "We won't be able to find Clifton if we're sleepwalking. I've posted the duty rosters for next week. Gonzalez and Wagner will be moving to the day shift. Odom to nights. Logsdon, I know you were on the night shift last week. Do you mind doing it again next week?"

"No, Sir. Maddie needs to take care of her son."

"Thank you. I'll see everyone in the morning."

The Sheriff drove home with too much on his mind. The bartender at the Kiowa Casino remembered Drew but said he hadn't been there for a couple of weeks. The same was true at the Comanche Casino.

Drew wasn't the type of man to stay out all night without letting his wife know his whereabouts. The situation was baffling.

Wade opened the back door and saw Lizzie standing in the kitchen.

"I heard you drive up," she said, walking toward him. She kissed him gently and held him close. "Hard day?"

Wade let the warmth of her embrace flow through him before he spoke. "I've had better."

"Did you find Drew?"

"No," he said and moved toward a barstool. "We haven't been able to find any trace of him."

"Are you hungry?" Lizzie asked and went to the refrigerator.

Wade shook his head and rubbed his tired eyes.

Lizzie took a pitcher from the fridge, poured two glasses of iced tea, and sat beside him.

Wade sipped his tea and said, "I'll be covering for Maddie this weekend. She doesn't have anyone to keep Brody."

"Is there anything I can do to help?"

"Not that I can think of," Wade said and took her hand. "I'm sorry about our weekend."

"It's disappointing, but I understand," she said and kissed him.

Wade wrapped her in his arms and said, "We still have our nights alone."

"Hmmm, yes, we do," Lizzie replied. "Why don't you hurry up and finish your tea?"

Wade grinned and pushed his glass away. "I'm not that thirsty."

"In that case, I'll race you to the bedroom," she said and sprinted down the hall.

Wade jumped up, knocking the bar stool he'd been sitting on to the floor. He ignored it and dashed after his bride.

He climbed into bed and reached for Lizzie. He cursed under his breath when his cell phone rang. Rolling over, he grabbed the phone.

"I'm sorry to bother you, Sheriff," said Wagner. "A 2015 Chevy Tahoe has been found on State Highway 240, three miles east of Harrold."

"Is it Clifton's?"

"The license plate matches."

"Any sign of Drew?"

"No, Sir," replied Wagner.

"I'm on my way. Better call the team."

"Yes, Sir."

Wade ended the call and turned to Lizzie. "I have to go. I'm sorry."

"I hope you find him," she replied. "And I hope he's okay."

"So do I," Wade said with a sigh. "So do I."

# CHAPTER THREE

DREW MOANED and twitched while he slept.

"No! No! I tried to save him! Don't you remember? There was nothing I could do! I tried to save him! Noooo!"

He jerked, toppling himself and the chair he'd been sitting on to the floor.

Dazed, he looked around the room. He lay back and covered his face with one arm. He stayed there until the pain of the sudden fall eased.

He rolled off the chair and got to his hands and knees. Crawling to the kitchen table, he pulled himself up and stared at an empty glass and a half-empty bottle of whisky.

He picked up the chair, sat down, and poured himself another glass of Jack Daniels. He gulped it down and wiped his mouth on his shirt sleeve.

Drew got up and staggered across the kitchen. He rummaged through the fridge until he found lunch meat and a water bottle. A fresh loaf of bread lay on the counter.

He made himself a sandwich and wobbled toward the table. Finishing his meager meal, he closed his eyes.

*Oh, my head! I wonder if there's any aspirin in this place.*

He stood and teetered to the kitchen cabinets. While searching the cupboards, he glanced out the kitchen window.

*It's dark out. I wonder what time it is.*

Drew groped his way into the next room and fumbled for a light switch. Nothing happened when he flipped it on.

He took three steps before he tripped. In his drunken stupor, he couldn't catch himself and fell onto something that collapsed under his weight.

He lay on the floor, confused. Light from the kitchen allowed him to see shapes. He could see the outlines of a couch and some other furnishings.

Struggling to his feet, he limped toward the couch and fell onto it. He rubbed a sore spot on his hip, laid his head back, and closed his eyes. The sound of snoring reverberated through the house.

* * *

Drake Wagner finished calling the team and frowned at the telephone. He wanted to be part of the crime scene team. Instead, he was stuck in the office on the night shift.

His green eyes flashed with frustration. He slammed his desk drawer and lifted his muscular six-foot frame from the chair. It was the first action the department had seen in weeks. It galled him that he hadn't yet had the opportunity to use his training. He wondered if he would ever be part of the team.

He grew up on his family's farm, and he'd worked for ten years with the National Park Service in Colorado. The outdoor life was what he loved the most. He craved sunshine and fresh air. He hated being stuck inside.

Drake moved home a year ago to be nearby after his father's stroke. He'd had hopes of rekindling his romance with Lizzie Fletcher.

Visions of Lizzie passed through his mind. Those vivid blue

eyes, the freckles across her nose, and the soft silkiness of her red hair were a few of her attractive qualities.

He ran his hands through his dark hair and began to pace. He might have been able to win Lizzie back if it hadn't been for Wade. But she made her choice, and he had to live with it. It was time to move on.

His thoughts returned to the present when the first member of the team entered the office. Sherri Logsdon tried to hide her looks at work. She wore little makeup and pulled her long blonde hair into a tight bun. Despite her efforts, she was an attractive woman.

Logsdon stopped and looked at her uniform when she saw Drake staring at her. "Did I spill something on my shirt?" she asked.

"No, I was...I'm surprised you got here so fast," Drake said, trying to disguise his reason for gawking.

"Am I the first one back?"

"You're seconds ahead of Odom," Drake answered and nodded toward the door.

The rest of the team soon followed and quickly gathered their equipment. Drake watched them leave before returning to his desk.

It was a dark night. The waning crescent moon did little to help. The Sheriff's team parked their vehicles so the headlights would shine on the scene.

The outside of the white Tahoe was in perfect condition. There were no dents or scratches to indicate an accident. It looked as though the driver parked on the side of the highway, intending to return.

Using a flashlight, Odom peered through the passenger side window and said, "The doors are locked, but the keys are in the ignition."

"See if you can get one of the doors open, Lodge," Wade directed.

Lodge examined the Tahoe. He took a long thin bar from his

toolkit and went to work. Ten minutes later, he opened the driver's door and said, "Tada!"

"I'll call the tow truck," Wade said. "Look for any evidence that might lead us to Drew Clifton. I'd like to have some good news for Maddie."

"There are some personal effects inside," reported Lodge

"Outside is clean," said Odom.

"Nothing of concern on the inside," added Baker.

"No other vehicle tracks," said Logsdon. "And no footprints."

It was almost one a.m. when the team returned to the office.

"Go home and get some rest," Wade told them. "We'll start processing Drew's vehicle in the morning."

The Sheriff sighed and went to his office. He picked up the phone and dialed Maddie's number. She answered after the first ring.

"Did you find him?"

"No, but we found his Tahoe."

"And?"

"There was no sign of Drew and nothing in the vehicle to help us locate him."

"Do you think he's hurt?"

"I don't know," Wade admitted. "There was nothing in the SUV to suggest he's injured."

"Where did you find it?" Maddie asked, confused.

"It was parked on the side of the road east of Harrold. The keys were still in the ignition."

"He may have had engine trouble and walked to a nearby house for help," Maddie suggested.

Wade could hear the hope in her voice. He hated to dash her spirits.

"It would have been a long walk, Maddie, especially if it was dark. The only lights we could see were cars on 287."

"Do you think Drew left it there?" she asked.

"We'll know more when we've finished processing. Does he know anyone in the Harrold area?"

"Not that I'm aware of," Maddie said in a whisper. "I don't understand any of this. Where could he be?"

Wade crept through the back door of the inn to avoid waking Lizzie. He tiptoed to their bedroom, undressed in the dark, and slipped under the covers beside his wife. He was about to doze off when Lizzie rolled over and snuggled close to him.

"Did you find Drew?" she asked.

"No, we hope something in his SUV will give us a clue."

"I know you're exhausted," she said, kissing him on the cheek. "We'll talk in the morning."

Wade nodded and drifted off before Lizzie could say, "I love you."

Lizzie was up at six-thirty cooking sausage and eggs. She didn't want Wade to miss breakfast again. He tended to delay or skip meals when working on a case. And this wasn't a typical case. Drew Clifton was a friend.

She poured a cup of coffee and carried it to the bedroom. She set the cup on the nightstand and looked at her husband.

His dark blonde hair curled around his ears and at the nape of his neck. Lizzie would have liked nothing more than to crawl into bed beside him and stay there all day.

She knew he wouldn't want to be late again. But he was sleeping so peacefully that she hated to wake him.

Wade opened one green eye and smiled. "Are you watching me sleep?"

"Yes, but I was about to wake you. Your breakfast is ready."

"What time is it?" he asked, stretching.

"It's almost seven."

"That's plenty of time," he said with an exaggerated yawn.

"Time for what?"

"For this!"

All at once, he sat up and grabbed her, pulling her onto the bed beside him.

"Wade!" she squealed. "You'll be late again!"

"It'll be worth it," he said, covering her lips with his.

At seven-thirty, Lizzie converted Wade's sausage and egg meal into a breakfast burrito. She poured coffee into a travel mug and waited while he finished getting dressed.

He was still tucking in his shirt when he ran to the kitchen. He put on his hat, kissed Lizzie goodbye, and rushed out the door with his breakfast in hand.

Lizzie ate her breakfast alone and cleaned up the kitchen. She looked around the inn for something to do. She'd spent the previous week doing all the chores so that she could enjoy the weekend alone with Wade. There was nothing else to be done.

*I need to find something to keep myself busy.*

She went to her office and checked the upcoming event schedule. It was going to be crazy for the rest of the year. The next three weeks would kick off the holiday season with a wedding the following weekend. A luncheon, an anniversary party, a dinner party, and two Halloween parties were also planned for the remainder of October. Overnight guests would stay at the inn for the wedding and anniversary party.

*If I do my shopping today, I can start decorating for the wedding earlier.*

Lizzie picked up the phone and dialed her parents' number. Lois Fletcher answered the call.

"Hi, Granny," Lizzie began. "I'm going to do some shopping in Wichita Falls this afternoon. Would you and Mama like to go with me?"

"I'll go with you. Hold on, and I'll check with Ellen."

Lizzie held the line and waited for her grandmother to return. She heard her mother's voice on the line instead.

"We'll both go with you," said Ellen. "But, I thought you had plans for the weekend."

"Wade has to work all weekend, after all. I thought I'd start preparing for this month's events."

"What happened?" asked Ellen.

"I don't know if it's public knowledge yet, but Drew Clifton is missing," Lizzie replied. "Maddie needed to be off with Brody."

"Do they have any idea where Drew might be?"

Lizzie shared the information she had with her mother. They talked a few minutes longer and arranged to leave after they'd had lunch.

After making her shopping list, Lizzie showered and dressed. She made the bed and straightened up the bedroom.

She went to the office and turned on the answering machine. Then she gathered her things and drove the quarter mile to her parents' house. She arrived in time to help make lunch.

"What are we having?" Lizzie asked, hugging her grandmother.

"Spaghetti and meatballs," Ellen said. "We'll have salad and garlic bread too."

"Sounds good," Lizzie said. "What do you want me to do?"

"You can make the salad," suggested Granny. "I'm in charge of the garlic bread and dessert."

Lunch was on the table when James Fletcher and Dan Hayes walked into the kitchen. James wrapped his daughter in a bear hug and said, "I didn't expect to see you today."

"We had a change of plans," Lizzie said, explaining the situation while the two men washed up.

"I'm sorry your weekend was spoiled," James said. "I hope they find Drew in time for you to salvage part of it."

"I do, too, Daddy," Lizzie replied. "Dan, how are things going with Deanna?"

Dan looked at his friend, annoyed. "Nothing has changed since you asked yesterday."

Lizzie gave him a sly grin and said, "I'm just making conversation."

"What happened to the days when we had more to talk about than my love life?" Dan said with an exaggerated sigh.

"All right, you two," Granny said, grinning. "If I didn't know better, I'd think you were kinfolk. Stop razzing each other so we can eat in peace."

"Yes, Ma'am," Dan replied with a wink and dug into his food.

"I'm glad you're here, Lizzie," Ellen said. "We were going to wait until Monday to say anything, but we have some news.

Lizzie was suddenly alert. In the recent past, the word news meant trouble. She relaxed when she saw the smiles on the faces of her loved ones.

"What kind of news?" she asked.

"Your Daddy and I are taking a trip," Ellen said, beaming.

"You are? Where?" Lizzie asked with excitement.

"I bought a raffle ticket months ago," James began. "I forgot all about it until I got a phone call yesterday. It turns out I won an all-expense paid trip for two to Cancun."

"That's awesome!" exclaimed Lizzie.

"Yes, and no," said James.

"What do you mean?"

"We have to take the trip before the end of this year," said Ellen. "And we'll be gone a week."

"Oh," Lizzie said, realizing the implications. "When are you planning to leave?"

"Right after the wedding next Saturday," James replied. "It's the best time. The longer we wait, the harder it will be for you."

Lizzie's mind reeled. She was happy and excited for her parents. But she wondered how she would manage without their help.

"Dan will be in charge of the farm," James continued. "He'll be looking after the cattle and doing maintenance on the equipment.

"And I'll be available to help at the inn," Dan added.

"Lizzie, we won't go if it will put you in a bind," James offered. "We can cancel, and it won't cost us a thing."

"I wouldn't dream of keeping you here. You're right. It's better to go now. I want y'all to go and have a good time. You deserve it."

James reached for Ellen's hand and squeezed it. "Well, Honey, I guess we're going to Cancun."

"Have you packed yet?" Lizzie asked.

"Your mother packed her bags as soon as I got the phone call," James teased. "I haven't started."

"I keep telling him we won't have much time for last-minute packing," Ellen said. "He may have to wear whatever I pack for him."

"I don't need much," James said. "A couple of pairs of overalls will do."

"What about clean shirts and...and underwear?" Ellen asked.

"It's hot down there. I'll be cooler if I go commando," he said with a wicked grin.

"James Fletcher!" Ellen exclaimed, astonished. "You most certainly will not!"

The entire group roared with laughter. None louder than James. His wife reacted as he'd expected.

Ellen blushed and grinned at her husband when she realized he'd been teasing. Still, she planned to make sure he'd packed more than overalls before they left.

"I have some news, too," said Granny with a twinkle in her eye. "Grace is coming."

"Aunt Grace will be here?" said Lizzie. "We haven't seen her since the wedding reception."

"She has some vacation time and wants to come for a long visit," Granny added. "When I told her about the trip, she offered to help."

"I can't wait to see her!

The group discussed the vacation plans. James and Ellen would drive to the airport in Dallas and meet Grace. They planned to have dinner and visit for a while before going to their hotel for the night.

Grace would drive their car back and stay with Granny while

James and Ellen were away. The process would be reversed when it was time to return home.

"It sounds like you're all set," Lizzie said, smiling.

"I'd like to bring Deanna for dinner before it gets crazy around here," Dan said. "Would one night this week be a good time?"

"How about Monday?" Lizzie suggested. "I won't start decorating for the wedding until Tuesday. There won't be as much stuff scattered around."

"That works for me. The usual time?"

Lizzie nodded. "Six o'clock, but Wade may not be there."

"I understand," Dan replied. "Monday should be good. I'll check with Deanna and let you know."

When the two men returned to work, the women put away the leftovers and cleaned the kitchen. Soon, they were on the road to Wichita Falls.

They began their shopping at the craft store. The anniversary party and the wedding decorations were chosen first. The other events had a Halloween theme. Those decorations could be reused or remade.

Their next stop was the specialty supermarket. There, they purchased all they would need to make the month's catered meals. They treated themselves to ice cream before returning to the inn.

The ladies put away their purchases and talked about Grace's visit, James and Ellen's trip, and dinner with Dan and Deanna.

"I wonder why Dan made a special appointment for dinner," asked Granny. "He knows he's always welcome to eat with us."

"We're going to be so busy that he probably wanted to make sure we'd have the time," Ellen pointed out.

"And he's bringing his girlfriend," said Lizzie. "He wouldn't want to bring her out here for leftovers or sandwiches."

"I hadn't thought of that," said Granny.

Her mother and grandmother went home, leaving Lizzie alone at the inn. She picked up the phone and dialed Wade's number. It rang twice and went to voicemail. She dialed the number to his office and waited.

"Sheriff's office," said a familiar voice.

"Hi, Baker. Is Wade around?"

"Hello, Fletcher. He's out of the office. I'll tell him that you called."

"Thanks, Baker. By the way, my name is Adams now.

Baker chuckled. "Yea, I know. But you'll always be Fletcher to me."

Lizzie laughed and ended the call. She looked at the clock and decided she'd try to call him again after a short nap.

She wanted to share the day's news with him. Their alone time would be more limited than anticipated. She knew he would need time to relax, especially since he'd be working late until he found Drew Clifton.

# CHAPTER FOUR

THE SOUNDS of birds chirping penetrated the fog in Drew's brain. He opened his eyes and saw a ray of sunlight. Getting up from the couch, he went to the window and pulled back the curtains.

The sunlight hurt his bloodshot eyes and made his head pound. Despite the pain, he left the curtains open.

He turned toward the kitchen and saw remnants of a demolished side table on a rumpled green and yellow throw rug.

*That must be what I tripped over. And it explains why my hip hurts.*

Drew took stock of the room. A couch and chair were covered in dated earth-tone upholstery. An abundance of Knick knacks, vases of plastic flowers, and lace doilies decorated the space.

It struck Drew as odd that there were no photographs on the walls. There was nothing that indicated an actual person lived there.

His gaze fell on a floor lamp between the couch and chair. Limping toward it, he tried the lamp switch. Nothing.

He followed the chord and discovered it wasn't plugged into the outlet. He plugged it in and tried the switch again. Still nothing.

He looked under the lampshade. There was no bulb. Looking

up at the ceiling, he saw the bulbs were also missing from that light fixture.

*No wonder the lights didn't work.*

He didn't want to be in the dark more than necessary. He explored every room, opening curtains and looking for lightbulbs. The only lightbulb in the place was the fluorescent one in the kitchen light fixture.

Besides the kitchen and living room, the house had one bath and two bedrooms with full-sized beds. Drew vaguely remembered the bedroom he'd been in when he woke.

*How long ago was it? Last night? The night before?*

His stomach growled, and Drew went to the kitchen in search of food. He made himself another sandwich and sat at the table to eat.

He stared at the empty whisky bottle. He wanted another drink, but he knew there was no more. He sighed, took a bite of his sandwich, and drank a bottle of water.

\* \* \*

The Sheriff and his team met in the conference room to discuss their plan for the day. Baker's task was to process Drew's vehicle. Odom and Lodge were assigned to interview the residents near the area where the Tahoe was found.

The meeting ended, and the team began their assignments. Sheriff Adams and Deputy Logsdon visited open establishments in town. They spoke with the business owners and their patrons. Many who were interviewed knew Drew but had not seen him in several days.

They left flyers with Drew's photo at each business with a phone number and a request that anyone with information should call.

Wade grew more concerned as time went on. He knew Drew to be a loving husband and father. He was responsible and well-respected in the community. It wasn't like him to disappear.

"What's on your mind, Sheriff?" Logsdon asked when they'd finished interviewing a restaurant owner and staff.

"Hmm?"

"You seem distracted. What's on your mind?"

"I was thinking about Drew and how this makes no sense," Wade replied. "I've known him for a long time, and I know his background. This isn't like him at all."

"Don't you think we'd make more progress if we consider him a stranger rather than someone we know well? Maddie said he hasn't been himself."

"I'm listening. Go on."

"What we've done so far is a good start, but we need to expand the search. We've been places Clifton would likely frequent because you're familiar with his lifestyle. What about those places you wouldn't expect to find him?"

"Gonzalez saw him at a casino bar," Wade recalled. "I wouldn't have expected him to be there. Where do you think we should go next?"

"We need to visit those places we'd least expect Clifton to be," said Logsdon. "Maddie said he's been leaving at night. She smelled alcohol on him. We know he was seen in at least two bars."

"I supposed he could have gone to one of the local bars. We'll interview at those establishments when they open."

"You aren't going to like this, but there are other possibilities," Logsdon began. "He may be seeing another woman, or he could be involved in something illegal."

"To be honest, those thoughts have crossed my mind," admitted Wade. "I can't imagine that either is the case. We need to find something to point us in the right direction."

"I think you should interview Maddie and see what else you can learn about Drew's condition," suggested Logsdon.

"You're right," Wade said. "There could be a detail she forgot to mention or missed. I think Dr. Hughes might be able to provide some insight."

The two officers interviewed more business owners and stopped for lunch. When Wade's phone rang, they had finished their meals and were about to resume their search.

"Sheriff Adams."

"Sheriff, I've finished processing Drew's Tahoe," said Baker. "Lodge and Odom finished their interviews and went back to the scene to see if there was anything we missed. They came back five minutes ago."

"We're on our way," Wade said and ended the call.

"Any news?" Logsdon asked.

"We'll find out when we get back to the office."

Baker was on the phone when Wade and Logsdon returned. He ended the call and said, "They're waiting in the conference room."

Wade nodded and followed Logsdon and Baker inside. He closed the conference room door. He turned to his team and asked, "Are we ready to record our discussion?"

Everyone agreed, and Wade started the tape. "This is Saturday, October 14, 2017. We're discussing evidence in the case of Andrew Clifton."

Wade looked at his team and asked, "What were the results from yesterday's interviews?"

"Logsdon and I talked with every person on Maddie's list of friends and acquaintances," said Lodge. No one had anything to tell us."

"Addie Sims works at the bank with Clifton," added Logsdon. "She suspects something has been bothering him, but she didn't know anything specific."

"Should she be brought in for an in-depth interview?" asked Wade.

"I felt she wanted attention more than to share information," said Logsdon.

"All right, let's move on."

"Sheriff Adams and I canvassed the area from Clifton's home to the city limits," Odom informed the team. "After talking with

Deputy Gonzalez, we drove to Devol, Oklahoma. We discovered that Drew has been drinking at both casinos in the past few weeks."

"There's been no cell phone or credit card activity on Drew's accounts since Thursday," said Baker. "And there have been no reports from other agencies before his vehicle was found last night."

"What did you find in the SUV?" Wade prompted.

"As you know, the SUV was perfect." Baker began. "There was no evidence of an accident or violence. The doors were locked, keys were in the ignition, and the gas tank was empty."

"An empty gas tank explains why the Tahoe was parked on the side of the road," Wade pointed out.

"Yes, it does," Baker agreed. "A wallet and cell phone were found in the driver's side door storage compartment. Seventy-three dollars in cash, a debit card, and two credit cards were inside the wallet. The driver's license and names on the credit cards indicate that it belongs to Andrew Clifton."

"What about the cell phone?" asked Wade.

"The battery was dead. That could be why Clifton wasn't responding. The last call was to Maddie Thursday afternoon," Baker replied. "There were a lot of incoming calls and texts from Maddie and a few from his parents."

"Were there any prints?" Lodge asked.

"There were four different sets inside the SUV," Baker replied. "I have a computer search running to identify them all."

"What about prints on the wallet and cell phone?" Wade asked.

"Those prints matched one set of prints on the driver's side. I assume they belong to Andrew Clifton, but that needs to be verified."

"What about the keys?" asked Odom.

"There were layers of prints on those," Baker said. "It will be faster to concentrate on the other prints."

"Thank you, Baker. Deputies Lodge and Odom, what can you tell us?" asked Wade.

"We spoke with all residents within a five-mile radius of where we found Clifton's SUV," Odom began. "No one had seen him or knew anything about his vehicle."

"We went back to the scene to see if we might have missed something in the dark," said Lodge. "We found traces of oil on the asphalt near the area where Clifton's vehicle was found."

"It could have been from a vehicle parked behind the SUV," Odom added. "We brought in a sample to be analyzed."

"We also found a driver's license in the grass near the edge of the pavement," Lodge told them. "It belongs to a local teenager by the name of Daniel Holden. We plan to visit with the young man this afternoon. It's doubtful, but he might have information."

"Let's hope he does," said Wade. "What are your thoughts about the case to this point?"

"The case started as the result of a quarrel," said Baker. "But something went wrong. It's strange that Clifton's personal belongings were left behind untouched by anyone else."

"I've been wondering about that too," said Odom. "Why leave his stuff behind if he went for help?"

"What if he didn't get out voluntarily," suggested Logsdon. "He could have been carjacked."

"But why leave the wallet?" pondered Lodge.

"The thief might not have known it was there," said Baker. "Most men keep their wallets in a pants pocket."

"That brings us back to why they were left in the truck," said Wade. "And if he went for help, why hasn't anyone seen or heard from him."

"Is it possible that Drew parked the SUV and walked away?" mused Lodge.

"Anything is possible," said Wade. "The only thing we know for certain is that Drew Clifton is missing and that he left a lot behind."

The meeting concluded, and the deputies returned to their tasks. Wade went to his office and made a phone call while Logsdon typed notes from their interviews.

"Good afternoon," said Dr. Hughes when he entered the office.

"Hello, Doctor," answered Baker. "What can I do for you?"

"I'm here to see Sheriff Adams."

"He's in his office. I'll let him know you're here."

"No need, Baker," Wade said from his office door. "Come in, Doc."

The doctor strode into Wade's office and sat in a chair in front of the desk.

"Can I get you anything?" asked Wade. "There's a fresh pot of coffee brewing."

"Coffee would be nice, thank you," said the doctor, eyeing Wade with suspicion.

Wade left and returned with a steaming cup of coffee. He brought sugar and creamer as well. He gave the items to his guest and closed his office door.

"Thanks for coming. I'm sorry to bother you so late in the day," Wade said. "But I need your advice."

"This must be serious," observed Dr. Hughes. "You normally get right to the point."

Wade grinned at his friend and sighed. "It is serious. I need to interview one of my deputies. I'd like you to be there to listen and ask the right questions."

"Which deputy? What's happened?"

Wade explained the situation and shared the facts. Dr. Hughes nodded while he listened.

"I can't make a diagnosis without examining the patient," said the doctor when Wade finished. "However, I may be able to find a few clues based on his wife's interview."

"I understand," Wade replied. "Maddie should be here soon. I called and asked her to meet us in the conference room."

Wade stood and led the way to the conference room. He stopped by Baker's desk on the way.

"Send Maddie to the conference room when she gets here," Wade told him.

"Yes, Sir," Baker replied.

Maddie arrived with Brody in tow. She went to her desk and said, "Brody, I want you to sit here and be good. Deputy Baker will tell me if you aren't."

Brody looked at Baker wide-eyed and grinned when the deputy winked at him.

"He'll be fine," Baker promised. "Wade's in the conference room."

Maddie nodded. She opened the door and said, "Wade, do you have any news?"

"Not really," Wade replied. I've asked you here because I need to ask you some questions. Dr. Hughes is joining us. He may have some questions too."

Maddie swallowed hard and nodded. She sat down across the table from both men.

"Maddie, I'd like to record this interview. I want something to refer to if needed. Do you agree to be recorded?" asked the Sheriff.

She nodded, and Wade turned on the recorder.

"This interview is being recorded on Saturday, October 14, 2017," Wade began and looked at the clock. "It's five-thirty-five in the afternoon. Dr. Gerard Hughes and Sheriff Wade Adams are interviewing Deputy Maddie Clifton regarding the disappearance of her husband, Andrew Clifton."

Wade looked at Maddie and smiled. He knew her nerves were on edge. He didn't want her to feel threatened. "Are you ready?"

Maddie nodded, "As ready as I'll ever be."

"Tell us what happened the night Drew disappeared," Wade said. "We need every detail you can remember."

Maddie repeated what she'd told Wade and her team before the investigation began.

"What do you mean when you say he hasn't been himself," asked Dr. Hughes.

Maddie described the differences between her husband's usual behavior and his recent actions.

"You said the annual personality change began earlier than usual. Can you be more specific?" prodded the doctor.

Maddie closed her eyes and cast her mind to the past. "It was the week before labor day. He came home from work and said he'd had a bad day. The nightmares started a day or two later."

"Did he mention what happened that day?" asked Wade.

"No, he said he didn't want to talk about it."

"When was the first time you noticed the scent of alcohol?" asked Dr. Hughes.

"I'm not sure," Maddie said. "It might have been the following week."

"Is that when he began leaving at night?" Wade inquired.

"Yes, I think it was."

"Maddie, I hate to ask this," Wade began. "Is it possible that Drew is having an affair?"

Tears filled her eyes, and she looked up at the ceiling. "I've been wondering the same thing," she admitted. "It would explain the late-night disappearances and some of his behavior. I never imagined that the man I married eight years ago would ever betray me. But now, I'm not sure."

"Do you have any other questions, Dr. Hughes?" Wade asked.

"Not at the moment," answered the doctor.

"I have one more," said Wade. "Does Drew go to the casinos often?"

Maddie stared at her boss in surprise before answering. "I've never known him to gamble. He says it's like throwing your money in the fireplace just to watch it burn."

Wade shared the information they had gathered with Maddie. He waited while she processed the news before he asked, "Is there anything you can think of that will give us a clue."

"I...no...I can't believe this. It's like Drew is a total stranger."

"I have one more request," Wade said. "I'd like to have the team thoroughly search your property. There might be something you wouldn't notice that could give us a clue."

"Yes, of course. Anything to find Drew."

Wade ended the recording and thanked Maddie for her help. "I want you to go home now. I'll let you know when we have any news."

"I'm going," Maddie replied. "This is no place for Brody."

Wade waited until Maddie and Brody had left the building to discuss the interview with Dr. Hughes.

"Well, what do you think?" Wade asked the doctor.

"Maddie believes Drew's nightmares and behavior are related to the past," replied Hughes. "Something else may be going on. Something that makes him feel the same emotions he felt then, fear and possibly guilt."

"Why would he feel guilty?"

"He may feel that he should have known who was responsible and prevented the murders. There's also the possibility that Drew has serious mental health issues. The longer it takes to find him, the more danger he could be in," said Dr. Hughes.

"Do you have any suggestions?" Wade asked, worried and frustrated.

"I believe something new triggered this episode. I suggest you start at Drew's place of employment."

"It's as good a place as any, but it will have to wait until the bank opens Monday morning."

Sheriff Adams escorted Dr. Hughes to his car and returned to his office. He dialed Lizzie's number and waited.

"Hello," said a sleepy voice.

"Did I wake you?"

"That's okay," Lizzie replied, more alert. "I'm glad you called. How's the search going?"

"Badly," admitted Wade. "I'm going to be late getting home. We're going to check out the local nightlife. Drew might have been in a bar recently."

"Are you sure?"

"No, but those are the only places we haven't been today. We saved those for last."

"You sound exhausted," Lizzie said with concern.

"I'm okay," he said. "I'd rather be home with you, though."

Baker tapped on his door.

"I'll get back to you," he told his wife. "Something's up."

"Sheriff, there's a body in Oklaunion," Baker told him.

"Better round up the team and call Dr. Hughes."

"Yes, Sir."

The Sheriff went to the conference room and waited for his deputies.

"What have you got for us, Baker?" Wade asked when everyone arrived.

"Dennis and Annette Handley have been out of town. They got home this evening to find light and music coming from inside the house. Mr. Handley went inside and found the victim. Mrs. Handley called 911."

Baker handed a sheet of paper to each team member and said, "This page has the Handley's address, phone numbers, and directions to the scene. They're waiting outside the house. Dr. Hughes will be here shortly with his van."

"Good work, Baker," said Wade. "Logsdon and Odom are with me. Lodge and Baker with Dr. Hughes."

"Do you think it's Clifton?" asked Odom.

"I sincerely hope not," Wade replied. "For Maddie's sake."

# CHAPTER FIVE

DREW FINISHED his meal and thought about his predicament.

*What day is it? How long have I been here? Will anyone ever find me?*

He stood up and paced around the kitchen.

*Did Foust plan this, or did he take advantage of an opportunity, like he said? Putting the security bars on the house would take a lot of time. He must have done that before bringing me here.*

He stopped pacing and looked at the kitchen light.

*He could have taken the lightbulbs before I woke up. Did he go grocery shopping, or was the food already here?*

Drew opened the refrigerator and inventoried his food supply.

*Foust said this would last three or four days. Will he be back by then? If he doesn't come back, I'll eventually run out of supplies and starve.*

A frightening thought passed through his mind. Drew knew he would have realized it sooner if he hadn't been so drunk.

*Why was Foust at that house? How do I know he isn't the killer? He might be planning to kill me when he comes back.*

Drew closed the fridge and resumed pacing the kitchen while he organized his thoughts.

*Maddie and Brody will never know what happened to me. I can't just sit here and take this. I've got to do something. I have to find a way out!*

Drew spent the rest of the day looking for an escape. During his search, he noticed a possible weakness in the bathroom. Three screws holding the security bars over the window were sticking out. If he could loosen them, he might be able to escape. He knew it would take time, but it could be his only chance.

He raised the bathroom window and reached through the opening. He tried to turn one of the bottom screws with his fingers. It wouldn't budge.

A growing sense of urgency drove him. He searched the house for anything he could use as a screwdriver or wrench. Foust had left nothing behind.

*I wonder if wiggling the bars will loosen the screws.*

He reached through the open window and grabbed the bars with both hands. He started shaking them will all his strength. He tried pulling and pushing them from side to side, backward and forward. The screws held fast. Exhausted, he sat down to rest.

*This isn't working. I need something to pry the screws out.*

He got up and searched the house again. Nothing he found was strong enough to use as a pry bar. The wooden handle of a broom snapped. The mop handle bent.

Discouraged, he went to the kitchen and made something to eat. He ate slowly and contemplated his situation.

*I can't get out. I need to make this food last as long as possible. It might last a week if I eat once a day.*

The house grew dark as sunset approached. Drew left the drapes and curtains open. He hoped that moonlight and the light from the kitchen would be enough so that he could see objects in his path.

He wandered into the living room and sat on the couch. There was no television and no radio. There was nothing he could use to find out what was happening outside his prison.

He found an old copy of People Magazine under the couch

cushions. Kate Middleton smiled at him from the cover dated December 6, 2010.

It was the only thing he could use to occupy his mind.

He read a few pages and tossed the magazine aside. It was getting too dark to read anymore. He leaned back and closed his eyes. He cast his mind back to the last things he could remember clearly.

The fight with Maddie was his fault. He felt horrible about the way he'd treated Brody. He should never have left the house. He should have told Maddie everything. He promised himself he'd make it up to them if he had the chance.

He let his mind drift. *Are the police looking for me? Who was in the tanning bed? Why was I there? How did I get there?*

Drew opened his eyes and sat up. He remembered leaving the bar. The woman he'd been talking to was a brunette. She called a friend to pick her up.

"She left first!" Drew shouted to the empty room. "I went to my truck and got in. I was about to close the door when someone called my name. They said they'd take me home. Why didn't they?"

He leaned back and tried to relax his mind again. He wanted to remember more. No matter how he tried, he couldn't remember anything between getting into the car and waking up on that twin bed.

Drew woke himself with a loud snore. He sat up and looked around the room. Flashing lights outside the large picture window caught his eye. He went to the window and saw blue and red lights blinking in the distance. He knew what those lights were. Law enforcement or emergency vehicles were nearby.

He ran toward the bathroom and opened the window. He shouted at the top of his lungs.

"Help! I'm trapped! Somebody help! I'm over here!" Drew shouted until his throat was raw, his voice reduced to a whisper.

He sprinted to the kitchen and flashed the kitchen light. He repeatedly turned it on and off. Then, he started using the morse code signal for S.O.S. He hoped and prayed that someone would see it.

* * *

The team arrived at a farmhouse southwest of Oklaunion, Texas. They parked their vehicles so the headlights would illuminate the dark areas around the Handleys' home. Bright light and loud music emanated from a west window.

Wade strolled toward the couple waiting inside their car while his team unloaded their gear and gloved up. The couple got out when he approached.

"I'm Sheriff Wade Adams," he said, extending his hand.

The man shook Wade's hand and said, "I'm Dennis Handley. This is my wife, Annette."

"I understand you've been out of town," Wade began. "How long have you been away?"

"Almost a week," answered Dennis.

"Did anyone know you weren't home?"

"People at both our jobs knew," offered Dennis. "Some of our friends and neighbors too."

"I told my hairdresser," added Annette. "One of the other ladies there may have overheard."

"Do any of those people know where you live?"

"Some of them do," answered Dennis.

"Does anyone else have a key or access to your home?"

"Our boys have keys for emergencies," Annette replied.

"Did their friends know you weren't home?"

"None that live in this area," Dennis told Wade. "Our boys are grown with their own families."

"Tell me what happened when you got here," Wade prodded.

"We could see the light when we turned off the farm-to-market road," Annette began. "I thought we might have left it on accidentally."

"We got out of the car and started toward the house. We stopped when we heard that music," Dennis said. "We got back in the car, and I got my pistol out of the console."

"He has a license to carry," Annette assured Wade.

Wade smiled and said, "I'm sure he does."

Dennis glared at his wife before he continued. "I told Annette to stay put and get ready to call 911. I went inside and saw someone that didn't look too good in the tanning bed. I got out of there as quick as I could."

"Then we called you," added Annette.

"Did you give anyone permission to use your tanning bed?"

Both of the Handleys shook their heads.

"Did you touch or disturb anything while you were inside?"

"I might have," Dennis admitted. "I was nervous going in and scared to death coming out."

"Do you have another place to stay?" Wade asked. "We'll finish with your home as quickly as we can, but it will be a day or two,"

"We've already discussed that," Dennis informed him. "We'll stay at one of the hotels in Vernon tonight."

"There's no need for you to stay while we work," said Wade. "You'll need to come by the office tomorrow. One of my deputies will take your statements and your fingerprints."

"Why do you need our fingerprints?" Annette asked, alarmed.

"We need to be able to distinguish your prints from those of the victim and the intruder," Wade told her and smiled. "It's a routine procedure."

"Oh, well, I guess that makes sense," she said.

Wade took a business card from his wallet and handed it to Dennis.

"Call me if you think of anything else we should know before tomorrow," said Wade. "It looks like my crew is ready to start, " Wade said. "I hope the rest of your evening is less exciting."

"So do we!" Annette exclaimed.

Wade joined his deputies, and they divided the tasks to be done. "Start outside the house. Lodge and Baker will work the west and south sides. Logsdon and Odom, east and north."

The team went to their assigned posts and went to work. They photographed and made notes of everything they saw. They joined Wade and Dr. Hughes when they'd finished.

"Let's get inside and find out what we've got," ordered Wade.

"Nothing more to see out here tonight anyway," said Lodge.

The team moved to the back door and entered the house. Bright light and music led them in the right direction. They moved slowly through the house, checking every doorway and room before moving to the next.

"What's that smell?" asked Odom sniffing the air.

"It smells a little like pot roast," commented Logsdon.

"Did these people start dinner before they called us?" Lodge joked.

"Maybe they left it in a slow cooker so they could eat when they got home," Baker joined in.

Wade knew the banter helped ease the tension, but sometimes he found it annoying. "The homeowners have been gone for a week," he growled.

"That's one dry pot roast," Lodge said under his breath.

Wade and Dr. Hughes were last to reach the lighted doorway. They looked into what was once a bedroom. A tanning bed was positioned to the left of the door and opposite the bedroom window. A gray upholstered armchair sat in the corner of the room. Feminine clothing lay on the seat cushion.

"Is the house secure?" Wade asked his deputies.

"Yes, Sir," answered Lodge.

"Good. You can start processing the other rooms," Wade ordered. "I'll help Dr. Hughes."

"We need to turn this thing off before our eyes burn or our hearing is damaged!" shouted the doctor.

Wade walked toward the bed and searched for the power outlet. He squeezed behind the machine and pulled the plug. The assault on their eyes and eardrums ended.

"Ah! That's better," said Dr. Hughes. "I'll see if I can find the light switch. I'd prefer to have my hands free to examine the victim."

The sound of someone searching the wall ended with a faint click and soft white light.

"I'll get out of your way, Doc," Wade said, moving away from the tanning bed. "We'll process this room when you've finished."

Dr. Hughes lifted the lid of the tanning bed and examined the body. He talked while he worked so that Wade could take notes.

"This is an adult female," he began. "Based on her skin condition, she's been here for some time."

"Did she die in there?" asked Wade.

"I won't know for sure until I start the autopsy," the doctor answered, distracted. "I won't be able to determine her time of death here. She's badly burned and dehydrated. The heat from these lamps elevated her body temperature."

Dr. Hughes completed his preliminary examination and asked for help to remove the body. The team worked together to place the victim into a body bag and load it into the van.

"I'll take her back and start the autopsy," Dr. Hughes told Wade. "I'll call you when I have anything to share."

"Thanks, Doc," Wade said and turned to his team. "Have you finished with the house?"

"All except the room where we found the victim," said Odom.

"Let's get to it," Wade said and rubbed the back of his neck. "Only two at a time in there, so you have more room to work."

Logsdon and Odom entered the space first. They collected and bagged everything other than the tanning bed and chair.

Baker and Lodge were the next to enter the room. Lodge examined the tanning bed while Baker dusted for prints.

The team packed up their gear and the evidence they had

collected. They drove back to the office and put everything away before meeting in the conference room.

"It's been a long day," Wade began. "I'd like you all to go home and get some sleep. We'll start processing the evidence first thing in the morning. Dr. Hughes won't have anything to tell us tonight."

"Will he be able to identify the victim soon?" asked Logsdon.

"I don't see how he could," said Odom. "The body was so blistered and burned that it didn't look human."

"He may not be able to use fingerprints," added Wade. "The skin was baked onto the glass. We had a hard time getting the body out."

"That's not a sight I'll forget anytime soon," Lodge said, shaking his head.

"Was there anything that you feel we should discuss tonight?" Wade asked, trying to change the subject.

"Baker and I altered the scene," said Lodge. "The front door was open. We closed it to keep the interior of the house intact."

"Anything else?" asked Wade.

The deputies shook their heads.

"In that case, go home. I'll see you in the morning," Wade ordered. "I'm going to make some phone calls before I go."

The deputies said goodnight and left the conference room. Wade stopped to talk with Wagner and Gonzalez before going to his office.

"I have a job for the two of you," he began. "How do you feel about running some background checks?"

"Anything's better than sitting here doodling," said Drake.

Wade ignored the comment and said, "Gonzalez, I need you to run background checks on Dennis and Annette Handley. There has to be a reason their home was used."

"Yes, Sir," said Gonzalez.

"Wagner, your job has to be done quietly. I don't want Maddie to find out."

"You want me to check into Clifton's background?"

"Yes, there might be a clue to help us find him."

"Why don't you want Maddie to know?" Drake asked.

Wade hesitated before he answered. "She has enough to worry about right now. I want to make sure that Drew isn't involved in something that he shouldn't."

"Is there anything specific you want me to look for?"

"No," Wade said. But I need you to be very thorough."

"I'll start right away," Drake replied and went to work.

Wade went to his office and dialed Maddie's number. It rang three times before she answered. He could tell she'd been crying.

"Maddie, it's Wade."

"Is it bad news?" she asked, sniffling.

"No, I wanted to see how you're doing."

"I'm okay," Maddie lied.

"How's Brody?"

"He misses his dad, and he's been asking questions. It kills me that I don't have any answers."

"It could be a while before we have answers," Wade began. "A body was found in Oklaunion. It was an adult female. She's Jane Doe until the doc can identify her. The team will be a lot busier with this new case. We'll have less manpower working to find Drew."

"Is there anything I can do to help?" Maddie asked.

"No, Brody needs you more than we do," Wade told her. "There's one more thing, Maddie. I'm going to send the team to your place tomorrow. It would be best if no one is there."

"I understand," Maddie said. "We'll find something to do, and I'll leave the door unlocked when we leave," Maddie said.

"Goodnight, Maddie."

Wade ended the call and dialed another number. The phone rang several times before Dennis Handley answered.

"This is Sheriff Adams," Wade began. "I'm sorry to wake you, Mr. Handley. I wanted to ask you a couple of questions."

"That's okay," said Handley, yawning. "What can I help you with, Sheriff?"

"Your front door was open when we went through your home. Is there any chance that you left it open?"

"The front door?" asked Handley, sounding confused. "Are you sure?"

"Yes, Sir."

"We didn't leave it open. We seldom use that door. The back door is our main entrance."

"When was the last time you used that entrance?" Wade asked. "There's evidence of recent use."

"I don't know," Handley said. "Let me ask my wife."

Wade could hear the muffled conversation while he waited. At last, Mrs. Handley spoke to him.

"I think it was back in the spring," said Mrs. Handley. "A young woman came to the house asking for directions. Everyone who knows us comes to the back door."

"What can you tell me about the woman?" Wade inquired, alert.

"She was about twenty. She said she was trying to find her college roommate. She took a wrong turn and ended up out here instead of across the state line where she intended."

"Did she mention any names or places?"

"She wanted to be somewhere between here and Davidson, Oklahoma," Mrs. Handley informed the sheriff. "I don't remember much else. I told her how to get to the right road, and she left."

"I see," Wade replied. "Thank you for your help. We'll go back to your house tomorrow to make sure we have everything we need. I'll let you know when you can go back inside."

The call ended, and Wade drummed his fingers on his desk.

*Who was the woman at the Handleys' house? Why was she there? Did she have anything to do with the body in the tanning bed?*

# CHAPTER SIX

THE SMELL of coffee brewing and bacon frying woke Wade from a fitful sleep. He would have preferred to stay in bed, but he got up and dressed.

Lizzie was cooking breakfast when he walked into the kitchen, ready for another day of work. He moved behind her and nuzzled her neck.

"Good morning," Lizzie said and turned to kiss her husband.

"Good morning. You didn't have to make breakfast for me."

"I wanted to," she replied. "You need a good meal. Besides, it will give us time to talk."

Wade gave her a sidelong glance and asked, "What about?"

"It's nothing serious," Lizzie said, flipping a pancake on the griddle. "Most of it is good news."

Wade sat down at the bar and sipped his coffee. "What's the bad news?"

"Who said anything about bad news?" Lizzie asked, not meeting his eyes.

"You said mostly good news," Wade reminded her. "That means there has to be some bad news, too."

Lizzie filled the serving platters and placed them on the bar. She moved beside Wade and sat down before she started talking.

"Mama and Daddy have won an all-expense paid trip to Cancun," Lizzie told him with an air of nonchalance.

"And?"

"The trip has to be used before the end of this year," Lizzie said. "They leave at the end of the week."

"That's great!" Wade said. "They deserve to have a nice vacation. What aren't you telling me?"

Wade stared at his wife while she told him about their trip and the plans they'd made to compensate for her parents' absence.

"It sounds like you have it all worked out," Wade said.

"Yes," Lizzie confirmed. "But, it's about to get crazy around here. There won't be much time for the two of us."

"Honey, it's crazy at the office, too," he told her about the murder case and the lack of progress in the Clifton case. "It should improve when Reed gets back tomorrow. Maddie can't be involved, and we need the help."

"Are you sure you don't mind the sudden change in plans?" Lizzie asked, concerned.

"Not enough to be upset about," Wade told her. "I may not be home much until these cases are closed anyway."

"Do you think you'll be here for dinner tomorrow night? Dan is bringing Deanna."

"I can't promise anything," said Wade. "I don't know where the cases will lead us."

"I don't like this at all," Lizzie said gloomily.

"We'll have to make the best of it. We might have to steal a few minutes alone between events," Wade teased.

Lizzie smiled at him and said, "You'd better eat your breakfast. I don't want you to be late."

* * *

When Maddie walked into the office, Wade was about to call his team to the conference room. Brody followed close behind her. She put her things on her desk and instructed her son to sit in her chair.

"Maddie, I'd like to see you in my office," Wade said, annoyed.

She followed him to his office and waited while he closed the door.

"What are you doing here?" Wade demanded his hand on his hips.

"I'm going crazy sitting at home," she replied, waving her hands around her head. "I need to keep busy."

"You can't get involved in this case," Wade began. "It's...

Maddie cut him off. "I know what you're going to say. It's a conflict of interest. With two cases, you need all the help you can get. I could run the office and free up another deputy to investigate. I won't do anything that might cause a problem."

"What about Brody?" Wade asked.

"My dad should be here any minute. He's going to take Brody home with him. He has all sorts of things planned to keep Brody occupied."

"Maddie, I don't know about this," Wade said.

"Wade, I don't want Brody here if Drew is...." Maddie didn't finish her sentence. "We both know the odds of finding him alive get smaller as time passes."

Wade nodded and said, "We could use the extra help. But you have to stay out of it, Maddie. I'll have to send you home if you can't."

"I promise I won't do anything to get in the way."

"In that case, you'll be running the office and nothing more. Do we agree?"

Maddie nodded, and the pair joined the rest of the team.

"Maddie will be running the office until further notice," Wade told them. "Gather your notes, and we'll meet in the conference room in ten minutes."

A tall thin man wearing a brown plaid flannel shirt, khaki pants, and a ball cap strode into the Sheriff's office.

"Poppy!" Brody shouted and ran toward his grandfather.

"Hello, Peanut!" the man said, hugging his grandson.

"Hi, Dad," Maddie said, smiling as she walked toward him. "Thanks for helping out."

"I'm happy to do it," Bill Furgeson said and hugged his daughter. "Any word?"

Maddie shook her head and wiped a tear from her eye. "Come and meet my friends."

She introduced her dad to the team. Wade couldn't help but notice that Maddie had his brown eyes and curly hair.

"It's nice to meet you, Mr. Furgeson," Wade said.

"It's a pleasure to meet you finally," said Furgeson. "My Maddie girl talks about y'all all the time."

The group engaged in polite small talk until Maddie interrupted. "I have Brody's suitcase in the car," Maddie said. "I'll walk out with you so these guys can get to work."

The three walked outside. Maddie transferred Brody's belongings to her father's truck and settled Brody into his car seat.

"Call me if you hear anything," said Bill. "Or if you need to talk."

"I will, Dad. Let me know if he gets to be too much."

"Don't worry about us. We'll have a grand ole time," Bill said and hugged his daughter goodbye.

Maddie hugged and kissed Brody before closing the door. She watched them drive away before going back inside. Her coworkers were already in the conference room when she returned.

Wade started the recording and said, "Today is Sunday, October 15, 2017. We currently have two cases. I want to start with the Jane Doe autopsy report so that Dr. Hughes may leave if necessary."

"Thank you," said Dr. Hughes with a nod. "I'm on call at the hospital this weekend."

Dr. Hughes was a short, stout man with a full head of brown

hair. He didn't look a day older than he had when Wade joined the Sheriff's department fourteen years ago.

"Based on my examination," the doctor began. "Jane Doe was five feet ten inches tall. She was between thirty and forty years old. Her weight is more difficult to determine due to the body's dehydration. A healthy woman of her height should weigh between one hundred thirty and one hundred sixty pounds."

"Have you been able to identify her?" Wade asked.

"Not yet," admitted Dr. Hughes. "Her face is unrecognizable. I believe that dental records will be the best chance we have. I don't expect to have those for several days. All I know for certain is that she had brown hair and brown eyes."

"How did she die?" asked Logsdon.

"Miss Doe was killed by blunt force trauma to the back of the head," the doctor answered. "The weapon left a circular indentation. I estimate the object to be two to two and a half inches in diameter. There was blood around the wound and cotton fibers in her hair. I believe she was dead before being placed in the tanning bed. She had third, and fourth-degree burns over her entire body. Her skin is completely dehydrated. She was literally cooked in that contraption."

"How long was she in there?" Wade inquired.

"Based on the burns and level of dehydration, I'd say between thirty and forty hours. That's as close as I can get to the time of death."

"Were there any clues as to where she might have been before she was killed?" Odom asked.

"Her blood alcohol was slightly over the legal limit," replied Dr. Hughes. "The excessive heat would have increased alcohol metabolism. Her stomach contents consisted of peanuts, pretzels, and a generous amount of gin and tonic."

"That sounds like she may have been in a bar," Lodge pointed out.

"Our victim would have been an easy target in her condition," said Dr. Hughes. "That's all I have at the moment. "I'll let you know when I have more to report."

"Thanks, Doc," said Wade.

Wade waited unto Dr. Hughes left the conference room to continue the meeting.

" I know there hasn't been enough time to get results from last night's crime scene," said Wade. "I'd like to table that discussion until this afternoon. Where are we on the Clifton case?"

"Someone needs to talk with the kid who lost his driver's license," said Lodge.

"Logsdon and I still have people to interview," said Wade.

"Sheriff, we have two open cases now," said Odom. " How will the casework be divided? We've all worked both cases to this point."

Wade pondered the question before answering. "I'll take the lead on the Clifton case. I'll have Reed work with me when he gets back tomorrow. Lodge will take the lead on the Jane Doe Case. I'd like everyone else to work with him. We may have to switch from one case to another depending on the evidence we find."

"Where do you want to start?" asked Baker.

First, I need all of you to search Maddie's home thoroughly.

"You can't be serious," said Lodge.

"I am," said Wade. "There may be something there that will help us find Drew. Maddie has given permission for the search. The door is unlocked, and no one is home."

"What do you expect to find that Maddie didn't?" asked Baker.

"You may not find anything," Wade told him. "Maddie has been dealing with Drew's odd behavior for a while now. She searched for drugs, but there could be something that she didn't consider while searching."

"That makes sense," said Lodge.

"After you've finished there, I'd like one of you to go with Odom to interview the teenager and one of you with Lodge to double-check the crime scene."

"I'll go with Lodge," said Baker. "I'd like to have another look while we can see better."

"I guess you're stuck with me, Odom," Logsdon joked.

"That leaves me to finish interviews," said Wade. "If there's nothing else, this meeting is adjourned."

Wade left the conference and asked Maddie to follow him to his office. She obeyed and closed the door behind them.

"The team is on the way to your house," he told her. "I need to emphasize how important it is that you don't get involved. You can answer any questions they have, but that's all."

"I understand," said Maddie, leaving the office only to return five minutes later.

"Sheriff, Mr. and Mrs. Handley are here."

"Good. I need to ask them a few more questions," Wade said and followed Maddie to the outer office. "Mr. and Mrs. Handley, thank you for coming in."

He shook hands with both of them and said, "If you'll follow my deputy, she'll get your fingerprints first so the lab can eliminate yours from those found at your home."

Maddie led them to a small room where the fingerprinting equipment was housed. She rolled each of their fingers onto the fingerprint scanner and stored them in the computer. Then she led them to the conference room and provided them with legal pads and pens.

"I'd like you both to describe what happened last night," Maddie told the couple. "Write down everything you can remember in as much detail as possible. I'll type them up when you've finished and bring them back for your review and signature."

"We'll do our best," said Annette Handley.

"Would you like anything to drink? We have coffee, soft drinks, and water."

"I'd like a cup of coffee, black," said Dennis Handley.

"Certainly, and for you, Mrs. Handley?"

"Water, please."

Maddie left the room and soon returned with the requested beverages. "I'll be right outside if you need anything," she said, leaving the couple to their task.

Half an hour later, Mr. Handley stepped into the doorway and said, "Deputy, I think we've written about all we can remember."

Maddie stood and followed him back into the conference room. She tore the used pages from both pads and said, "Sheriff Adams wants to talk with you while I type these. I'll let him know you're ready."

Dennis and Annette Handley didn't have long to wait. Wade soon joined them with a pad and pencil.

"I appreciate your help with this," Wade said. "I have more questions for you after collecting the evidence."

"We'll help anyway we can," said Mrs. Handley.

"First, I'd like to double-check my notes. You said you've been away for a week. Is that correct?"

"Yes," she replied. "We went to spend some time with our son and his family in Amarillo. We were on our way to see our son in Pflugerville. It was getting late, so we decided to spend the night at home and leave in the morning."

"How long are you planning to be there?"

"A week. We're spending our entire vacation visiting our boys and spoiling our grandkids," Annette said with a smile.

Wade smiled back at her and said, "That sounds like a great vacation. When did you leave?"

"We left last Sunday afternoon and planned to be back next Saturday," Dennis said.

"You said there were people at both your jobs who knew you'd be away. Did they know you planned to come home this weekend?"

"No, that wasn't part of our plans," Annette replied. "Dennis ran out of his medication. He needed to get more for the rest of the trip."

"Is the medication at your home?" Wade asked, concerned.

"No, I stopped at the pharmacy and had the prescription refilled before we went home last night," Dennis answered.

"That's good," Wade said, relieved. "Now, Mr. Handley, you said you went inside the house last night. Can you describe to me exactly what you did while in there?"

"I went in the back door," Handley began. "I could see the light and hear the noise coming from the tanning room. I tiptoed to the door and looked inside. Then I went out the back door and back to the car."

"You weren't in any other room of the house?"

"No, I was scared somebody might still be in there. I wasn't going to hang around to find out."

"Did you notice the house's condition while you were inside?"

"What do you mean?" Dennis asked.

"Was anything out of place, missing, or broken? Did the house look the same as it did when you left?"

"To tell you the truth, I didn't notice."

"I don't mean to pry, but I need to know how you left the house," Wade said apologetically.

"I made sure the house was in perfect condition before we left," said Annette. "I didn't want to clean when I got home."

A thought occurred to Wade as he jotted notes on his pad. "How much cleaning did you do? Was it routine or a deep cleaning?"

"Nothing major. I dusted, vacuumed, washed the dishes, and made the beds. That sort of thing."

"I'm going to need a list of the people who knew or might have known your plans," said Wade. "People you work with, friends, neighbors, anyone."

"I'm sure no one we know would do something like this," Annette said confidently.

"We'd all like to believe that," Wade said. "The truth is that we don't know what people are capable of doing. It may not have been anyone you know. Maybe it was someone who overheard a conversation and saw an opportunity. We have to start somewhere looking for leads."

"I hadn't thought of that," said Annette.

"I'll need the names, phone numbers, and addresses of your coworkers, friends, and neighbors," Wade told them.

Wade waited while the couple listed everyone who might have known they would be away. When they'd finished, he began questioning them again.

"Tell me about your neighbors."

"Our closest neighbor is David Foust, but he's seldom home," Dennis said. "He lives about a half mile away. He's a truck driver and hauls stuff all across the country. It's been at least a month since we've seen him."

"We don't see our other neighbors often," Annette added. "They're mostly young families busy with their own lives."

"What about friends?" Wade asked.

"We have some friends from church and a few others who knew we were leaving," said Dennis.

By the time the interview concluded, Maddie had returned with the statements ready for signatures.

"Sheriff, may we continue our trip?" Dennis asked. "Since we can't go home, I thought we'd go on to Pflugerville."

"Yes, there's no reason for you to stay," Wade assured him. "I have your phone number. I'll call you if I have more questions. We should be finished with your home before you get back."

"Do you know who was in our tanning bed?"

"Not yet," Wade admitted. Right now, we're calling her Jane Doe."

"Is there going to be…anything to clean up when we get back," Annette asked, dreading the answer.

"We'll clean up after ourselves when we've finished," Wade promised. "We've determined that Jane Doe didn't die in your home. We believe she was placed in your tanning bed after she was killed."

"Why on earth would anyone do that?"

"That's what we're trying to find out."

# CHAPTER SEVEN

THE DEPUTIES FOUND nothing in Maddie's house to help them in their search for Drew. They brought back a few items that might be useful in verifying his fingerprints but nothing else.

Odom and Logsdon went to the home of Daniel Holden. He was a seventeen-year-old male living near the high school with his mother.

They parked in front of the house and walked to the front door. Odom knocked while Logsdon stood back.

A woman wearing heels and a sheath dress that was a bit too tight answered the door. "Hello, officers. What can I do for you?"

"Does Daniel Holden live here?" asked Odom.

"I'm Diana Holden. Daniel is my son," said the woman, surprised. "What's wrong?"

"Probably nothing," said Logsdon trying to reassure the woman. "We need to ask him some questions. You're welcome to listen."

"Oh, well, I guess that's all right," the woman replied, unsure what to do. "Come in. He's upstairs. We've only been home from church for a few minutes."

She led the deputies to the living room and invited them to sit down.

"Daniel! I need you to come downstairs!" she yelled toward the ceiling.

"Why?" a voice called from above.

"Don't ask questions. Get down here!"

The teen was not pleased and protested as he made his way down the stairs. He froze when he saw the deputies in the living room.

"Daniel, these officers want to ask you some questions," said his mother, obviously annoyed with him.

"I'm Deputy Odom, and this is Deputy Logsdon. We need to ask you about an incident involving a white Chevy Tahoe."

The boy's eyes grew wide with fear, and his knees trembled.

"I...I...don't...know anything," he stammered.

His mother looked at him sharply and said, "Daniel Lane Holden, if you know what's good for you, you'll tell these officers the truth."

Daniel hung his head and whispered, "Yes, Ma'am."

"Why don't we sit down and talk," Logsdon suggested.

When everyone was seated, Odom began asking questions.

"When were you last on Highway 240 east of Harrold?"

The boy looked up in surprise. "How did you know...?"

"Why were you there?" Odom asked.

"We were goofin' around," Daniel replied.

"Who's we?" asked his mother, her eyes flashing.

"Me and some of the guys," he said.

"What were you doing?" asked Logsdon.

"Drivin'."

"Daniel, did you and your friends steal that Tahoe?" asked Odom.

Ms. Holden gasped as Daniel nodded.

"Tell us about that night," said Logsdon.

"We were out drivin' around in my car. Russ needed to make a pit stop, so I parked behind a building. When he came back, he said there was an SUV sitting empty. The door was open, and the keys were inside."

"Then what happened?" Odom prodded.

"We hadda check it out. It was dope," Daniel said, smiling. "We took turns sittin' in the driver's seat and the passenger seat. Tim turned the key, and the engine started. That's when Russell said we should take it for a test drive."

"I can't believe you'd steal a car! What were you thinking?" demanded Daniel's mother.

"I didn't drive it," he said, his eyes pleading with his mother. "Sitting in it was one thing, but driving it didn't feel right."

"What did you do?" asked Logsdon.

"I came home and went to bed," Daniel replied.

"How did your driver's license end up on that highway?" Odom asked sternly.

Daniel swallowed hard before he answered. "Tim called me and said they were out of gas. He asked me to pick them up. I guess my license fell out of my pocket when I got out of the car."

"Was the vehicle damaged?" asked Ms. Holden.

"No," Logsdon said. "It was in perfect condition when we found it. Daniel, did you see anyone near the SUV when you found it behind the building?"

"No, we looked all around. We didn't see anybody."

"Do you remember which building it was behind?" Odom inquired.

"I'm not sure," Daniel said, squinting his eyes, trying to remember. "It was pretty dark."

"Do you remember what the building looked like?" Odom asked, excited.

"No, I was too busy looking at the SUV."

"I'm afraid you'll have to come with us," Odom said and stood.

"Are you arresting my son?"

"Not yet, Ma'am," Odom assured her. "We need to get his statement and his fingerprints." He turned to Daniel and said, "We'll also need the names and addresses of your friends."

"I thought you said the car was fine. Why does he need to be fingerprinted?"

"The man who owns the vehicle is missing," said Logsdon. "These boys may be charged with grand theft, possibly more. Their cooperation could be helpful when facing a judge."

"Since he's a minor, you have every right to accompany your son to the office and during questioning," added Odom.

"Mom, I'm sorry," Daniel said.

"You go ahead with the deputies," said Ms. Holden. "I'll call our lawyer, and we'll be there as soon as we can."

Daniel nodded and obeyed his mother. Odom escorted him to the car and opened the back door. The three rode in silence to the sheriff's department.

Logsdon and Odom escorted the teenager to an interrogation room. They waited until the boy's mother and attorney arrived to ask more questions. They soon had the names and addresses they needed to pick up the other boys for questioning.

Christian Daberkow, Tim Florez, and Russell Favors were questioned individually. All had the same story as Daniel Holden. None of the boys saw anyone near the Tahoe. Christian was sure that it had been parked near The Watering Hole Bar.

The boys were fingerprinted and allowed to go home with their parents until charges were filed. Daniel Holden's driver's license was returned to him.

"I'll take that," said Ms. Holden. "You won't be needing it for a while. You're grounded for six weeks."

Daniel looked at his shoes and handed his license to his mother.

"I understand how you feel," Logsdon told the woman. "But he did the right thing by choosing not to follow his friends. And he cooperated with us."

"Thank heaven for that," answered Ms. Holden. "He's really a good boy. Maybe I'll ground him for a month instead."

Logsdon smiled at Ms. Holden and waved goodbye. She returned to the interrogation room to assist Odom with their report.

Wade returned to the office no closer to finding Drew than he had been earlier in the day. He went to his office and sat at his desk. He was preparing to write his report when Clint Odom tapped on his door.

"We've had a break in the case," Odom told him.

"Tell me," Wade replied with excitement.

Odom told him everything he and Logsdon had learned from Daniel Holden and his friends. "Logsdon thought you'd want to go along to interview the bar owner and patrons," he said.

"The bars were the last places on my list," Wade said. "I planned to go as soon as they opened. We'll start with The Watering Hole. Have you told Maddie anything?"

"Not yet," Odom replied. "We thought it best to leave that decision to you. I'm sure she's curious. She saw those kids when they were brought in."

"I'd rather have more information before I share anything with her," Wade said. "We may have more news after going to the bars."

"Logsdon is calling to find out when they're open," Odom said.

"Let me know."

"Yes, Sir," Odom replied and left the office.

The intercom on Wade's desk buzzed. "Baker and Lodge are back," Maddie told him.

"Have everyone gather in the conference room in fifteen minutes," Wade replied.

When everyone had gathered, Wade started the recording and said, "We'll discuss the Oklaunion crime scene evidence first. What about the tire tracks?"

"There were two sets of tire tracks on the north side of the house," Odom reported. "One appears to be from the homeowner's car, a Ford Escape with Michelin tires. The other has a tread pattern matching the Bridgestone brand tires, common on mid-sized sedans."

"There was one set of tire tracks on the south side of the house, as well," said Lodge. "The tread pattern matches the Goodyear tires common on cars made between 2010 and 2015."

"Two vehicles other than the one belonging to the Handleys were at that house," Wade said. "Were the tracks old or new?"

"The tread patterns were too clear to have been old," said Lodge.

"What else did you find outside?"

"We found three sets of footprints," Odom continued. "All led from the vehicle tracks to the house and back. Two sets were made by men's shoes and one by women's shoes."

"A woman?" Wade asked with surprise. "I thought our victim was already dead."

"Yes, Sir," Odom replied. "High heels, to be specific. Pointy toes and narrow heels that left holes in the ground. They didn't match the victim's shoes."

"I see," Wade said, frowning. "Anything else? "

"There was another set of tracks," Odom said. "It looks like someone or something was dragged from a vehicle toward the house. The trail was between two sets of footprints, one male and the other female."

"Did two people drag the victim inside?" asked Wade.

"The victim's shoes were clean," said Baker. "There would have been scuffs or dirt on them if she'd been dragged to the house."

"Then who, or what was dragged toward the house?" Wade asked. He paused in thought before continuing. "Were there footprints on the south side of the house?"

"There were two sets of footprints, both appearing to be male," said Baker. "There were also signs of a struggle between the two."

"Baker and I went back to finish the scene," said Lodge. "It seems there were several people at that house. Four men and two women were there based on the shoe print sizes and patterns. One of them was Mr. Handley and one Mrs. Handley."

"We compared shoes from the Handleys' closet to the prints

outside and were able to eliminate theirs," Baker added. "Mrs. Handley didn't have high heels in the closet, and Mr. Handley has relatively small feet. Neither of them was on the south side of the house."

"Evidence of six people at that house, and only two belonged there," Wade said. "Did you find anything else?"

"The back door was forced open," answered Logsdon. "The tool marks are similar to a crowbar or tire iron. I didn't find the tool at the scene."

"The front door was open," added Baker. "Someone vomited outside near the front porch. It had a strong odor of alcohol. There were peanuts and pretzels in it. The lab report shows the alcohol to have been whisky, most likely Crown Royal."

"It sounds like there was a lot of action at the Handley house," Wade observed. "Could there have been a party while they were away?"

"If so, it wasn't a big party," Baker pointed out.

"True," Wade agreed. "Let's talk about inside the house."

Lodge spoke first. "Someone tampered with the tanning bed. Most have timers that turn the whole thing off after a specified time, usually twenty to thirty minutes max. The timer on that bed had been removed."

"Is there a way to find out how long it had been running?" asked Wade.

"There might be," Lodge replied. "It will likely be tomorrow before we can find out."

"Stay on that, Lodge. What else?"

"Most of the house was undisturbed," said Odom. "There was evidence that someone else was there. The bedding on one of the beds was rumpled. The others were untouched."

"There was also evidence of some sort of altercation or an accident in the living room," said Logsdon. "An ottoman was overturned, and a broken lamp was on the floor."

"Was there evidence of the victim in the house?" Wade prodded.

"Everything connected to Jane Doe was in the room where she was found," said Logsdon. "The clothing we found on the chair appears to be hers."

"There was no blood in or outside the house," said Odom.

"What about prints?" Wade asked.

"We dusted the entire house," said Baker. "There was one set on the back door. The next prints were in the bedroom with the twin beds. There was a print on the inside of the doorframe. A print was found on the door to the tanning room. And another on the tanning bed lid. The last set of prints was on the inside door knob of the front door. The same person made all except those on the back door."

Wade pondered the information before he spoke. "Let me get this straight. There were at least six people there, but only two of them left prints in the entire house?"

"That's right," answered Baker.

"The Handley's prints should have been everywhere!"

"Maybe they cleaned before they left," Logsdon suggested.

"Mr. and Mrs. Handley came in while the rest of you were out," Wade began. "Mrs. Handley says they left the house clean and neat. Based on her description, their prints should be on at least some surfaces."

"Did someone wipe the house?" asked Logsdon.

"But why wipe the entire house and leave only a few prints?" asked Odom.

"Either someone was in the house after it was wiped," Wade began. "Or the perpetrator wanted to incriminate someone. The question is, who and why?"

"Maybe someone was in the house at the time," suggested Odom.

"Are you saying someone was already in that house when the body was moved inside?" asked Logsdon.

"Or left behind," Baker replied. "Whoever left those prints was there after the house was wiped."

"Do you have any matches?" asked Wade.

"Not yet, the program is running, but I haven't had any hits yet."

"Does anyone have anything to add concerning the Jane Doe case?" Wade asked.

The deputies shook their heads.

"Mr. and Mrs. Handley gave me a list of people who might have known they weren't at home," Wade added. "Lodge, I'll get that to you so you can decide how to divide the tasks."

"Yes, Sir," replied Lodge.

"Our investigations will overlap," Wade pointed out. "Mrs. Handley works at the same bank and knows Drew. I didn't mention his disappearance to her. She and her husband were out of town at the time."

"On to the Clifton case. Did you find anything at their home?"

"Odom and I searched the barn and garage," said Lodge. "We didn't find anything useful."

"The same in the house," said Logsdon.

"I did take an item that belongs to Drew for fingerprint comparison," said Baker. "I need to verify that some of the prints we found in his Tahoe are his."

"I hoped you'd find a clue, but I didn't expect he'd left anything for us to find," said Wade. "It occurred to me that if he were doing anything illegal, he wouldn't leave evidence where Maddie might find it."

"That's true," said Lodge. "Maddie would have sniffed that out in no time."

"You don't think...never mind," said Logsdon shaking her head.

"What are you thinking?" Wade prodded.

"I was wondering if Maddie might have found something and disposed of it before we got there," Logsdon said apologetically.

"Not a chance," said Baker angrily. "If anything, she'd have turned it over to Wade."

"You're right," Logsdon said. "Maddie wants to find her husband. I know she wouldn't jeopardize the investigation."

"Moving on," Wade said to diffuse the tension. "We may have a break in the case. I'll let Odom and Logsdon tell you about it."

Odom and Logsdon gave their report about the teenagers finding Drew's SUV.

"Sheriff Adams, Logsdon, and I will interview the bar owners and patrons in the next few hours. With any luck, we'll have a lead to Andrew Clifton's location."

"Speaking of which, I think it's time to adjourn and continue our investigations," Wade said and turned off the recorder. "Don't mention anything to Maddie or answer any of her questions. I'll fill her in after we've completed interviewing at the bars."

"Yes, Sir," the deputies replied.

* * *

Sheriff Wade Adams, Deputy Clint Odom, and Deputy Sherri Logsdon walked into The Watering Hole shortly after the Sunday afternoon football games began. The bar was filled with loud, excited football fans.

The three split up and began interviewing the occupants. Odom and Logsdon interviewed the patrons while Wade spoke with Trey, the owner and bartender.

"Hello, Sheriff, what can I do for you?" asked Trey, eyeing Odom and Logsdon as they made their way around the room.

"Hello, Trey," Wade replied. "We're looking for a missing person."

Wade took a photo of Andrew Clifton from the folder he was carrying and handed it to Trey.

"Yea, I've seen him," said Trey. "I don't know his name. He's not a regular."

"When did you last see him," Wade asked, excited.

Trey wiped the bar while he tried to remember. "I'm pretty sure it was Thursday night."

Wade could hardly contain himself when he said, "What do you remember about that night?"

"He was my first customer," Trey began. "I think he came in around seven-thirty. He sat at the end of the bar and ordered a Crown and Coke. He didn't say anything except to order more drinks. How long has he been missing?"

"No one has seen or heard from him since Thursday," Wade replied. "Is there anything else you can tell me?"

"There was a woman who came in around nine. She sat at a table behind him and ordered a gin and tonic. She invited him to join her. They started talking. She was mad at her boyfriend. He was mad at his wife. They sat there complaining and drinking."

"Did you know the woman?" asked Wade.

"She's been in a few times. I don't know her name either. She's a good-looking woman. The kind you don't forget, long brown hair, tall, and built. Hot, you know what I mean?"

Wade's stomach knotted while Trey described the woman. He nodded and asked, "Did they seem to know each other?"

"No, I don't think so. She asked his name, but I didn't hear the rest. I had to wait on another customer. I cut them both off around midnight. They were disturbing my other customers."

"Then what happened?"

"She called a friend to come and pick her up," Trey said. "He didn't have a cell phone, so I offered to let him use the bar phone. He said his phone was in his car, and he'd call for a ride when he got outside."

"Did they leave together?"

"No, she left a few minutes before he did."

"Have either of them been here since then?" Wade asked.

"Not while I've been here," Trey replied.

"How did Clifton pay for his drinks?" Wade asked.

"He paid cash," Trey replied. "He bought some of the woman's drinks too."

"Thanks, Trey. You've been a big help."

"Anytime, Sheriff. I hope you find that guy."

Wade signaled Odom and Logsdon that he'd finished and would wait for them outside. *Who was the woman? Could she be the woman found in the tanning bed?*

# CHAPTER EIGHT

WADE ARRIVED at the office early on Monday morning. He brought donuts and made coffee for everyone. He dreaded telling Maddie what he'd learned at The Watering Hole.

Deputy Gordon Reed walked into the Sheriff's office with a bright smile. He'd had a great vacation and couldn't wait to annoy his coworkers with the stories. His smile faded when he saw the look on Wade's face.

"What's going on?" he asked.

"Good morning, Reed. How was your vacation?" asked Wade.

"It was awesome," Reed said, his smile returning. "I think this time of year is the best time for a beach vacation. It's not crowded, and you don't have to stand in line for hours."

"That's great," Wade replied, distracted. "I'm glad you had a good time."

"How are things here?" asked Reed.

"Not great," Wade replied. "Drew Clifton has been missing since Thursday evening.

"Wow! How is Maddie taking it?"

"She's trying to stay busy and in the loop without getting

involved in the investigation," Wade answered. "I need to update her when she comes in."

"Is everybody working the case?"

"We were until a body was found in Oklaunion on Saturday night. It was a Jane Doe. Lodge has the lead on that case. You'll work with me on Drew's case. Maddie is running the office."

"When do you want to get started," Reed inquired.

"We learned some new information last night," Wade said. "I'll update the team in the conference room after I've informed Maddie."

"The expression on your face tells me it isn't great news," Reed observed.

"It could be better," Wade admitted. "It could be a lot worse."

Maddie walked into the office and stopped at her desk. She put her things away and smiled at Reed.

"Welcome back," she said. "Did you have a good time?"

"I had a great time," Reed said, smiling.

"Maddie, I'd like to see you in my office before everyone gets here," said Wade.

Deputy Clifton nodded and followed her boss into his office. She sat down in front of his desk and waited.

"How are you holding up?" Wade asked.

"I'm okay," Maddie lied.

"Come on, Maddie," Wade prodded. "I know what you're going through."

"I'm sorry. I'm afraid I'll have a meltdown if I tell the truth."

"I understand," Wade said. "I wanted to tell you privately what we learned yesterday and last night."

Maddie nodded and said, "I'm ready."

"Drew didn't leave his truck on the highway," Wade began. "Some kids found it and took it joyriding until they ran out of gas."

"So, he didn't park it and walk away," Maddie said with tears in her eyes.

"No, he didn't."

"What did happen?"

"The boys found the truck behind The Watering Hole. I spoke with the bartender. Drew must have driven there from your house on Thursday. He was there until after midnight drinking heavily."

"Where is he now?"

"We don't have any other leads right now," Wade admitted. "Maddie, he was drinking with a woman. Reed and I will try to locate her and find out what she knows."

"I see," Maddie said with anger flashing in her eyes.

"Trey said they didn't seem to know each other, and they didn't leave together," Wade said quickly. "They were talking. We don't know that anything else was going on."

"Why didn't he talk to me? I've been right there all along, yet he never confided in me," she said as angry tears dripped from her chin.

"I don't know, Maddie," Wade said and shook his head. "Trey said they were both angry and venting to each other. That may be all that happened."

"What did this woman look like?" Maddie asked, trying to conceal her jealousy.

"All I have is a general description," lied Wade. He knew repeating Trey's description of the woman would be a mistake.

"What now?"

"Reed and I will keep searching," Wade told her. "We'll find him, Maddie."

"I know you will," she said with a weak smile. "But I'm worried Drew will be dead when you do."

Their conversation ended, and Maddie returned to her desk. Wade joined the rest of the team in the conference room. Updates were given on both cases and the day's tasks assigned.

"We don't know much about Jane Doe," said Wade. "I'll have Maddie run a search for missing women matching the description that Dr. Hughes gave us. Reed and I will go to the bank and interview Drew's coworkers. Lodge, what assignments do you have for your team?"

"Baker and Gonzalez will analyze evidence from the crime scene. Wagner and I will start interviewing people from the list provided by Mr. and Mrs. Handley."

"All right, time to get to it," Wade said.

The team went to work when the meeting adjourned. Wade and Reed drove to the bank and went inside.

"I read the case reports while you were talking with Maddie," said Reed. "Haven't these people already been interviewed?"

"Yes," Wade replied. "But I have different questions this time."

"Oh? Care to fill me in?"

"Dr. Hughes thinks something may have happened at work that triggered Drew's behavior. We need to find out what that might have been."

"How is that going to help us find Drew?"

"If we can get an idea of what happened, it might give us a lead," Wade explained. "He could be hiding because he's involved in illegal activities or staying in a hotel somewhere with a woman."

"Do you think he left with that woman from the bar after all?" Reed asked, surprised.

"The Drew I know wouldn't be involved in anything illegal or with another woman," Wade assured his deputy. "The problem is that he isn't the man I know right now."

"So, you're telling me that I know as much as you do, and you're hoping to get a lead from the interviews," Reed said, grinning.

"I was trying not to say that, but yes," Wade admitted, smirking.

Wade parked his truck at the bank, and the two men went inside. They went directly to the bank president's office.

"Good morning," said the secretary. "How may I help you?"

"We'd like to speak with Mr. Dillingham," Wade told her.

"Do you have an appointment?"

"No, but it's important," Wade said politely. "We're investigating the disappearance of Andrew Clifton."

"Please, have a seat, and I'll see if he's available."

The secretary went into Dillingham's office and closed the door. She returned a few minutes later and said, "He'll be with you as soon as he finishes his phone call. Would you like some coffee?"

"No, thank you," said Wade.

Reed shook his head.

They waited fifteen minutes before Dillingham opened his office door and invited them inside.

"What can I do for you?" Dillingham asked and indicated that they should sit down.

"We need to interview everyone again about Andrew Clifton," Wade told him. "We like to conduct the interviews here rather than asking everyone to come to our office."

"That sounds like a good idea. What will you need?"

"We'll need a space that allows for private conversations," Reed said. "We want everyone to feel comfortable."

"I understand. We don't have any empty office space, but you could use the board room," Dillingham suggested.

"That will do," Wade said, nodding. "We'd also like to search Drew's office."

"Search his office? Why?"

"There might be something inside that will help us locate him," said Reed. "We can get a warrant if you'd prefer."

Garrett Dillingham blanched and said, "That won't be necessary. I hope you find something useful. When would you like to start the interviews?"

"Now," said Wade. "My deputy will search Clifton's office while you and I talk."

Surprised, Dillingham said, "Oh…well…yes…of course. I'll ask Miss Lozano to show you to Drew's office."

He opened his door and said, "Janet, will you take Deputy Reed to Drew's office, please? Answer any questions and get him anything he needs."

"I'd be happy to," said the secretary with a sweet smile. "Right this way, Deputy."

Dillingham returned and sat behind his desk. He looked at the Sheriff with a worried expression and said, "I'll be happy to answer your questions, Sheriff Adams."

"How closely do you work with Drew?"

"We work together on occasion, but we have different responsibilities."

"Have you noticed anything odd or unusual about his behavior in the past two months?"

"Odd or unusual?" Dillingham asked and shook his head. "No, I haven't."

"Any personality change? Did he come in late or leave early more than usual?" Wade queried.

"Not that I'm aware of," said Dillingham. "But I did notice that he seemed to be tired lately."

"What do you mean?"

"Dark circles under his eyes, yawning a lot, and once I caught him dozing at his desk."

Wade jotted notes while Dillingham spoke, then asked, "Is there anything at the bank that might cause him to lose sleep?"

"We have a bank audit coming up. Everyone's a little nervous about it because of our assigned auditor. I don't think that would cause Drew sleepless nights."

"What's so bad about the auditor?" asked Wade.

"He likes to intimidate people," said Dillingham. "Perfect audits don't exist as far as he's concerned. He digs for things to write up."

"Has Drew had any visitors that weren't here for bank business?"

"Not that I'm aware," said Dillingham with one eyebrow raised. "What exactly do you mean?"

"Nothing, exactly," Wade replied, trying to avoid potential

gossip. "I'm looking for a needle in a haystack and hoping it will point us to Drew."

Garrett Dillingham relaxed and said, "I understand. I can't imagine where he is or why he disappeared."

"Has he had any issues with anyone working here?"

"I don't believe so."

"Would Drew have any information that would warrant kidnapping?"

Dillingham sat up, suddenly alert. "I hadn't thought about a kidnapping. Drew has vault access and access to the building after hours. He knows our cash delivery schedule."

"I suggest you make some changes to be on the safe side," Wade told him.

"And as soon as possible," agreed Dillingham.

"That's all I have at the moment," Wade said. "I'd like to interview everyone here, but I don't want to disrupt your routine."

"I'll take care of that," Dillingham volunteered. "I'll print out an employee roster. We don't want to miss anyone."

"Thank you," Wade said and extended his hand. "I appreciate your cooperation."

Dillingham shook Wade's hand and said, "We need to do whatever it takes to find Andrew."

The two men left the bank president's office, and Reed joined them. Dillingham led them to the board room.

"Make yourselves comfortable," Dillingham said. "I'll have coffee brought in. Is there anyone, in particular, you'd like to interview first?"

"I'd like to start with those who knew him best or worked closely with him."

"I'll see what I can arrange. I may have to send people as they become available. Let me know if you need anything."

"Thank you," said Wade.

Reed waited until Dillingham had closed the door to speak quietly with Wade.

"I didn't find anything in Drew's office," he said. "I texted his office phone number to Baker. He might find something useful there."

"I don't know if anything Dillingham said is useful," Wade admitted. "He didn't seem to be the observant type."

A tap on the boardroom door interrupted their conversation. Reed opened the door, and Dillingham's secretary entered.

"I understand you have questions about Mr. Clifton," she said.

Wade nodded and said, "Please, sit down. Tell me your full name and your job title."

"My name is Janet Lozano. I'm a secretary for Mr. Dillingham, Mr. Hallmark, and Mr. Clifton."

Wade asked the secretary the same questions he'd asked her boss. Her answers were similar.

"Has Mr. Clifton had any problems with anyone working here?" Wade asked.

Janet Lozano avoided looking at Wade when she answered, "I don't think so."

"Miss Lozano, we're doing everything we can to find Mr. Clifton," he coaxed. "If you know something that might help, we need to know."

Janet nodded and said, "I came back from lunch one day and overheard part of an argument between Mr. Clifton and Mr. Hallmark. I didn't hear much, but it sounded like they were arguing about the audit."

"Do you think they're worried about the audit?"

"I know Mr. Clifton has been concerned. I'm not sure about Mr. Hallmark."

"Why would Mr. Clifton be worried about the audit?"

"I don't know," replied Janet. "He's never worried about them before."

"Thank you, Miss Lozano," said Wade. "Call us if you think of anything else that might help."

The Sheriff and his deputy interviewed several more people

with no results. No one had noticed anything or knew anything helpful.

A tap on the boardroom door alerted the two men that their next interview subject had arrived. Wade invited her to sit down.

"My name is Addie Sims. I'm a receptionist for the bank officers."

"How closely do you work with Mr. Clifton?"

"We work together every day."

"Have you noticed anything odd or unusual about his behavior in the past two months?"

"Yes, I have," Addie whispered and nodded.

"What did you notice?" Wade asked, trying to hide his annoyance.

"I can't explain it," she began. "But I'm pretty sure something has been bothering him."

"Why do you say that?"

"He seems so sad and tired," she said, shaking her head. "I'm pretty sure I smelled alcohol when he came back from lunch one day. I think he might have a bottle in his desk."

"Has he come in late or left early more than usual?" Wade queried.

"He's been late a few times, but not more than five or ten minutes."

"Has Mr. Clifton had visitors who weren't here for bank business?"

"I haven't seen anyone," she replied, whispering. "But I heard a woman has dropped by a few times."

"Do you know if Mr. Clifton has had disagreements with anyone working here?"

"Hmmm," Addie said and paused. "I don't know anything for sure, but things do seem a little icy between him and one of the girls on the teller line."

"Has Mr. Clifton been worried about the upcoming audit?"

"Not that I've noticed," she said. "I mean, everyone's worried, but Mr. Clifton never mentions it."

"Thank you, Miss Sims. "Don't hesitate to call us if you think of anything else."

Wade breathed a sigh of relief when Addie Sims left the room.

Reed chuckled and asked, "Do you think anything she said was true?"

"I don't know," Wade said. "Did you find any alcohol in Drew's desk?"

"Not a drop."

"Still, she could have smelled alcohol on him," said Wade.

They interviewed everyone from the teller line, the cafeteria, and the bookkeeping department. No one had anything new to share.

Wade and Reed discussed the case while they waited for the last interview of the day. The man sauntered in and shook their hands with a toothy smile.

"I'm Mitchell Hallmark," he told them. "I'm one of the vice presidents of the bank. I'll be happy to help you in any way that I can. Drew is one of my good friends."

"Please, sit down, Mr. Hallmark," said Wade.

Mitchell Hallmark's answers matched most of the people's interviewed that day. He hadn't noticed anything unusual and wasn't aware of any problems Drew might be having with coworkers.

"I understand you had a disagreement with Mr. Clifton," Wade prodded.

"What? Who told you that?" Hallmark asked a little too casually.

"I'd rather not say," Wade told the man with an air of authority. "It seems the two of you were arguing about being audited."

"We discussed the audit several times but never argued about it."

"I see," Wade said and stared at Hallmark for a moment. "That's all for now, Mr. Hallmark. "Please, call us if you remember anything that could help our investigation.

"I will, and I hope you find Drew soon," said Hallmark. "We miss him around here."

"What do you think?" asked Reed after Hallmark had gone.

"I think we need to find some lunch. Then we'll go back to the office and talk to Maddie about some of these people, especially Drew's good friend, Hallmark."

The two men returned to the office to find Maddie sitting at her desk with an odd expression on her face. She was staring at her computer screen.

"Are you all right, Maddie?" asked Reed.

"We might have a problem," she said without looking up.

"What kind of problem?" Wade asked warily.

"There are two missing women that match the description of Jane Doe," she said and raised her eyes to meet Wade's. "One of them is…."

Maddie was interrupted before she finished her sentence. A Vernon Police detective strutted into the office.

"Well, well, well," said Officer Allen Joyner. "Sheriff Adams, you're the man I need to see."

"What can I do for you, Joyner," Wade said coldly.

Joyner smirked through his cookie-duster mustache. Slightly shorter and heavier than Wade, his receding hairline accentuated his bushy brows and brown eyes.

"I'm working on a missing persons case," Joyner replied.

Deputies Brandon Lodge and Drake Wagner burst through the office door.

"Sheriff! You'll never guess …," shouted Lodge. He stopped abruptly when he realized they had a visitor.

"And Wagner, the other man I need to see," sneered Joyner.

"Why do you need to see me?" asked Drake.

"Oh, I'm here to see you and Sheriff Adams," Joyner gloated. "You're both persons of interest in my case."

"We don't have time for your games, Joyner," Wade growled. "We've got cases of our own."

"Game? Game? This is no game. But I have to admit that I am enjoying this."

"What do you want?" demanded Wade.

"As I was saying," Joyner said with a wide grin. "You are of interest in my missing persons case."

"Why is that?" asked Drake.

"You both dated her," said Joyner with glee.

"Who?" asked Wade.

"Tiffany Pruitt," said Joyner with a mischievous grin. "She's missing."

# CHAPTER NINE

"DID you say Tiffany Pruitt is missing?" Wade asked, shocked.

"I did," replied Joyner, smirking. "I guess that means you haven't seen the bulletin yet."

"We've been out of the office, working," Wade retorted.

"Ah, yes," Joyner said with a malicious gleam in his eye. "Wouldn't it be a hoot if Clifton and Pruitt ran off together?"

Maddie glared at Joyner but didn't have a chance to reply before her coworkers spoke up.

"That's enough!" Reed shouted. "It's time for you to leave!"

"Baker and I will show you the door," said Lodge with a menacing tone.

"You need to keep your dogs penned up, Adams. They should know by now that threatening a peace officer could get them into trouble."

"You weren't threatened," Wade said, seething with anger. "You were asked to leave."

"I'm not leaving until I've questioned you and Wagner," Joyner said with authority.

"Why question us?" Wagner snapped. "Wade's a happily married man, and I haven't seen or spoken to her in over a year."

Wade looked at Drake as if seeing him for the first time. He never expected Lizzie's ex to stand up for him.

"You know the drill," Joyner answered. "I've got to interview everybody. Trying to avoid questioning makes me think you have something to hide."

"We don't mind answering your questions," Wade informed the officer. "However, we do object to your unprofessionalism."

Joyner grinned and said, "Please, accept my apology for my behavior this afternoon."

Wade ignored the apology and said, "You can use the conference room. Who would you like to interview first?"

"I'll start with Wagner," Joyner said. "I have a few questions for Maddie when I finish with you, Sheriff."

Wagner led Joyner to the conference room and closed the door.

Wade whispered, "Do you have a picture of Tiffany, Maddie?"

"Yes, I was trying to tell you she was missing when Joyner blew in here."

"We were about to tell you that Pruitt works at the insurance company with Dennis Handley," added Lodge. "She hasn't been to the office for over a week."

"All right," Wade said. "Lodge and Baker, go to her house and see if you can find anything. If asked about it, it's part of your investigation."

"Yes, Sir," replied Lodge.

"Do you mind if we wait until that idiot leaves?" Baker asked. "I don't want him to insult Maddie again."

"It's better if you go now while he's busy," Wade said. "He doesn't need to know what you're doing."

"I can handle Allen Joyner," Maddie assured her friends. "We dated years ago. He wasn't happy when I broke it off. He uses every opportunity to take jabs at me."

"It's still not right," said Baker angrily.

"Can we focus on our current situation, please?" Wade asked impatiently. "We don't have much time. Maddie, make half a dozen of copies of Tiffany's picture. Don't let Joyner see them."

Maddie pressed the print button, took the photo from the printer, and went to the copier.

"Reed, don't let Maddie or Joyner know what you're doing. Take a copy of that photo to The Watering Hole and find out if she's the woman with Drew."

"You don't think...," Reed began.

Wade interrupted and said, "No, I don't, but we have to make sure. Take it to the bank too. See if anyone there recognizes her. Report back to me in person, privately."

Maddie returned with the photocopies and handed one to each of her friends. She put the rest inside her desk and locked it. Baker, Lodge, and Reed immediately left the office.

"What do you think he's asking Drake?" Maddie queried.

"I imagine the same things we'd ask if we were questioning a potential suspect," Wade replied. "He said he wants to talk with you. Do you want one of us to be there with you?"

"Of course not," Maddie said, insulted. "I'm a big girl, and I can take care of myself. Thank you very much."

Wade blushed and grinned, "I'm sorry, Maddie. Sometimes I'm an overprotective ass."

"Yes, you are," Maddie said with a grin. "But I forgive you."

The door to the conference room opened, and Drake Wagner walked out. His jaw and his fists were clenched.

"The others have gone to lunch," Wade said. "Why don't you take a break too? Maddie and I can handle things here."

Drake nodded and mumbled, "Thanks." He left the office without looking back.

"It's your turn, Sheriff," Joyner said with an evil grin.

Wade went into the conference room and shut the door. He sat down in his customary seat at the head of the table, forcing Joyner to move. With one quick motion, he started the recorder without the police officer's notice.

"Sheriff, You were…"

"Before you get started, I'd like to ask you some questions," said Wade.

"That's not how…."

"Who filed the missing persons report?"

"All right, I'll play it your way," Joyner said, irritated. "Her parents filed it this morning."

"What are the particulars?"

"I don't see how that concerns you."

"We're fellow peace officers, aren't we?"

"Yes, but…"

"Since I haven't seen the report, I'd like to know the details so that my department can help with the search," said Wade enjoying the frustration on Joyner's face. "We recently shared information with your department."

"Fine!" Joyner said with gritted teeth. "Tiffany Pruitt and her son have been visiting her parents in Abilene, Texas. She left there on Thursday morning to investigate an insurance claim. She told them she'd be back Saturday afternoon. They haven't heard from her since she left."

"Where is her son?" Wade asked, attempting to irritate Joyner further.

"He's with her parents," growled Joyner. "Can we get on with this?"

"Shouldn't he be in school?"

"Why? Are you his dad?" Joyner said with a smirk.

"No," Wade answered calmly. "Checking the facts of the case."

"He was excluded from school because he has chicken pox," Joyner said. "Now, if you don't mind, I'd like to finish here."

Wade smiled and said, "By all means. What did you want to ask?"

"Is it true that you were once engaged to Ms. Pruitt?"

"Yes, it is," Wade replied. "That relationship ended before I moved here and joined the Sheriff's department."

"Who ended it?"

"She did," answered Wade. "I'd been injured on the job. She didn't handle it well."

"How did you feel about that?"

"I was hurt at the time, but I moved on."

"How long has it been since she broke off the engagement?" Joyner asked, looking for a reaction from Wade.

Wade looked at the ceiling, trying to recall the approximate dates, and said, "It's been fourteen or fifteen years."

"I understand that she wanted to reinitiate a relationship with you after moving to this area," Joyner said, trying another tack.

"Yes, she approached me more than once," Wade admitted. "I told her that I wasn't interested because I love Lizzie."

"When did you last speak with Ms. Pruitt?" asked Joyner.

"She came to my house a few days before I married Lizzie," Wade said. "I didn't invite her inside. We had a short discussion, and she left."

"You haven't seen or spoken with her since then?"

"No, I haven't," said Wade.

"I'll contact you again if I have more questions later," Joyner said.

"I'll be happy to answer them. Are we finished?"

"I still need to speak with Maddie," said Joyner with a smug expression.

Wade wanted to say a lot of things on Maddie's behalf. Instead, he said nothing and left the conference room, leaving the recorder running.

Maddie didn't give Joyner a chance to say anything. She held her head high and walked into the conference carrying a file folder. She sat down and said, "I'm ready."

Joyner grinned and said, "I'd like to clarify some things in the missing persons report you filed."

Maddie tossed the folder to him and said, "It's all there. A copy of the report and my statement for your records. What else do you want?"

"A copy of the investigation records would be nice," Joyner jeered. "Oh, wait, you don't have access to those, do you?"

"No, I don't," said Maddie calmly.

"Then you don't know, do you?" Joyner said maliciously.

Maddie glared at the officer and said with conviction, "I know a lot of things. I know my husband loves me and our child. He would never intentionally cause us worry or pain. He's a man of integrity."

"I also know," Maddie shouted. "That you're a manipulative, backstabbing weasel who has to torment others to make yourself feel like a man."

"Are you implying…?"

"I'm not implying anything," Maddie said, cutting him off. "I've tried to be courteous to you for professional reasons. That's over. I'm telling you face to face that I've had enough of your insults, innuendos, and snide comments. It's been ten years. Get over it and get a life."

Stunned, Joyner didn't immediately reply. He looked at Maddie and blinked several times before saying, "I think that's all I need, but I hope we can get past this and be more civil next time."

"There won't be a next time," Maddie informed him. " I've had enough."

"I may have more questions," Joyner said, trying to regain control of the conversation.

"Then send someone else to do the interview. Preferably, someone who is a professional and knows how to behave," Maddie said as she stood up. "We're done here."

Maddie opened the door and walked out of the conference room, leaving Joyner sitting alone with his mouth hanging open.

"I'm going to lunch," Maddie told Wade. "I won't be back until that weasel is gone."

Wade grinned as he watched Maddie pick up her purse and keys. She stomped out of the office without looking back. He turned toward the conference room when he heard Joyner clear his throat.

"Thank you for your cooperation, Sheriff," said Joyner meekly. "I'll send you a copy of that missing persons report."

"I'd appreciate that," said Wade fighting the urge to laugh.

Joyner hurried out of the office, leaving Wade alone. Drake Wagner returned five minutes later.

"Is Joyner gone?" he asked.

"He's gone," Wade replied. "I take it he gave you a hard time too."

"I wanted to knock his teeth out," growled Drake. "I had to get out of here before I lost control."

"If you want to file a complaint, write up what happened during your interview," Wade suggested.

"Will it do any good?" Drake asked, doubtful.

"It might," Wade said. "I turned the recorder on before he started our interview. I left it on during Maddie's. I wish I'd thought to turn it on before yours. We might have enough to warrant disciplinary action."

A smile spread across Drake's face. "I'll start writing while it's still fresh on my mind."

"That reminds me," Wade said and got up from the chair he'd been occupying. "I need to turn the recorder off."

Reed hurried into the office and asked, "Is Wade here?"

Wade heard his name and said, "In the conference room."

Reed went into the conference room and closed the door behind him. "We need to talk."

"What's wrong?" asked Wade, fearing the worst.

"I went to the bank first. No one recognized Tiffany. Either she hasn't been inside, or she banks elsewhere."

"Go on," Wade said, putting his hands on his hips.

"Trey was unlocking the door to The Watering Hole when I got there," Reed continued. "He identified Tiffany as the woman talking with Drew the night he disappeared."

"Damn!" Wade swore and hung his head. "How am I going to break this to Maddie?"

"There's more," Reed said and hesitated. "Trey pointed out a car sitting in the parking lot. He said it's been there for days and asked me to find out who owns it. I ran the plates."

"It's hers," said Wade.

Reed nodded and asked, "What do you want to do?"

Wade crossed his arms and tilted his head in thought. Finally, he said, "Run her phone records. Trey told me she called a friend to pick her up. We need to know who she called. That person may have picked up Drew as well."

"Yes, Sir," Reed said and left the room.

Wade started toward his office but was interrupted by Lodge and Baker.

"There's no one at Pruitt's house," said Baker. "No sign of her car either."

"It was a long shot," Wade replied. "Did you boys have lunch?"

"We did," answered Lodge. "We knew it was safe to come back when Joyner walked into the restaurant. How's Maddie?"

"She was in better shape than Joyner when that interview ended," Wade said, grinning.

The deputies smiled their approval and returned to their work.

Wade went to his office and closed the door. He went to his desk and sat down. Picking up the phone, he tapped in a number and waited.

"This is Sheriff Adams. Is Dr. Hughes available?"

"Yes, I'll transfer you to his office," said his secretary.

"Hello, Sheriff, what can I do for you?" answered the doctor.

"Doc, I need you to check into something for me."

"Of course."

"This has to be kept quiet if possible," Wade said. "At least for now."

"All right," said the doctor with curiosity in his voice.

"I may have a lead on the identity of our Jane Doe."

"Don't keep me in suspense," joked Hughes.

"I think you should compare Tiffany Pruitt's dental records with Jane Doe."

"Oh my!" exclaimed the doctor. "Wasn't she…"

"Yes, she was," answered Wade. "I'll have to hand the case over to someone else if it's her."

"I understand," said Dr. Hughes. "I'll let you know as soon as possible."

"Thanks, Doc."

The call ended, and Wade tapped in Lizzie's number.

"Hi, Sweetheart," Lizzie said when she picked up her phone.

"Hi, how's your day going?"

"It's going well. How about yours?"

"It could be better," Wade said. "There's something I need to tell you before you hear it through the grapevine."

"Do I need to sit down?" Lizzie joked.

"You might."

"Now, you're scaring me," Lizzie replied as she sat in the nearest chair.

"Tiffany Pruitt is missing," Wade began. "A police detective was at my office to question Maddie, Drake, and me."

"Why would they want to question you?"

"You know how it goes," said Wade. "Everyone connected to the victim is questioned at first."

Lizzie didn't say anything. Her silence made Wade so uncomfortable that he asked, "Are you still there?"

"I'm still here," Lizzie replied. "I was thinking about Tiffany. Do you think she's missing or up to something?"

"It could be either," Wade replied. He wanted to share his suspicions but knew he couldn't.

"Could she and Drew be together?" Lizzie asked in disbelief.

"I don't know, Honey," Wade admitted. "I'd rather not talk about the case."

"Okay, I'll change the subject. Will you be home for dinner?"

"I'm not sure," Wade replied. "I still have a couple of leads to follow before the day ends."

"Don't forget that Dan is bringing Deanna," Lizzie reminded him.

"Oh, that's right. I'll do my best to be there on time. I'll talk to you later."

"Okay, I love you."

"I love you too, Lizzie."

The call ended, and Wade remained in his chair, drumming his fingers on his desk. His thoughts vanished when he heard a tap on his door. He got up and walked across the room. Drake Wagner handed him a sheet of paper when Wade opened the door.

"Wagner, come in," said Wade. "We need to discuss something. Have a seat."

Drake obeyed while Wade closed the door. "What do you want to talk about?"

Unsure how to start the conversation, Wade sat down before answering. Finally, he said, "I don't know of a good way to say this."

"You aren't about to fire me, are you?" Drake asked with defiance.

Wade looked at his deputy, surprised. "No! Why would you think that?"

"It's no secret that we aren't fond of each other," Drake pointed out. "My past relationship with Lizzie is a source of contention."

Wade sat back in his chair and sighed. "I knew this would come up eventually, but I didn't expect it to be today."

"My mistake," Drake apologized. "I jumped to the conclusion…"

"The mistake was mine," said Wade. "We should have gotten this out in the open months ago. Drake, you're a good deputy and an asset to this department. My personal feelings have made it difficult to form a professional relationship. I apologize."

"Thank you, Sheriff," said Drake. "It's nice to know that my work is appreciated regardless of the past. I apologize for my lack of professionalism."

Wade grinned at this deputy and said, "Now that that's settled, I want to discuss the Tiffany Pruitt case."

"What about it?" asked Drake. "I don't have anything to hide. You can read that report."

"No, that's not what I'm getting at," Wade said, frustrated. "This is harder than I thought it would be."

Drake waited while Wade collected his thoughts.

"I have a hunch about this case," Wade said at last. "There's no proof, and I could be wrong."

"Understood," said Drake, nodding.

"If I'm right, we'll find ourselves in a difficult position," Wade told his deputy.

"Are you talking about the whole department?"

Wade leaned forward in his chair and said, "It could affect the whole department, but I'm talking about the two of us. We may have to exclude ourselves from all investigations connected with Tiffany Pruitt."

"I see what you mean," said Drake. "Joyner would love to tie us to Tiffany's disappearance."

"Yes, he would," Wade admitted. "And any case this department builds related to her could be thrown out due to conflict of interest."

"What do you have in mind?"

"I think you and I should avoid any aspect of our cases that involve Ms. Pruitt. Let one of the other deputies take over if her name comes up."

"I agree," said Drake.

"Did you finish that background check on Drew Clifton?"

"Yes. I didn't find anything that would help us," Drake replied. "He hasn't had so much as a traffic ticket in the last ten years."

"It was worth a try," Wade said. "We need a good lead if we're going to find Clifton."

"Maddie seems to be holding up," Drew pointed out.

"She is, but I'm not sure how long that will last," Wade said with concern. "The more we uncover, the worse it looks for Drew."

# CHAPTER TEN

WADE DROVE to the inn that night, thinking about Maddie and Drew. He wanted to break the news to Maddie gently. The facts led to the assumption Tiffany and Drew were together.

He parked behind the inn and noticed Dan's truck. He walked to the back door, opened it, and stepped inside.

"Wade! You made it," said Lizzie happily.

Wade smiled at his wife and kissed her. "Did I miss dinner?"

"You're just in time," said Granny. "We haven't finished filling our plates yet."

Wade joined the family at the table. They passed bowls and plates of food to him as they talked.

"How's the search for Drew Clifton going?" asked James.

"It's at a standstill," Wade admitted. "We've exhausted every lead."

"How is Maddie taking it?" Ellen asked.

"On the surface, she's handling it pretty well. It may be a different story when she's away from the office," Wade replied. "I understand you're going on a trip," Wade said, changing the subject.

Ellen Fletcher beamed at her son-in-law and said, "We're so excited. We've had our passports for years, but we've only used them once."

"It'll be nice to see beaches," added James.

"Where are you going?" asked Deanna Garnett.

"To Cancun for a week," Ellen explained.

"James will have some interesting tan lines if he wears his overalls," Dan joked.

"He's not going to be wearing his dirty old overalls," replied Ellen. "I'll make sure he packs something suitable for the beach."

"Yeah, my idea was vetoed," James said with a twinkle in his eye.

"If Ellen hadn't stepped in, I would have," said Granny. "No son of mine is going commando in his overalls."

Wade laughed so hard that he choked on his potato salad. Lizzie patted him on the back until he could talk.

"I'm sorry," he said. "I had a mental image of Lois and Ellen chasing James with a shirt and underwear."

Laughter erupted around the table. The group talked while they ate and enjoyed each other's company.

"Who wants cake?" Lizzie asked.

"Lizzie, if you don't mind," Dan began. "There's something we need to talk about first."

"It sounds serious," said Lois, concerned.

"It is," Dan said and reached for Deanna's hand. "We have something important to tell you." He looked into Deanna's eyes and smiled. "Deanna has agreed to be my wife."

Joyful screams and shouts of congratulations filled the inn.

"I've been dying to tell you since we got here," said Deanna.

"Show us the ring!" said Lizzie beaming.

Deanna proudly displayed the diamond ring on her left hand. "I was afraid you'd see it before Dan could tell you."

"It's gorgeous," Lizzie said. "Dan, you did good! Who would have guessed?"

Dan laughed and said, "Thank you, thank you. Does this end the nosey questions about my love life?"

"I won't make any promises," Lizzie joked.

"Have you set a date yet?" asked Ellen.

"That's what we wanted to talk with you about.," Dan replied. "We thought about getting married at city hall. But this place is like a second home for me, and y'all are part of my family. We want to be married here as soon as possible."

"My dad is terminally ill," said Deanna. "We don't know how much time he has left. I want him to be there when we get married."

"We know there aren't many open dates," Dan added. "We can get married during the week if necessary. It'll be a small wedding, with family and a few friends. It doesn't have to be anything fancy."

"I'll get my calendar, and we can look at available dates," Lizzie said and hurried to her office.

"I'll cut the cake," said Granny.

"Do we have champagne?" James asked. "This calls for a celebration."

"There's a bottle in the pantry," said Ellen.

Wade sat back and watched his in-laws congratulate and celebrate the happy couple. The room brimmed with pure joy and love. It lifted the gloom he'd felt since Drew's disappearance.

Lizzie returned with her calendar and said, "There aren't any Saturdays available until after the New Year. I have a couple of Fridays and most Sundays open until December. There are more options if you consider earlier days of the week."

"I think a Sunday would be best," said Deanna. "Don't you, Dan?"

"Whatever you want," Dan replied and smiled at his fiancé.

The couple looked at Lizzie's schedule and discussed their options. They settled on an afternoon wedding on Sunday, November fifth.

"Are you sure?" asked Lizzie. "That's less than two weeks away."

The couple looked at each other and smiled. Deanna turned to Lizzie and said, "We're sure."

"There's a lot to decide," Lizzie told them and handed Deanna a checklist. "Look this over and call me in the next few days with your choices."

Deanna looked at the list and back at Lizzie, "Does all of this need to be done?"

"No, you don't have to do everything. It's a guide to help you make decisions. Scratch off what you don't want and make notes about the rest. I'll be happy to help if you need it."

"I'm gonna need it," Deanna said with wide eyes.

"This is your wedding," Lizzie said, patting Deanna's hand. "We'll do what the two of you want. You can throw that list in the trash if it isn't helpful."

"Okay, that makes me feel better," Deanna said and looked at Dan.

"Don't look at me," said Dan with a grin. "Tell me what to wear and where to stand. The rest is up to you."

After cake and champagne, everyone said goodnight leaving Wade and Lizzie alone.

"What are you smiling about, Sheriff Adams?"

"They remind me of us not so long ago," Wade answered, wrapping her in his arms.

"They're so happy," said Lizzie holding him close. "It's a shame that her dad is ill."

"He may live longer than they think."

"That's true. Wouldn't it be great if Deanna's dad lived long enough to meet his grandkids?"

Wade kissed Lizzie on the forehead and held her tight.

"What's wrong?" she asked.

"It's been a rough weekend," he replied. "I'm afraid things will get worse before they get better."

"Why don't we go to bed and watch a movie," Lizzie suggested. "I won't mind if you fall asleep in the middle of it."

"A movie? I had something else in mind," he said, grinning.

"I thought you were tired," Lizzie teased.

"I have a little energy left," he said, leading her to their bedroom.

* * *

Wade arrived at the office early the following day. He'd needed the brief respite from work. Now it was time to focus on solving these cases.

Gonzalez was the first of the deputies to arrive. Wade called her into his office.

"I haven't had a chance to talk to you about that background check you were running for me," Wade said apologetically. "Did you find anything interesting about the Handleys?"

"Nothing that would explain what happened at their home," said Gonzalez.

"I didn't expect there would be," said Wade with a sigh. "We'll meet in the conference room to compare notes when everyone gets here."

Gonzalez went back to her desk. Wade went to the coffee machine to refill his cup when Maddie entered the office.

"Wade, can we talk?" she asked.

"Do you want some coffee first?" Wade asked, stalling.

"No, thanks," Maddie replied nervously. "In your office?"

Maddie didn't wait for an answer before she turned around and walked away. Wade followed and closed his office door. Maddie was already sitting down, tapping her foot.

"What's going on, Maddie?" Wade asked, concerned.

"I did something stupid yesterday," she replied. "I want you to know about it in case there are repercussions."

"What did you do?"

"I told Allen Joyner off during my interview. It was unprofessional, and I shouldn't have done it."

"Maddie, I'm sure there won't be a problem."

"You don't know him like I do! He's conniving and manipulative. He twists people's words and uses them as weapons or to further his interests."

Wade smiled and said, "He can try, but it won't work."

"You don't understand! He's been backstabbing people for so long that he's an expert."

"Maddie, we have proof of what was said during your interview."

"What are you talking about?"

"I turned on the video recorder before I sat down," Wade explained. "I wanted a record of any information I could get from him about Tiffany's disappearance. I didn't turn it off when I left. It recorded both our interviews."

A smile spread across Maddie's face. She began to relax, and then her eyes opened wide.

"Did you watch it?"

"No, I haven't yet. I plan to before our meeting so that I can jot down notes about Tiffany Pruitt's disappearance."

"I was furious with him," she admitted. "I'm not even sure what I said."

"Do you want to watch it with me? I'd like to know what you said that made him tuck his tail between his legs," Wade teased.

Maddie blushed and said, "I'd like to hear it."

Wade found the recording on the server and ran it forward to Maddie's interview. Maddie gasped and covered her mouth, but Wade roared with laughter.

"Maddie, you were right," Wade said with pride. "You are a big girl, and you can take care of yourself."

Maddie laughed and said, "I told you so."

"Would you mind if I showed this to the others during our

meeting? It will boost their morale and let them know they don't have to defend you."

"I don't mind," said Maddie. "Honestly, it felt good when y'all came to my defense. I've felt like I've been fighting this battle alone. No one wants to upset me, so they don't say anything."

"I'm sorry about that, Maddie. We care about you and don't want to cause you more pain."

"I understand and appreciate your concern," Maddie began. "But you have to remember that I've been a deputy sheriff for a long time. I've seen a lot over the years. When I'm out of the loop, my past experiences and imagination fill in the information gaps. I'd rather know the truth than imagine what it might be."

Wade looked at his deputy and said, "I hadn't thought of it that way. I apologize.

"It's okay," Maddie said. "All I'm asking is to be in the loop."

"In that case, I have some news."

Wade updated Maddie on the investigation into Drew's disappearance. He shared the facts but kept his suspicions and hunches to himself.

"Thank you for telling me," Maddie said when he'd finished, anger and pain showing in her expression.

"I'll keep you updated in the future," Wade promised.

Maddie nodded. "If you don't mind, I need a few minutes alone. I'd like to skip the meeting."

"There's no need for you to be there," said Wade.

Maddie left Wade's office and went to the ladies' room to regain control of her emotions. Wade joined the rest of his team in the conference room and turned on the video recorder.

Today is Tuesday, October 17, 2017. We're meeting to discuss progress in the Andrew Clifton and Jane Doe cases. Lodge and Wagner, do you have anything to report concerning Jane Doe."

"We interviewed the employees at the insurance company where Dennis Handley works as office manager," said Lodge. "Everyone we spoke with believed the Handleys' would be away two weeks, and all of them know or could easily find out where they live."

"It's a small office with six staff members, including Mr. Handley and Tiffany Pruitt," said Wagner. "We verified the alibis of all but one of the people we interviewed. Elaine Cabrera said she was home alone watching television on Thursday night and went to bed after the ten o'clock news."

"We've started a background check on Ms. Cabrera," added Lodge. "We'll conduct interviews at the bank today and then contact the Handleys' family and friends."

"Start with the bank president, Garrett Dillingham," Wade suggested. "He proved to be helpful yesterday. Gonzalez and Baker, do you have any new information concerning the evidence?"

"I got in touch with the right person at the electric company," Baker said. "A definite power spike occurred between two-thirty and two-forty-five Friday morning. The power usage remained steady until Saturday night at approximately the same time we were on the scene."

"That puts Jane Doe's time of death between midnight and two-forty-five the morning of Friday the thirteenth," Wade observed. "That's within the time frame that Dr. Hughes gave us. Gonzalez, do you have anything?"

"I tested the fibers Dr. Hughes found in the victim's hair," said Gonzalez. "They were likely fibers from a gold cotton bath towel."

"What color were the towels at the crime scene?" asked Wade.

"They were all white," replied Lodge. "Those gold fibers came from somewhere else."

"Have you matched any of the fingerprints from the scene," Wade inquired.

"I've matched the print on the back door to Mr. Handley," Baker reported. "I'm still working to find the other person's identity."

"I promised the Handleys we'd clean up after ourselves, especially in the tanning room," Wade informed them. "Lodge and Wagner have a lot more interviews to do. The rest of us will make another sweep for evidence and clean up so the homeowners can have their house back."

The deputies nodded their approval, and Wade continued. "Unless anyone else has new information on the Jane Doe case, we'll move on to the Clifton case. Reed, I'll let you discuss our results."

"Sheriff Adams and I interviewed everyone at the bank concerning Andrew Clifton," reported Reed. "There were three people of interest. One woman, who seems to be a credible witness, reported that Drew argued with another bank officer several weeks ago. That bank officer denies arguing but wasn't convincing. Another woman made some statements that have been disproved, but others haven't. I've started background checks on these three."

"Most of the people at the bank didn't work closely with Drew and didn't notice anything different," Wade added. "Those who did said that he seemed tired and didn't look well. One mentioned smelling alcohol on him after lunch."

Reed looked at Wade. Wade nodded, indicating that he should continue.

"When we learned that Tiffany Pruitt is missing, Wade suggested I take her photograph to The Watering Hole. Trey confirmed that she was the woman drinking with Andrew Clifton the night he disappeared."

"I'd like y'all to see this," Wade said and started the video of his conversation with Joyner. He stopped the recording before Joyner began questioning him.

"Pruitt has been missing since Thursday?" asked Lodge.

"According to Joyner, she has," Wade replied. "I haven't seen a copy of the report. I think a call to Pruitt's parents is in order. However, it has to be done by someone other than Wagner or myself."

"I'll make the call."

"Thank you, Reed," said Wade. "I've informed Maddie about the new evidence. I made a mistake by telling you not to discuss the case with her. I'd still prefer that she gets new information from me, but feel free to talk with her."

"Why do you think it was a mistake?" asked Gonzalez

"Maddie should be feeling supported by her coworkers. Instead, she's feeling frustrated and alone because of my orders. Coming to her defense the way you did yesterday lifted her spirits. She appreciated it more than you can imagine. I think it gave her the boost she needed to deal with Joyner. I'd like you to see this," Wade said and ran the recording to Maddie's confrontation with Joyner.

Maddie worked at her desk and heard laughter coming from the conference room. She smiled and giggled when she heard them cheering.

The meeting ended, and the deputies went to work. But not before congratulating Maddie for cutting Allen Joyner down to size.

Reed went to his desk and looked up the number for Tiffany Pruitt's parents. He tapped the number into the phone and waited.

"Hello?"

"Is this the Douglas residence?"

"Yes, this is Sharon Douglas."

"Mrs. Douglas, my name is Gordon Reed. I'm a deputy with the Wilbarger County Sheriff's office. I'd like to verify some information about your daughter, Tiffany Pruitt."

Reed gathered as much information as he could and ended the call. He went directly to Wade's office.

"I spoke with Tiffany's mother," he told Wade. "Joyner's information was incomplete, to say the least."

"What did you find out?" Wade asked.

"According to Mrs. Douglas, Tiffany wasn't on vacation," began Reed. "She was investigating insurance claims in their area and decided to stay with her parents. Her son, Ross, did have chicken pox, but he didn't break out until they arrived in Abilene on Saturday the seventh."

"Someone is misinformed or lying about Tiffany's absence from work," said Wade.

"The afternoon of Thursday, the twelfth, Tiffany said she had to go to the office to turn in her reports. She said she'd be back to spend the weekend with them."

"That's a vague timeline," Wade pointed out.

"Mrs. Douglas said she wasn't sure when Tiffany planned to be there. When she hadn't shown up by Sunday, they tried to get in touch with her. Tiffany didn't answer her home phone, and her cell phone went to voice mail," said Reed.

"That sounds familiar," said Wade shaking his head.

"Mrs. Douglas called the insurance office this morning. No one there had heard from Tiffany. That's when she filed the report," Reed said.

"Mrs. Douglas isn't one to panic," Wade recalled. "She'd have tried everything before calling the police."

"She mentioned something else that I think you'll find interesting," Reed began. "She said she would have called Tiffany's boyfriend if she'd known his name or number."

"Did she know anything about the boyfriend?" Wade asked, suddenly alert.

"Not much. Mrs. Douglas said they'd been dating for three or four months but didn't see each other often. Tiffany never gave her a satisfactory explanation about it," said Reed. "She suspects Tiffany may have gone to see the boyfriend after leaving the office. Could Drew be the boyfriend?"

"Trey said Tiffany was complaining about her boyfriend to Drew," Wade recalled. "He said they didn't seem to have met before Thursday night."

"If that's true, Drew couldn't have been the boyfriend," Reed said, grinning.

"Why wouldn't Tiffany see her boyfriend often?" Wade pondered.

"Could be because of his job," Reed suggested. "Or a long-distance relationship."

"I suppose so," Wade said. "I got the missing persons report a few minutes ago. Detective Joe Fleeks sent it instead of Joyner. It agrees with what you found out except for the part about a boyfriend."

"Should we tell them?"

"I'm sure he'd appreciate the information," said Wade. "Besides, it isn't our case."

# CHAPTER ELEVEN

ANDREW CLIFTON DOZED on the couch. He'd been awakened by
sunlight streaming through the bedroom window where he slept.
Rather than close the curtains, he moved into the living room. It
was time to start his day.

But there was nothing to do. He'd kept himself busy trying to
find an escape from his prison. When he grew tired, he began
cleaning dust and cobwebs from the small house.

Each day he worked to loosen the security bars over the bathroom window. Each day they were as tight as the day before.

He was losing hope of ever seeing his family again. The
memory of Brody's mischievous smile and Maddie's beautiful face
tormented him.

*I can't imagine what they're going through. I wish I could see them,
talk to them, hold them.*

The sound of a car on the dirt road beside the house brought
him back to the present. He listened, expecting it to drive past.
Instead, the sound of crunching gravel reached his ears.

He got up and went to the kitchen. Looking out the back door,
he saw David Foust.

Foust got out of an older model Cadillac and disappeared behind the open trunk. A few minutes later, he reappeared with a box and his Glock. He waved the gun, indicating that Drew should move away from the door.

Drew knew that today could be his last day on earth. He was no match for Foust. There was no chance of overpowering him. His only hope was to stay alert and wait for an opportunity to escape.

Backing out of the kitchen, Drew stopped in the hallway and waited. His body buzzed, and his heart pounded with anticipation.

Foust opened the back door, the screen slamming shut behind him. He put the box on the kitchen table. Pocketing the gun, he wrinkled his nose.

"Phew! Kinda ripe, ain't ya'?"

Drew didn't reply.

"Got some hot food. Sit down."

Drew's stomach growled. The smell of something delicious was more than he could resist. He stepped into the kitchen, keeping his eyes on his visitor.

"Is this my last meal?" Drew asked.

Foust laughed. "Not today," he said, taking a white paper bag from the box and handing it to Drew. "Eat!"

Drew sat down and took a hamburger and fries from the paper bag. He watched Foust and took that first glorious bite.

"Got some news," Foust said, joining Drew at the table. He wrinkled his nose, got up, and opened a window.

"Is it good news?"

Foust crossed his arms and leaned against the wall. "Depends."

"On what?" Drew asked with his mouth full.

"Your point of view," replied Foust. "Cops lookin' for ya. Missin' person case."

Drew stopped chewing and looked at his captor. "Missing person? They don't think I killed anyone?"

Foust shook his head. "Found the body, still investigatin'. Remember anything yet?"

"Bits and pieces. Nothing helpful."

Foust nodded. "Might have a lead. Meetin' tonight."

"Does that mean you'll let me go?"

"Might tell cops where ya are after leavin' town."

Drew nodded and finished his meal. He wiped his mouth and leaned back in his chair. "Thanks for the burger."

Foust nodded.

Drew briefly considered throwing the box at Foust and running out the door. At that moment, Foust moved away from the wall and took the Glock from his pocket. He pointed it at Drew's chest.

"Don't try it!"

Drew shook his head and stayed in his seat. He watched Foust back out the door and lock the security bar. He didn't move until he heard the car drive away.

He stood and inspected the contents of the box Foust had left. More lunch meat, a loaf of bread, a bottle of whisky, and a newspaper.

Drew put the food away, leaving the whisky and the newspaper on the table. Taking a glass from the cabinet, he returned to the table and opened the bottle.

He was about to pour himself a drink when he hesitated. Drinking had gotten him into this mess. It certainly wasn't going to get him out of it. He needed to keep his mind sharp.

Putting the cap back on the bottle, he sat down to read the latest issue of the Vernon Daily Record. On the second page, he saw a photo of himself. He read the article giving his description and details about the investigation.

After reading the article, Drew concluded that he'd been a prisoner for four or five days. Foust brought enough food to last another four.

Images began to flit across his mind. They were gone before he could make sense of them.

He continued reading in the hopes that it would trigger his memory. It was then that he saw another article with a familiar face.

*That's her! The woman at the bar!*

Drew thought about that night. He still couldn't remember what had happened after leaving the bar. He could see Tiffany Pruitt's face in his mind. But that was all.

The food and the news spurred Drew into action. He went to the bathroom and worked on the security bars again. He worked until thirst and darkness forced him to stop.

A foul odor reached his nostrils on the way to the kitchen. He sniffed the air and realized Foust was right. He reeked of stale alcohol and sweat.

A washing machine and dryer stood in the corner of the kitchen. Drew stripped off his clothes and tossed them into the washer. He added detergent he found in the pantry and started the machine.

He went to the bathroom and took a long hot shower. He went to bed feeling refreshed but exhausted. He fell asleep thinking of his wife and son.

* * *

Sheriff Adams sat in his office going over the case files. They'd searched for clues in the disappearance of Drew Clifton and Tiffany Pruitt all day. Nothing new came to light. He hoped he'd spot something they'd missed by rereading the files and reports.

"Sheriff, you have a visitor," said Baker.

"Who is it?"

"Detective Joe Fleeks with the Vernon Police Department," Baker replied.

"What now?" Wade replied with irritation. "All right, I'll go see what he wants."

Joe Fleeks was a tall African American man who looked like he could have played professional football. A rim of graying hair circled his bald head. He had an easy manner and a warm smile that made him feel like an old friend. His eyes didn't miss anything.

"What can I do for you, Detective?"

"Do you have a few minutes to discuss the Tiffany Pruitt case?"

"Have you had some new developments?"

"No, I'd like to ask you some routine questions," answered Fleeks.

"Certainly, but I don't know what else I can tell you that I haven't already told Detective Joyner," Wade replied.

"What are you talking about?" asked Fleeks, his eyes narrowing.

"Allen Joyner was here yesterday. He interviewed two of my deputies and me."

"Oh, he did, did he?" replied Fleeks angrily. "May we talk in private, Sheriff?"

"Baker, hold all my calls," Wade said, leading Fleeks to his office.

"Would you like something to drink?" Wade asked and offered the detective a chair.

"No, thank you. I'd like to get right to it," replied Fleeks with an edge to his voice. "Exactly when was Joyner here?"

"It was during the lunch hour yesterday," Wade told him and sat behind his desk. "Is something wrong?"

"Joyner isn't working this case," said Fleeks. "He had no business interviewing any of you."

"I see," Wade said, unsure of what was going on. "I noticed the information he gave us didn't match the missing persons report you sent."

"Joyner's desk is close to mine, and he overhears most of my conversations. He left in a hurry while I was taking the call," said Fleeks. "I didn't think anything of it at the time."

"I take it that he didn't share the interview information with you," Wade said shrewdly.

"No, he didn't."

"As it happens, I have video recordings of two of the interviews and a detailed report of the other," Wade informed the detective. "Would you like to see them?"

"Yes, I would," replied Fleeks.

Wade stood and went to his file cabinet. He took Wagner's report from a folder and handed it to the detective. While Fleeks read the information, Wade cued up the videos.

Detective Fleeks watched the videos with growing irritation until he reached Maddie's tongue-lashing. His laugh was deep, loud, and hearty.

"I like her," said Fleeks, grinning. "Would you mind sending me a copy of these?"

"I'll get them to you right away. Do you have any other questions for me?"

"What was your impression of Joyner?"

Surprised, Wade took a moment to answer. "He seemed to be more interested in causing trouble than getting answers. Maddie thinks he'll use the information he gathered as a weapon against us. Especially after the things she said."

"She's right about that," Fleeks admitted. "Joyner is a piece of work. He doesn't care who he hurts or steps on to get what he wants."

"If he wasn't assigned to this case, why was he here?"

"I don't know unless he was looking for someone else to blame."

"Someone else?" asked Wade, suspicious.

"Until a few months ago, Joyner was dating Tiffany Pruitt. He says he ended it, but that might not be true."

Wade raised an eyebrow and nodded, unable to come up with the right words.

"I'll make sure he doesn't bother you about this case again," Fleeks said. "I plan to speak with the chief about this when I get back. The videos and Deputy Wagner's report will help keep him out of the way during this investigation."

"Let us know if we can be of any help," said Wade. "Do you need to speak with my deputies?"

"Not right now."

"I have some information that might help your case," said

Wade. "Deputy Reed contacted Pruitt's mother. It seems that Tiffany had a boyfriend that she didn't see often. Mrs. Douglas thinks she may have gone to see him."

"Is that right? She didn't mention that when giving me the report."

"She may have remembered it after she spoke with you," Wade suggested. "She said they'd been dating for three or four months but didn't know any details. Could it have been Joyner?"

"I'll check that out," replied Fleeks and extended his hand. "Thank you for your time, Sheriff. I don't think I'd have been so cooperative after dealing with Joyner."

The two officers exchanged small talk as Wade escorted him from the office. Wade felt he had a new ally in the police department.

He returned to the office and emailed the requested information to Fleeks. He called his team to the conference room and informed them about Joyner.

"He's not on the case?" asked Wagner. "At all?"

"No, he isn't. He'll likely be working a desk for the foreseeable future," Wade said with a grin. "Fleeks has copies of our interviews."

"Do you think he'll come here again?" asked Baker.

"He will if he can get away with it," Maddie assured them.

"I suggest that no one in this office discuss anything with Joyner," said Wade. "We're dealing only with Detective Fleeks in the Pruitt case."

"Can we punch Joyner if he gets in our way?" joked Lodge.

"No, you can't, tempting as that might be," Wade said, grinning. "I think it would be best if we avoided Joyner altogether. We don't want any issues with the police department."

The team reluctantly agreed, and the meeting continued.

"Let's discuss the background checks," suggested Wade.

"There was nothing to suggest that Elaine Cabrera would be involved in the break-in at the Handley home," said Gonzalez. "I talked with her coworkers. They describe her as a quiet person who rarely changes her routine."

Reed spoke up next. "Addie Sims has had six jobs in the past two years. She was laid off from one and quit the others. I spoke with her former employers. All of them said she tended to be nosy. One of them said she took every opportunity to stir the pot."

"That matched my impression when we interviewed her," observed Wade. "What else?"

"Janet Lozano has been with the bank for years," said Reed. "Everyone I spoke with thinks highly of her. Nothing in her background suggests a connection to either case."

" What about Hallmark?"

"He's hard to pin down," replied Reed. "There were some issues with the law years ago. There's nothing that points to him as a suspect. His coworkers have mixed feelings about him. Some like him, and some don't."

"Keep digging on Sims and Hallmark," said Wade. "It wouldn't hurt to run background checks on everyone at the bank and insurance company. Someone may have slipped under our radar."

"Baker, did Drew's office phone provide anything useful?"

"No, Sir. All the calls in the past month have been loan related."

"Reed, any luck finding out who Tiffany Pruitt called?"

"I haven't gotten any results back yet," Reed replied.

Wade nodded and said, "I mentioned the possibility of kidnapping to the bank president during my interview with him. The intention was to keep him guessing about our investigation. His reaction convinced me that it could be a motive for Drew's disappearance. I don't think that happened, but you never know."

The briefing ended, and the team returned to their duties until time to leave for the day. Wade returned to perusing the files and reports but found nothing useful. He filed them away and picked up the phone.

"Sheriff, are you busy?" asked Baker from the doorway

"Nothing earth-shaking," Wade replied, putting the phone down. "Come in."

Baker obeyed and closed the door behind him. He held a file in his hand and sat in front of Wade's desk. The pained expression on his face concerned Wade.

"What's wrong, Baker?"

"You won't like what I have to say, but I can't ignore the evidence."

"Talk to me," said Wade.

"I've run every possible test half a dozen times. The results are always the same."

"Baker, I can't help if you don't tell me what you're talking about."

Baker looked Wade in the eye and handed him the file. "I can't say it."

Wade stared at his deputy and took the file. He opened it and read silently. Finally, he looked at his deputy and said, "Are you sure?"

"Sure enough," Baker answered, obviously distressed. "It's not a hundred percent accurate but close enough for an arrest, maybe a conviction."

Wade reread the file and leaned back in his chair. "This is insane! It can't be!"

Baker nodded and said, "I know. That's why I ran the tests so many times."

"Walk me through your process," Wade said, trying to come to grips with the startling news.

"The prints on the wallet and cell phone matched one set of prints in the Tahoe," Baker began. "Maddie verified that the phone and wallet belonged to Drew. Most of the crime scene prints were smudged. The ones on the tanning bed were the best and matched the best prints we had from Drew's cell phone."

"That should have been enough," said Wade. "But I notice you took it one step further."

Baker nodded and said, "I thought it might be possible that someone had wiped Drew's prints from his personal effects, and then someone else handled them. I know it was a long shot, but I had to make sure."

"Go on," encouraged Wade.

"I brought a bottle of Polo Black cologne from Maddie's house. She identified it as Drew's," Baker said, not wanting to continue.

"And?"

"There were two different sets of prints," said Baker. "Maddie's and one other. The second set of prints matched the others, leaving me to conclude…"

"That Drew was in that house," Wade said, finishing the sentence.

Baker nodded and hung his head. "How am I going to tell Maddie?"

"Don't worry about that," said Wade. "I'll tell her."

Wade stood and walked around his desk. He placed his hand on Baker's shoulder and said, "You've done nothing wrong. You did your job and did everything possible to verify your findings. It was excellent work."

"Thank you, Sir," said Baker. "But I still feel like I've let Maddie down."

"You haven't let anyone down," said Wade.

Baker nodded and stood. He started toward the door and turned toward Wade. "Thanks for taking this off my shoulders."

Wade smiled at his deputy and joked, "That's why I get paid the big bucks."

Baker left the office, and Wade paced around the room. He searched his mind for the best way to break the news to Maddie. Finally, he left his office and walked to her desk.

"Maddie, will you come to my office, please?"

Maddie looked at her boss and knew she wouldn't like what he had to say. She got up and walked past him to the chair in front of his desk. She sat down and waited for him to begin with her hands clenched in her lap.

"Does Drew have any close friends at the bank?"

"A few," she replied.

"What about Mitchell Hallmark?"

"Their friends at work. We've never socialized with him, so I wouldn't say they were close."

"I had a feeling that was the case," Wade said. "I called you in here because there's been a development."

"What's happened?" she asked, sounding much braver than she felt.

"Maddie, I've been trying to find the best way to tell you this," Wade began. "There's no easy way to say it."

"Tell me," Maddie ordered.

"All right, brace yourself," Wade said. "The prints at the Jane Doe crime scene matched those on Drew's personal effects."

"That's not possible! There has to be some mistake!"

"Baker ran every test available," Wade assured her. "He checked and rechecked the results. I'm sorry, but the evidence says Drew was in that house."

Maddie nodded and sat quietly, taking in the information. Finally, she said, "Is there anything else we can do, another test to run?"

"Not unless we find more evidence," said Wade.

"You're right," Maddie said. "Do you think he was involved?"

"What I think doesn't matter. We need proof."

"I know that. I'm asking what you think?"

Wade looked into his deputy's eyes before he answered. "The Andrew Clifton that we know would never be involved in a murder."

"But?"

Sighing, Wade continued, "But the evidence we have makes me wonder about his state of mind. We know he was drunk when he left the bar, and we know he didn't drive. How did he get to that house? It was dark and too far to walk, especially in his condition."

"Someone drove him there," said Maddie, understanding Wade's point.

"We don't know what happened after he left the bar," said Wade. "He might have been in danger, or he may have been protecting someone. If we can find out who picked him up, we'll get answers, and we'll find Drew.

# CHAPTER TWELVE

AT THE END of the day, Wade drove home thinking about both cases. Finding out that Drew was at the crime scene was a shock. He hadn't been expecting that.

But it did provide another piece of information. They knew where Drew had been after he left the bar. There were still a lot of questions to be answered. This bit of information gave them a new starting point.

Wade parked his truck and got out. He went in the back door, hoping Lizzie had saved him some dinner. Instead, the dining table was covered with silk flowers and crafting supplies. Lizzie was twisting silk greenery around twinkle lights.

"Hi, Sweetheart," Lizzie said with a bright smile. "How was your day?"

"I've had better," Wade grumbled. "I'm hungry. Have you already had dinner?"

"No, I was waiting for you," replied Lizzie. "I'll whip up something when I get this garland finished."

"Fine, take your time," Wade said, disappointed. "I'll go watch television and relax for a few minutes."

He left Lizzie to her work and opened the bedroom door. Flowers and craft supplies covered every surface of the bedroom. Frustrated, he shoved a box off his side of the bed and lay down.

Picking up the remote, he turned on the television and flipped through the channels. He turned it off when he found nothing interesting to watch.

"Wade," Lizzie said, shaking him gently. "Dinner's ready."

Wade opened his eyes and looked at her, confused. "What?"

"Dinner's ready."

"I must have fallen asleep," Wade said, sitting up. "What time is it?"

"It's almost seven," Lizzie replied. "I can bring your plate in here if you'd like."

"No, that's okay," Wade began. "Unless this is the only place available."

"I cleaned off the bar," Lizzie said, annoyed. "I thought you might want to stay in here and rest."

"I'll eat at the bar," Wade said. "It feels like a jungle in here."

Lizzie glared at him but said nothing. She stomped out of the bedroom and into the kitchen. She was filling her plate when Wade wrapped his arms around her waist and nuzzled the back of her neck.

"I'm sorry, Honey," Wade said. "I wasn't expecting you to be in full decoration mode tonight."

Lizzie turned and looked at him, surprised. She made air quotes with her fingers. "Full decoration mode?" she retorted.

Wade stepped back and grinned sheepishly. "Okay, that was a bad choice of words."

"I have less than four days to get everything done," Lizzie began. "My parents are busy getting ready for their trip. They're leaving Saturday night. Aunt Grace won't be here until Sunday. Why wouldn't I be in full decoration mode?"

Wade pulled her close and said, "I'm sorry. I shouldn't have said any of that. We're both tired and stressed. Why don't we start over?"

Lizzie nodded and said, "Hi, Sweetheart. How was your day?"

"It was good," Wade replied. "How was yours?"

"It was great!" Lizzie said, giggling. "Are you hungry? Dinner's ready."

"Starved," Wade replied. "What are we having?"

"Leftover lasagna!"

"Sounds great!" Wade replied.

They sat down to eat but said little to each other. Neither wanted to talk about work and risk another argument.

"I'll clean up so you can finish what you've been working on," Wade offered when they'd finished.

"Thank you," she said, kissing him on the cheek. "I'll move that stuff out of our room so you can rest."

"Thank you," Wade said. "I am sorry about before. I shouldn't vent my work frustration on you."

"That's okay. That goes for both of us," Lizzie said. "I'm sorry too."

They kissed and held each other tight for a few minutes. Lizzie broke the silence when she said, "I could clean the stuff off our bed first. The other stuff can wait a little while, don't you think?"

"Baby, you read my mind," Wade replied with a smirk. "It'll be faster if I help you."

"Then what are we waiting for?" asked Lizzie, taking him by the hand and leading him down the hall.

* * *

David Foust sat in a corner booth at a restaurant in Vernon. Most of the law officers in the area frequented the establishment. It was the best way to keep tabs on the investigation. His chances of successful blackmail depended on how close the authorities got to the truth.

At sundown, he drove to Oklaunion and parked beside an abandoned barn near Highway 287. There he waited for his quarry.

He thought about Drew Clifton while he waited. Clifton seemed to be a nice man. Was he an innocent bystander, or was there another reason for leaving him at that house?

Either way, it was a stupid thing to do. Now, they had no choice. He might be able to identify them.

Foust liked Clifton. It was a shame he'd be dead soon.

A vehicle drove slowly along the access road and flashed its headlights. Foust flashed his lights in reply and waited. The car stopped on the side of the road. Someone wearing a hooded jacket got out and stood beside the car.

Foust got out of his car and walked toward his quarry. He put his hand in his jacket pocket and wrapped his fingers around the grip of his Glock.

* * *

Wade went to work the following day, leaving Lizzie neck-deep in wedding décor. Her mother and grandmother were there early to help. When he returned, he expected to see flowers and twinkle lights strung throughout the inn.

He parked his truck and went into the office. Odom was halfway through a jelly donut when Wade walked in.

Odom wiped jelly from his chin and said, "My sister was here. She brought donuts for everyone."

"That was nice of her," said Wade. "How is Megan?"

"She's good," Odom replied. "She has a new boyfriend and seems to be happy."

"I'm happy for her," Wade said sincerely. "Have you met him?"

"No, she says she doesn't want to rush things. She won't even tell me the man's name."

"How long has she been seeing him?"

"I'm not sure," Odom said. "Long enough that they decided to take a trip together."

"Well, I hope it works out for her," Wade said, taking a donut from the box.

"How are the investigations going?" asked Logsdon.

"We're going to discuss that as soon as everyone gets here. There's some new information. I'd like you both to stay for the briefing if you don't have plans," Wade told them.

"We were talking about feeling left out of things earlier," Logsdon replied. "I'll stay."

"Me too," said Odom.

The meeting began when the coffee cups were filled and the donuts distributed. Everyone took their customary places and waited for Wade to start.

"We have a new development that involves both our current cases," Wade began. "Baker, you're up."

Deputy Calvin Baker reluctantly shared his discovery. The room was silent for a moment before it came alive with questions. Wade stood and held up his hand.

"I know y'all have questions," he said. "I had them when Baker first came to me with this. Now that I've had time to think about it, I have specific questions for Maddie."

"For me?" asked Maddie, surprised.

Wade nodded. "Do you remember what Drew was wearing when he left your house?"

"What does that have to do with finding his prints at the crime scene?" Maddie asked, confused.

"It might be important," Wade replied.

"Okay," Maddie said and closed her eyes, picturing her husband. "He wore a light blue button-down shirt, a red and navy blue striped tie, and navy dress pants."

"What about his shoes?"

"His shoes? He always wears cowboy boots."

"I see what you're getting at," said Lodge. "What kind of toe do his boots have?"

"What do you mean?" Maddie asked, still confused.

"Pointy, square, or rounded?"

"They're kind of a rounded point."

"What kind of heel?" Lodge asked.

"He prefers a riding heel," said Maddie beginning to understand.

"I'll be right back," Lodge said, leaving the room. He returned a few minutes later with a laptop.

"What size boot does he wear?" he asked Maddie while typing on the keyboard.

"Size eleven."

"Do any of these resemble the pair he was wearing?" Lodge asked, showing her the screen.

"Those," she said, pointing at an image.

Lodge tapped the laptop keys, and the printer in the outer office went into action. He excused himself again and returned with photocopies of the shoe prints from the crime scene and the boots that Maddie had indicated. He handed copies to each member of the team.

"The shoe prints that match the boots were near the front of the house," observed Baker. "There aren't any in the back."

"Look at the trail going to the back door," said Wagner. "Could that have been made by this type of boot?"

"I believe it could," Lodge replied.

"Reviewing what we know," said Wade. "Andrew Clifton left his home and went to The Watering Hole. He left there shortly after midnight. He left his vehicle there, meaning that someone had picked him up. We know he was at the Handleys' house sometime between midnight Friday morning and the time the body was found Saturday night."

"No boot prints behind the house means he didn't walk," said

Gonzalez. "It appears that someone dragged him inside. Why did they do that?"

"He'd had a lot to drink," said Logsdon. "Maybe he passed out."

"That would explain the rumpled covers on the twin bed," said Odom. "Whoever dragged him into the house left him there."

"But why would they take him into the house?" asked Reed.

"That's a good question," said Wade. "We'll table it for now. What do you think happened next?"

"Was Jane Doe carried into the house and put in the tanning bed before Drew was taken inside or after?" asked Gonzalez.

"If I were going to try to disguise a murder," Wagner began. "I'd move the body first. It must have taken time to disable the tanning bed timer and wipe the entire house down."

"You're saying leaving Drew there was an afterthought," Wade observed.

"Maybe he was coming around, and they didn't want him to identify them," Wagner added.

"That's possible," said Baker. "It would explain the prints we found, the overturned furniture in the living room, and the vomit outside."

"So, you think Drew woke up in a strange house," Maddie began. "He found the body and ran outside where he got sick."

"It's a strong possibility," said Logsdon.

"Then, why didn't he call for help?" Maddie queried.

"Don't forget there was another set of tire tracks and shoe prints," Lodge said. "And signs of a struggle. Someone else must have picked him up."

"But who and why?" Maddie asked. "Where is Drew now?"

"It sounds like some excellent detective work is happening here," said Joe Fleeks. "I'm sorry to interrupt your briefing. I was driving by and thought I'd share some news on the Tiffany Pruitt case."

"Come in," said Wade with a grin. "I'd like you to meet my team."

Wade made introductions before he asked, "Did you hear enough to give us some insight on our case?"

"I heard something about disguising a murder and your thoughts on the matter," admitted Fleeks. "I apologize again for disturbing you. I'm not comfortable talking about my case at the office now."

"Is Joyner still an issue?" asked Wade.

"He's in a lot of trouble," Fleeks replied with a satisfied grin. "He'll be on desk duty for a long while. Unfortunately, he can still overhear my conversations."

"Would you like some coffee and a donut?" Wade offered.

"No, thank you. I've got to follow a lead on the Pruitt case," Fleeks answered. "I wanted to tell you that I've been to see Elaine Cabrera. She found a voicemail from Ms. Pruitt on her phone."

"Was she Ms. Pruitt's ride?" asked Reed.

Fleeks shook his head. "Miss Cabrera had gone to bed and didn't hear her phone. The voicemail was recorded five minutes after twelve on Friday the thirteenth. Ms. Pruitt asked for a ride and said, never mind, someone else is here. I'll see you at work."

"Then, we still don't know who gave her a ride that night," said Reed.

"Not yet," said Fleeks.

"Thanks for keeping us updated," said Wade. "We know you don't have to do that, considering the circumstances."

"I don't mind sharing information," said Fleeks with a grin. "The time may come when we have to work together. I'd rather it be a pleasant experience. I do have one question for you."

"Okay," Wade said, alert.

"Why the interest in Ms. Pruitt's ride from the bar?"

"It turns out our missing person and your missing person left that bar within a few minutes of each other," Wade informed the

Detective. "We've been wondering who picked them up and if it was the same person."

"It sounds like we could be working together sooner rather than later," said Fleeks. "I'll keep you posted if you agree to do the same."

"Agreed," Wade said, extending his hand.

Fleeks shook Wade's hand and left the office.

"I'm sorry, Wade," Maddie said. "I should have been running interference."

"It's not your fault," said Wade. "I wanted you to be part of this meeting."

"Do you think Detective Fleeks will work with or against us?" Reed asked.

"I believe him to be a man of his word," Wade said. "However, we won't share everything we have unless it's pertinent to his case. No point in sharing too much."

"Crossing Fleeks could be a bad idea," said Lodge. "He's got a lot of power in the Police Department. From what I've heard, he'll be the next head of criminal investigations."

"I've heard that too. Fleeks is a good man and a good investigator. I'd prefer to have him as a friend rather than an adversary," said Wade.

"Where should we start today?" asked Reed.

"We need to find out who transported Clifton from the bar and away from the crime scene," Wade replied. "Double check alibis for midnight until six a.m. Friday morning. We'll continue background checks and verify or discredit our conclusions."

The team went to work when the briefing ended. They verified the alibis of most of the people they'd interviewed and eliminated them from the list of possible suspects.

The stories and backgrounds of the remaining people of interest were checked more closely. Mitchell Hamilton, Addie Sims, and Elaine Cabrera had no one to vouch for their whereabouts. All said they were home asleep during the time in question.

The type of boots Drew wore matched the shoe prints and drag marks at the scene. Without Drew's boots to make an actual comparison, the deputies' assumptions couldn't be proved. Nor could they be ruled out.

Wade sat in his office, drumming his fingers on the desk. He felt they were right about what happened, but it didn't look good for Drew without proof. The fact that he was in that house and vanished could be enough to make him the prime suspect in Jane Doe's murder. He'd at least be a person of interest in the case.

*Two people in one vehicle left Clifton and Jane Doe at the house. Why did they leave Drew behind? Did they come back to get him in a different car? Who would have driven Clifton away from the scene?*

Although it wasn't his case, Wade couldn't help wondering about Tiffany Pruitt.

*Is it possible that Tiffany and her friend are responsible for the death of Jane Doe and Drew's disappearance? I wonder if there's another missing person that hasn't been reported. They may have left the country together.*

Wade got up and went to Maddie's desk. He waited for her to finish what she was doing before asking, "Does Drew have a passport?"

"Yes, we had to have them when we went on our honeymoon," she replied. "Why?"

"It was just a thought," Wade admitted. "Have there been any other missing person reports?"

"I haven't seen anything," said Maddie. "What's going on?"

"Nothing," Wade said, distracted. "The pieces of this puzzle don't all fit. I'm trying to figure out why."

"Our passports are in a safe deposit box at the bank. I can check to see if Drew's is still there if you like," Maddie offered.

"That's a good idea," Wade said. "It'll eliminate one possibility. Take Baker with you."

"We'd better go before they close," Maddie said to Baker.

The two deputies left Wade to run the office in their absence. It was a slow afternoon, and Wade let his mind wander over the case.

*Someone picked Tiffany up from the bar. It could have been the boyfriend. But would she have gone with him? She was upset with him, according to Trey.*

The phone rang, and Wade's thoughts evaporated.

"May I speak with Deputy Reed?" asked a female voice.

"Deputy Reed is out of the office," Wade replied. "I'd be happy to take a message."

"That's all right," said the woman. "I'll try to catch him later."

The call ended, and Wade stared at the receiver. "She sounded familiar," he said to the empty room.

He hung up the phone and returned to his thoughts.

*Tiffany and her boyfriend leave the bar. They offer to give Drew a ride. Drew passes out, and they take him to the scene. Is Jane Doe in the car? She'd have to be. That would mean that the boyfriend killed her. Tiffany helped dispose of the body and Drew. Who is the boyfriend, and where are they now?*

"Are you still trying to fit the square pegs into round holes?" joked Maddie when she and Baker returned.

"They still won't fit," Wade answered with a grin. "What did you find out?"

"Drew's passport is still in the safe deposit box," said Baker.

"It wouldn't have done him much good anyway," Maddie added. "It's expired."

"What's on your mind, Sheriff?" Baker inquired.

"Possibilities," answered Wade. "I thought it might be possible that Tiffany and her boyfriend were behind this and left the country. I thought they might have taken Drew with them."

"That's why you asked about other missing persons reports," said Maddie.

"It's a long shot, but it would explain her disappearance and the fact that we can't find the person who picked her up at the bar," Wade said.

The phone rang again, and Maddie answered it. "It's Dr. Hughes," she said, handing the receiver to Wade.

"Hello, Doc," said Wade. He listened for a minute and said, "You're absolutely sure? All right, thanks for letting me know."

Wade hung up the phone and looked at his deputies. "Get everyone back to the office immediately, including the night shift people. We'll meet in the conference room. I have some phone calls to make."

"What's wrong?" asked Baker.

"I'd rather tell everyone at the same time. These phone calls can't wait," Wade said, walking to his office.

He closed his door leaving Maddie and Baker staring after him. They split the list and contacted their coworkers. Half an hour later, everyone gathered in the conference room.

"I'm sorry I had to call this meeting," Wade began. "But it was urgent that I speak with each of you as soon as possible. Texas Rangers will be here tomorrow."

"Why are the Texas Rangers coming," asked Lodge.

"I called them," Wade said. "Finding Andrew Clifton's prints at the crime scene changed things. The two cases are connected, and we're in a conflict-of-interest situation. I want you all to stop working on both cases until the Rangers arrive. They'll be taking over."

"Were you considering this earlier, or has something changed?" asked Reed.

"I'd thought about making the call after hearing Baker's evidence," Wade replied. "I hoped we'd have more evidence before it was necessary. However, I learned something today that left me no choice."

"What happened?" asked Lodge.

"Dr. Hughes identified Jane Doe," Wade told them. "The victim in the tanning bed was Tiffany Pruitt."

"No!" Maddie moaned.

"I'm sorry, Maddie," said Wade. "It's out of my hands."

# CHAPTER THIRTEEN

WADE WAS at work early the next morning. He wanted to talk with Maddie and Wagner before the Texas Rangers arrived. He called them both into his office and closed the door.

"Maddie, I hope you don't mind, but I'm going to refer to Drew as a victim during this conversation," said Wade.

"I don't mind," she replied. "As far as I'm concerned, he is a victim until someone proves otherwise."

"My thoughts exactly," Wade replied. "The three of us are more closely linked to the victims than the rest of the team. We'll probably be excluded from the investigation. It will be up to us to keep the department running and investigate all other cases until this is solved. That means we'll work together more than we have in the past. Will that be a problem for either of you?"

Both deputies shook their heads.

"Do you think the Rangers will question us?" asked Wagner.

"I would if I were in their position," Wade answered. "They'll at least ask for our statements."

"What are the Rangers going to do while they're here?" queried Maddie.

"I can't answer that," Wade replied. "I've never worked with them before. The person I spoke with on the phone said they'd need access to everything we have. If you don't have any more questions, we'd better get ready for our visitors."

During the lunch hour, three people wearing khaki pants, white button-down shirts, ties, and white Stetsons arrived at the Wilbarger County Sheriff's department.

"We'd like to see Sheriff Adams," said the older member of the group. He was thick around the middle, had a double chin, and a full head of salt and pepper hair.

"Certainly, if you'll follow me," Reed said, leading them to the conference room. "Would you like anything to drink?"

"Not right now, thank you," said the man in charge.

"I'll let the Sheriff know you're here," Reed replied. "Make yourselves comfortable."

Reed tapped on Wade's door and said, "The Texas Rangers are here."

"Thanks, Reed."

Wade went to the conference room and introduced himself.

"I'm Sheriff Wade Adams," he said, extending his hand. "Thank y'all for coming."

"I'm Dale Mints," said the older man shaking Wade's hand. "This is Collin Lindsey and Cassidy Farrington."

Ranger Lindsey was short and slim with thick curly strawberry-blonde hair. He looked like a freckle-faced kid with laugh lines around his eyes.

Ranger Farrington's features were opposite those of Lindsey. Her long, auburn locks accentuated her fair skin and hazel eyes. The standard Texas Ranger uniform didn't hide her voluptuous figure.

"It's nice to meet you," Wade said. "I hope you had a pleasant trip."

"It wasn't a bad drive," said Mints. "These two slept most of the way. They kept me awake with their synchronized snoring."

"We still weren't as loud as you," said Lindsey with a grin.

"Have you had lunch?" Wade asked.

"No, we thought we'd come here and talk with you first," said Mints. "We'd like to spend the afternoon familiarizing ourselves with the case and your crew."

"Most of my crew is on their lunch break," Wade replied. "They should all be back in less than an hour."

"Tell us about the case," Mints prodded.

Wade gave them the case highlights and why he'd called the Texas Rangers.

"Have you contacted the folks in charge of the missing woman's case?" asked Lindsey.

"Yes, I called Detective Joe Fleeks immediately after I called your office," Wade replied. "He agreed to contact Ms. Pruitt's family and serve as liaison."

"Good," said Mints nodding. "We'll need a large area to work in today. We may want desks or individual workspaces as the case progresses."

"This is our largest room," Wade said. "You're welcome to work in here. We have some unused office spaces that you can use."

"That should do," said Mints. "We'll get settled in our hotel and have lunch. We'll be back here around two o'clock. We'll meet your crew then. It would be helpful if everything pertinent to the case is waiting for us."

"It's ready for you," Wade replied. "We'll move the files in here before you get back."

"Now that we have that settled," said Mints. "Where's a good place to eat?"

"That depends on what you want," Wade said with a grin.

"Anything but barbeque," said Farrington.

Wade made several suggestions, and the Rangers left the office.

"What do you think?" asked Reed.

"It's too soon to tell," said Wade. "I'll have to put Lodge and Baker on a leash when they see Ranger Farrington."

Reed grinned and said, "She is pretty. What's her specialty?"

"I don't know," Wade replied. "We didn't get past the pleasantries. I guess we'll find out this afternoon. What about you? Do I need to put you on a leash too?"

"Naw, she's not my type."

Wade raised an eyebrow and smirked. "I thought any woman between the ages of twenty-one and fifty was your type."

Gordon Reed smiled mischievously but said nothing.

"That reminds me," said Wade. "A woman called yesterday looking for you but didn't want to leave a message. She sounded familiar, but I couldn't come up with a name."

Reed blushed and said, "I'm sure it wasn't important."

"Then why are you blushing?"

"I'm not blushing. It's hot in here."

Wade smirked, shook his head, and changed the subject. "Get someone to help and move all the case files into the conference room. The Rangers are going to work in there this afternoon. I'm going to see if the empty office spaces are fully equipped."

At two o'clock, Wade and his entire team gathered in the conference room to meet the Texas Rangers. Ranger Mints addressed the group after introductions were made.

"We're not here to place blame or find fault with anyone's work," Mints began. "We're here to preserve the integrity and credibility of the Wilbarger County Sheriff's department. That includes all of you. After we've read through your evidence and files, we'll be working with you as the lead investigators on this case. Does anyone have any questions?"

"How will this affect those who work the night shift?" asked Odom.

"It shouldn't change your routine," said Mints. "You might be asked to run background checks or do computer work regarding the case, but nothing more."

"I'll speak with those of you who have been on the night shift this month after this meeting," said Wade.

"Are there any other questions?" asked Mints.

No one spoke up.

"In that case, we'll get started on the case files," Mints said.

Wade and his deputies left the room to the Rangers. Odom, Gonzalez, Logsdon, and Wagner followed Wade to his office.

"This will affect Gonzalez and Logsdon more than the rest of our team," Wade began. "I believe it would be in the department's best interest if Wagner and Maddie were not assigned the night shift until this case is closed. I'd prefer the three of us to work under the supervision of one of the rangers at all times."

"What do you have in mind?" asked Gonzalez

"I have two proposals," said Wade. "First, I can ask for volunteers to work the night shift exclusively until this case is closed. Second, we can continue as usual, except two men will be on duty, and one of you ladies will be on call. There's no need for either of you to be here when there are no female inmates. You'll be called to attend to the prisoner if a female is arrested. What do you think?"

"Both are good ideas," said Gonzalez. "I'll volunteer. I don't mind being on the night shift because Antonio works nights too.."

"Thank you, Marina," said Wade, smiling at her.

"I'll take over anytime Marina needs a break," said Logsdon.

"Thank you, Sherri. That means that Marina will take over the night shift as of now.

"I'd like to volunteer for the night shift as well," said Odom. "I'll need a break once in a while."

"Clint, you don't have to do that. We have more than enough men on staff," said Wade.

"I know, but Baker and Lodge are better at forensics. Reed has the weekend shift. With Wagner eliminated, that leaves me. I can run the computer with the best of them."

"Thank you," Wade said sincerely. "This is a tough situation. And it's likely to get tougher before it's over. I truly appreciate your help. Let me know when you need a break, and I'll see that you get it."

The deputies left Wade's office, and Maddie went in.

"Do you have a minute?" she asked.

"What's on your mind?"

"Dad called. Brody is homesick. I've missed him so much that I need to see him too," Maddie said. "I thought I'd go get him this weekend unless I need to be here."

"There's no need for you to stay," Wade said. "Reed has the weekend duty."

"Dad said he'd bring Brody home, but he's done so much already," Maddie said. "He needs a break, and I might have to call him again before this is over."

"Get away from all this and spend time with your family," Wade told her.

"Okay, but if something comes up, I'll stay," she said.

"I know, Maddie. You've been incredibly strong through this. Take some time."

"Thank you, Wade."

No sooner had Maddie left than Baker and Lodge knocked on Wade's door.

"What can I do for you boys?" asked Wade suspecting the answer.

"Baker wants to know the policy about dating a fellow officer on temporary assignment as a coworker," said Lodge.

Wade laughed and said, "I knew it, I knew it. I told Reed I'd have to put a leash on you two."

"We'll behave," said Baker. "We made a bet and need you to settle it for us."

"Was the bet which one of you she'd go out with first?"

The looks on the deputies' faces gave Wade his answer. He roared with laughter.

"Boys, I hate to burst your bubble, but coworker is the operative word. Dating a coworker, even a temporary one, is against department policy."

"Yea, we know," replied Lodge. "We were hoping this would be the exception."

"I'm sorry, but there are other women in town," Wade reminded them.

"None of them look like her," Lodge mumbled.

"Sheriff, what are we supposed to do while the Rangers are going through our stuff?" asked Baker.

"Now that you mention it," said Wade. "The Rangers will be using the empty office spaces. Will you check the computers and internet connections to see that they're working properly?"

Baker and Logsdon left the office, and Wade finally had a moment to call Lizzie. He picked up his phone and punched in the number.

"Hi, Sweetheart."

"Hi, how is the decorating going?"

"I've almost finished," Lizzie replied. "Will you be home for dinner?"

"I'll pick up something," Wade replied. "I want to stay available here in case the Rangers have questions. I don't know how long they plan to work."

"Okay, I'll find something here when I take a break. What are the Rangers like?"

"It's too soon to tell," Wade said. "I'll see you when I get home."

The three Texas Rangers worked for several hours combing through the evidence, reports, and files. When they finished, Mints tapped on Wade's door.

"Come in," said Wade. "What can I do for you?"

Mints sat in the chair in front of Wade's desk and said, "We've finished with your files. We didn't find anything that would compromise the investigation. Distancing your deputies and your-self from the case was smart. I want to ask you a couple of questions."

"Okay."

"Why did you distance yourself and Deputy Wagner from the case?"

"I thought it best when we learned that Ms. Pruitt was missing."

"What prompted you to send Deputy Reed to the bar with her photo?"

"The bartender gave me a general description of the woman with Andrew Clifton," Wade told him. "I asked Deputy Clifton to search missing women of that description on a hunch. She found two women. One was Pruitt. Detective Joyner came to the office soon after and informed us that Ms. Pruitt was missing."

"And what was your relationship with Ms. Pruitt?"

Wade told Mints about his previous involvement with Tiffany and that he hadn't seen or spoken to her in more than a year."

"What can you tell me about Ms. Pruitt, her personality, her habits, anything?"

"The woman I was engaged to in 2002 was very different from the woman who walked into my office two years ago," Wade said. "She was once a sweet, naïve woman who loved with all her heart. Something must have happened to her. She'd become a manipulative woman determined to get what she wanted. I don't know enough about her life here in Vernon to tell you more."

"What about Deputy Wagner's relationship with her?"

"I know they went out a few times before he joined the department. I understand they didn't see eye to eye."

"How long has Wagner worked here?"

"Slightly over a year. I can look up the exact hire date if you need it."

"We can tend to that later. Do you know anything about Detective Joyner's relationship with the deceased?"

"No, I don't," replied Wade. "I didn't know they had been involved until Detective Fleeks mentioned it."

"How well do you know Andrew Clifton?"

"He and Maddie were married about eight years ago," said Wade. "We've attended some of the same social functions and had dinner together over the years. I'd consider him a friend but not a close one."

"What about Deputy Clifton?"

"Maddie is as tough as they come," said Wade, smiling. "She can hold her own with any man in this department. She's a top-notch deputy, a good mom, and a loving wife."

"How would you describe the Cliftons' relationship?"

"It's good," said Wade. "Like all relationships, it's had its up and downs. They've been going through one of the downs recently. That makes Drew's disappearance more difficult for Maddie."

"Given what you know about Mr. Clifton, would you say his drinking and disappearance are normal?"

"Not at all," Wade replied. "I've never seen him with a drink in his hand and certainly not intoxicated. He's a well-liked and respected man in this community. He's always been a good husband and a good father."

"I think we're done for the night," said Mints. "I'll want to interview Deputy Wagner and Deputy Clifton tomorrow. We'll split into groups and make assignments after that. Who's your best technology person?"

"That would be Calvin Baker, and a close second is Brandon Lodge," said Wade. "They're both meticulous with technology and forensic evidence."

"Excellent," said Mints, standing to leave. "Well, we're going to call it a night. I expect we'll have some long days ahead of us. Goodnight, Sheriff Adams."

"Goodnight."

Wade waited until Gonzalez and Odom returned to the office before calling Lizzie.

Hi, Honey. I'm about to start home. Have you eaten?"

"No, I'm still decorating. What time is it anyway?"

"It's just after six. How does pizza sound for dinner?"

"That sounds amazing!"

"I'll be home soon," Wade said and ended the call.

He left the office and drove to the local pizza parlor. He placed his order and sat down to wait.

"Hi, Wade! How are you doing?" asked Megan Ford when she entered the restaurant.

Wade tried not to cringe. Megan had caused a lot of trouble in the past. She was a blue-eyed blonde with an hourglass figure. She'd used her looks to manipulate every man she met. She particularly liked the men in his department.

"I'm fine, Megan. How are you?"

"I'm great, thanks for asking," she said with a sweet smile. "How's married life treating you?"

"It's great!" Wade said, thankful that his order was ready. "I'd better get our dinner home while it's hot. It was good seeing you."

"It was good seeing you, too," Megan replied and moved toward the counter.

Wade hurried to his truck and got in. He left the parking lot as fast as he could. He didn't want to talk to Megan again.

Something niggled in the back of his mind on his drive home. He couldn't put his finger on it, but the conversation with Megan reminded him of something.

Suddenly it dawned on him. "No, it can't be," he said aloud with a broad grin. "I'm going to have to check into this."

He parked behind the inn and went inside, pizza in hand.

"What are you grinning about?" Lizzie asked.

"I'm glad to be home," Wade said, sidestepping the question.

"Was it a hard day?"

"It could have been worse," admitted Wade. "I work with a great bunch of people."

"What happened?"

"I'll tell you while we eat," he said. "I'm starved."

Lizzie poured drinks for the two of them while Wade put slices of pizza on paper plates. They ate and shared the details of their day.

"What time is the rehearsal dinner tomorrow night?" asked Wade

"It's at seven. The guests will start arriving around six thirty. Will you be home by then?"

"I might be. I'm not in charge right now, so I can't give you a definite answer."

"Is it going to be hard watching someone else do your job?" Lizzie asked.

"It could be," Wade admitted. "I might go out on patrol to have something to do."

"How is Maddie taking this?"

"She misses Brody and Drew, of course. Other than that, she seems to be holding up. I expected her to break down every time we got bad news, but she's holding on."

"I wonder if she's angry about all of this?"

"What do you mean?"

"I'm sure she's hurt and worried," Lizzie explained. "But I'd be angry if I were in her shoes."

"Why?"

"I don't know all the details, but from what you've told me, it looks like Drew was having an affair and that he took off because he didn't have the guts to face her."

"I see what you mean," said Wade, thinking about Lizzie's comment. "That could be where she's finding the strength to deal with this. Everything we find makes it look worse for him."

"What do you think she'll say to Drew when he's found?"

"Your guess is as good as mine. I just hope he's alive to hear it."

# CHAPTER FOURTEEN

ANDREW CLIFTON WOKE when the sun rose and lit the bedroom he'd claimed as his own. Since Foust's last visit, he'd showered and laundered his clothes nightly. He wanted to be clean when he died.

He got up and dressed before going to the kitchen for a meal. He sat at the kitchen table and reread the newspaper while he ate. He noticed the date on the front page.

*Monday, October 16, 2017. The papers are usually delivered in the afternoon. If Foust brought this the next day,* he stopped and counted the days on his fingers. *I've been here a week!*

Drew leaned back in his chair and let his mind absorb the discovery.

*Foust said he had a meeting when he left. He can't risk letting me identify him. He'll either kill me himself or leave me here to starve.*

He got up and paced the kitchen. There had to be a way to tell Maddie what had happened. He noticed the white paper bag in the trash can. He stopped and took it out.

*This should work. I saw a pencil somewhere.*

Searching the kitchen cabinets and drawers, he located a pencil.

He used a butter knife to separate the bag's seams and laid it flat on the table.

He sat down, picked up the pencil, and began to write.

*Dear Maddie,*

*I'm so sorry. I wish I could tell you this in person, but I don't think I'll have the chance.*

Drew wrote until he'd filled both sides of the paper bag. He told Maddie everything he could remember. He read over it twice before he folded it up.

He stood and looked around the kitchen. *I can't hide it in here. I have to put this somewhere so the right people will find it.*

He went from room to room, rejecting every hiding place he considered. Standing in the living room, he heard the crunch of tires on the gravel drive.

He stuffed the letter deep in his pants pocket and went toward the kitchen. He waited in the hallway expecting Foust to wave him away from the back door. But it wasn't Foust.

Drew stepped into the kitchen for a better look. Then he saw the gun.

\* \* \*

Wade arrived at the office to find the Texas Rangers already at work.

"Good morning, Sheriff," Ranger Mints greeted him. "I hope you don't mind. We wanted to get an early start."

"Not at all," Wade replied. "I see you found the coffee. Is there anything else you need?"

"No, not right now," said Mints. "We'd like to meet with you and your deputies when everyone arrives. We discussed your case last night, and we've made a plan."

"Certainly, they should all be here shortly," Wade answered.

When the deputies arrived, they settled themselves in the conference room. Ranger Dale Mints called the group to attention.

"We've been through all the evidence and case records," Mints began. "I want to commend you for the detailed work you've done. It makes our job much easier. The three of us discussed the case last night and developed a plan of attack, if you will. There will be three squads. One squad will investigate Ms. Pruitt. One will question people she knew. The other squad will remain at the office to handle daily business and any other case that may arise."

"Hello? Is anyone here?" said a voice from the outer office, interrupting the meeting.

"Excuse me," said Maddie, who went to greet the visitor.

"Yay! Someone's here," said Megan Ford with a bright smile. "I brought donuts for y'all. I haven't seen my brother in a few days. Is he here?"

"Clint's on the night shift," Maddie told her. "I'll let him know you dropped by."

"I thought he finished with that," Megan said.

"He volunteered to work that shift for a while," said Maddie. "We're in the middle of an important meeting, so if you don't mind."

"Oh! I didn't realize," said Megan. "I'll go. I hope y'all enjoy the donuts."

Maddie waited until Megan had gone and locked the main door behind her. She picked up the box of donuts and carried them back to the conference room.

"We have donuts, courtesy of Megan Ford," she announced to the group, taking one and passing the box.

"That was thoughtful," said Mints, choosing a chocolate-covered pastry. "As I was saying, we'll have three squads. Lindsey will lead the questioning squad. Farrington will take the lead here at home base. I'll lead the investigation of Pruitt. Does anyone have any questions?"

"What about Clifton?" asked Reed. "He's still missing."

"Yes," Mints replied. "The fact that Mr. Clifton is missing and there is evidence that he was at the scene makes him a person of interest. I believe we'll find him as we gather more evidence."

Reed nodded, and the other deputies glanced at Maddie to see her reaction. She shifted in her chair but said nothing.

Wade could see the anger in her eyes. *Lizzie might be right.*

"My squad will begin by searching Ms. Pruitt's home," Mints continued, ignoring the tension in the room. "Deputy Baker and Deputy Lodge will work with me."

"Deputies Reed and Logsdon will work with me. We'll question everyone associated with Ms. Pruitt," said Ranger Lindsey.

"That leaves Sheriff Adams and Deputies Wagner and Clifton with me here at home base," said Ranger Farrington. "We'll work with evidence gathered in addition to computer searches."

"Unless you have questions or complaints," Mints began. "Let's get to work."

Mints approached Baker and Lodge, saying, "I chose the two of you because the Sheriff says you're meticulous about finding evidence. That's what we need today. I want to go through the victim's house like we're looking for specks of gold dust on the beach."

"Yes, Sir," said Baker. "But hasn't the police department already been there?"

"I talked with the detective last night. He said they went in to see if the victim was inside but nothing more."

"What are we looking for?" asked Lodge.

"We'll know when we find it," Mints replied. "Gather your gear, and we'll get going."

Baker and Lodge obeyed and met the Ranger outside. The three men climbed into the Ranger's truck and drove to Tiffany Pruitt's home.

Mints talked while he drove. "Everything we can learn about Pruitt could be a potential lead. I want to know her likes, dislikes, preferences, and habits. I want to know everything from what her neighbors thought of her to what she had for dinner the night before she disappeared."

"Yes, Sir," said Baker and Lodge in unison.

"Start with her neighbors," Mints suggested, parking the truck. "Then we'll work from the outside in."

The three men split up and interviewed Tiffany's neighbors on both sides of the block and the block behind her. Many weren't home, but one observant neighbor gave Mints a wealth of information.

Edmond McKay spent most of his time on his front porch. Little happened in the neighborhood without his notice.

"That pretty lady took good care of her son," McKay said. "But she didn't stick around when he was away for the weekend. That boy would be gone during the summer for at least a month. She'd come home from work, change clothes, and be gone again."

"Did anyone ever stay the night with her?" Mints asked.

"Not that I noticed."

"Did she have dates at the house?"

"I never saw anyone there except when her folks came, or she had a party."

"Did she have parties often?"

"Once or twice," said McKay. "They weren't loud or anything. "Small crowds, and they didn't stay long."

"Have you noticed anyone hanging around the house?"

"Well, the other night," McKay began. "I noticed a Cadillac parked down the street. Somebody was inside smoking. I could see the smoke coming from the driver's side window. I woke up later that night and looked outside. The Cadillac was gone."

"What woke you?" Mints asked.

"I'm an old man," replied McKay shaking his head. "I have to get up a lot at night."

"Did you happen to get the license plate number?" Mints asked hopefully.

"It was too dark."

"Could you show me where the Cadillac was parked?"

McKay pointed to a house across the street at the end of the block. Mints thanked him and walked toward the house.

Taking his cell phone out, Mints photographed the house and the street in front of it. The accumulation of cigarette butts indicated the smoker had been there for some time.

Mints bagged the butts and walked to his truck. He deposited the evidence in a cardboard box in the backseat. Baker and Lodge joined him and reported their findings.

"Most of the neighbors aren't home," said Lodge. "The few I spoke with didn't know the victim very well. They like her son, though."

"Only one person was home in my section," added Baker. "She knew Pruitt and her son lived nearby but didn't know their names."

Mints shared his information and asked, "Have you had a chance to look around outside the property?"

Baker nodded. "No tire tracks or footprints to be found. I noticed a cigarette butt near the front window. Nothing else caught my eye."

"Better bag it," said Mints. "Could be from whoever was in the Cadillac down the street. We can work out here. Detective Fleeks is supposed to meet us here with the key they used to get inside."

"How'd he get a key?" asked Lodge.

"Said he found it under a decorative rock near the back door," said Mints shaking his head. "I'll never understand why people do that. Every crook in the country knows about those rocks."

The officers searched the outside of the property while they waited for Fleeks. They found the side door to the garage unlocked and went inside.

"Ms. Pruitt liked things neat and tidy," observed Mints. "Garages tend to be used for junk storage."

A lawnmower was parked near the overhead door, ready to be used. A washing machine and clothes dryer stood at the opposite end. Laundry and cleaning supplies lined the shelves above, arranged neatly by height.

A mop and push broom hung on the wall near the side door. The garage floor had no dirt or debris.

"I don't think we'll find much in here," said Baker, taking out his flashlight.

"I don't either," said Mints. "But that speck of gold dust could be hidden anywhere."

They searched the garage but found nothing interesting until they opened the dryer. A load of bath towels waited to be folded and put away.

"Weren't the fibers in the victim's hair from a gold towel?" asked Mints.

"Yes, Sir," said Lodge. "Did we find that speck?"

"Maybe," admitted Mints. "Bag those for comparison."

"Ranger Mints?" called a voice from outside.

"In here!"

Joe Fleeks appeared at the side door. "I'm sorry it took so long. We had a situation to deal with this morning."

"Anything serious?" asked Lodge.

"It could have been. It's under control now. Did you find something?"

"We aren't sure," said Mints. "Do you have the key?"

Fleeks dug in his pocket and pulled out a key with an evidence tag attached. He handed the key to Mints and said, "I'd like to stay and help, but I need to get back. Let me know if you find anything useful."

"We'll do," Mints replied as Fleeks walked out the door. "Boys, let's finish up in here and have a look inside."

They completed their search of the garage and moved to the house. Mints opened the back door with the key, and they stepped inside.

At first glance, the house appeared to be as clean and tidy as the garage. The bedrooms were immaculate. The kitchen sparkled, and nothing was out of place except for a black marble orb near the sink.

"Why would someone as neat as Pruitt leave this here?" Mints asked. "It doesn't look like it belongs."

"It matches the desk set over there," Lodge said, pointing at a corner desk. "It could be a paperweight."

A black marble desk set sat at the front edge of the desk. Tiffany's purse lay beside it.

"I don't know many women who'd leave their purse behind," Mints pointed out.

"I've got something," Baker called from the bathroom. "The towels on the shelf look like they've been knocked off and put back in a hurry. One was between the tub and the toilet along with this."

Baker held a large black coat button in his gloved hand.

"Was the victim wearing a coat?" Mints asked.

"Not when we found her," said Baker.

"It could still be hers," Mints said. "Check the closets for a match."

The men searched every closet but found no coat missing a button. They moved to the living room, but nothing seemed to be out of place. They went over the room as carefully as they had the rest of the house.

Baker was near the fireplace when he noticed something different about the carpet. It appeared to have been recently cleaned.

Kneeling for a better look, he said, "I think we might have something."

"What is it?" asked Lodge.

"Does the carpet here look different to you?"

"Yea, it does. We should test it," Lodge suggested.

They closed the curtains and blinds, making the room as dark as possible. Baker took a spray bottle from his bag and sprayed the questionable area of the carpet.

Lodge shined a black light on the spot. The carpet glowed light blue.

"Something out of the ordinary happened in here," said Mints. "Bag up that piece of carpet. We'll take it, the paperweight, and the button back with us."

Lodge and Baker cut a section of the carpet away from the fireplace. They bagged it and the stained carpet pad for analysis.

"That looks like blood to me," said Lodge.

"It does to me, too," said Baker. "Those towels in the bathroom bother me. I think I'll look around outside a bit more. I'll take this stuff to the truck."

Mints watched Baker and Lodge work. He listened to their conversation as they discussed what they'd found. They were good.

Lodge and Mints continued combing through the house. Baker searched the length of the alley behind the house and around the dumpsters. He didn't expect to find anything in the dumpsters after a week, but he looked anyway.

His determination paid off when he found a gold towel on the ground between a dumpster and fence at the end of the alley. He bagged it and carried it with him back to the house.

"Found it!" Baker said when he entered the house.

"What did you find?" asked Mints.

"The speck of gold dust," Baker said, handing him the evidence bag with the blood-soaked towel inside.

"That's a gold nugget!" Mints said, beaming. "I think it's safe to assume that Ms. Pruitt was killed here. Dust for prints and get this stuff to the lab."

The men spent the remainder of the morning dusting Tiffany's house for fingerprints. The only prints found were in the bedrooms. The rest of the house had been wiped clean.

The law officers returned to the Sheriff's department and took the evidence to the lab. Mints slapped Lodge on the back.

"Lunch is on me, boys! Where would you like to go?"

Baker and Lodge looked at each and grinned. Baker was the first to speak.

"There's a Mexican food restaurant at the edge of town," he began. "There's a waitress there that takes good care of us."

"She's gorgeous," said Lodge.

Mints laughed and said, "I want to see this little lady for myself."

While Mints and his squad were searching the Pruitt house, Lindsey and company interviewed people at the insurance company. This time the questions concerned Tiffany's death.

No one socialized with Tiffany outside of work except at the occasional office party. Her coworkers weren't aware of her dating anyone and didn't know her friends. They left the building knowing little more than they did when they entered.

Reed suggested they have lunch before going back to the office. Reed and Logsdon led the way inside and found themselves face-to-face with Megan Ford.

She glanced at Logsdon and smiled at Reed. "Hello, Gordon," she said. "I haven't seen you in a long time. How have you been?"

"Fine," Reed replied stiffly. "Have you met Deputy Sherri Logsdon?"

"No, I haven't," Megan said with a biting tone.

"Sherri, this is Megan Ford. Odom is her brother."

"Oh! You brought the donuts this morning," Logsdon replied. "Thank you so much. I can't tell you how much we appreciated that."

Megan ignored Logsdon and took hold of Collin Lindsey's arm. "I haven't met you either."

"This is Ranger Collin Lindsey," Reed said, irritated. "He's on temporary assignment with us."

"Ranger?" asked Megan impressed. "Do you mean Texas Ranger?"

"Yes, Ma'am," said Lindsey with a grin.

"Oh my, that's impressive," Megan gushed. "How long will you be in town?"

"I'm not sure," Lindsey replied. "I'd like to take you to dinner while I'm here."

"That sounds wonderful," Megan said, glancing at Reed. "I'd better get back to work. Enjoy your lunch."

"She's Odom's sister?" Logsdon asked with disbelief.

"Yea, half-sister," Reed replied. "They discovered each other a couple of years ago."

The hostess led them to a table, and the conversation continued.

"They're so different," Logsdon continued. "I'd never have guessed they were siblings."

"I know what you mean," said Reed.

"What's her story," Lindsey inquired with a smile. "Is she single?"

"I think so," said Reed. "It would take days to tell her story. She was once engaged to Deputy Wagner and later married another local guy. She dates a lot."

"What happened between her and Wagner?"

"I'd like to hear that story myself," said Logsdon.

"I don't feel comfortable sharing a story that isn't mine," Reed said. "Besides, I don't know all the details. Wagner would be the best person to ask."

"Do you think Odom will give me her phone number," Lindsey queried.

"It won't hurt to ask," Reed replied, looking at the menu. "A crispy chicken sandwich sounds good to me. What are y'all getting?"

The three officers ordered their meals and discussed the interviews at the insurance company.

"I find it hard to believe that no one at that office knew Tiffany

Pruitt well enough to know who her friends were and whether or not she had a boyfriend," said Lindsey.

"I got the impression that Elaine Cabrera knows more than she's telling," said Logsdon. "Why would Pruitt call her for a ride if they weren't friends?"

"That's a good point," replied Reed. "I think we should check her phone records a little closer."

"We can start that process when we get back to the office," said Logsdon. "Unless you have something else in mind, Ranger Lindsey."

"Please, call me Collin. I think Cabrera's phone records are a good place to start. Not only her personal accounts. We should check calls to the office as well."

# CHAPTER FIFTEEN

THE MORNING WAS uneventful for the squad at home base. They answered the phone and double-checked the evidence.

Ranger Farrington interviewed Wagner about his past relationship with Tiffany Pruitt. She also interviewed Maddie about Drew's disappearance.

The squad took turns going to lunch. Wade sent the other three to eat while he took care of the office. He planned to take his turn when one of them returned.

The phone rang as Maddie and Wagner walked in the main door.

"Sheriff's Office," Wade answered.

"You folks need to get out to Oklaunion," said a male voice.

"May I have your name, please?"

"This is Vollie McMahan. My dog found a body out here close to the water tower."

"A body? Is it a man or woman?" asked Wade taking notes

"It looks like a man. It stinks too bad to get any closer. Are you going to send somebody out here?"

"We'll be there right away," Wade assured him. "Do you mind staying until we get there?"

"All right, but hurry," said McMahan. "This stench is turning my stomach."

"Thank you, Mr. McMahan," said Wade. "We're on our way."

"What's happening?" asked Wagner.

Wade shared the news with his deputies and said, "The other squads aren't back yet. Maddie, will you stay and keep the office running?"

Ranger Farrington entered the office and heard Wade's comment to Maddie. "Do you have a call?"

"Yes, but the others aren't back. Someone has to stay here to run the office."

"I'll stay," said Maddie. "If it's Drew, I don't want to see him that way."

"I had the same thought," Wade replied. "I don't want you to see him that way either. Call Dr. Hughes and ask him to meet us near the water tower in Oklaunion."

"Would you like some help?" Farrington asked.

"We could use an extra pair of hands," admitted Wade. "We usually call out the whole team."

"I'll get our gear," said Wagner, leaving the room.

"I'll get mine from the conference room," Farrington said.

"I'll meet you at my truck," Wade shouted behind them.

"Maddie, are you sure you're okay with staying behind?"

Maddie nodded with tears in her eyes. "I can't even think about it without getting emotional," she said. "I wouldn't be any help to you if it's him."

"I'll call you as soon as I know anything," Wade promised.

"I'd appreciate that," Maddie admitted. "Dr. Hughes is on his way."

When Sheriff Adams, Ranger Farrington, and Deputy Wagner arrived in Oklaunion, Vollie McMahan waved from beside an abandoned barn. They got out and walked toward him.

"I'm sorry, I couldn't take the smell over there," McMahan told them. "Besides, I couldn't keep my dog away from it."

A brown and white Bassett Hound strained at the leash while sniffing the air.

"How did you find the body?" asked Wade.

"Bailey found it," McMahan said, pointing at the dog. "She got loose and took off in this direction. I couldn't keep up. All of a sudden, she let out a howl that made my skin crawl. I knew something was wrong."

"Is the body directly under the tower?" asked Wade.

"No, it's about fifty yards away. I'll show you," McMahan said, leading the way.

Wade continued to ask questions while they walked. Do you live nearby?"

"I live across the road over there," McMahan said, pointing at a white house. "Bailey likes to run out here when she gets loose. Sometimes she scares up a rabbit."

"Have you heard or seen anything unusual around here lately?"

"Nah, it's pretty quiet out here. That's why I like it. This is the first time anything like this has happened, as far as I know."

McMahan stopped and covered his nose.

"I'll wait here," he said with a muffled voice. "It's not far now. You should be able to see it pretty soon. Bailey will be right in the middle of it if I let her get any closer."

"Thank you, Mr. McMahan. You can go home if you'd like," Wade told him. "I'll stop by your place if I have more questions."

"Thank you!" McMahan said and tugged Bailey's leash. The dog reluctantly followed her master home.

"He wasn't kidding about the stench," said Farrington.

"It makes me wish I hadn't eaten lunch," Wagner agreed.

"There's Dr. Hughes," said Wade. "I'll help him get his equipment."

"You want some fresh air," Wagner accused, only half joking.

Wade grinned and retraced his steps toward the access road.

"What's the situation?" asked the doctor as Wade approached.

"Body near the water tower. "I'd say it's been here a while from the smell," said Wade. "I haven't gotten close enough to see it yet. Let me help you with your gear."

"Will the gurney make it through the vegetation?"

"I don't think so, Doc. It's tall and thick over there."

"We better take the stretcher instead."

The men opened the stretcher and loaded the doctor's equipment onto it. Carrying the stretcher between them, Wade led the way.

Ranger Farrington was standing back from the body with one hand over her mouth and nose. Wagner was trying to take pictures while his eyes watered.

"Dr. Gerard Hughes, meet Texas Ranger Cassidy Farrington," said Wade.

"It's nice to meet you, Ranger Farrington," said the doctor. "It would have been nicer under different circumstances."

The Ranger nodded at the doctor in response.

"Why don't y'all move and get some fresh air while Dr. Hughes works?" Wade suggested.

The two deputies didn't have to be told twice. They moved away, thankful for the respite.

"I'll make notes while you talk, Doc," Wade said, taking a pad and pen from his pocket and holding his breath.

"The victim is male," said Hughes. "He's been here for two or three days, based on the insect larva. It looks like some of the local wildlife found him too."

"Any idea what the cause of death might be?" Wade inquired and held his breath again.

"Nothing on his back," said the doctor. "Would you help me turn him over?"

Wade reluctantly moved toward the doctor and helped roll the victim. The odor of decay seemed to engulf the two living men.

"There's some blood here," said Dr. Hughes. "There are some

wounds on his legs and torso. I'll have a better answer after I get him cleaned up."

"Are you ready to take him in?" asked Wade.

"Yes, that's all I can see here."

Wade waved at Wagner and Farrington. They took one last clean breath and helped put the victim in a body bag.

Wade checked the man's pockets for identification before loading him in the medical examiner's van. He looked at the driver's license in the man's wallet before bagging it as evidence.

The three law officers photographed the scene, picked up, and bagged all possible evidence.

"There's a blood trail here," said Wagner.

"Follow it and see where it leads," said Farrington.

"I'll join you in a minute," said Wade. "I have a promise to keep."

Wade took out his cell phone and punched the speed dial for the office.

"Sheriff's office," answered Maddie.

"Maddie, it's Wade. The victim isn't Drew."

"Oh, thank God!"

"We'll talk when I get back," Wade told her. "Wagner and Farrington found something."

The call ended, and Wade hurried toward the other squad members.

"We've got skid marks on the pavement over here," said Wagner. "It looks like someone veered off the road toward this spot."

"I've got a gun over here," called Farrington. "And a couple of hundred-dollar bills."

"This could have been a drug deal gone wrong," said Wade.

Wagner continued to search the area while Wade and Farrington photographed the marks on the pavement and bagged the gun and cash.

There are footprints and tire tracks by that old barn," said Wagner.

"Are they McMahan's?" asked Wade.

"These are on the opposite side of where McMahan stood," said Wagner. "There's a car parked there too. It doesn't look like it belongs here."

"Call Maddie and have her run the license plate," said Wade. "I'll photograph these tracks."

Wade studied the footprints and tire tracks as he photographed them. One set of footprints led from the car beside the barn toward the pavement.

A second set of shoe prints joined the first. The first set of prints moved away from the second. It appeared the person was running. But why?

Wade followed the running shoe prints and noticed they stopped where the skid marks on the pavement ended.

"Ranger Farrington, do you see a place where it looks like our victim landed hard?" asked Wade.

"Yes, there's a place close to where I found the gun and the money. The grass is mashed down, and there's some blood."

Wade joined Farrington. They searched and photographed the area.

"Do you have the gun handy?" Wade asked.

Farrington handed the clear evidence bag containing the gun to Wade. Wade examined the gun and handed the bag back to Farrington.

"He emptied it," said Wade. "I think some sort of deal was going down. Something went wrong. Either he started shooting, and someone ran him down, or vice versa. The car hit him over there, and his body landed here. He must have crawled to get away and died where the dog found him."

Wagner joined Wade and Farrington while they talked. "Maddie says the car is registered to David Foust. He lives in this area."

"Did she happen to get his address?" asked Wade.

"Yea, I wrote it down," Wagner replied.

"We'll check out his place after we've finished here," said Wade. "I'll call the tow truck."

The squad members photographed and collected evidence until they were sure they'd found everything related to the case. They climbed into Wade's truck. Wagner read the address aloud so that Wade could program it into the navigation system.

Wade drove the farm to market road and realized he'd gone down it in the recent past. "Do either of you remember the name of the Handleys' truck-driving neighbor?"

"I know it was in the file," said Farrington. "Let me think."

"That," Wade said, pointing at the Handley house. "Is where we found Tiffany Pruitt's body. I'm almost certain their neighbor's name was Foust."

"That can't be a coincidence," said Wagner.

Wade turned and drove past the earlier crime scene. A half mile later, the navigation systems announced, "You have reached your destination."

"Looks like this guy was afraid of something," observed Farrington. "What's with the security bars?"

"We'd better find out," Wade said. "Search the perimeter first. There might be someone in there with a weapon."

"Bullet hole in the back door window," announced Wagner as he approached.

"Wait until we've cleared the outside before getting any closer," ordered Wade. "The shooter could be inside."

Wagner stayed where he was until Wade and Farrington returned.

"All right, Wagner. We'll cover you."

Wagner crept toward the back door and peered through the window. "There's another body in there," he said quietly. "The security bars are padlocked."

"I'll get the bolt cutters," Wade said. "Keep your eyes open. There could be someone else inside."

"No kidding," said Wagner, adding "Sir" as an afterthought.

Wade retrieved the bolt cutters from his truck and ran toward the house. The lock was off in seconds, and Wagner carefully opened the bars and the back door.

Wagner stood aside with his gun ready to fire while Wade and Farrington entered the house. They made sure the house was empty before tending to the victim.

"Damn!" said Wade when he saw the victim's face.

"What's wrong, Sheriff?" Farrington asked, seeing Wade's pained expression.

"It's Drew Clifton."

Wagner bent down to examine the victim. He saw a slight rise in the chest and checked for a pulse. "He's still alive!"

Wade took out his phone and called an ambulance while Wagner and Farrington administered first aid. He was torn between calling Maddie now and waiting until he knew more about Drew's condition.

Farrington decided for him when she said, "It's a good thing we found him when we did. He doesn't look good."

"The two of you keep working with him," said Wade. "I'll see what evidence I can find while we wait for the ambulance."

The house held few clues other than Drew had been imprisoned in the house for days. The trash can overflowed, but the rest of the house was spotless.

A newspaper lay open on the kitchen table. The refrigerator had enough food to last a couple more days. A whole bottle of whisky sat on the kitchen counter.

Drew had been sleeping in one of the bedrooms. Going into the bathroom, Wade noticed a mop with a bent handle and a broken broom on the floor. He moved closer to examine the open window. *Drew must have been trying to work his way out through here.*

There was no sign that anyone else had been in the house. But someone had to have brought the food and the newspaper.

Wade turned when he heard the siren and went outside to greet the ambulance. He recognized the EMTs Rashad Weaver and Tanya Balderas.

"The victim is inside. He's been getting first aid since we found him," said Wade.

"It's been a while since we've seen you, Sheriff," said Balderas.

"Yes, it has," said Wade, smiling. "That's a good thing, isn't it?"

"We wouldn't mind running into you outside of work," said Weaver with a grin.

"I wouldn't mind that either. I'd appreciate it if you kept this quiet until I've had a chance to inform his family."

"Do you know the victim?" asked Weaver.

"Yes, he's been missing for several days," Wade told them.

"Is he the guy from the bank?" asked Balderas. "What happened to him?"

It looks like a gunshot wound to the right shoulder."

"We know how to keep our mouths shut," said Weaver. "We'll take good care of him."

"I know you will," Wade said and followed them inside.

The EMTs attended to Drew and loaded him into the ambulance.

"Why don't you go with him, Sheriff?" suggested Farrington. "If he wakes up, it would be best if he saw a friendly face."

"We'll finish here and take your truck back to the office," said Wagner. "You need to know his condition before you talk to Maddie."

"You're right," Wade replied. "I'll see you back at the office."

Wade rode in the ambulance to the hospital with Drew. He breathed a sigh of relief when Dr. Hughes walked into the emergency room.

"What happened?" the doctor asked.

"We found him in a house near Oklaunion," said Wade. "We don't know how long he'd been lying there or how much longer he would have lasted."

"Does Deputy Clifton know?"

"Not yet. I wanted to find out Drew's prognosis before calling her."

"I'll examine him immediately and let you know," said the doctor, disappearing into the examination room.

Wade paced the waiting room floor for what seemed like hours before hearing someone say, "Sheriff?"

He turned and saw a nurse holding a piece of paper.

"Dr. Hughes found this in Mr. Clifton's pocket. He asked me to give you this and tell you that it's time to call Mrs. Clifton. The bullet went through without causing serious damage."

Wade took the paper from her and said, "Thank you. I'll call Mrs. Clifton right away."

The nurse nodded and returned to her work. Wade took out his cell phone and called the office.

"Sheriff's office."

"Reed, is Maddie still there?"

"Yea, but she's getting ready to leave."

"I need to talk with her," Wade said. "Stay close. She might need you."

"Is it bad?" Reed asked, dreading the answer.

"It could be worse," said Wade.

Wade heard Reed call Maddie to the phone and waited a few seconds before she answered.

"Maddie, we found Drew. He's at the hospital in the emergency room. He's been shot, but the doctor thinks he'll make it."

"What?"

Wade repeated the information and added, "Get Reed or one of the others to drive you. I'll stay until you get here."

"He's alive?"

"He's alive, Maddie," Wade assured her, smiling.

The phone call ended abruptly, and Wade sat down to read the note. He read the first two words. He stopped, folded it up, and put it in his pocket. He wasn't comfortable reading a letter from a husband to his wife.

Wade took out his cell phone again and called Wagner.

"Are you still at the scene?"

"Yes, Sir. How is Clifton?"

"Dr. Hughes thinks he'll make it," Wade told his deputy. "He says the bullet went through without doing any major damage. Have you found the slug?"

"No, but we'll look for it before we leave," Wagner promised. "How is Maddie taking it?"

"I haven't seen her, but she's on her way," said Wade. "Shocked would be the best description of her initial reaction."

"I didn't expect to find him alive," Wagner admitted.

"Neither did I," said Wade. "Maddie's coming in now. "I'll see you at the office."

Maddie ran into the emergency room and went directly to Wade.

"How is he? Where is he? Can I see him?"

"Slow down, Maddie, slow down," Wade said slowly, hoping she'd mimic him. "Dr. Hughes is with him now. Talk to the receptionist at the desk. She'll find out when you can see Drew."

Maddie turned and went to the reception desk. The young woman disappeared and returned a few minutes later. She led Maddie to the examining room to see her husband.

"Wade, I never want to go through that again," said Reed. "Maddie came unglued after talking to you. I've never seen her like that."

"What do you mean?"

"Happy one minute, mad as hell the next, and crying the next," said Reed. "She couldn't sit still. And she talked so fast that I couldn't understand anything she said."

"She's kept a tight rein on her emotions through all of this," Wade told him. "She had to let go eventually."

Maddie returned to the waiting room and sat down beside Wade and Reed. She covered her face with her hands and sighed deeply.

"Are you okay, Maddie?" Wade asked, concerned.

"Yes, and no," she said. "I'm thrilled that Drew's alive, but we still don't have any answers. I won't be able to relax until I know the truth."

Wade remembered the letter and took it from his pocket. He handed it to Maddie, "This was in Drew's pocket. I read the beginning and stopped. It's to you."

Maddie opened the letter and read. Silent tears fell onto the white paper. She handed it to Wade when she finished.

"You should read it," she said. "There's some personal stuff, but there's also information that might be useful in the investigation."

Wade read the letter before folding it and putting it back in his pocket. "I'll make a copy of it if you'd like. The original needs to be included in the case files."

"I know," said Maddie, wiping tears from her face. "I don't need a copy. Oh! I have to call my dad. Will you excuse me?"

Maddie didn't wait for an answer. She went outside to have some privacy.

"What's in the letter?" asked Reed.

"Aside from the personal stuff, it answers some of our questions," said Wade. "We know who took him from the murder scene and why. We still don't know how Drew got there."

"Is Drew still a person of interest in the case?"

Wade nodded and said, "Until we can prove otherwise. Yes."

# CHAPTER SIXTEEN

WADE AND REED went back to the office when Drew was moved to a room. Maddie insisted she'd stay with him until her dad arrived with Brody.

The Sheriff's department buzzed with activity. Evidence collected from all three scenes had to be analyzed. The daytime workers left it all in the capable hands of the night shift. The briefing would be held the following day.

Wade drove home that night exhausted. It had been a rough week. He wanted to relax in front of the television with Lizzie by his side.

He arrived at the inn to find the parking area filled with cars. He leaned back in the seat and sighed. "The rehearsal dinner," he said aloud.

Parking his truck in his usual spot, he got out and crept to the back door. *I might be able to slip in unnoticed if they're not in the dining area.*

He looked through the kitchen window, and his hopes faded. People were everywhere.

Wade was about to move when Lizzie saw him. She excused herself and went outside to meet him.

"Why aren't you coming in?" she asked after kissing him.

"I didn't want to crash the party," he replied. "Is there any way I can sneak in through the office?"

"It's almost time for dinner," Lizzie replied. You can come in through the front door."

"I'll go around front and wait," Wade said.

"Have you eaten today?" Lizzie asked, knowing the answer.

"No, it's been crazy."

"You look exhausted," she said with concern. "We'll make you a plate and put it on the office desk. I'll send Daddy to get you when everyone is seated."

"Thanks, Baby," Wade said and kissed her.

Lizzie watched him until he rounded the corner. She went back inside and spoke with her family.

James cleared his throat and said in a loud voice, "Everyone, please, make your way to the dining room and find your seats. Dinner is about to be served."

Lizzie and Ellen helped shepherd the guests into the dining room and to their seats. Granny filled the guests' plates and an extra one for Wade.

While Lizzie and Ellen served, James opened the door and told Wade it was safe to come in. Wade was steps away from the office when he heard an irritating voice coming from the direction of the men's room.

"Well, well, well," said Allen Joyner. "If it isn't the Sheriff."

Wade turned and said, "Joyner."

"Why are the Texas Rangers here, Sheriff?" Joyner taunted. "Can't do your job?"

Wade's jaw and fists clenched, but he said nothing.

"Mr. Joyner, dinner is being served," James said sharply. "I think you should join the other guests in the dining room."

"Got your father-in-law fighting your battles now?" Joyner

continued at the top of his voice. "I almost got fired because of you!"

"Allen!" said a gruff voice from the hallway. "That's enough!"

Joyner looked at his father's angry face and then back at Wade with a smirk. "This isn't over!" he said and went to the dining room.

"What's he doing here?" Wade asked.

"He's the groom's cousin," James replied. "And one of the ushers."

"Thanks for dealing with him," Wade said. "I'm in no mood for him tonight."

"It's part of my job as host and father-in-law, " James said with a grin. "Have some food and relax. We can talk later."

Wade smiled at James and went into the office. He hadn't realized how hungry he was until he smelled the food.

He sat at the desk and picked up the tv remote. He flipped through the channels until he found a favorite sitcom and dug into his food. His plate was clean when Lizzie opened the door adjoining their bedroom.

"Are you all right?" Lizzie asked. "Do you need anything?"

"I'm better now," Wade assured her. "I'm not hungry anymore, but I'm still tired."

"Daddy told me about Allen Joyner. What's his problem?"

"He got caught doing something he shouldn't have and wants to blame me."

"Did you almost get him fired?"

"No, that's all on him," Wade replied with a grin. "One of his fellow detectives pulled the trigger. We supplied some ammo."

Lizzie smiled at his joke and said, "We're about to serve dessert," Lizzie told him. "Do you want some?"

"No, I've had enough. How long will the dinner last?"

"It shouldn't be much longer. The rehearsal part is over. All that's left are the toasts and speeches during dessert."

"I'll hang out here a little longer," Wade said. "I'll move to our room when this tv show is over."

Lizzie blew him a kiss and left. He leaned back in the executive desk chair and relaxed. It was almost as comfortable as a recliner.

Wade must have been dozing when his phone rang, startling him. He looked at the caller id and answered.

"Maddie? What's wrong?"

"It's not Drew," she said. "He's doing okay. He's still sleeping. Dr. Hughes said that was expected."

"Has he been awake to talk to you?"

"Not yet," Maddie replied. "That's not why I'm calling. Dad brought Brody and me home a little while ago. I had a strange phone call."

"How strange?" Wade asked, alert.

"The man said he was supposed to meet with Drew this weekend. He wanted to reschedule because of a family emergency. I explained Drew's situation and asked why they were meeting. He said it was a bank matter."

"Did he leave a name and number?"

"Yes. The man wants Drew to call him next week. His name is Walker Thiele," Maddie said and gave Wade the number.

"I'll give him a call tomorrow," said Wade. "You aren't planning to come in tomorrow, are you?"

"No, Brody needs me this weekend," she replied. "He had a great time with Dad, but seeing Drew in the hospital scared him."

"Take all the time you need, Maddie," said Wade. "Let me know when Drew is ready to talk."

"I will. Goodnight."

The call ended, and Wade turned off the television. It sounded like the rehearsal dinner was coming to a close.

He went into the bedroom and stretched out on the bed. He closed his eyes and settled back on his pillow.

Lizzie rubbed his arm, waking him from a brief nap.

"Is the dinner over?"

"Yes, and we've almost finished with the cleanup."

"I didn't think I'd been in here that long," Wade said, surprised.

"Daddy wants to see you for a minute," Lizzie said, smiling.

Wade got up and followed Lizzie into the kitchen. Ellen and Lois were finishing the dishes while James swept the floor.

"James, thanks again for stepping in with Joyner."

"You're welcome," said James. "I wanted to ask you about that. Is he going to be a problem tomorrow?"

"Was he a problem before I got here?"

"Nothing more than being obnoxious," said Ellen.

"That's his normal personality, from what I understand," said Wade. "I won't be here tomorrow during the wedding. He shouldn't be a problem, but don't hesitate to call the office."

"Why didn't you say anything to him?" asked Ellen.

"Ordinarily, I would have," Wade began. "But this isn't an ordinary circumstance."

Wade explained the situation with the conflict of interest, the Texas Rangers, and the unpleasant incident with Joyner. They understood his silence when he'd finished.

"You're in a tight spot, aren't you?" James observed.

"The entire department is walking on eggshells," Wade admitted. "I'm ready for this to be over. The good news is that we found Andrew Clifton alive. He's in the hospital now."

"That's wonderful!" said Ellen. "Where was he?"

"I can't tell you that," said Wade. "But I can tell you that his disappearance wasn't his idea. He never intended to leave Maddie and Brody."

"I'm sure that's a relief for Maddie," said Granny. "It must have been a horrible week for her."

"I think it was more difficult than any of us realized," agreed Wade.

"We'll leave you two alone," said Ellen. "We still have some packing to do. We'll be here bright and early in the morning to help set up for the wedding."

Lizzie's family left, and the young couple retired for the night. They snuggled under the covers and talked about the day before drifting off to sleep.

The following morning, Wade and Lizzie skipped breakfast. They both had busy days ahead of them.

"Call me when the wedding and reception are over," Wade told Lizzie. "I don't want to ruin the event by getting into another scene with Joyner. I'll probably be working late anyway."

"I'll call you when we start the cleanup," she told him. "And I'll call you if Joyner causes trouble."

The newlyweds embraced and kissed before Wade drove into town. They knew they'd be exhausted when they saw each other again.

Wade walked into the main office, followed by Drake Wagner.

"That was good work yesterday, Wagner," Wade said.

"Thank you, Sir," Wagner replied with some surprise. "It felt good to be working outside."

"I know what you mean. I don't like being stuck inside either."

The conversation ended when the Texas Rangers entered the office.

"Good morning," said Mints. "Looks like we've got a busy day ahead of us. I'm going to need coffee to get my brain going."

"It's brewing now," said Baker. "Lodge went to get breakfast burritos for us."

"That sounds like the perfect brain fuel," said Lindsey.

"I suggest we enjoy our food in the conference room," said Wade. "We'll set up a table for the burritos and move the coffee maker in there."

"That sound like a fine idea," replied Mints. "We have a lot of evidence to discuss. How do you feel about working lunches?"

"I have pizza on speed dial," Wade said, grinning.

"Do we have someone to man the office?" asked Mints. "I understand Deputy Clifton will want to be with her husband."

"We have an arrangement for the times like this," Wade

answered. "Only emergencies will get through. All others will leave messages or call again at a later time."

"Has it been successful?"

"It works for us. It eliminates the frivolous calls and visits," Wade replied.

"Do it then," said Mints.

"Dr. Hughes is on his way," said Wade. "I'll lock the door when he gets here."

The conference room was set up, and the emergency contact protocol was implemented. All staff members informed their families to call only in an emergency.

Wade introduced Dr. Hughes to Ranger Mints and Ranger Lindsey before asking, "Do you need to get back to the hospital?"

"As a matter of fact, I do," replied the doctor. "I want to check on Mr. Clifton.

Wade raised his voice and asked for everyone's attention.

"Dr. Hughes would like to present his findings first so that he can return to the hospital," Wade began. "Please, continue to enjoy the burritos. Thank you, Lodge and Baker, for buying."

Everyone applauded their thanks. The two deputies stood and bowed in unison.

"Please, don't encourage them," Wade joked. "If there are no objections, I'll start the video recorder, and we'll get started."

No one objected, and Wade started the meeting. "This is Saturday, October 21, 2017. We'll begin today's briefing with Dr. Hughes."

"I'd like to start with Andrew Clifton," said Hughes. "He received a single gunshot wound to the right shoulder. Based on the blood loss and the clotting at the wound, I'd estimate the shooting occurred before noon yesterday. He also had blisters on his hands and several bruises that have almost healed, including a black eye. There's a nasty bump on the back of his head, most likely from falling to the floor."

"What is Mr. Clifton's prognosis?" asked Mints.

"It'll take time, but I expect him to make a full recovery," replied the doctor. "However, I am concerned about infection. I'll be watching him closely."

"When will he be able to talk with us?" asked Lindsey

"Later today or tomorrow," said Hughes. "Now, on to the body found yesterday. Based on the insect larva and body decomposition, I believe he was killed late Tuesday or early Wednesday."

"Were you able to determine his cause of death?" asked Wade.

"He died from internal bleeding. He had both external and internal injuries that suggest a car hit him. His hand and knees had cuts and abrasions. Considering that he had one broken leg and the other lacerated, he must have crawled several yards before he collapsed and died."

"Is there anything else you can tell us about him, doctor?" asked Mints.

"The condition of his lungs indicates that he was a heavy smoker, and his liver showed the beginning signs of alcoholism. Otherwise, he was relatively healthy."

"Thank you, Dr. Hughes," said Mints.

"If there's nothing else, I need to be going," said the doctor.

Wade escorted Dr. Hughes to the door and locked it behind him. The others were waiting for his return to continue the briefing.

"Now that we've heard the medical and autopsy reports, what would you like to discuss next?" asked Wade.

"It's your house," said Mints.

"In that case, I'd like to discuss Andrew Clifton," Wade began. "I received some information yesterday that I want to share with you now."

Wade told the team about Maddie's phone call from Walker Thiele and Drew's letter. He handed copies of the letter to each of them and waited for questions.

"According to this letter," began Lodge. "Drew woke up in the house, found the body, and ran outside."

"That would explain his fingerprints and the toppled furniture," said Baker.

"Yes, it would," said Wade.

"Foust shows up and takes Drew to his house," said Logsdon. "He leaves him locked up there for the money. Who would pay him?"

"Foust may have expected us to offer a reward," said Wade. "Or he may have discovered who killed Tiffany and tried blackmail."

"That was a big mistake," Wagner pointed out.

"It would explain the money we found," said Farrington. "He could have met with the guilty party. The perpetrator paid him, ran him over, and retrieved the money."

"That's a strong possibility based on the evidence," said Mints. "Clifton was convinced that Foust was going to kill him. But he couldn't have been the shooter since he was dead when Clifton was shot."

"And if Foust was blackmailing someone for Pruitt's murder, he didn't kill her either," said Logsdon.

"Before we get ahead of ourselves, look at the evidence from both scenes," said Mints.

"Were there any tire tracks at the house where we found Clifton?" asked Wade.

"Yes, there were two different tread patterns," said Wagner. "One matches the tires of the Cadillac that belonged to Foust."

"That tread also matches the pattern at the front of the Handley house," said Lodge.

"The other tread pattern matches the unidentified pattern at the back of the Handley house," Wagner continued. "And it matches the pattern near the barn where we found Foust."

"Were there any shoe prints to compare?" asked Reed.

"One set at the house and one near the barn," said Wagner. "They appear to be the same."

"Do they match any from the Handley house?" asked Wade.

"Athletic shoes left these tracks," answered Wagner.

"Were the shoe prints made by a man's or woman's shoe?"

"Could have been either," said Wagner. "The tracks weren't clear enough to compare size."

"Were there any fingerprints in the house other than Drews?"

"There were some that belonged to Foust," said Farrington. "The rest belonged to Clifton."

"Were you able to find the bullet?" Mints inquired.

"Yes, it was a nine-millimeter round," Farrington replied. "We also found the casing outside. The shooter fired one shot and left."

"Did you find any bullets or casings near the barn?" asked Mints.

"We found ten casings and seven slugs," said Wagner.

"The other three slugs could be in the car or its occupants," added Farrington.

"We need to be on the lookout for people seeking treatment for gunshot wounds," said Wade.

"What about the phone call from Thiele?" pondered Mints. "Could that have something to do with this case?"

"I called and got his voicemail," said Wade. "I left a message asking him to call us."

"I think it's time we discussed the evidence at the Pruitt house," said Mints, nodding at Baker.

"We found blood residue on the living room carpet and a significant amount of blood on the pad underneath," said Baker. "After searching the alley and dumpsters, we found a gold towel soaked in blood. The two samples match."

"We also found blood on a marble paperweight that matches the blood on the carpet and towel," added Lodge. "The shape and size of the paperweight match the wound on Pruitt's skull."

"I found a button in the bathroom that doesn't match any of the victim's belongings," said Baker. "The bathroom showed hasty cleaning, while the rest of the house was in perfect condition."

We found Pruitt's purse in the house," said Lodge. "Her keys and wallet were inside, but no cell phone. We didn't find a cell phone in her house. However, there was an address book with names of people we haven't spoken with yet."

"We believe that Ms. Pruitt was killed in her home and then moved to the Handley house," said Mints. "Either her cell phone was lost in transit, or someone took it."

"There was a partial print on the paperweight and a trace of blood under the paper label on the bottom," said Baker. "The label looks like it had been wet. Someone washed it."

"The other prints we found inside were in the bedrooms," said Lodge. "They appear to belong to Ms. Pruitt and her son. The rest of the house was clean."

"The house was wiped?" asked Wade, surprised.

"It looks that way," said Mints.

"Does this mean Andrew Clifton is innocent?" asked Logsdon.

"Not necessarily," said Lindsey. "He could have killed her and cleaned up afterward. We only have his word for it that he doesn't know how he got to the Handley house. He must have known the Handleys weren't home."

"Counterpoint," said Farrington. "I spent most of yesterday morning looking at those crime scene photos. The position of the fingerprints on the tanning bed is wrong."

"Wrong?" asked Mints.

"Have you ever been in a tanning bed? When you're inside and ready to tan, you close the lid by grabbing the edge and pulling down," she said, demonstrating the action.

"If you're standing beside it, you'd have to push the lid down," she continued demonstrating again.

"The prints on that lid were underneath, as you'd do if you were opening the lid while standing. Clifton lifted the lid instead of closing it."

"That doesn't make him innocent of murder," said Lindsey.

"It doesn't make him guilty either," said Mints. "I'd like to discuss one more point before we take a break. I believe Foust was watching Pruitt's house."

"What makes you think it was Foust?" asked Wade.

"Pruitt's neighbor saw a Cadillac parked down the street and smoke coming from the passenger side window. I found a pile of cigarette butts there, and Lodge found one of the same types near Pruitt's front window."

"Go on."

"There were cigarettes in Foust's car that match the butts found near Pruitt's house," said Mints. "I need to verify that Foust's car is the one the neighbor saw parked on the street. But I took the liberty of running a thorough background check on Foust. He's never been a truck driver. He's got quite a rap sheet but no violent crime."

"Are you saying that he killed Pruitt, took her to his neighbor's house, and tried to frame Clifton?" asked Reed.

"No, that doesn't add up with the evidence we have," said Mints. "I'm saying Foust was hired to watch Pruitt. That person killed her and moved her body. Foust suspected and planned to double cross his employer."

"If Foust didn't kill anyone and Clifton didn't kill anyone, who did?" asked Lindsey.

"That's what we need to find out," said Mints.

# CHAPTER SEVENTEEN

THE SHERIFF'S department and the Texas Rangers took a break from the briefing. They needed time to make sense of all the information.

Wade tried to call Walker Thiele again. He left another message and leaned back in his chair.

Foust was at all four of the crime scenes. Was he the key to solving these murders?"

The meeting resumed, and Wade gave Mints the lead.

"Now that you've had some time to consider the evidence, does anyone have any suggestions as to how we proceed?"

"I have a question about that partial print," said Wade. "Can we match it to anyone?"

"There's not much there," answered Baker. "It could be used to eliminate or confirm a suspect."

"What's on your mind, Sheriff?" Mints inquired.

"The evidence we have indicates that two people dragged someone, we assume Drew, into the Handleys' house. That suggests two perpetrators. The shoe prints indicate one male and one female."

"I think so, too," said Baker. "There were definitely four unidentified sets of shoe prints at the scene.

"We've been looking at these cases as though they were planned. But what if they weren't?" asked Wade.

"I don't quite follow," said Mints.

"Someone picked up Pruitt at the bar. That person offered Clifton a ride. Assume that the driver took Pruitt home. Clifton doesn't remember anything after getting into the car. He could have passed out," Wade said.

"Okay, we're with you."

"Pruitt and the driver go inside. The victim turns her back to the driver. He or she picks up the marble paperweight, hits Pruitt on the head, and kills her.

The driver panics and calls someone for help. Help arrives, and they decide to hide the body. One or both of them know the Handleys are on vacation. They may or may not know about the tanning bed. Either way, they don't expect anyone to find the body for at least another week."

"I see what you're saying," said Reed. "They worked together to clean up Pruitt's house and move her body to Oklaunion. But why take Drew."

"If he passed out in the car, they had no choice but to take him with them," said Wade.

"They had to have known he'd wake up before the Handleys came home," said Lindsey. "Why take him inside?"

"That part still doesn't make sense," said Wade. "Unless they wanted to set him up for the murder."

"It's plausible," said Mints. "Where does Foust fit in?"

"If he'd been watching Pruitt's house, he might have needed a break. They may have left while he was gone. He drove home and saw the activity at the crime scene."

"Do you believe this has all been a series of murderous opportunities?" asked Mints.

"It could be," said Wade. "The driver took the opportunity to murder Tiffany. The two culprits took the opportunity to leave Drew behind. Foust took the opportunity to blackmail. I think

Foust gave up Drew's location for the cash. One or both then went to the house to kill Drew."

"Why would they want to kill Drew?" asked Wagner.

"Because he might know too much," said Mints. "They couldn't take the chance that he'd remember what he'd seen. He had to have seen the driver. He might have witnessed a lot more."

"He's going to need protection," said Wade.

"I'll go," said Reed.

"No one sees him without clearance," said Wade. "Go now. It won't be long before his location is all over town."

Reed rushed out of the office, and the rest of the team got their assignments.

"We need to find out as much as we can about Foust," said Mints. "We need to know where he went, who he talked to, and who he worked for in the past. We have to find out who hired him to watch Pruitt's place and why."

"We also have to find that driver and the helper," added Wade. "Go through Tiffany's friends, past and present, male and female."

"We still don't know if Pruitt had a boyfriend," said Farrington. "I'll run her phone records and check her background."

"There's an interesting entry in Pruitt's address book," said Lodge. "The name Snuggles with two hearts and a phone number. No address."

"That sounds like a boyfriend," said Wade. "Check him out for sure."

"Speaking of boyfriends," Mints began. "We haven't interviewed Allen Joyner."

"I'm going to leave that to you," said Wade. "I happen to know where he'll be this afternoon, but I shouldn't be a part of it."

"Oh?"

Wade told Mints about the incident with Joyner at the inn.

"I think you're right," said Mints. "Lindsey and I will handle him. I'm going to run a background check on him first. The more ammunition I have, the better."

"You might want to speak with Detective Fleeks as well," Wade suggested. "He works with Joyner quite a bit."

"I'll do that," Mints said with a mischievous grin. "This'll be fun."

Wade and Wagner ran the office while everyone else tended to their tasks.

* * *

The Paradise Creek Inn was in preparation mode for the Hartin-Cullar wedding. An arch covered with rust-colored cushion mums, purple daisies, sunflowers, and red roses stood at the end of the room. Chairs draped with purple sashes faced the arch.

Greenery with twinkle lights and matching flowers framed the walls and the entry doors. Twelve tall vases of fall mums and flameless candles were spaced evenly against the walls.

The bridal party began arriving at noon. The bride and her bridesmaids were housed upstairs in the original part of the inn. The groom and his attendants used rooms in the new wing.

"Lizzie, the hall is gorgeous," said the bride. "It's better than I imagined."

"I'm glad you like it, Libbi. Is there anything you need?"

"I can't think of anything," answered the bride. "Mom, can you think of anything?"

"Everything is absolutely perfect," answered Mrs. Hartin. "All you need to worry about is getting dressed."

"I'd better get upstairs," Libbi replied. "There isn't much time left."

Lizzie and Mrs. Hartin watched Libbi run up the stairs. They heard the door close, and they smiled at one another.

"I'll tell you what I'm worried about," said Mrs. Hartin. "Benny's cousin is a loose cannon."

"Which cousin?" asked Lizzie, trying to be polite. She already knew the answer.

"Allen Joyner," replied Mrs. Hartin. "He caused the ruckus at the rehearsal dinner last night."

"Oh yes," Lizzie replied. "I don't think we'll have to worry about him. My dad will be watching."

"So will we," said Mrs. Hartin and went upstairs to help her daughter.

The groom and groomsmen arrived, and Lizzie led them to their changing rooms. To Lizzie's relief, Joyner behaved himself.

"Lizzie, dear," said Mrs. Cullar. "Where is Libbi?"

"She's upstairs," Lizzie replied. "I'll show you."

Lizzie led the way to the bride's rooms. Mrs. Cullar stopped her at the top of the stairs.

"I wanted to apologize for my nephew's behavior last night. I pressured Benny into including him in the wedding. I should have stayed out of it."

"There's no need for you to apologize," said Lizzie. "It wasn't your fault. No one could have known that would happen."

"Thank you," said Mrs. Cullar. "You're very sweet. I'd better get in there and make some more apologies."

Mrs. Cullar opened the door and joined the bridal party. Lizzie went downstairs and waited for the wedding guests to arrive.

"How are things with the groomsmen?" she asked her dad.

"They're all being perfect gentlemen," James replied. "How about the bridal party?"

Mrs. Cullar apologized for Joyner's behavior last night," Lizzie told him.

"She isn't the one who needs to apologize," James pointed out.

At half past one, the ushers took their places in the foyer, and James went to help Dan in the parking area. Lizzie, Ellen, and Granny made sure everything went according to plan until time for the ceremony to begin.

Promptly at two o'clock, Lizzie began the music. The bride had chosen classical violin music for the bridesmaid's processional. The minister, groom, and groomsmen entered and took their places near the arch.

The flower girl and ring bearer were next. They were dressed like a prince and princess in champagne-colored attire.

The bridesmaids followed, wearing rust-colored dresses with sweetheart necklines, long sleeves, and A-line skirts. Each carried a bouquet of sunflowers and red roses.

The bride and her father stood at the door. They waited for the bridesmaids to take their places at the arch.

Libbi looked like a princess in her ballgown-styled wedding dress. The long sleeves were tapered from the shoulder to the wrist. She held a bouquet of rust, purple, yellow, and red roses in her hands. She wore a tiara in her curly brown hair and a pearl necklace around her neck.

Lizzie started the bride's processional and smiled at the young bride signaling it was time for Libbi Hartin to become Mrs. Benny Cullar.

The wedding went off without a hitch. While photographs were being taken, the event room was transformed from a wedding chapel to a reception room.

James and Dan set up tables and moved chairs. Lizzie and Ellen pushed a rolling table holding the cake and punch under the arch. The wait staff they'd hired decorated the tables under Granny's supervision. A buffet table was set up, and the food service began.

The music for the reception was anything but classical. The young couple wanted music suitable for dancing.

Lizzie kept her eye on the guests. She had the wait staff remove empty dishes and refill glasses. Eventually, no one went to the buffet. Then, Lizzie stopped the music and announced it was time to cut the cake.

The cake was three-tiered, with red roses and greenery cascading down the sides. Atop the cake was a bride dragging a groom by the collar to the altar.

When the last guests had gone home or to their rooms, James and Ellen were ready to be on their way.

Lizzie, Dan, and Granny walked them to their car and hugged them goodbye.

"I wish we could have seen Wade before we left," said Ellen.

"He may not be home for several more hours, Mama."

"Tell him we'll see him when we get back," James said. "I might bring back a souvenir for him."

"I'll tell him," Lizzie replied. "Have a safe trip and a good time."

James and Ellen waved goodbye and drove away excited about their new adventure.

"I think we deserve a break before we start the cleanup," said Lizzie.

"It was a lovely wedding," said Granny. "We did a good job."

"Yes, you did, ladies," said Dan.

The trio sat at the dining table, drinking iced tea and having a small meal while they talked. It had been a busy day, and it was time to relax.

"I almost forgot. I promised I'd let Wade know when the wedding was over," said Lizzie.

"He didn't seem happy last night," said Granny. "Is something wrong?"

"He's stressed over the case and the Texas Rangers being here," Lizzie replied. "He's got a lot on his mind, and he came home hoping to relax but met up with Joyner instead."

"Is living here putting a strain on your relationship?"

"It's either that or the fact we've both been working hard," Lizzie replied, shrugging her shoulders.

"Your jobs have always been an issue," Dan pointed out.

"That's true," Lizzie admitted. "I'd better call him before we start cleaning up."

Lizzie tapped in Wade's cell phone number. It went to voicemail, and she sent a text message telling him the coast was clear.

Dan and Granny were already washing dishes when she joined them.

"Let's leave the flowers and greenery until tomorrow," Lizzie suggested. "We can wait to move the chairs and tables to the basement tomorrow too."

"I like that idea," said Dan. "I'm tired. Directing traffic isn't easy when no one pays attention to you."

"You won't have to direct traffic at our next wedding here," said Lizzie. "You'll be standing under that arch."

"Are we going to have an arch?"

"Deanna will be here on Monday," Lizzie said, laughing. "You might have an arch, and you might not."

Dan grinned at Lizzie and said, "Either way is okay with me."

When the chores were finished for the day, Dan said, "I'm going home. I'll be here in the morning to help move stuff to the basement. Lois, do you want me to take you to your house?"

"Yes, I'm tired too," Granny replied. "Will you pick me up in the morning?"

"Yes, Ma'am," Dan promised.

Lizzie walked them to the door and said goodbye. She was tired, but it was still early. She couldn't relax entirely with overnight guests at the inn.

She changed into more comfortable clothing and went to the office. Picking up the phone, she tried to call Wade at the office.

*They must be busy if they're using the emergency contact system.*

* * *

Wade read Lizzie's text and told Mints that Joyner had left the inn. Mints and Lindsey drove to his apartment building and waited.

Joyner didn't see them when he parked his car and walked toward the building. The Rangers got out and followed him.

"Allen Joyner?" said Lindsey when they caught up with him.

Joyner turned and said, "What do you want?"

"I'm Ranger Dale Mints, and this is Ranger Collin Lindsey," Mints said as they showed Joyner their credentials. "We'd like to talk with you about Tiffany Pruitt."

"Well, well, well, Texas Rangers," Joyner sneered. "Did Adams put you up to this?"

"No, Sir," replied Lindsey. "We're working on this case. The Sheriff has nothing to do with it."

"Yea, right!"

"We understand that you and Ms. Pruitt were recently romantically involved," said Mints.

"We went out a few times," Joyner said. "It was no big deal."

"When did you last see her?"

"How would I know? I don't keep track."

"Mr. Joyner, I don't think you understand the gravity of the situation," said Lindsey. "We've been informed that Ms. Pruitt might have been to see a man before she disappeared."

"We've also been informed that you might be that man," said Mints.

"You know what that means, don't you?" asked Lindsey

"It means you're our number one suspect," said Mints.

"This is some kind of joke," said Joyner. "The Sheriff wants to get back at me for confronting him at the inn, doesn't he."

"We told you. This is our case," said Mints. "This is no joke."

"You can either talk to us here or at the Sheriff's department," Lindsey threatened.

Joyner's eyes darted from Mints to Lindsey and back again. "I know what you're doing. I've used the same intimidation tactic. Well, it won't work. I know my rights. I'm not saying anything without my lawyer."

"In that case, you need to come with us, Mr. Joyner," said Mints. "You can call your attorney on the way."

"What? You can't do this!"

"Yes, we can," said Mints. "We brought a warrant for your arrest in case we needed it."

"You have the right to remain silent," Lindsey began, taking a pair of handcuffs from his pocket.

"Let me see that warrant!" Joyner demanded.

Mints took a piece of paper from his shirt pocket and showed it to Joyner.

"That's real! You're not joking!"

"We told you we're serious," said Mints. "Lindsey, finish reading his rights."

"You have the right to an attorney."

"Wait! Wait!" shouted Joyner. "I'll answer your questions."

"We'll talk at the Sheriff's office," said Mints. "I want a record of our conversation."

Joyner nodded and followed the Rangers to their truck. He got into the back seat and said nothing during the ride. Lindsey texted Wade informing him that they were bringing Joyner in for questioning.

The Sheriff and his deputies were nowhere to be seen when Joyner entered the office. Mints and Lindsey escorted him to an interrogation room. Wade sat behind the two-way mirror and ran the video recorder.

"Were you romantically involved with Tiffany Pruitt?" Mints asked.

"Yes."

"How long were you involved?"

"About two months."

"When were you last together?"

"It was the middle of May."

"Of this year?"

"Yes."

"Who ended the relationship?"

"She did."

"Why?"

"We were at the rodeo. Tiffany said I ignored her and talked too much to the girl beside me."

"Did you argue?" asked Mints

"We argued a lot," replied Joyner with a smirk. "I like to argue and make up afterward."

"Tell us about that argument," ordered Mints.

"I drove her home. She yelled at me all the way," said Joyner. "I walked her to the door, and we argued some more. This time she wouldn't let me in the house. I was expecting make up sex, but she said she didn't want to see me anymore."

"Then what happened?" Lindsey prodded.

"I got mad. We yelled and cussed at each other until Tiffany slammed the door in my face."

"I'll bet you didn't like that did you?" said Mints.

"No, I didn't. I pounded on the door and yelled until a patrol car showed up. I don't know if she called it in or one of her neighbors. Either way, I left."

"Did you see her again?" Lindsey queried.

"Nope, we never went out again," said Joyner. "I tried to call her a few times, but she blocked my calls."

"Where were you the night she disappeared?" asked Lindsey.

"I was at home watching a movie," Joyner replied.

"Can anyone verify that?" Mints asked.

"Just my goldfish."

"Are you sure you didn't get a call from Ms. Pruitt asking for a ride home?" asked Lindsey

"She wouldn't have called me."

"Maybe you drove by, saw her coming out of the bar, and decided to offer her a ride," said Mints

"She'd have had to beg me on her hands and knees before I gave her a ride."

"Do you know Andrew Clifton?" asked Lindsey

Joyner's expression changed from amusement to irritation. "Yea, I know him."

"Did you see him that night?" asked Mints

"I was at home that night."

"Do you know David Foust?" Lindsey asked.

"Never heard of him."

Wade heard a tap on the door. He left the recorder running and answered it.

"Reed called the emergency line," said Wagner. "Clifton's awake and wants to see you."

"I'd better take Farrington with me," said Wade. "Will you take over here? Tell Mints and Lindsey where we are when they've finished."

"Yes, Sir."

# CHAPTER EIGHTEEN

SHERIFF ADAMS and Ranger Farrington arrived at the hospital and found Andrew Clifton's room. They spoke with Reed before going inside.

"How is he?" Wade asked.

"He seems to be on the mend," replied Reed. "Maddie and Brody are in there now. She wants to be here while the two of you talk."

Wade nodded and tapped on the door. He heard little feet running across the floor. It stopped when Brody pulled the door open.

"Sheriff Wade! My Daddy's back!" the little boy exclaimed.

"I heard! I know you were glad to see him." Wade smiled, tussled the boy's curls, and looked into his shining blue eyes.

"Uh, huh," Brody replied. "Who's she?"

"This is Texas Ranger Farrington," Wade said. "She's helping us find out what happened to your Daddy."

"Peanut, let's go to the cafeteria and see if they have ice cream," said Bill Furgeson.

A smile spread across the boy's face. "Can I have chocolate,

Poppy?"

"I don't see why not," Furgeson said and winked at his grandson.

Brody ran toward the elevator leaving the grownups behind.

"I'm supposed to keep him occupied so that y'all can talk," said Furgeson. "Ice cream won't distract him for long."

"We'll finish as soon as we can," Wade said, grinning at Furgeson.

Furgeson followed his grandson, and they disappeared behind the elevator doors. Wade and Farrington stepped into Drew's room. Maddie sat on the edge of her husband's bed, holding his hand.

"Drew, this is Ranger Farrington," Wade began. "I assume Maddie explained our situation."

"She did," Drew replied. "I'm sorry I've been so much trouble."

"I told him about the conflict of interest but nothing more," said Maddie. "I knew you'd want to discuss the details."

"Sit down," said Drew. "I can buzz the nurse to bring us something to drink if you'd like."

Wade smiled at his friend and said, "We promised Maddie's dad we'd make this quick."

Drew grinned and said, "Brody's a handful when he's excited."

"We've read the letter that you wrote explaining what happened," Wade began. "Is there anything else you can remember?"

Drew told them everything in greater detail than he had in the letter. "I know the woman I met at the bar is also missing. Have you found her?"

"We have," replied Farrington. "Had you ever met her before that night?"

"No, I think I'd have remembered her," said Drew. "She has a forceful personality."

"What can you tell us about her?" asked Wade.

"She was mad at her boyfriend," Drew recalled. "She said this was the third time he'd broken a date in the past month. She'd made a special trip back to town because he promised he'd be there."

"Did she mention a name or tell you anything about him?" asked Farrington.

"I don't think so, but she said she was tired of sneaking around. She didn't want to hide their relationship anymore. If he wouldn't tell his wife, she would. The bartender cut us off right after that."

The room was silent except for the scratching of Farrington's pencil on her notebook. They let the new information sink in.

"What happened after you left the bar?" Wade asked.

"I walked across the parking lot," said Drew. "I remember dropping my wallet twice before I got to my Tahoe. I put it in the door panel with my cell phone when I opened the door."

"Why did you leave your phone in the SUV?" Farrington queried.

"I knew Maddie would call, and I didn't want to talk to her," Drew admitted. "I didn't want to argue. I wanted to be left alone. I'm sorry, Honey."

Maddie nodded and smiled at her husband with tears in her eyes but said nothing.

"Then what happened?" Wade asked.

"I climbed into the driver's seat and put the keys in the ignition. Then, I heard my name. I remember getting out of my car and into another. After that, nothing."

"What can you tell us about the person who picked you up?" asked Farrington.

"I don't know who it was, but I think I knew her," said Drew. "I don't usually get into a car with someone I don't know."

"Was it a woman?" asked Wade.

Drew looked at Wade with a stunned expression before answering, "I think so. Yes, it was a woman's voice. She called me by name and said that I shouldn't be driving. She said she'd take me home."

"Did you give the driver your address, or did she already know?" Wade asked.

"I...I don't know," Drew replied. "She might have asked. I think I mentioned it was a long drive."

"Do you remember any details?" Farrington prodded. "What she wore, hair color, facial features?"

"I'm pretty sure she was wearing a hoodie," said Drew. "I can't remember a face."

"What color was the hoodie?"

"It was a dark color, navy or black."

"Do you remember anything about the car?" asked Wade.

Drew closed his eyes and pictured the bar parking lot. "It was a sedan. I got into the back seat...it was a four-door sedan."

"Can you remember the color or make and model?"

"It was light colored, maybe silver or white. I'm not sure. I was hammered, and it was pretty dark that night."

"You don't remember anything from the time you got into the car until you woke up in the house, is that correct?" asked Farrington.

"Yes," said Drew. "I'd rather have forgotten that part. Did you find out who was in the tanning bed?"

"We did," Wade said, looking at Maddie and Farrington. "It was Tiffany Pruitt."

Drew gaped at the Sheriff. He looked at his wife and Ranger Farrington for confirmation. After a few moments, he said, "Does that mean I was there when...?"

"It's possible," said Wade.

"It must have been Foust," Drew shouted. "He never told me why he was at that house or why he held me prisoner. It had to be him! Find him!"

"We did find him, Mr. Clifton," said Farrington. "We found his body shortly before we found you."

"His...his body? Foust is dead?"

"I'm afraid so," Wade replied. "When did you last see Foust?"

Drew told them about Foust's last visit and what he'd said. His tale confirmed what the officers had already surmised.

"Did you see who shot you?" asked Farrington.

Still reeling from the news of Foust's death, Drew was slow to answer, "No, I couldn't see the face. I saw someone through the kitchen door. Whoever it was wearing a hoodie."

"Was it the same person?"

"I don't know."

"What about the hoodie? Was it the same?"

"Maybe, I'm not sure. It was either navy or black."

"Did you see a car or vehicle of any kind?" asked Wade.

Drew closed his eyes and pictured the scene. "I heard someone drive up. I thought it was Foust. I hung back so I didn't see a car. Someone walked up to the back door with a gun. I remember being surprised that it wasn't Foust. The last thing I remember was the gun pointing at me."

"Is there anything else you can remember?" Farrington asked. "Any detail that seems insignificant?"

"I can't think of anything else," said Drew with a tired voice. "Why is Reed standing guard? Am I in danger?"

"We think the person who shot you believes you can make an identification," said Wade. "When word gets out that you're still alive, there may be another attempt to kill you."

"When will you be released from the hospital?" asked Farrington.

"Dr. Hughes wants to keep him for a couple of days," said Maddie. "He wants to be certain there's no infection in the wound."

"You'll have a guard round the clock while you're here," said Wade. "In the meantime, we'll make a plan for your protection when you're released."

"If you remember anything else," said Farrington. "Call us. We want to find who did this as soon as possible."

Wade and Ranger Farrington said goodbye and stepped into the hallway. Wade stopped and spoke with Reed.

"Do you have plans tonight?" Wade asked his deputy.

"None that can't be postponed," Reed replied.

"I'll arrange for someone to relieve you when I get back to the office. I want a round-the-clock guard until he's released or we catch the culprit."

"I understand," said Reed and smirked. "Should I cancel or delay my date a couple of hours?"

"Someone will be here to relieve you at six," Wade replied, grinning. "I won't have one of my deputies disappointing a young lady."

"Thanks," said Reed, smiling and blushing.

The Sheriff and the Texas Ranger left the hospital and drove back to the office in silence. Both were thinking about what they'd heard. Drew Clifton was lucky to be alive. He'd be luckier still if he survived until the case was closed.

Wade and Farrington walked through the office door to the sound of laughter.

"What did we miss," asked Farrington.

"We've been discussing the interview with Detective Joyner," said Mints. "Lindsey had him expecting to spend the night in one of your cells, Sheriff."

"I'm sorry I missed that," Wade said, smirking.

"You can watch the recording if you'd like," Lindsey replied.

"What did you find out at the hospital?" asked Mints.

Farrington read her notes aloud while the others listened.

"She may have been seeing a married man," Lindsey began. "But that doesn't rule out the single men."

"It's made our list of possible suspects bigger rather than smaller," said Wade.

"Unless," Wagner began. "The wife killed Tiffany and called the husband to help."

"Maybe the wife hired Foust to follow Pruitt," added Lindsey.

"Or the husband," said Mints.

"The interview with Clifton didn't tell us anything we haven't already discussed," said Farrington. "But we know more about the driver and the car."

"And this person likes to wear dark-colored hoodies," added Wade.

"Anything new on Foust?" asked Farrington.

"I've tried to get in touch with his next of kin," said Wagner. Patty Starnes is his sister and lives in Kansas. "I've left a message for her to call us."

The rest of the team returned to the office, and Wade asked for their attention.

"As you know, Andrew Clifton is in the hospital," Wade addressed his deputies. "We'll provide round-the-clock protection until further notice. Reed is now on guard duty at the hospital, and I need a volunteer to relieve him at six."

"I'll do it," said Lodge. "Talking with pretty nurses beats sitting at home alone on a Saturday night."

"Thank you," Wade said, smiling. "But you'll be there to protect Drew, not flirt with the nurses. I'll relieve you at midnight. Who would like to take the six a.m. to noon shift?"

"I'll take it," said Wagner. "I wouldn't mind meeting a pretty nurse myself."

The group laughed, and Wade thanked Wagner for volunteering.

"If that's all we need to discuss, we'll meet with the full team tomorrow morning," said Mints. "We'll review today's findings and decide our next move."

* * *

Lizzie heard Wade's truck while putting away the dishes. It felt like ages since she'd seen him. She couldn't wait to tell him about her day.

"Hi, Honey," said Wade when he entered the back door. "How was the wedding?"

"It was gorgeous and went off without a hitch," Lizzie replied. "How was your day?"

"It was all right," Wade replied and took her in his arms. "I spoke with Drew. He seems to be recovering well."

"I know Maddie is relieved. Are you hungry? I can make you something if you'd like."

"A sandwich will do," Wade told her. "I have to go into town and relieve Lodge at midnight."

"What's going on?"

Wade explained the situation and said, "I thought I'd nap for a while before going back to town."

"Why don't you go into our room and relax," Lizzie coaxed. "I'll bring your dinner to you when it's ready."

"Thanks," Wade replied and kissed her. "You're a good wife and a wonderful woman."

"And don't you forget it," Lizzie teased.

Wade showered before going to their room and turning on the television. Lizzie joined him with two sandwiches, two sodas, and a bag of chips.

"I'd thought we'd have dinner together," she told him.

They talked while eating, ignoring the television. The couple discussed the day's events and the plans for the following day.

"When is Grace supposed to be here?" Wade asked.

"I'm not sure," Lizzie replied. "Sometime tomorrow. I thought we'd all have dinner together if you don't mind."

"Why would I mind?"

"We haven't had much time to ourselves lately," Lizzie began. "And it could be a while before we do."

"Honey, until this case is over, I won't have a normal work schedule. Especially since we're protecting Drew."

"I know it's just...."

"What?"

"Granny said something to me earlier today that's been bothering me."

"What did she say?"

"She asked if living here was causing a problem with our relationship."

"Do you think it is?" Wade asked, surprised.

"Maybe. What do you think?"

"I asked you first."

"Our jobs have always been an issue for us," Lizzie said. "I know you'd like to have more privacy. You'd tell me if there were a problem, wouldn't you?"

"Of course, I would," Wade assured her. "You're right about our jobs. But they'd be a problem regardless of where we live. More privacy would be nice, but it hasn't been anything I can't handle."

"You shouldn't have to deal with your work when you get home," said Lizzie. "There might be other times that events here and your work overlap. Not just the Joyner incident."

"I'll try to avoid those situations," Wade promised. "I'll crawl through our bedroom window next time."

They laughed at his joke before returning their plates to the kitchen. Lizzie cleaned up while Wade lay down to rest. She waited until she was sure her guests were in for the night before joining him.

Wade's alarm went off at eleven fifteen. He got up and dressed before tiptoeing out of the inn to his truck. Lodge was pacing in front of Drew's room when Wade arrived at the hospital.

"Did you have any excitement?" asked Wade.

"No, it was quiet," Lodge replied. "Maddie and Brody left at eight. Drew's been snoring since then."

"Did you meet a pretty nurse?" Wade teased.

Lodge grinned and said, "I'll take this shift again tomorrow if you need me to."

Wade laughed and said, "Go home and get some sleep. You'll want to be alert for the meeting with Mints in the morning."

Wade sat in a chair beside Drew's hospital room door. He thought about the case and the evidence they'd found. Some of the pieces fit together, but many were still missing.

He was getting drowsy when screams from inside startled him.

"NO! NO! AAAH!"

Wade rushed into Drew's room with his gun drawn. There he found Drew sitting up, his hand over his heart, panting for air.

"Are you all right?" Wade asked, holstering his gun.

"It was...a nightmare," Drew said breathlessly.

"Do you feel like talking about it?"

"You don't want to hear about my crazy dreams," said Drew.

"I've got nothing else to do," Wade replied. "Guard duty isn't an exciting assignment. Besides, It might help."

"How could it help?"

"I used to have nightmares after Craig Dodson died," said Wade.

"Do you still have them?"

"Sometimes, but not as often as I did. It helped to talk about it with a counselor I met in the hospital."

"How did it help?"

"My counselor helped me to understand my feelings about Craig's death. Once I understood those emotions, I could deal with them."

"I'm not going back to sleep anytime soon," Drew replied. "I'll tell you about the nightmare if you think it'll help."

"It can't hurt," Wade replied with a smile.

Picturing the people and the crime scenes as Drew shared his nightmare helped Wade to relate to Drew's fear. He said nothing more than encouraging words to his friend.

"Those are my nightmares," Drew said when he'd finished. "I've never told anyone, not even Maddie."

"Do you feel better now that you've shared?"

"I'm not sure," Drew admitted.

"Maddie said your nightmares started earlier this year than usual," Wade began. "She said you'd had a bad day at work that you didn't want to discuss. Did something happen at work that might have triggered your dreams?"

"I don't understand," said Drew.

"Dr. Hughes and I had a conversation about your dreams while you were missing," said Wade. "He thought something might have happened that made you feel the same emotions you felt in the past."

Drew stared at Wade for a moment before saying, "I don't know if it had anything to do with my dreams, but I remember that day.

"What happened?"

"I found some discrepancies at the bank. I've been trying to sort them out, but I don't have access to all the files and records. I set up a meeting with the toughest bank auditor I could find. Instead of meeting with me first, he decided to do a full audit."

"What's the auditor's name?" Wade asked, suspecting the answer.

"It's Walker Thiele. We were supposed to meet this weekend."

"What were you going to meet about?"

"I wanted to discuss what I found and find out if a full audit was necessary," said Drew. "Thiele is known for his tenacity."

"What do you suspect?"

Drew hesitated and sighed before answering. "It looks like someone has been embezzling and moving funds from other accounts to hide the activity."

"How did you find it?"

"One of my customers called about an error on his loan statement. He made his payments in person and had receipts. His checking account showed the withdrawals, but some of his payments weren't credited to his account. I did some digging and discovered his account wasn't the only one."

"Who do you think is responsible?" asked Wade.

"At first, I thought it might have been one of the tellers," admitted Drew. "But I couldn't find any evidence pointing to any of them. That's why I called Thiele."

The two men talked until Drew began to yawn. Wade excused himself and went back to his post outside the door.

*This puts a new spin on things.*

# CHAPTER NINETEEN

WADE LEFT the hospital when Drake Wagner relieved him at six a.m. He considered driving back to the inn but dismissed the idea. He wouldn't be there long before he had to go back to work.

It was times like this that Wade missed having a place in town. He could have gone home for a shower, a quick bite, and maybe a short nap.

He stopped at a local fast-food establishment and ordered his breakfast and coffee. He would need all the caffeine he could get to make it through the day. He relaxed while he ate and thought about Andrew Clifton.

The Sheriff's department wouldn't be able to protect Drew indefinitely. There was a lack of manpower and funds.

Eventually, Drew would return to work. That would make watching him more difficult. This case had to be closed, and the sooner, the better.

The absence of concrete leads hampered their efforts. Every answer they found led to more questions.

Wade finished his meal and drove to the office. Gonzalez and Odom were at their desks when he entered the main door.

"Good morning," he said. "How was your shift?"

"It was quiet," said Odom. "We've been compiling the information from the computer searches."

"Did you find anything helpful?"

"We might have," said Gonzalez. "Tiffany Pruitt's ex-husband, Roger, sued for full custody of their son."

" And?"

"They haven't gone to court yet," said Gonzalez. "It will be easier to get more details during business hours."

"Have you been able to talk with the ex-husband?"

"I've called several times and left messages," said Odom. "Have you considered talking with Pruitt's son? I know he's a minor, but kids see and hear more than parents think. He might know something."

"I hadn't considered talking with Ross," Wade admitted. "We'll discuss that during the briefing."

"Who's Ross?" Mints asked when he entered the room.

"Ross Pruitt is the victim's son," Wade answered.

"How old is he?"

"According to vital statistic records, he's ten years old," said Odom.

"Do you think he might know something useful?" Mints inquired.

"He lived in the same house with his mother," said Odom. "It's possible."

"Where is he now?"

"He was with his grandparents when Reed spoke with Mrs. Douglas," Wade answered. "Detective Fleeks may have more up-to-date information."

"It's worth a try," said Mints.

The rest of the team arrived and convened in the conference room. Mints began the briefing with a discussion of Tiffany Pruitt.

"Did anyone find a lead as to who Pruitt's boyfriend might have been?"

"I ran the phone number from her address book for Snuggles," Baker said. "It's a burn phone that's no longer active. There was only one phone number in the call log, and that belonged to Pruitt. The last outgoing and incoming calls were Thursday the twelfth."

"We still don't know who the boyfriend was," observed Mints. "I think we should interview Pruitt's parents and son. They may have more information than they realize."

"I'll call and set up an appointment with them," said Lindsey.

Mints nodded his approval and said, "Do we know anything more about Foust?"

"He's never had a steady job for more than a year," said Lodge. "There have been several arrests but no history of violent offenses. Foust's father died when he was a child. His mother passed away in a nursing home ten years ago. He has one sister who is listed as his next of kin. He was married to Randilyn Lord. They divorced after two years and had no children."

"What's he been doing all this time?" asked Farrington.

"Foust did odd jobs around town," Lodge replied. "Anything from lawn maintenance and household repairs to criminal activities. He did anything to make money. He built himself a nice little nest egg."

"Were you able to find out who paid him?" Wade asked.

"All were cash deposits made by Foust," Lodge answered. "The last deposit was made two days before Clifton and Pruitt disappeared."

"Are we sure he was watching Pruitt? Wouldn't he have been at the bar or following her while she was out of town?" asked Baker.

"That's a good point," said Wade. "But he may not have known she was out of town and decided to watch her house. We can find out if he was in the bar."

"Or he was watching the boyfriend and expected him to show up at Pruitt's," added Reed.

"Have we talked to his next of kin yet?" Mints inquired.

"No, Sir," Farrington replied. "We've called and left messages but haven't heard back. I'll try again."

"Did you learn anything useful in your interview with Joyner?" Wade asked.

"A few things," replied Lindsey with a smirk. "He has a chip on his shoulder about this department and Andrew Clifton. Pruitt ended the relationship, and he wasn't happy about it. He has no alibi for the evening of Thursday the twelfth or the following morning."

"Pruitt may have been seeing someone else, but Joyner's the type to hold a grudge," Mints added. "He's at the top of my suspect list."

"I spoke with Clifton yesterday," Wade began. "He'd remembered more than he'd written in that letter to Maddie."

Wade shared the information he'd gained from the conversation at the hospital.

"Pruitt was seeing a married man?" asked Mints. "Maybe the wife hired Foust to follow Pruitt or the husband."

"The female driver confirms our theory that a woman was at the crime scene," said Logsdon.

"I'll check DMV records and contact body shops in the area," said Baker. "The car may have been taken in for repairs."

"There's more," said Wade. "Drew and I talked last night while I was on guard duty. It could change our whole perspective on this case."

Wade shared the information about the discrepancies at the bank and Walker Thiele.

"Does someone at the bank know Clifton is behind the audit?" asked Farrington.

"If so, that could mean that Clifton was the target rather than Pruitt?" said Lindsey.

"Then why kill Pruitt and leave Clifton alive?" asked Lodge.

"There are still too many unanswered questions," said Mints.

"I have a thought," said Maddie from the doorway.

"How long have you been here?" asked Wade. "You should be at the hospital with Drew."

"I've been here a while," Maddie replied. "I didn't want to interrupt. Drew had another nightmare this morning and tore open his sutures. Dr. Hughes gave him a sedative."

"Deputy Clifton, we'd be happy to hear your thoughts on the case," said Mints.

"We've been trying to figure out why Drew was left behind at the crime scene," said Maddie. "To be clear, I mean the department."

"Understood," said Mints with a grin.

"What if the culprits intended to discredit Drew?" Maddie pointed out. "Who would believe a man suspected of murder? It would cast suspicion on Drew for the embezzlement."

"That's plausible," said Mints. "And it fits into the scenario that Sheriff Adams proposed about this being a series of opportunistic events."

"That puts the focus on someone at the bank," said Wade.

"Yes, it does," replied Mints. "Deputy Clifton, in your opinion, what are the odds that Detective Joyner might be involved?"

"Joyner's problem is with me," said Maddie. "He doesn't take rejection well. I began seeing Drew shortly after we broke up. I wouldn't put it past him to try getting back at me through Drew."

"Did Joyner know the Handleys?" asked Wade.

"That's something that didn't occur to me to ask," said Mints.

"How long did you date Joyner?" asked Baker.

"We went out three or four times," said Maddie. "All he wanted to do was argue. Since then, he has tried to start an argument every time I see him."

"Did he ever mention make up sex?" asked Lindsey.

"Ewww, No!" Maddie replied. "We never had sex at all. Why would you ask that?"

"He told us he likes to start arguments in hopes of having make up sex," Lindsey replied, grinning.

"You mean he does that on purpose?" Maddie asked with a surprised and repulsed expression. "And he...Ewww!"

Everyone in the conference room began to laugh. After a moment, Maddie joined in.

"I'm sorry, Maddie," said Wade. "The look on your face was hilarious."

"I'm glad you enjoyed it," Maddie said, chuckling.

"Why don't you join us officially, Deputy Clifton," said Mints. "There's no point in standing in the doorway."

Maddie smiled at the Ranger and took a seat.

"Other than Joyner, which of the people interviewed don't have alibis for the murder of Pruitt?" Mints asked the group.

"Elaine Cabrera doesn't," said Lodge.

"What about Foust's death?"

"We haven't spoken to everyone about that yet," said Logsdon.

"It's difficult to find everyone on the weekend," said Mints. "What about people of interest who have alibis?"

"There were two men and a woman at the bank," said Wade. "I felt that both Dillingham and Hallmark were holding something back, and the Sims woman was...odd for lack of a better word."

"I think we should return to our three-squad plan," said Mints. "Tomorrow morning, my squad will continue investigating Ms. Pruitt. We'll speak with her parents, son, and ex-husband. Lindsey's squad will interview everyone at the bank, paying specific attention to alibis for both murders. Find out as much as possible about the three people mentioned by the Sheriff."

"That leaves us to run searches and analyze evidence," said Farrington. "And keep the office running, of course."

"Before we adjourn," Wade began. "I need volunteers to stand guard outside Clifton's hospital room in six-hour shifts. Wagner is there now and should be relieved at noon."

"I'll take the noon shift," Baker volunteered.

"I like that six o'clock shift," Lodge said with a grin.

"And I've got the midnight shift again," said Wade. "Maddie, do you know when Drew will be released?"

"It could be tomorrow afternoon," Maddie replied.

"What are our plans for Clifton's protection when he's out of the hospital?" asked Mints.

"We've kept people in protective custody here in the past," Wade replied. "I'll need to discuss that with Maddie and Dr. Hughes. Drew should be in the best place to recover and be safe."

"Because today is Sunday, and our ability to investigate is hampered," Mints began. "I suggest we take the rest of the day off, with the Sheriff's approval, of course."

"I agree," said Wade. "It's been a long week, and you've all worked hard. Take some time to rest and come back ready to go in the morning. Only those scheduled to work today should remain on duty."

The meeting ended, and the team dispersed. Wade drove to the inn, hoping to relax before he had to report for guard duty.

* * *

Lizzie woke up earlier than usual that morning. She had so much to do that her mind wouldn't let her rest.

She began her day by checking the supplies she'd need for Wednesday's luncheon, Thursday's dinner party, and Saturday's anniversary party.

The luncheon would be small and take place in the dining room. The dinner party and anniversary party were to be in the event space.

She decided to leave the tables and chairs from the wedding in place. Moving them to the cellar and out again would be extra work.

Lizzie cleaned the guest rooms as soon as the overnight guests checked out. When Dan and Granny arrived, she was carrying the linens to the laundry room.

"Good morning," Granny said. "Are you already working?"

"Good morning! I couldn't sleep any longer and decided to get started. Dan, we're going to leave the tables and chairs for now. It will save time and effort."

"That sounds like a plan to me," Dan replied. "I assume your guests have gone."

"Yes, they left half an hour ago," Lizzie replied.

"What do you want us to do?" Granny asked.

"Would you mind making something quick and easy for breakfast? I'm starting to get hungry, but I didn't want to stop working."

"How about pancakes?"

"Perfect! That'll give me time to sort these sheets and put them in the washing machine."

"What about me?" asked Dan.

"You can start taking down the flowers and décor in the event room? I'll help you move the vases and the arch back to the cellar. Leave the greenery and twinkle lights. I may use those for the dinner party."

"Got it," Dan replied and went to work.

Breakfast was ready by the time Lizzie had finished vacuuming and dusting the vacated guest rooms. Dan had removed the flowers from the arch and the doorways.

The three sat at the bar and enjoyed their pancakes. They discussed the plans for the upcoming events until Granny's cell phone rang.

"Good morning!" Granny answered, smiling. "Are you on your way?"

Granny listened before saying, "Okay, we'll see you soon. I'm at the inn."

"Is Aunt Grace on her way?" Lizzie asked when the phone call ended.

"She'll be here by lunchtime."

"We'd better get to work then," said Dan.

"We can finish our breakfast first," Lizzie said. "Aunt Grace is coming to help. She'll need something to do."

"Since you put it that way, work can wait," Dan said, stuffing his mouth with pancake.

They finished breakfast and went to work. The guest rooms were clean and equipped with fresh linens.

All of the silk flowers and chair sashes had been placed in a bin for sorting and storage. The tablecloths had been laundered and put away.

When Wade arrived, Dan and Lizzie were moving the vases and arch to the cellar.

"Let me help you with that," he said and rushed to take Lizzie's load. "You can open the door."

"What are you doing home so early?" she asked, surprised.

"We decided to take the rest of the day," Wade told her. "There isn't much we can do until tomorrow."

The two men moved the items into the cellar. They emerged to find Lizzie waving at someone familiar stepping out of James and Ellen's vehicle.

"Aunt Grace!" Lizzie exclaimed and hurried toward the car.

"There's my favorite niece," said Grace, hugging Lizzie. "And my favorite nephew."

Wade hugged Grace and stood back while she greeted Dan. Granny ran out the door to greet her daughter.

"Oh, I'm so glad you're here," Granny said, wrapping Grace in a hug.

"It's good to be here," Grace said with tears in her eyes. "I've missed y'all so much, and I have so much to tell you."

"We were about to take a break for lunch," Granny said. "Are you hungry?"

"I am," Wade said, smirking. "What are we having?"

"I started a pot of beef stew after breakfast," Granny replied. "It should be ready by the time the cornbread bakes."

"That sounds wonderful," said Grace.

"Let's go inside. We can visit while I mix up the cornbread."

The group went inside and chose to congregate at the bar because bins of wedding décor covered the dining table. Granny began pouring cornbread ingredients into a bowl.

"What did you want to tell us?" Granny asked while she stirred.

"I was going to wait until dinner, but since everyone's here," Grace began. "The story that I did about corruption in Las Vegas got the attention of one of the top publishers in the country. They researched my career and then asked if I'd be interested in writing about my exploits."

"That's wonderful," said Granny. "What did you tell them?"

"One thing led to another, and I agreed to write my stories as fiction based on fact," Grace answered. "I'm using a pen name rather than my own for obvious reasons."

"That's a good plan," Wade snorted.

"I knew you'd approve," Grace said, patting Wade's shoulder. "They offered a nice sum for a series of books with a decent advance. The first book will be released in February."

"You've already written it?" Lizzie said, amazed.

"I've written four so far," Grace replied. "It doesn't take long to write about things that actually happened. I changed a few details and the names of the people involved, but it's basically my life story."

"That's awesome!" said Dan. "How long does it take you to write a book?"

"I spend about three months researching, writing, and editing before sending it to the editor with the publishing company," Grace replied. "I start writing the next book while they edit the previous. It's working well so far."

Granny put the cornbread in the oven and sat down beside Grace. "Doesn't that take time away from your job?"

"That's something else I wanted to tell you," Grace said, twisting the ring on her finger. "I quit my job."

"Why did you quit?" Granny asked. "I thought you loved being an anchor at the television station."

"I did, Mom," Grace replied. "But things haven't been the same since I went back. They fired Barry Townson and replaced him with a younger, more popular reporter. I've known my days as an anchor were numbered for a while now. I'd have been next when they found the right woman to replace me. I chose to leave on my terms rather than being fired."

"What are you going to do? How are you going to live?" Granny asked, concerned.

"I'm thinking of moving here," Grace said, waiting for her mother's reaction.

"What?" Granny sat with her mouth open while Grace's words sank in. "Are you serious? That would be wonderful!"

"I thought you'd come around," Grace said, chuckling.

"Would you look for work in Wichita Falls?"

"No, Mom," Grace hesitated. "I don't need to work anymore."

"Are you going to make enough money from your books?"

"That depends on sales," Grace answered. "But it doesn't matter. I've been saving for a long time, and I can finally afford to retire. I'll sell my house in Vegas and buy a place in Vernon."

"I can't believe it! Both my babies living nearby after all these years," Granny said with tears of joy in her eyes.

"Aren't we a little old to be called your babies, Mom?" Grace teased.

"You'll always be my babies," Granny said, beaming. "I can't wait. When do you think you'll move?"

The timer sounded, and Lizzie took the cornbread from the oven.

"We can talk about it while we eat," Grace suggested. "Wade and Dan look like hungry wolves."

"I could eat," Dan replied.

The conversation paused while they filled their bowls with stew and glasses with iced tea. It didn't resume until everyone began to get full.

"Is your house already on the market?" Lizzie asked.

"I'm shopping for a realtor right now," Grace replied. "I want to look around and see what's available before selling. Depending on what I find here, I may sell everything and start fresh."

Wade suspected that Grace wasn't telling them the whole truth. He chose to wait and talk with her privately rather than spoil Granny's joy.

The conversation was interrupted by the sound of Wade's cell phone. He looked at the caller id before answering.

"Adams," he said and listened. "I'm on my way."

"What's wrong, Wade?" Lizzie asked.

"It's Andrew Clifton," he said as he rushed out the door.

# CHAPTER TWENTY

WADE DROVE to the hospital with his lights flashing and sirens blaring. He parked in an emergency vehicle space and ran to Andrew Clifton's room.

Maddie sat in a waiting area with Brody in her arms. Both were crying while Bill Furgeson tried to comfort them. Wade knew the worst had happened.

Maddie passed Brody to her dad and stood to greet Wade. She wrapped her arms around his neck and wept uncontrollably.

"He's gone!" Maddie said through her tears. "I don't understand what happened. He was fine when we went downstairs."

Wade hugged her and said, "I'm so sorry, Maddie. I wish there were something I could do to ease your pain."

"Knowing you're here helps," Maddie said and stepped back. "I'm sorry, I got your shirt all wet."

"That's okay," Wade said with a teary smile. "What are a few tears between friends?"

Maddie smiled and turned toward Brody and her dad. "Can you sit with us?"

"I should talk with Baker first," Wade replied. "I'll be back soon."

Maddie nodded and sat beside Brody. Wade walked toward Baker, concerned. Baker looked more miserable than any human being Wade had ever seen.

"I'm sorry," Baker said, running the fingers of both hands through his hair. "Dr. Hughes was with him, so I went to the men's room. When I got back, all hell had broken loose. I would never have left my post if the doctor hadn't been with Drew."

"I know. No one is blaming you," Wade said. "Tell me what happened?"

"I looked in on him before the doctor came. He was asleep and seemed to be fine. All the monitors sounded and looked normal," Baker assured Wade.

"What happened when Dr. Hughes came?"

"I asked if I had time for a break. He said he'd be there for ten minutes or more. So I went down the hall. When I came back, people were running in and out of the room, and I could hear the monitors squawking."

"Where was the doctor?" asked Wade.

"He came down the hall after I got back," Baker said. "I swear he was in Clifton's room when I left."

"When did Maddie get here?" Wade asked.

"They've been here all morning. They went to the cafeteria for lunch," Baker answered.

Dr. Hughes made eye contact with Wade and indicated that he'd like to speak privately. Wade led Baker to a chair and asked a nurse to look after him before joining the doctor.

"What happened, Doc?"

"I'm sure you've heard Mr. Clifton is dead," Hughes replied. "He was sedated but in perfect health minutes ago."

"Baker said you were with Drew when he went to the men's room."

"Yes, I told him I wouldn't leave until he came back. But I was paged. I went down to the emergency room," said Dr. Hughes. "I'm sorry."

"You were back here pretty quickly, weren't you?"

"Yes, there was no emergency when I got downstairs."

"Do you think someone wanted you out of the way?" asked Wade.

Dr. Hughes nodded.

"Have you told Maddie?"

"She knows her husband is dead, but I haven't told her anything else," the doctor replied. "I'm almost certain it wasn't natural causes."

"Do you know how he died?"

"He was under sedation but was beginning to come around, " said the doctor. "It still would have been easy for anyone to walk in and tamper with the equipment."

"How would someone get out of the room without being seen? Wouldn't the monitor alarms get everyone's attention?"

"Not with all that commotion," said the doctor. "No one would notice an extra person when so many people moved in and out of that room."

"I'd better get Maddie out of here," said Wade. "Brody doesn't need to see what's going on."

"Your deputy could use your guidance, too," said the doctor, nodding at Baker.

Baker sat where Wade left him with his elbows on his knees and his face in his hands. He seemed to be sinking as Wade watched. Wade hurried to his deputy and patted him on the back.

"Baker, have you talked with Maddie?"

"No, I...I can't."

"You two work side by side every day," Wade reminded him. "She'd appreciate a kind word and a hug from her friend."

"Are you sure?"

"I talked with Dr. Hughes," said Wade. "He had an emergency call and stepped out. This isn't your fault."

Baker nodded and joined Maddie in the waiting area. Wade could hear her sobs and the muffled conversation while they hugged.

When Baker returned, he looked ready to work and less miserable than he had a few minutes earlier.

"Baker, one of us needs to call the team, and one of us needs to look after Maddie and her family," Wade said.

Baker looked at the heartbroken family and said, "I'll call the team. I can't stand to see Maddie cry."

"All right, let's get to it," Wade said, smiling at his deputy.

Baker found an empty room so that he wouldn't be overheard. He took out his cell phone and began calling the team.

Wade sat beside Maddie and put his arm around her shoulders.

"Why don't you go home," Wade suggested. "There's nothing you can do right now."

"I want to stay here with Drew," Maddie said.

"Maddie girl, I know what you're going through, " said Furgeson. "The Sheriff is right. We should go home."

"Why? Nothing's going to change," Maddie answered angrily. "He'll still be gone."

"No, it won't change a thing," Furgeson agreed. "But staying here won't either."

Maddie looked at her father and said, "I know you're right, but I can't leave him."

Maddie burst into tears, and her dad held her close.

"He's not here anymore," Bill whispered to his daughter. "Drew's gone on to a better place. He'll be waiting to greet us alongside your mother when it's our turn."

Wade felt helpless watching the exchange between Maddie and her father. He wished there was something, anything he could do to help. But he knew there wasn't.

"Come on, Maddie girl," Bill said. "You know there's work to be done here," said her dad. "We'll be in the way."

Maddie nodded, wiping tears from her face. Brody snuffled in his mother's arms.

She looked at Wade and said, "We'll go but call me as soon as you know what happened."

"I promise to call you as soon as we know anything," said Wade. "It might be tomorrow before you hear from me."

Wade walked the family to the elevator, hugged Maddie and Brody, and shook hands with Bill. He waited until the doors closed to return to Drew's room. It was time to get to work.

He went inside, took out his cell phone, and photographed the room. He took pictures of everything, whether or not it looked important. Baker joined Wade when he'd finished calling the team.

"They're on the way," Baker told him. "The Rangers are too."

"Thank you, Baker," said Wade. "Find out if they have a security camera on this floor, will you?"

"It would be nice to have some video evidence for a change," said Baker as he left the room.

Dr. Hughes entered the room and said, "I want to have a look at these monitors before I examine the body."

"Why did you have the monitors on him, Doc?"

"I was concerned about infection and concussion," answered the doctor. "I wanted to keep an eye on his condition."

"He had a nightmare while I was on guard duty," Wade told the doctor. "We talked for a while afterward."

"Was there any sign of bleeding or confusion?"

"I didn't see any blood, and he seemed coherent."

"Then it must have been this morning's episode that caused him to rip out his sutures," said Hughes. "I can't find anything wrong with these monitors. They'll have to be sent in for a more thorough examination."

Dr. Hughes turned his attention from the monitors to his former patient. "That's odd," he said.

"What's odd?"

"I don't remember that plant being there before," said the doctor pointing at an ivy on the bedside table.

Wade moved toward the table and photographed the plant. He looked for a card but found nothing. "There's no card or florist's label."

"It had to have been brought by someone," said the doctor. "Flower shops don't deliver on Sundays, and the auxiliary ladies aren't here either."

"Are there any clues about Drew's death?" Wade asked.

"There aren't any puncture wounds on his arms or legs. No bruising other than those he already had. The only abnormality I can see is that his lips are blue."

"What does that mean?"

"It usually indicates a lack of oxygen," said the doctor. "But could have any number of causes."

"Are pillows usually kept on the floor, Doc?" Wade asked, pointing at a pillow beneath the bed.

"No, they aren't," replied the doctor. "However, that one could have been tossed aside while trying to resuscitate the patient."

"I'll bag it for evidence to be sure," said Wade.

"I won't have a cause of death until I've done an autopsy," said Hughes. "There's no question about the time of death."

"The team should be here any minute," Wade told the doctor. "Considering the circumstances, the Texas Rangers need to look at the scene before you remove the body."

"I understand. Page me when you've finished. I'll have some orderlies move the body."

"Speaking of pages," Wade began. "Were you paged through your cell phone?"

"No, it was over the intercom," said the doctor.

"Do you remember anything about the page?"

"It was a female voice. The woman said my name and to report to emergency stat."

"Is that how pages usually sound?"

"Yes, it sounded like any other page."

The deputies and the Rangers arrived at the scene. Wade went to meet them and explained the situation. He called Maddie before getting back to work.

"Any news?" Maddie said when she answered the phone.

"No, but I wanted to ask something," Wade told her.

"Okay."

"Who brought the plant that's in Drew's room?"

"What plant?"

"There's an ivy plant on the bedside table," Wade said, suspecting the answer.

"No one brought a plant," said Maddie. "Unless it came after we went to the cafeteria. What does a plant have to do with Drew's death?"

"Probably nothing," he said. "Dr. Hughes didn't remember seeing it, and I thought you might have left it there. I was going to save it for you."

"Wade, are you keeping secrets from me?" Maddie asked with anger in her voice.

"No, I'm not. I'm trying to make sense of the whole situation."

"You think the shooter came back to finish the job, don't you," Maddie said bluntly.

Wade sighed and admitted, "I think it's possible. We won't know anything until we've processed the room and Dr. Hughes has done the autopsy."

"Finally, a straight answer," Maddie said.

"Sheriff!"

"I have to go, Maddie. Baker wants to talk to me."

The call ended, and Wade joined his deputy near the nurse's station.

"They have security footage," Baker said with a huge grin. "I've gotten to the point that Maddie and her family go downstairs."

"All right. Let's see what happened."

Wade and Baker watched Maddie and her family leave Drew's

room and walk toward the elevator. Several minutes later, someone got off the elevator wearing a black hoodie and carrying an ivy plant. That person went into a patient room across from Drew's.

Dr. Hughes approached Drew's room and spoke with Baker. Baker left, and the doctor went inside. A short time later, the doctor left.

Someone wearing nurses' scrubs and carrying the plant exited the patient room across the hall and entered Drew's room. Then nurses ran in and out of the room while someone wearing scrubs got onto the elevator.

"Which room is that?" Wade asked, pointing at the screen.

"It looks like it's across the hall and two doors down from Drew's room," said Baker.

"Make sure we have a copy of that video," Wade ordered as Farrington stepped into the hall. "Farrington, this way!"

The Ranger followed Wade to an empty patient room. "What are we looking for?"

"Someone waited here until everyone was out of the way," said Wade. "Then, went to Drew's room. The clothing is different on the way out."

They searched every drawer and under every piece of furniture. It wasn't until Farrington searched the bathroom that they found the black hoodie.

"We need to dust for prints," said Farrington, bagging the hoodie. "Did you see who it was?"

"No, a plant was used as a face cover," said Wade, frustrated. "This person knew where the security cameras are and hospital procedures."

"Did we get a break, or is this case getting more complicated?" Farrington queried.

"That's a good question," said Wade. "I wish I had an answer."

The team collected all the evidence and took it to the Sheriff's office for analysis. There were no prints on the plant container.

There were too many prints in the vacant room to isolate those of the person carrying the plant.

Analysis of the evidence began in the lab with the pillow found under Drew's bed and the hoodie found in the empty patient room.

The entire team watched the security video again and again.

"I think it's woman," said Lodge. "Look at the height and build."

"And the way she walks," added Reed. "Baker, can you zoom in on the hands?"

"I don't see any jewelry or tattoos," said Lodge.

"That's because she's wearing gloves," said Baker.

"I don't see it," replied Reed.

"She's wearing those latex gloves that doctors and nurses wear," Baker insisted, pointing at the screen. "You can see a wrinkle right there."

"Did she have the scrubs and gloves, or did she steal them at the hospital?" Farrington posed.

"Was she wearing the scrubs when she got off the elevator?" asked Lindsey.

"Back it up to the elevator, Baker," said Farrington.

Baker obliged and waited.

"Zoom in on her clothes."

"Those could be scrubs," said Lindsey. "Navy blue scrubs under a black hoodie."

"Can we see her hair when she leaves?" asked Lodge. "It looked blonde, but the hairstyle was hard to see."

Baker zoomed out and ran the tape back to the point the person was waiting for the elevator. "She's wearing a surgical cap with her hair stuffed inside."

No matter how many times they watched the security footage, they couldn't find an identifying image. Eventually, they decided to take a break and look at it again with fresh eyes the next day.

There was nothing more they could do until the lab results were completed. They went home for the evening to rest and grieve the loss of Andrew Clifton.

Wade returned to the inn, steeling himself for the questions he knew Lizzie would ask. He didn't feel like answering any of them.

"Hi, Sweetheart," Lizzie said when he opened the door. Her face fell when she saw Wade's expression. "What happened?"

Granny and Grace stopped talking, looked at Wade, and waited for his answer.

"Drew is gone," Wade said. "We aren't sure, but it looks like he was murdered."

Lizzie ran to him and held him close for a few minutes before asking, "Are you hungry? I'm warming up the leftover stew."

"Stew sounds good," Wade replied.

"Sit down and relax. It's almost ready."

"Do you want something to drink?" asked Grace.

"A coke would be great."

"I know what you need," said Granny as she headed for the liquor cabinet. She returned with a glass of bourbon and coke.

"Thanks," Wade said with a weak smile and sipped his beverage.

"How is Maddie?" asked Granny.

"Not good," Wade replied and took another swallow. "They were having lunch in the hospital cafeteria when it happened."

"Wasn't someone guarding him?" asked Grace.

"Yes. Someone took advantage of a short time frame when no one was with Drew."

"Was it planned?" asked Grace.

"It looks that way."

"Do you have any leads or suspects?"

"Not right now," Wade admitted. "We won't be certain he was murdered until the autopsy is done. We've been sifting through a lot of useless information, looking for the clues we need."

Lizzie spooned stew into bowls and set them in front of her

family. She took fresh cornbread from the oven and put it on a plate.

"Wade?"

Wade looked up from his bowl at his wife.

"I promise I won't ask any questions if you'll tell me one thing," Lizzie said.

"Okay, what do you want to know?"

"Is there anything I can do to help?"

Wade smiled at his wife and said, "Maddie may need some companionship. It would be a big help to know she and Brody are okay while we work."

"I'll call her tomorrow," said Lizzie. "Is anyone staying with her and Brody?"

"Her dad is here," said Wade. "He lost his wife a few years back. He knows what Maddie's going through."

The family finished their meal and talked about everything except Andrew Clifton.

"You look exhausted," Grace told Wade. "Go get some rest. We'll help Lizzie clean up."

Wade didn't argue. The warm stew and the liquor made him feel relaxed and sleepy. He went to their bedroom and closed the door. He flopped onto the bed and was snoring a second after his eyes closed.

"My heart is breaking for that poor girl," said Granny after Wade had gone.

"I can't imagine the pain Maddie must be feeling," said Lizzie. "And Brody! How do you explain something like this to a four-year-old?"

Grace sat quietly, listening with tears in her eyes. It wasn't that long ago that she'd experienced the same kind of pain. Although they weren't married, Todd had been the love of her life.

After they finished cleaning up, Lizzie sent her grandmother and aunt home so Wade could rest. She knew the rest of the week would be chaotic.

She went to her office to check her schedule for the next day. Deanna Garnett would be there at ten to discuss her wedding plans. She was sure Dan would be there too, although she hadn't asked.

The rest of the day would be spent making décor for the upcoming luncheon and dinner party. She could squeeze in time to make a meal and deliver it to Maddie and her family.

Lizzie sat at the desk and thought about Wade. The coming week would be particularly hard for him. The activities at the inn would give him little time to rest. It would test the strength of their marriage.

# CHAPTER TWENTY-ONE

A COLD RAIN fell on Wilbarger County, adding to the somber atmosphere at the Sheriff's department.

The loss of Andrew Clifton was a hard blow. Not only because he was Maddie's husband but because they'd failed to protect their friend.

Deputy Calvin Baker was having a more difficult time. He blamed himself for Drew's death. No words of encouragement or pardon would change his mind.

Mints began the morning briefing with a moment of silence in honor of Andrew Clifton. He got right to business when that moment ended.

"Dr. Hughes, we need to hear from you first. Was it an accident or murder?"

"It was murder," replied the doctor. "Andrew Clifton was smothered with a pillow from his bed. I found bruising inside his mouth and lint in his nostrils."

"Wouldn't he have fought his attacker?" asked Logsdon.

"I ordered sedation for him earlier that morning," said Hughes. "I doubt that he knew what was happening."

"The pillow found at the scene had traces of saliva and skin cells matching the victim," said Lodge.

"The hoodie found in the unused patient room had several stains," Baker said. "They were a combination of chili, cheese, and jalapeno."

"Does our suspect crave chili cheese treats?" asked Mints.

"Either that or it was one messy meal," Baker replied.

"After discussions in this office yesterday, I think it would be wise for us to interview Tiffany Pruitt's family and ex-husband," Mints began. "I realize my squad members are Baker and Lodge, but I'd like Sheriff Adams to go with me. I understand you have a good relationship with the son."

"I think so," said Wade. "But I haven't seen him in a while."

"We'll make the trip to Abilene and Breckenridge after this meeting," said Mints. "I'd like Baker and Lodge to stay here to do their magic with the evidence."

"Yes, Sir," replied both men.

"My squad will look for links between the hospital and any of our victims," said Lindsey. "Well, also be checking the backgrounds of all the employees. It may be a long shot, but the woman in the video knew her way around the hospital. She could be a current or former employee."

"We'll keep trying to contact Foust's sister," said Farrington. "And assist with the evidence analysis and background checks."

"Until we have more evidence or answers, this meeting is adjourned," said Mints. "Sheriff, how far is it to Abilene from here?"

"It's a little over two hours from here and then an hour from Abilene to Breckenridge," Wade replied. "It's two hours from Breckenridge to Vernon."

"Five to six hours round trip, then," said Mints. "It's almost nine now. We'd better be prepared to stay overnight. We may not be able to interview everyone today."

"I'll have to go home and pack a bag," said Wade. "I can be back by ten-thirty."

"My bags are at the hotel," said Mints. "I'll meet you back here. Do you mind taking your truck? I don't want to leave my people without transportation."

"I don't mind at all," Wade said as he walked out the door."

Wade was back at the office before Mints. He'd thrown two sets of clothes into a bag and explained the situation to Lizzie. He knew she didn't like the idea of him being gone overnight, but she didn't complain. Instead, she told him to be careful and gave him a long goodbye kiss.

"What are you smiling about, Sheriff?" Mints asked with a wink when he returned.

"Nothing," Wade replied, embarrassed.

"That lipstick on your face says otherwise," Mints retorted, laughing.

Wade wiped his face and grinned at the Ranger. "It's the first time we've been apart since we married."

"Hopefully, it won't be long," said Mints. "How long have you been married?"

"A year," Wade answered. "Well, thirteen months if you asked Lizzie."

Mints chuckled and said, "Those months matter in the beginning. Not so much when you've been married for decades."

"How long have you been married?"

"It's getting close to thirty years," Mints replied, grinning. "I think we've stayed together this long because I'm gone more than I'm home."

"Ain't that the truth," said Lindsey, grinning.

Farrington chuckled but stayed out of the conversation.

Mints laughed and said, "These two are stuck with me when my wife isn't. We'd better be on our way. As my dad used to say, we're burnin' daylight."

Wade led the way to his truck, and Mints tossed his bag into the backseat beside Wade's.

"Keep track of your mileage," said Mints. "And your gas receipts. This is my idea. The Texas Rangers will pick up the tab."

"Yes, Sir," said Wade and started the truck. "Who are we meeting first?"

"I thought we'd start with Pruitt's parents in Abilene. We won't make an appointment. I think surprise interviews are better, don't you?"

"I prefer an unrehearsed response," agreed Wade. "We may have trouble talking to anyone if they aren't home."

"That's true, but I have a feeling that we need to talk to the boy before the opportunity is gone."

"Is that a gut feeling, or do you have reason to suspect," Wade asked as he drove.

"Roger Pruitt's background check has a few blemishes. If he wants custody of his son, it's a matter of time before he goes to get him."

"The courts won't stop him since he's the boy's father," added Wade. "Chicken pox might."

"That's what I'm hoping for," said Mints. "You've had them, haven't you?"

"Yep, I should be safe."

"Me too."

The men didn't talk again until they reached Seymour, where they stopped for gas and a soft drink. When they got back on the road, Mints wanted to discuss the murders.

"Do you have any theories about this case?" Mints asked.

"I have one," Wade answered. "It won't hold water without evidence."

"Tell me about it. I'd like to find out how your mind works."

Wade looked at the Ranger with a raised brow.

"Humor me," said Mints, winking.

"All right," Wade said. "The information we've learned about

Foust indicates that he was about making a quick buck. He told Drew that he was a man of opportunity."

"I'll agree with that."

"I think self-preservation was important to him too. There's no record of violent offenses, yet he carried a gun and wasn't afraid to use it."

"The fact that he emptied his gun before he died backs you up on that point," said Mints.

"He took the precautions to protect Drew and himself, but he agreed to meet his mark on a lonely road in the dark," Wade said. "That suggests that he didn't feel threatened."

"That's possible. If Foust were surprised, that would explain the wild shots and empty magazine."

"Drew remembered a woman in a hoodie at the bar. I'll call her Suspect A to keep track."

"That helps," said Mints.

"Someone in a hoodie shot him. A woman in a hoodie was at the hospital. What if it was Suspect A each time?" Wade posed. "And what if she was Foust's mark?"

"That's logical," said Mints. "It would be helpful if we had descriptions of the woman."

"We do, in a way," said Wade. "But not a physical description."

"You're talking about a psychological profile, aren't you."

Wade nodded and continued, "Assume that Suspect A killed Tiffany Pruitt. Based on the cause of death, Suspect A has a violent temper. She panicked when she realized what she'd done and called for help. She called someone she could convince to help her regardless of the consequences. That leads me to believe she's manipulative."

"That's plausible."

"Suspect A is intelligent. She managed to get into the hospital, kill Drew, and leave without anyone seeing her face. She left no prints behind at any of the crime scenes. She hid her face from Drew at the bar and Foust's home."

"Do you think she was responsible for moving Pruitt to the tanning bed?"

"It's possible," said Wade. "One of the two knew the Handleys well enough to know where they lived, that they were out of town, and had a tanning bed. I assume it was her because women use tanning beds more than men. At least the men in our area."

"What else?"

"Suspect A is probably attractive and appears naïve and helpless," said Wade. "Those qualities make it easy to manipulate people."

"Do you know anyone who fits that description?" Mints asked.

"I do," Wade admitted. "But I can't find any connection to our victims."

"Aha, so you've done some digging," said Mints. "Why haven't you mentioned this woman before?"

"I wanted to look into it without drawing attention," Wade said. "She has a history with our department and members of it. Because of that, I'm biased against her. It's the only reason I thought of her in the first place. She's also Odom's half-sister."

"Are you talking about the gal who brought donuts?"

"Yes. Megan Ford has been linked to a couple of our cases in the past."

"But no arrest or convictions?"

Wade shook his head, "She was a suspect but eliminated as we uncovered evidence."

"I see," said Mints. "You don't believe Miss Ford is part of this case."

"There's no evidence that indicates her involvement," said Wade. "And she's been trying to change her life. She's been pretty quiet for the past couple of years."

"Are there other women like her in Vernon?"

"I think there are people like her everywhere," said Wade. "It's their way of surviving. Some were taught, and some learned along the way. Others come by it naturally."

"What do you make of the person who helped Suspect A?"

"It's a man, based on the little evidence we have," said Wade. "We'll call him Suspect B."

"Agreed."

"He could be a man that Suspect A has power over. She may have some knowledge that he doesn't want to be exposed."

"Okay," said Mints. "Suspect B is afraid."

"Yes. Suspect B could be afraid of losing his wife, job, or community position. He might be afraid Suspect A will expose a crime he's committed either in the past or recently."

"That means he could be a man of power or influence," said Mints.

"We don't know as much about him because we found no evidence other than the Pruitt crime scene. He may not be involved in the rest. Unless…"Wase paused.

"Unless?"

"What if it was his idea to leave Drew at the house to implicate him, as Maddie suggested? He could have been driving the car that ran down Foust."

"You believe that Suspect B could have been the driver at three crime scenes, while Suspect A is responsible for the deaths."

"Yes," said Wade. "But without evidence, the whole theory is speculation."

"It seems our minds work the same way," said Mints. "Your theory matches up with mine minus the psychological profiles. I lean toward the dual suspect scenario with Joyner as Suspect B. He has enough police experience to know to destroy forensic evidence. Wiping prints, washing away blood, and disguising the time of death are things a cop would have at least read about in police journals."

"That still doesn't tell us who Suspect A is," Wade pointed out.

"Like yours, it's a theory that won't hold up without evidence," Mints said. "Do you know where the Douglas family lives?"

"It's been too long. What's the address?" Wade asked.

Mints read the address aloud, and Wade nodded. "It's the same. My parents live in Abilene. I'll be in big trouble if we don't stop to see them. It's a good place for a meal and a bed if we need it."

"I was going to ask if you knew of any good places to eat. We should be there about lunchtime."

"I'll call and let them know we're coming," Wade said, grinning. "They're both at work. We'll grab a hamburger for lunch and have dinner with my folks."

Sheriff Adams and Ranger Mints enjoyed a burger and fries and discussed the upcoming interview.

"You make the first contact," said Mints. "They might be more receptive to you than a stranger."

"I don't know about that," said Wade. "It's been a long time."

"If it doesn't go well, I'll take over."

The officers finished their lunch and drove to the Douglas' house. They got out of the truck and walked to the front door. Wade knocked and waited.

Forrest Douglas opened the door and said, "Well, I'll be damned."

"Hello, Mr. Douglas," Wade said. "I wonder if we could have a few minutes of your time."

"Is this about Tiffany?"

"Yes, Sir," Wade replied. "I wish we were here under better circumstances."

"Me too! It's been a long time, Flatfoot," said Douglas, smirking. "Get in here."

Wade grinned at the man and the familiar nickname. He went inside, followed by Mints.

"Sharon, come see who's here," Forrest called to his wife.

Sharon Douglas stepped into the living room, wiping her hands on a dish towel. She gaped when she saw Wade.

"Hello, Mrs. Douglas."

Sharon didn't reply. She walked directly toward Wade and hugged him. "It's good to see you."

"It's good to see you, too," Wade replied. "This is Texas Ranger Dale Mints. We'd like to talk with you about Tiffany."

"Of course, please, sit down," Sharon said. "Can we get you some coffee or tea?"

"No, Ma'am," Mints replied. "Thank you. We just had lunch."

"Ranger Mints is in charge of Tiffany's case," Wade said and explained the reason. "We have some questions and hope you'll have answers that could lead us to an arrest."

"We'll do whatever we can to help," said Forrest with anger in his eyes.

"You mentioned to Deputy Reed that Ms. Pruitt may have gone to see her boyfriend," Mints began. "Do you know anything about him?"

"No, not really," said Sharon. "She mentioned she'd been seeing someone for three or four months but didn't tell us anything more. She said she didn't want to jinx it."

"Did she jinx relationships often?" Mints asked.

"Every relationship she ever had," Forrest said, looking at Wade. "Including yours."

Wade chose to smile at the man rather than reply. He didn't want to get off topic.

"Were there any former boyfriends who might have been angry or jealous?" Mints continued.

"According to Tiffany, most of the breakups were mutual," said Sharon. "I had a feeling that most were more one-sided and the man's decision."

"Why do you think so?" asked Mints.

Sharon looked at Wade as she spoke. "Tiffany changed after Roger left her. It didn't happen overnight, but she was a different girl when she died than the one you knew."

Forrest nodded and said, "She wasn't happy. She was always angry and never satisfied with anything."

"Did her unhappiness extend to her son?" Mints probed.

"No, that was the one area where she shined," said Forrest. "He was the light of her life. She'd have gone through hell and high water for him."

"I'm glad she had some joy in her life," Mints replied. "Did she mention any good friends or coworkers?"

"There was a girl at work," said Sharon. "I think her name was Elaine. Tiffany liked her even though she was quiet and shy. There was another girl. Ooooh, Forrest, what was her name?"

"I don't know who you're talking about," Forrest replied.

"You remember. Tiffany used to talk about her all the time. She worked at the bank."

"Oh, I know who you mean," Forrest said, wrinkling his brow, trying to remember. "I don't remember her name either. She hadn't mentioned her in a while."

"Do you remember which bank?" Mints inquired.

"Tiffany called it the bank," said Forrest. "We assumed there was only one in Vernon."

"There are four, and one of those has a branch office," Wade told them.

"Oh, that doesn't help you much, does it."

"Did your daughter belong to a church or a social group?" Mints continued.

Sharon shook her head and said, "She took Ross to church on special occasions. I don't think she had any friends there."

"Do you know which church?"

"No, but I'm sure Ross does," said Forrest.

"Is he here? May we talk with him?"

"He's upstairs trying to catch up on his schoolwork," said Sharon. "I'll go get him."

Mrs. Douglas left the room and disappeared up the stairs.

"How long will you be able to keep Ross?" Wade asked.

"We don't know," replied Mr. Douglas. "We heard Roger married wife number four recently. I expect he'll have his lawyer call us."

"We understand he filed suit for full custody," said Mints.

"He did. Tiffany told us she hadn't heard anything new about that when she was here."

"Sheriff Wade!" Ross shouted when he came down the stairs.

"Hello, Sheriff Ross," Wade replied with a wide grin.

Ross ran toward Wade and jumped into his lap, hugging him tightly. Wade took a moment to catch his breath when Ross released him.

"Sheriff Ross," Wade began. "I'd like you to meet my friend. This is Ranger Mints. He's a Texas Ranger."

"You don't look like a baseball player," Ross said.

Dale Mints roared with laughter.

"He's part of the state law enforcement Texas Rangers," Wade explained, trying not to smile.

"Wow!" said Ross with wide eyes.

"Ross, Ranger Mints wants to ask some questions about your mom," Wade told him. "Is that all right with you?"

"Somebody hurt my mom, didn't they"

"Yes, they did," Mints answered. "I'm sorry that happened. It's our job to catch the person who did it."

"What do you want to know?" Ross asked like a grown man.

"Did your mom have any special friends?"

"Do you mean a boyfriend?"

"Well, yes," said Mints, grinning.

"Mom had two boyfriends, but I never met them," the boy replied. "She said she wanted to be sure they liked each other a lot before introducing them to me."

"That was a smart idea," said Mints. "Did you ever see any of them? Did they come to your house to pick her up for a date?"

"Na, she only went on dates when I was at my dad's."

"Did she have any close friends from work or church?"

"Mom didn't go to church," said Ross. "She'd drop me off and pick me up after. She had a friend at work, though."

"Did you ever meet your mom's work friend?"

"Yea, she's nice, but she doesn't talk much. Her name is Elaine."

"Were there any other friends that she talked about?"

"No," Ross said. "Why are you asking about Mom's friends?"

"We think your mom had a boyfriend, and we want to ask him some questions," explained Mints. "We were hoping her friends might know his name. Do you know?"

"It was a long time ago, but I overheard her talking on the phone one night," said Ross. "She said something about Allen. Oh, and there was someone she called Snuggles."

"Did she mention any last names?"

"No."

"Do you know who she was talking to?"

"I think it was Elaine, but I'm not sure."

"I have a hard question for all of you now," warned Mints. "I wouldn't ask if it wasn't important."

"We're ready," Forrest replied.

"Did Tiffany ever mention being afraid of someone or someone hurting her?"

Forrest and Sharon Douglas looked at each and shook their heads. "She never said anything to us."

"Ross?"

"I think she was scared of something," the boy replied. "Mom liked fresh air, especially at night. But she started keeping the doors and windows locked."

"When did that start?"

"The last time I went to visit Dad. When I got home, she told me we had to keep everything locked."

"When did you visit your dad?"

"It was before I got sick. Two weeks ago, I think."

"I think that's all for now," said Mints. "Thank you for taking the time to talk with us."

"Please, call my office if you think of anything we should know," Wade added.

The two officers stood to leave and shook hands with Forrest and Ross. Sharon hugged them both.

"It was good to see you, Wade," she said. "Call us when you find out what happened to Tiffany, please."

"Detective Fleeks is nice, but you're family," added Forrest. "We'd rather hear it from you."

"I have to follow protocol, but I'll call you afterward."

"Fair enough," said Forrest.

Tiffany's family stood on the porch and waved goodbye.

Mints looked at his watch and said, "We have time to go to Breckenridge if you're up for it."

"Let's go," Wade replied and backed out of the driveway.

# CHAPTER TWENTY-TWO

SHERIFF ADAMS and Ranger Mints arrived at the construction company where Roger Pruitt worked. They were escorted to a small waiting area.

"Mr. Pruitt will be with you in a moment," said the young secretary.

"What is Pruitt's job here?" Mints asked.

"Mr. Pruitt owns the company," the girl replied. "Would you like some coffee while you wait?"

Both men declined and sat in armchairs.

"Do you know anything about Pruitt?" Mints asked Wade.

"Nothing more than what we've read," replied Wade. "Tiffany once told me he wasn't a good father, but that may not be true."

The secretary returned and said, "Mr. Pruitt will see you now. Please, follow me."

The men followed her down a corridor to an elevator. They got inside and rode to the third floor. The elevator doors opened, and they stepped into a large, expensively furnished office.

A distinguished-looking man sat behind an ornate wooden desk. He looked up when the secretary spoke.

"Mr. Pruitt, this is Ranger Mints and Sheriff Adams," she said before stepping back onto the elevator.

"Come in, come in," said Pruitt, standing and moving around the desk. He shook their hands and said, "Make yourselves comfortable. Would you like a drink?"

"No, thank you," said Mints.

"We can talk over here," said Pruitt, leading them to a sitting area. "It's more comfortable than those desk chairs."

After they were seated, Pruitt said, "I assume this isn't a social visit. What can I do for you, gentlemen?"

"We're here to discuss your ex-wife, Tiffany Pruitt," said Mints.

"Tiffany? She was married to my son."

"It appears there's been a mistake," said Mints. "We asked to speak with Roger Pruitt."

"My secretary is new and probably doesn't know. I'm Roger Pruitt, Senior. We call my son Junior. It eliminates the confusion. Well, most of the time."

"I see," Mints said, nodding in understanding. "Do you mind if we ask a few questions while we're here?"

"Not at all," said Pruitt, senior. "What's happening with Tiffany?"

"You haven't heard?"

"Heard what?"

"Ms. Pruitt was found dead at a coworker's home last weekend," Mints said and watched the elder Pruitt's face.

"What! I can't believe it," said Pruitt, surprised. "What happened?"

"She was murdered."

Pruitt stared at Mints, then turned toward Wade and back at Mints. "Murdered? Are you sure?"

"Yes, Sir."

"Where is Ross? Was he hurt?"

"He's safe," said Mints. "We understand that your son has filed a custody suit. Is that correct?"

"I believe he did," admitted Pruitt. "There hasn't been a court date set to my knowledge. What are you insinuating?"

"I'm not insinuating anything," Mints replied. "I'm checking facts. Do you know why your son waited so long? I understand they've been divorced for several years."

Pruitt senior sighed and rubbed both temples with his hands.

"Tiffany is, was, a good mother," he said. "To be honest, I don't believe my son had a prayer of taking Ross from her. In my opinion, it wasn't his idea."

"What do you mean?" asked Mints.

"His new wife wants him to have custody of all of his children. He has three, including Ross."

"That's unusual," said Mints. "Is your daughter-in-law the motherly type?"

"Hardly," said Pruitt. "Debra is all about the money. She gets a nice child support check monthly but wants Junior to stop paying his child support."

"I'm sure his previous wives would have something to say about that," Mints said.

"They would, indeed," said Pruitt. "The idea of suing for custody came from realizing they would receive child support if the children lived with Junior. I don't believe any judge would give him custody."

"What sort of man is your son?" asked Wade. "Why don't you think he could win custody?"

"I love my son," said Pruitt. "But I'm not blinded by that love. Junior wouldn't be able to provide a stable home. He left Tiffany for his second wife, the second wife for the third, and so on. Two of the new brides were pregnant at the time of their marriage. To my knowledge, Debra isn't expecting."

"I assume he hasn't chosen his brides well," Mints observed.

"No, he hasn't," said Pruitt. "Tiffany was the exception. He regretted leaving her, but the damage was done. She wouldn't talk to him about getting back together."

"He wanted to reconcile?" Mints asked, surprised.

"Yes, he did," said Pruitt. "I believe he broached the subject with her before he married Debra."

"What did she say to that?" Wade asked.

"I assume she refused. You'll have to ask Junior for the details."

"Where can we find your son, Mr. Pruitt?" Mints asked.

"He's inspecting a job site near Abilene," Pruitt replied. "He should be back tomorrow evening."

"May we have the directions to that job site? We're headed back to Abilene ourselves," said Mints.

"The site will be closed for the night before you get there," said Pruitt. "I'll tell him you'll be there in the morning. He'll meet you in the office rather than on a scaffold."

"I appreciate that," said Mints. "Thank you for your time."

Wade and Mints left the elder Pruitt's office. They got into Wade's truck and discussed what they should do next.

"I want to talk to the current wife," said Mints. "She might let something slip."

"What's the address?" Wade asked and put the truck in gear.

They drove to a nice neighborhood and located the house where Roger Pruitt, Junior, lived with his current wife. They got out of the truck and started toward the front door when they heard a fierce growl.

The men froze in their tracks and looked around them. A Doberman Pinscher snarled at them from the corner of the house.

"Any suggestions?" asked Mints nervously. "We're as close to the house as the truck."

"We could run in different directions," said Wade. "He can't chase both of us."

"True, but which one of us will he catch quicker?"

"That depends on how fast you can run," Wade said, eyeing the dog.

"Why do you think I take younger officers with me?" asked Mints.

"Got it," Wade replied. "I'll take off for the truck. When he comes after me, run for the front door."

"What if he doesn't run after you?"

"Then, start yelling," said Wade, getting ready to run.

The front door opened, and a woman dressed in workout gear stared at them. "What are y'all doin' out there?"

"Are you Mrs. Pruitt?" Mints asked.

"Yea, what do you want?"

"We'd like to ask a few questions, but your dog seems to think we're trespassing," said Mints. "Would you call him off, please?"

"Her name is Peaches," said the woman. "Come 'ere, Peaches, Come 'ere."

The dog stopped snarling and trotted to the door. She barked at the officers before going inside.

Wade and Mints moved toward the door and stopped on the front step. They introduced themselves before going any further. Mrs. Pruitt didn't invite them inside.

"We'd like to talk with your husband," said Mints, knowing he wasn't home.

"My husband? Is this about the custody suits?"

"We need some information concerning his ability to provide a stable home," Mints said, evading the question.

"It would be more stable if he didn't have to pay so much child support," replied Debra Pruitt.

"We're particularly interested in the suit against Tiffany Pruitt," Mints continued. "Do you happen to know when he last saw her or spoke with her?"

"The last time was a couple of weeks ago when Roger took his kids home," she answered. "All three spent the weekend with us."

"Three?"

"He has two girls who live near here."

"Has your husband seen or spoken with Tiffany since then?"

"No, why would he?"

"Isn't your husband supposed to have his son every other weekend?" Mints probed.

"Yea, he should have been here this weekend," she replied. "He's got chicken pox, and I didn't want my kids exposed."

"That makes perfect sense," said Mints. "How well do you know Tiffany?"

"We've been friends for years," Debra replied in an offhand manner. "We lived next door to each other when she was married to Roger, and I was married to my first husband."

"Have you spoken with her lately?"

"Not since Roger and I started seeing each other. Why are you asking about Tiffany?"

"We're checking into her background," Mint's lied. "In your opinion, is she a good mother?"

"Well, she could be better," said Debra. "She tends to run around with a lot of men if you know what I mean."

"Does she run around, as you put it, while her son is home?"

"Well, I've heard she leaves him alone almost every night. What kind of a mother does that?"

"When was the last time you saw her?" asked Mints.

"I don't remember."

"She was seen with someone matching your description at a bar around midnight on Thursday of last week," lied Mints.

"It wasn't me," she said with suspicion. "I haven't seen her in ages."

"Where were you at that time?"

"I was at work. Where else would I be?" Debra retorted. "I work nights and deal with kids when I'm off."

"Can anyone verify that?"

"Call the hospital!" she said and slammed the door in the officer's faces.

Wade followed Mints back to the truck. Neither man said anything until they were on the road toward Abilene.

"Wonder if the newest Mrs. Pruitt knew Junior wanted to get back together with Tiffany," said Mints.

"I was wondering the same thing," Wade replied. "If her kids were with their dad that weekend, she could have been in Vernon."

"They both could have been. I'll have Farrington check into the visitation orders and call the other parents before we go further down that rabbit hole."

"We should talk to Ross again," Wade suggested. "He didn't mention Tiffany leaving him alone."

"Ross seems the type of kid who'd mention something like that," said Mints. "I wonder where the current Mrs. Pruitt got that information."

"It would be stupid to lie in the custody suit. That would hurt the chances of winning."

Wade parked his truck in the Douglas' drive, and the two men got out. This time Mints knocked on the door.

"Is something wrong?" Sharon Douglas asked when she answered the door.

"No, Ma'am," answered Mints. "We'd like to clarify something with Ross if that's okay."

"Of course, come in."

They followed her into the living room, where Ross and Forrest watched television.

"Back so soon?" Forrest asked when he saw them.

"We're sorry to bother you, folks," said Mints. "We need to speak with Ross again."

"Did you find out who hurt my mom?"

"Not yet," Mints replied. "I need to know if your mom ever left you alone at night."

"Nope."

"Not even once? Could she have gone out after you were asleep?"

"Uh uh," Ross replied. "I get up a lot at night. She was always there."

"Why do you get up at night?" asked Mints.

"Mom always said I drank too much water after dinner. But, I get thirsty."

"He breathes through his mouth when he sleeps," Sharon offered.

"Did you ever see anyone else in the house when you got up?"

Ross shook his head.

"Do you remember if your Mom and stepmom Debra were ever friends?" Mints queried.

"Deb says they were," answered the boy. "Mom said they weren't really. She didn't trust Deb."

"Did your mom tell you why?" Wade asked.

"She said she'd tell me about when I got older," Ross replied. "She said that a lot."

"When was the last time your dad and mom talked?" Mints probed.

"Dad took me home, and they talked for a while before he left."

"Did you hear what they were talking about?"

"They whispered so I couldn't hear and stopped when I got too close."

"But you still heard something, didn't you," Wade said, encouraging Ross to share.

Ross nodded and said, "Mom said she wanted to file charges. Dad said he'd take care of it."

"What kind of charges?" asked Mints.

"I don't know," Ross said.

"Did your mom and dad talk together often?" asked Wade.

"Sometimes," Ross replied.

"Thank you, Sheriff Ross," said Mints with a smile.

Forrest walked the officers to the door and asked, "What was that all about?"

"One of the people we interviewed gave us some information we had to verify," said Wade. "Roger Pruitt, Senior, didn't know about Tiffany's death. That leads us to believe that Junior hasn't told him or doesn't know either."

"Haven't you talked with Roger Junior yet?"

"No, he's working in this area," Wade said. "We'll see him in the morning."

"Did you tell Pruitt where Ross is?"

"No, we didn't," Wade replied. "We told him that Ross is safe."

"He's a smart man," said Forrest. "He'll find out one way or another."

Wade's cell phone beeped, and he looked at the screen. It was a text from his mother.

"Thanks again, Mr. Douglas. We'd better be going."

"Come back if you have more questions," Forrest said and waved goodbye.

"What's the rush?" asked Mints.

"Supper's ready," Wade replied, grinning.

Wade and Ranger Mints enjoyed dinner and conversation with Wade's parents. While Sean and Gloria entertained Mints, Wade stepped out and called Lizzie.

"Hi, Sweetheart! How was your day?" Lizzie answered.

"It was productive," Wade replied. "Mom and Dad said to tell you hello."

"Oh, give them hugs for me. I'm glad you're getting to spend some time with them, but I wish I could see them too."

"How was your day?" Wade asked.

"Deanna came this morning," Lizzie replied. "Everything's planned for their wedding. I took some food to Maddie's house. I feel so bad for her and Brody. It breaks my heart."

"I know. It's not going to be easy raising that boy alone," Wade replied. "Is it still raining?"

"No, it stopped this afternoon. It's been cloudy and cool since then."

"It's like that here, too," Wade replied. "I miss you more than I expected."

"I miss you too," Lizzie replied, smiling. "When will you be home?"

"I don't know. We'll interview Tiffany's ex in the morning. It depends on what we learn from him. I'll let you know."

"What did your mom make you for dinner?" Lizzie asked.

"She made her famous chicken fried steak with mashed potatoes, gravy, and fried okra," Wade said, smacking his lips. "It was de-e-e-licious."

Lizzie laughed and said, "It's always delicious. That makes me wish I was there even more."

"I'll talk to you tomorrow," Wade said. "I love you. Goodnight."

"I love you too. Goodnight."

Wade and Mints were at the construction site by ten the following morning. They approached a trailer on the site that served as the office. Climbing the steps, they heard laughter coming from a television.

Mints knocked on the door.

"Come in!" called a voice from inside.

Mints entered and made room for Wade in the small space. The man behind the desk muted the television.

"What can I do for you?" the man asked.

"We'd like to speak with Roger Pruitt," Mints said, introducing himself and Wade.

"I've heard a lot about you, Adams. I'm Roger Pruitt," he said, extending his hand.

The men shook hands, and Pruitt offered them a seat.

"My dad and wife told me you've been to see them," said Pruitt. "What's this all about?"

"Where were you on the night of October twelfth and the morning of October thirteenth?" Mints asked.

Pruitt looked at a desk calendar and ran his finger to the dates mentioned. "I was at a job site in Seymour."

"Can anyone verify that?"

"Why do you need to know where I was on those dates?" asked

Pruitt, irritated

"Because that's when Tiffany Pruitt was murdered," Mints said and waited for a reaction.

Roger Pruitt's jaw dropped. It took several minutes for him to recover and say, "Tiffany's dead?"

"I'm afraid so," Mints replied.

"What about Ross? Where is he? Is he okay?"

"He's safe," Mints said.

"I...I can't believe this," Pruitt stammered. "Are you sure she was murdered?"

"Absolutely," Mints assured him. "When did you last speak with your ex-wife?"

"Uh, I'm not sure," Pruitt said, still stunned. "It was the day she told me Ross had chicken pox, I guess."

"When did you last see her?"

"I took Ross back to her place after he spent the weekend with me two or three weeks ago, the seventh, I think."

"We understand that you had a private conversation with her at that time," Mints probed.

"It was nothing," Pruitt lied.

"Was Tiffany afraid of someone, Mr. Pruitt?" asked Wade.

Pruitt sighed before answering, "I didn't believe her at first. She said someone was threatening her. She thought it was me."

"Was it?" asked Mints.

"No! I'd never hurt Tiffany! She's the mother of my son and the only woman I..."

"The only woman you, what?"

"She's the only woman I ever loved," Pruitt said. "I made a horrible mistake. I shouldn't have left her."

"Does the current Mrs. Pruitt know how you felt about Tiffany?" asked Wade.

"I hope not!" exclaimed Pruitt. "I care about Debra, and we have a good time together. But she has a hell of a temper."

"I'll ask again," Mints said. "Where were you when your ex-wife was killed?"

"I was at a motel in Seymour," Pruitt answered.

"Can anyone verify that?"

Pruitt nodded. "I met a woman at a bar outside of town. We spent the night together."

"What is her name, and where can we find her," asked Wade.

Pruitt gave them the information and looked at Wade. "Does my wife need to know this?"

"Your wife lied to us," Wade said. "She said she was with you. That makes us wonder why. She may ask how we found out. We won't volunteer the information."

"I understand," said Pruitt. "She'll be mad as a hornet when she finds out. I may as well tell her about it and the custody suits."

"What about the custody suits?"

"I dropped them," said Pruitt. "I'm seldom home, and Debra isn't much of a mom. Their mothers are better parents than either of us."

"What about your son?" asked Mints.

"Is he with Tiffany's parents?"

"Yes," said Mints. "Ross is your responsibility now."

"I'll go and see him today," Pruitt promised. "He must be having a terrible time dealing with his mom's death. We have some things to talk about."

"Please, don't discuss our conversation with your wife. We'd like to speak with her again first," said Mints.

"Trust me! I'm going to put off talking with her as long as possible," Pruitt replied.

"Do you know who was threatening Tiffany?" asked Wade.

"No," said Pruitt. "After I told her it wasn't me, she thought it might be Debra and wanted to confront her. I told Tiffany I'd take care of it."

"Did you?"

Pruitt shook his head and said, "No, I haven't. That woman scares the hell out of me when she's mad."

# CHAPTER TWENTY-THREE

SHERIFF ADAMS and Ranger Mints spent the rest of the day driving and verifying alibis. They visited Mrs. Pruitt's place of employment and discovered that she was at work when Tiffany was killed.

The officers returned to the Wilbarger County Sheriff's department at noon the following day. Wade drove to the inn, planning to shower and change his uniform. A quiet lunch with Lizzie appealed to him as well.

Wade arrived at the inn and saw unfamiliar cars parked out front. He parked his truck behind the inn and went to the back door. Women of all shapes and sizes sat at the dining table eating lunch.

He opened the door and went inside. He hoped to make it to the bedroom without being noticed. His hopes evaporated when someone called his name.

"Sheriff Adams, please join us?" said the group leader.

"Thank you, Ma'am. But I can't," Wade replied. "I only came home to change my uniform."

"Isn't it terrible about Andrew Clifton," said another woman. "Do you have any suspects?"

"I can't discuss an ongoing investigation, "Wade replied. "If you'll excuse me, I'll leave you to your lunch."

Wade looked at Lizzie. She left the guests in the capable hands of Granny and Grace to follow him.

"How was your trip?" Lizzie asked.

"It was long and tiring," Wade said with an edge to his voice. "I came home to have a quiet lunch with my wife."

Annoyed, Lizzie replied, "I'm sorry you had such a difficult trip. But you knew about this luncheon before you left. It's been on the calendar for weeks."

"Is there anything planned for tonight?"

"No, but there is tomorrow night," Lizzie said, with her hands on her hips. "Granny and Aunt Grace will be here for dinner. They're going to help redecorate for the dinner party."

"Am I ever going to have a minute's peace in my own home?" Wade shouted.

"Shhhh, the guests will hear you," she whispered. "Can't we talk about this later?"

"When?" Wade whispered. "Never mind. I'm going to shower and change, then go back to work."

"Fine!" Lizzie said and stomped out of the room.

"Fine, she says," Wade muttered. "I'd like to know what's so fine about this."

Wade cleaned up and put on a fresh uniform. He went through the office to avoid Lizzie and her guests. He went out the front door and walked around to his truck.

Lizzie heard the truck start but didn't look outside. She pretended everything was as it should be while she tended to her guests.

Wade's temper began to cool as he drove into town. Lizzie was right. He'd known about the planned events for weeks. It wasn't her fault he'd forgotten about the luncheon.

*I'll call her and apologize this afternoon. I wonder what time the luncheon ends.*

Wade walked into the office to find Megan Ford talking with his deputies. Baker and Lodge had managed to look busy. Reed wasn't so lucky.

"I thought Clint would be back on the day shift by now," Megan said.

"He volunteered for the night shift until this case closed," Reed told her. "Why don't you call him at home?"

"I tried, but he didn't answer," Megan replied.

"He's probably sleeping," said Reed. "Try calling him later this afternoon."

"Miss Ford, we have a case to discuss," said Wade. "I'm afraid you'll have to leave."

"Hello, Sheriff," Megan said with a sweet smile. "I didn't see you come in. I'll be on my way, so you can do whatever you do."

Megan sashayed out the door, and Wade locked it behind her.

"What did she bring this time," asked Wade.

"Nothing," replied Baker. "It's disappointing."

"She's after somebody in this office," said Lodge. "Odom said he told her he was on night shift until further notice."

"It might be Lindsey," said Logsdon. "She seemed to like him when we ran into her at lunch the other day. He kind of liked her too."

"Is he here?" asked Reed, frowning. "We'll never get the briefing started if she catches him in the parking lot."

"He's in his cubicle," said Baker. "I think he's on the phone."

"Did you boys warn him about our Miss Ford?" asked Wade, smirking.

"I tried," said Reed. "He didn't seem to believe me."

"He's been warned," said Wade. "It's his fault if he gets tangled up with her."

"Yea," replied Reed, distracted. "Yea, it is."

The telephone rang, and Lodge answered. "Sheriff, it's for you."

"I'll take it in my office," Wade replied, expecting to hear Lizzie's voice.

"Hi, Honey."

"Hello to you too, Flatfoot," said a chuckling masculine voice. "I guess you were expecting someone else."

Wade laughed and leaned back in his chair, "How are you, Forrest?"

"We remembered the name of Tiffany's friend. Well, we think we did."

"The one that worked at the bank?" Wade asked, sitting up straight.

"Yea, it was Abby or Addie, something like that," Forrest replied.

"That's great!" Wade said. "That'll give us a place to start. How's Ross doing?"

"He's doing as well as can be expected," said Forrest. "Roger came by yesterday. We all had a good talk and a good cry. We decided to work together to do what's best for Ross."

"That's good to hear," said Wade. "I'll give you a call as soon as we know anything."

The call ended, and Wade went to the conference room. The team was already gathered, and Mints began the meeting.

"Sheriff Adams and I talked to several people of interest," said Mints. "We've eliminated Tiffany Pruitt's ex-husband and his wife. We have two names of people we need to interview again."

"Mr. and Mrs. Douglas remembered the name of another," said Wade.

"The friend from the bank?"

"Yes, Sir."

"That's good news," replied Mints. "Since people are inclined to lie to us, I think it's time to take a more aggressive approach. We'll bring people here for intensive questioning rather than a friendly chat elsewhere."

"I agree," said Wade. "The people we need to interview are Elaine Cabrera, Allen Joyner, and Addie Sims."

"What have you found while we've been away," Mints asked the team.

"Baker and I searched current and former hospital employees for a connection to our victims," said Lodge. "We didn't find anyone."

"We dug deeper into the backgrounds of the victims' coworkers," said Baker. "Two, Elaine Cabrera and Addie Sims were volunteers at the hospital when they were in high school. Janet Lozano was a nursing student."

"Would these women fit the profile, Sheriff?" asked Mints.

"It's possible," Wade replied and explained his theory to the group.

"What else do we have?" Mints inquired.

"Foust's sister, Patty Starnes, returned our call," said Farrington. "She's been away on business. She and her brother weren't close. They rarely spoke and thought he was driving a truck for a living."

"That must have been his standard line," said Mints.

"She'll be here in a couple of days to identify and claim the body," Farrington added."

A cell phone buzzed in the room. Everyone took out their phones to see who might be calling.

"It's mine," said Baker. "I'll be right back."

Baker left the room and returned a few minutes later.

"A car matching the description Drew gave us has been found abandoned on farm-to-market road 1811. The caller said the front end looks like it hit a deer."

"Let's go," said Mints.

Wade, Wagner, and Farrington watched as the rest of the team gathered their equipment and left the office.

Wade took the opportunity to call Lizzie.

"Hello."

"Hi, Honey," Wade said. "I'm sorry about earlier. My mind has been so full of this case that I forgot about the luncheon."

"I'm sorry too," Lizzie replied. "You've been working so hard. I could have been more understanding."

"I'm not sure when I'll be home tonight," Wade told her. "A car has been found that may be the one used during all three murders."

"I'll leave something for you in the oven if you aren't here for dinner," Lizzie promised.

Wade joined Wagner and Farrington in the outer office when the phone call ended.

"Did you have a good trip?" asked Farrington.

"The best thing about it was eating my mom's cooking again," said Wade. "Lizzie's a great cook, but it's different than Mom's."

"I know what you mean," said Wagner. "I've dated some good cooks, too, but nobody cooks like Mom."

"Don't mention that to your wife or girlfriend," said Farrington. "Those are fighting words."

"Wouldn't dream of it," said Wade.

"Don't I know it," said Wagner.

The trio laughed and discussed their favorite Mom made meals. When that topic was exhausted, the discussion returned to the case.

"How was your trip with Mints," asked Wagner.

"Exhausting," Wade replied. "I thought I was thorough. We checked and verified every statement no matter how long it took or how far we had to drive."

"He's like a pit bull sometimes," said Farrington. "He gets hold of an idea and won't let go."

"Speaking of dogs," said Wade. "We almost had a close encounter with a Doberman."

Wade shared the story to the amusement of Farrington and Wagner.

"I would have loved to see Mints run from that dog," Farrington said, laughing. "He can't run, and he doesn't like dogs."

"Where did he plan to go if the dog chased him?" asked Wagner with a chuckle.

"I thought the dog would chase the first one to move," said Wade. "I was just hoping I could beat it to the truck."

The group laughed until the phone rang. Wagner answered and made notes on his pad.

"Baker says they need the tow truck and asked us to run the car's license plates," he told Wade.

"Did he tell you where they are?"

"Here are the directions," Wagner said, handing Wade the note.

"I'll call the tow truck. You can start running the plates," said Wade. "This could be the break we need."

By the time the tow truck arrived with the silver Nissan Sentra, Deputy Drake Wagner had the registered owner's name.

"The car belongs to Lynda Dillingham," he told the team. "She's the wife of Garret Dillingham, the president of the bank where Andrew Clifton worked."

"It seems that bank is key to this investigation," said Mints. "Is there any evidence in the car?"

"We haven't started processing the inside," said Baker. "There's damage to the front passenger side and a broken headlight with traces of blood. We're comparing it to Foust's."

"How did it end up way out there?" asked Lindsey.

"Taking it to a body shop wouldn't be smart," said Logsdon. "Taking it home wouldn't be a good move either. The next option would be to dump it somewhere."

"I wonder how many people passed it before someone called it in?" asked Wagner.

"It depends on how long it was out there," said Lodge. "I don't understand why it was left there. It would have been better to drive off into some brush or a lake. It wouldn't be found for months or years."

"Maybe it was dumped there on purpose. Someone wanted it to be found," said Farrington.

"Why?" asked Logsdon.

"To throw us another red herring or to implicate another person," said Baker.

"It seems to me that someone is trying to cover their tracks by pointing us in other directions," said Mints. "Have you contacted the owner of the car?"

"Yes, Sir," replied Farrington. "She claims that the car was stolen. She's been out of state taking care of her mother for the past three weeks."

"Have you verified that?"

"Mrs. Dillingham's mother was in intensive care in Orlando, Florida, after a car accident on October fourth. The nurse that I spoke with said that Mrs. Dillingham arrived on the evening of October fifth. She hasn't left the hospital for more than a few hours since her arrival."

"Was there evidence of the car being tampered with?" asked Wade.

"No, Sir," answered Baker. "The key fob was in the console. It was one of those that has a push button start."

"Could Garrett Dillingham be involved?" asked Logsdon. "It's his wife's car. He worked with Drew."

"He could be," said Lodge. "Or someone could be setting him up. Who knew Mrs. Dillingham was out of town?"

"And who could have gotten hold of her key fob?" asked Baker. "Or taken the car without Mr. Dillingham's knowledge?"

"Will the blood analysis be finished by tomorrow?" asked Mints.

"It should be ready first thing in the morning," Baker replied.

"We'll wait for that to start the interviews. We need to have the evidence before questioning these people."

"Has anyone heard from Maddie today?" asked Baker.

"I thought I'd stop by her place on my way home," said Wade. "Should I give her an update?"

Mints looked at Wade a moment before answering, "She needs to know how her husband died. Tell her we have a list of people to interview. I don't want to raise her hopes until we have more concrete evidence."

"I don't think that'll be enough for Deputy Clifton," said Farrington. "She's too sharp to be put off."

"That's true," said Wade.

"Use your best judgment then," replied Mints.

A cell phone rang again. This time it was Wade's.

"Sheriff Adams."

"Sheriff, this is Walker Thiele. I'm returning your call."

"Mr. Thiele, thank you for getting in touch. Do you have time to talk?"

"Yes, I'd prefer to talk in person," Thiele replied. "I'm outside your office now."

"So would I," said Wade. "I'll open the door for you."

"Show him into an interrogation room," said Mints. "I want a record of what he has to say."

Wade nodded and went to open the main door. He greeted Mr. Thiele and locked the door behind him.

"I'm sorry about that," said Wade. "We're working multiple cases and are spread thin. We can talk in here."

Wade opened the door to an interrogation room and offered Thiele something to drink.

"I could use a coke if you have one," said Thiele. "It was a long drive."

Wade stepped into the hall. "Baker, would you bring a coke for Mr. Thiele, please."

"Yes, Sir."

Wade sat across the table from Thiele and said, "We'd like to record this conversation for our files. It's easier to review than a stack of papers."

"I understand," said Thiele. "It would be best considering the circumstances."

Baker brought a cold bottle of coke for Thiele and closed the door on his way out.

"I understand Andrew Clifton called you about a problem at the bank," Wade began. "What did he tell you?"

"Why don't you ask him?" Thiele inquired.

"That isn't possible," said Wade. "Mr. Clifton is dead."

"What? When?"

"He was murdered in his hospital room Sunday afternoon. Someone went in and smothered him with a pillow while he was sleeping."

"Why would anyone do that?"

Wade gave Thiele the highlights of the case and waited for a response.

"And you believe this is somehow connected to the bank," said Thiele.

"We aren't certain, but it looks that way," Wade replied. "That's why we need to know what you and Drew talked about."

"Mr. Clifton called me because he had reason to believe that funds were being moved from multiple accounts into a single account," said Thiele. "He sent me photos of the discrepancies he found."

"He told me about the money but not the photos," said Wade. "What do you suspect?"

"It appears the owner of an inactive account noticed a shortage," replied Thiele. "Someone with access to these accounts began moving small amounts over time to the account in question."

"Wouldn't the other account holders notice money disappearing?"

"Some account holders wouldn't notice a few dollars here and there," explained Thiele. "You'd be surprised how many people don't keep track of their funds."

"Why did you decide an audit is needed?"

"I suspect this has been going on for years," said Thiele. "The longer it continues, the bolder the embezzlement. Missing loan payments of hundreds of dollars prompted Clifton to look into the situation."

"Did Clifton suspect someone?" asked Wade. "He didn't mention anyone to me."

"He didn't mention a name," Thiele replied. "To access multiple accounts, it would have to be someone in a position of power."

"Like a bank officer?" Wade probed.

"That would be the first place I'd look," Thiele replied.

"When do you plan to begin the audit?" Wade inquired.

"I planned to start tomorrow morning unless there's some reason why I shouldn't."

"I'd like to talk with my colleagues about that," said Wade. "We have to question some of the bank staff soon. Will you excuse me?"

Wade left the room and closed the door behind him. Mints exited the adjoining room and met him in the hall.

"What do you think?" asked Wade. "Audit or no audit until questioning is done."

"I can see advantages and disadvantages to both," said Mints. "The audit could rattle our targets or make them clam up."

"We could bring all of them in at the same time. Questioning the secretaries first might shake up the officers," suggested Wade. "They might be rattled enough to talk with the audit happening at the same time."

"Let's see what Thiele has in mind before we decide," said Mints, opening the door.

"Hello, Mr. Thiele. I'm Dale Mints with the Texas Rangers."

"Hello," replied Thiele, obviously surprised.

"Will you explain how an audit works? What does it entail?"

Thiele explained the process and the specific things he intended to investigate.

"Did anyone at the bank know that Clifton contacted you?" Mints asked.

"Not that I'm aware," said Thiele. "He gave me his personal cell phone number. I assume that was so his coworkers wouldn't overhear."

"Go ahead and start your audit as planned," Mints told him,

handing him a business card. Call us if you feel unsafe or threatened at any time."

Wade escorted Thiele from the building and thanked him for his help.

"Do you think we should keep an eye on him?" Mints asked when Wade returned.

"He might turn up in the morgue if we don't," answered Wade.

# CHAPTER TWENTY-FOUR

THURSDAY MORNING BEGAN with a briefing to discuss the evidence and devise an action plan. Mints started the meeting as usual.

"Baker, what can you tell us about the car found yesterday?"

"It was the car used in David Foust's murder," said Baker. "The blood on the broken headlight matched the victim."

"Was there anything of use inside the car?" Mints prodded.

"There were no prints inside the car. Like the crime scenes, it had been wiped clean. But we did find something interesting," Baker said, grinning. "We found blood in the trunk and a cell phone. Both belonged to Tiffany Pruitt. There were also traces of cotton fibers that match the towel found in the alley behind Pruitt's house."

"Finally, we get a break in the case," Mints said, smiling broadly.

"The tire tread matches the tracks we found at three crime scenes," added Lodge.

"Do we have more information about the car's owner?" asked Wade.

"Lynda Dillingham said she left the car in the garage at her home. She has her key fob but her husband, Garrett, has one too."

"We need to interview him before he finds out the car has been discovered," said Mints. "But I want to give Walker Thiele time to start the bank audit."

"We could bring in Cabrera and Joyner first," Wade suggested. "That should give Thiele a nice head start."

"I think you're right," said Mints. "Those two names keep coming up. There has to be something they aren't telling us. Logsdon and Baker will pick up Cabrera. Farrington will interview her. Lindsey and I will bring in Joyner."

The meeting ended, and the team began their assigned tasks. Baker and Logsdon left the office and found Maddie waiting outside the door.

"Maddie? You shouldn't be here," said Baker.

"I wanted to see you," she said and hugged her friend. "I know you've been blaming yourself."

"Maddie, I…"

"No, I want you to listen. You aren't responsible for Drew's death. That responsibility belongs to the person who killed him. Do you hear me?"

Baker looked at Maddie and nodded. "I hear you," he replied. "It doesn't change the fact that he died on my watch."

"I was there too, remember?"

"That's different."

"How is that different?" Maddie asked with her hands on her hips. "I'm a deputy sheriff, the same as you."

"But…," Baker began.

"But nothing!" shouted Maddie. "According to Wade, the person who killed Drew waited for an opportunity and took advantage of it."

"She's right," added Logsdon. "It could have happened when any of us was on duty."

"But it didn't!" Baker shouted. "It happened while I was there! If I could go back to that day, that minute, I wouldn't have left Drew's side."

"Baker, Listen to me! Nothing is going to bring Drew back," Maddie said with tears in her eyes. "This can't be changed. None of this would have happened if we hadn't argued or if he hadn't left that night. There's only one thing you can do for Drew and our family. Catch the person who did this. Catch the person who murdered my husband."

"We will, Maddie," said Baker with a determined expression. "I promise."

"Now that that's settled," said Mints from the front entrance. "You two had better get to work if we're going to keep Baker's promise."

Logsdon and Baker nodded and headed for the car.

"How long have you been standing there?" Maddie asked.

"Long enough to know that you did a good thing," Mints replied. "Baker needed to hear that from you. He wouldn't listen to anyone else."

"I hope he listened to me."

"What are you doing here, Deputy?" Mints inquired.

"I came to town to make arrangements for Drew's funeral," Maddie replied. "I wanted to stop by to see Baker and find out if you had any news."

"Sheriff Adams is inside," said Mints. "Lindsey and I are on our way to ask Detective Joyner to join us."

Maddie grinned and said, "Can I watch?"

Mints chuckled and said, "I don't think that would be wise, but the interrogation recording will be available after the case is closed."

Maddie went inside, locking the main door behind her. She found Wagner and Farrington preparing the interrogation room. Wade prepared the observation room.

"Are you busy?" Maddie asked when she found Wade.

"You shouldn't be here, Maddie," he replied.

"So I've been told. I'm on my way to the funeral home. Do you have any updates?"

Wade sighed and said, "I planned to stop by your place last night. Instead, I decided to wait until I had more news. Why don't we go to my office?"

Maddie nodded and followed Wade. She sat in the chair in front of his desk and said, "Give it to me straight. I'm too tired and emotional to read between the lines."

"Dr. Hughes said that Drew was smothered with a pillow in his room," Wade began. "We found a car that matches the description that Drew gave me. We found evidence that it was used to move Tiffany Pruitt and kill David Foust."

"Are you bringing the suspect in?" Maddie asked. "What's the plan?"

"You don't need to know," Wade said sternly. "All you need to worry about is taking care of Brody and yourself."

"Yes, but…"

"I'm not going to give you any details. We have suspects, and they'll be brought in for interrogation."

Dozens of questions swirled through Maddie's mind. She knew Wade wouldn't answer most of them. She had one chance to get him to talk.

"May I ask if any suspects have been ruled out?"

"We've ruled out Tiffany's ex-husband and his wife."

Disappointed, Maddie said, "I didn't know they were suspects?"

"They were for a short time. You were hoping I'd give you a name so you could figure out the remaining suspects weren't you?" asked Wade, grinning at his deputy."

Maddie smirked and said, "I know Joyner is still on the list. Mints told me they were on the way to pick him up."

"Joyner is the prime suspect as far as Mints is concerned," said Wade.

"Oh? Who are you leaning toward?" Maddie probed.

Wade grinned and said, "You thought you had me, didn't you?"

Maddie smirked and said, " I thought I might catch you off

guard. Since you aren't going to tell me anything, I'd better go. I'm supposed to be at the funeral home in ten minutes."

"Do you want me to go with you?" Wade asked with compassion.

"No, I have to do this myself," Maddie replied, fighting back the tears. "Dad offered to come, but this is between Drew and me."

"I understand," said Wade. "We're here if you need us."

"I know, and thank Lizzie for the wonderful meals," Maddie answered. "Seeing her every day has been a nice break."

"Let us know when the service will be," said Wade. "We'd all like to be there."

"I will," Maddie said, wiping a stray tear from her cheek. "Catch the person who killed Drew, please."

"We will."

Wade walked Maddie to the door and locked it behind her. He returned to the observation room and finished his task. Everything was ready when Logsdon and Baker returned with Elaine Cabrera in tow.

They led the suspect to the interrogation room and left, closing the door behind them. Wade and Farrington watched Cabrera from the observation room.

"She seems to be scared," Wade observed. "And a little angry."

"Two emotions we can use to our advantage," said Farrington. "Do you think she could be Suspect A?"

"I don't know," Wade mused. "She's been described as quiet and shy, but it's possible."

"It's time we found out," said Farrington as she left the room.

Wade watched Farrington enter the adjoining room. He made sure the video recorder was working and made himself comfortable.

"Miss Cabrera, I'm Ranger Farrington. I have questions, and I want you to answer them."

"Do I need my lawyer?" asked Cabrera with a squeak.

"You have every right to call your attorney," Farrington replied.

"But you should know that you haven't been charged with a crime."

Cabrera nodded and said, "Okay, I'll answer your questions."

"How long did you know Tiffany Pruitt?"

"We met at work when she started working through our office," answered Cabrera. "I think it was two years ago."

"What kind of friends would you say you were?"

"I don't understand your question."

"Were you coworkers, office friends, best friends, or somewhere in between?" Farrington probed.

"I'm not sure. Office friends, I guess."

"Did you ever go to her home?"

"A few times," Cabrera replied. "We went out to eat together sometimes or went to a movie."

"Did you ever meet her son?"

"Yes, I met him once, I think."

"Did you ever meet her boyfriend?"

Cabrera hesitated before she said, "No."

"Do you know his name?"

The suspect began to fidget, "No."

"Are you sure?"

"I've answered these questions a dozen times. How many ways do I have to say it!" shouted Cabrera. "I don't know who her boyfriend was, and I never met him. She wasn't my friend!"

"What do you mean?" Farrington pounced. "You said a moment ago that you were office friends."

"A friend wouldn't do what she did to me!" Cabrera shouted.

"What did Ms. Pruitt do?"

"She knew I cared about him! She knew we'd been going out for months! She knew and went out with him anyway!"

"Who did you care about?"

"Allen Joyner!"

"You were dating Allen Joyner, and she took him from you, didn't she," Farrington pushed.

Cabrera began to cry and said, "Yes, he was everything to me."

"I'd be angry with her if I were in your place."

"I was furious," Cabrera replied. "She had no right to take him from me!"

"Did you want to get even? Did you want to kill her?"

Cabrera nodded and said, "I wanted to, but I didn't."

"Pruitt called you that night and asked for a ride. You went to get her and took her home. Then you argued, and you killed her."

"No! No! I didn't kill her! I swear!" Cabrera said with wide, frightened eyes.

"Why don't you tell me what happened that night," Farrington said.

"I was asleep when I heard my cell phone ring," Cabrera began. "I rolled over and saw Tiffany's name on my caller id."

"Then what happened?"

"It was late, after midnight," said Cabrera. "I didn't want to talk to her. I thought she wanted to talk about her new man. I ignored the call and went back to sleep. I didn't listen to the voicemail until I heard she was missing."

"How well did you know Andrew Clifton?" Farrington asked, changing tactics.

"Who?"

"Andrew Clifton. He was a vice president at one of the local banks."

"I don't know him at all," Cabrera replied, confused.

"I understand you volunteered at the local hospital when you were in high school. Is that correct?"

"Yes, I was part of a service organization. We were required to do community service. What does that have to do with Tiffany's death?"

"Were you at the hospital this weekend?"

"No, I was in Dallas visiting my cousin," Cabrera replied.

"I'll need your cousin's name and phone number," Farrington said. "And your fingerprints."

"Why do you want my prints?"

"Your prints will be compared to those found at the scene," Farrington told her. "If you didn't kill Ms. Pruitt, your prints won't match."

"I didn't kill her!" Cabrera said adamantly. "I want to call a lawyer!"

Farrington sighed, glaring at Elaine Cabrera. The intimidation tactic didn't work.

"I'm going to call your cousin," Farrington told her. "I may have more questions afterward."

Cabrera was left alone in the sparsely furnished room. Wade watched her wring her hands, tap her feet, and rock in her chair. She was scared.

Farrington opened the observation room door and asked, "How's she doing?"

"She's terrified. I can't tell if it's because she's been caught or if she's worried you'll find something else."

"I haven't found anything," Farrington admitted. "Her cousin vouched for her, but she's hiding something."

"Ask her if she's been threatening Tiffany," Wade suggested.

"That could be it," Farrington said, grinning. "Mints and Lindsey have Joyner cooling his heels in the waiting area. I'll wrap this up so they can have a turn."

Wade chuckled as Farrington left the room and rejoined Cabrera. She sat on the corner of the table, forcing Cabrera to look up at her.

"Why did you threaten Ms. Pruitt?"

Cabrera fell apart. She made the sign of the cross before covering her face with her hands, sobbing. "I wanted to make her pay. I wanted her to stay in her house, terrified to leave."

"I see," said Farrington. "You may be charged for making those threats. That will be up to the district attorney. Your cousin verified your statement. But without your prints, I can't eliminate you as a suspect in the murder of Tiffany Pruitt. I'll escort you out."

"You mean I can go?"

"Yes, for now."

Cabrera wasted no time leaving the premises. Allen Joyner called to her as she passed, but she pretended not to hear. He laughed and tossed his empty water bottle into the trash.

Ranger Farrington gave Mints and Lindsey a brief rundown of her interview with Cabrera before going to the waiting area.

"Mr. Joyner," Farrington said. "It's your turn. Follow me, please."

Joyner looked Farrington up and down, leering at her. "I'd follow you anywhere, Baby."

Farrington resisted the urge to body slam the detective. Instead, she showed him to the interrogation room and closed the door.

She went into the observation room and shivered. Frowning, she looked through the two-way glass at Joyner.

"Are you cold?" Wade asked.

"No, but I agree with Maddie. That man is disgusting!"

Waded chuckled and said, "Here come Mints and Lindsey."

"Why am I here again?" asked Joyner.

Mints sat across the table from Joyner. Lindsey stood in the corner, leaning against the wall with his arms crossed.

"We have more questions. You know how that can happen during an investigation," answered Mints. "Your name keeps cropping up."

"My name?"

"You are Allen Joyner, aren't you?" Mints asked, smirking.

Joyner rolled his eyes and said, "Yes, I'm Allen Joyner."

"During our last interview, you said you had been romantically involved with Tiffany Pruitt for two months. She ended the relationship in mid-May. Is that correct?" Mints asked.

"Yes."

"Were you seeing anyone when you met Ms. Pruitt?"

"What does that have to do with anything?"

"Humor me," said Mints.

"Yea, I was seeing a couple of women," admitted Joyner.

"What are their names?"

"Elaine Cabrera and Addie Sims."

"How did you meet these women?" asked Mints.

"I met Elaine and Tiffany at the insurance company where they work. I met Addie while doing business at the bank."

"How long did you go out with Cabrera?"

"I don't know, maybe six months," replied Joyner.

"Why did it end?"

"I started flirting with Tiffany to make Elaine mad. Before long, I was dating Tiffany instead."

"What about Addie Sims?"

"I went out with her for six weeks or so," said Joyner. "She was too flaky for me, so I stopped calling her."

"Would you come to the aid of either of those women if they called?" Mints probed.

"I don't know. It would depend on why they needed my help."

"What if one of them found themselves in a questionable legal situation?"

"And jeopardize my career?" Joyner asked. "No way! I haven't met a woman yet that was worth that."

"We've established that you were home alone at the time of Tiffany Pruitt's death," Mints began. "Where were you on the night of October seventeenth?"

"I was on duty," replied Joyner. "A robbery at one of the convenience stores."

"What about the afternoon of October twenty-second?"

"You're trying to pin Clifton's death on me, aren't you? I'm sorry to burst your bubble. I spent the day visiting my mother in the nursing home."

Joyner gave them the name and address of the nursing home in Wichita Falls.

"Will you consent to be fingerprinted?" asked Mints.

"Why should I?" Joyner answered with a sneer.

"To eliminate you as a suspect," said Mints. "We have prints from one of the crime scenes. If you weren't there, why protest? We can call your superiors if necessary."

"You'll have to get a warrant!"

"It's your decision," said Mints. "We'll let you think it over while we verify your whereabouts at the times in question."

They left Joyner alone and took their time checking his alibis. Both were verified.

"I hate to let that smug jerk go," said Mints. "You do it, Lindsey."

Lindsey grinned at his superior and went to the interrogation room. "Have you decided to be fingerprinted?" he asked Joyner.

"You can take my prints from my cold dead body," Joyner replied. "Until then, you'll need a warrant."

"I'm sure you know that we can't eliminate you as a suspect for the Pruitt murder without them," Lindsey said.

"Either charge me or release me!"

"Right this way," Lindsey said, leading Joyner to the door.

"I still think he's our man," Mints said after Joyner left. "Don't you, Adams?"

"Maybe," Wade replied. "He's arrogant and smug. He's also a womanizer and, as Maddie said, a weasel. But he isn't stupid."

"You may have a point," Mints said, annoyed. "Who do you think it is?"

"I'm leaning toward someone at the bank," Wade replied. "We have four possible suspects working in the same building. They work closely together. We know one of those suspects had access to the car used in two of the murders and probably the first assault on Drew."

"True, true," said Mints nodding his head and looking at the clock. "It's time for lunch. We'll take a break and give Thiele a chance to shake those folks up real good."

"Who do you want to bring in first?" Wade asked.

"The choice is yours," Mints replied. "You've been right so far. I'll trust your instincts."

"In that case," Wade began. "I think we should bring in Garrett Dillingham and Janet Lozano. His wife's car was used, and Lozano was a nursing student at the hospital. We don't want them to compare notes or discuss the interviews with Hallmark or Sims. We'll need to pick those two up before releasing Dillingham and Lozano."

"I like the way you think, Adams," Mints said. "Lindsey and Farrington will pick them up, and I'll do the questioning."

"Fair enough," Wade said. "I like being the fly on the wall."

# CHAPTER TWENTY-FIVE

WADE TOOK advantage of the relative peace and quiet of the lunch break to call Lizzie.

"Hi, Honey."

"Hi, Sweetheart," Lizzie replied. "How are things going?"

"We're making progress," Wade told her. "Maddie was here and said to thank you for the meals."

"I took another to her house this morning. Her dad said she had to make funeral arrangements."

"She's having a hard time with Drew's death," said Wade. "From what Baker told me, I get the impression that she blames herself."

"How could she have known?" asked Lizzie. "There wasn't anything she could have done."

"That's true. How are preparations for the dinner party coming along?"

"We've finished decorating," Lizzie answered. "The tables and chairs are set up. All we have to do now is set the tables and cook the food."

"It sounds like you've got it handled," Wade said. "Which room are you using tonight?"

"The large event room. You should be able to slip in the back door unnoticed."

"That's good. I don't know when I'll be home. We have at least four interrogations before we quit for the day."

"I'll fill a plate and put it in the microwave for you," Lizzie promised.

"Thanks, Honey. I'd better get some lunch. You're making me hungry."

The call ended, and Wade drove to a small restaurant on the edge of town. He wanted time alone to think.

The hostess led Wade to a booth in the corner of the restaurant. The waitress took his order, and he leaned back. He took a deep breath and let his eyes wander over the dining area.

Wade did a double-take when he saw a couple sitting in a booth on the opposite side of the restaurant. A broad grin spread across his face, and he chuckled.

It was at that moment that Reed looked up and saw his boss. His face turned beet red. He grinned and shrugged. Megan Ford leaned over to see what had caught his attention. She smiled and waved.

Wade waved back, enjoying the look on his deputy's face. His meal arrived, and he chuckled between bites until he'd eaten it all.

Reed was waiting for him when Wade returned to the office.

"Sheriff, can I have a word?" he asked.

Wade grinned and asked, "One?"

"Please? In your office?"

Chuckling, Wade led the way to his office. Reed closed the door and looked at Wade red-faced.

"Reed, as your boss, let me start by saying this," Wade began. "What you do and who you see on your own time is not the business of this department, as long as it isn't illegal."

"Thank you, Sheriff," Reed began. "I…"

Wade held up his hand to stop Reed in mid-sentence. "As your friend, I have to ask, are you out of your mind? You know what she's done, what she's capable of doing."

Reed looked at Wade with a sheepish grin. "I know you think I'm crazy. But she really has changed."

"How long have you been seeing her?"

"It's been almost six months," Reed replied. "We became friends while she was in protective custody here at the jail. We were both invited to a mutual friend's barbeque, and we've been going out ever since."

"Why all the secrecy?"

"We've given each other a hard time about Megan for years," Reed replied. "Can you imagine how Baker and Lodge would react? I'd never hear the end of it."

Wade barked with laughter. "You're right. They'll torture you relentlessly."

"The fact that her brother and ex-fiancé work here makes it even more uncomfortable," Reed explained.

"Someone else will find out eventually if you continue seeing her," Wade said. "I suspected something was going on with you two. I didn't know for sure until I saw you today."

"How? We've been careful to keep a low profile?" Reed asked, surprised.

"The familiar voice of a woman who wouldn't leave a message. She keeps showing up here, bringing goodies, and pretending she's here to see Odom. She knows he's on the night shift. Those habits haven't changed."

"Yea, I've talked to her about showing up here," Reed said. "Odom has too. She's stubborn sometimes."

"Sometimes?" Wade asked with a raised eyebrow.

"Okay, she's stubborn most of the time," Reed admitted. "Will you do me a favor?"

"You want me to keep your secret, don't you," Wade said.

Reed nodded.

"All right. I won't say anything," Wade promised. "But you'd better tell them before someone else sees you together."

"I will," Reed said. "It's been fun and kind of exciting sneaking around. But I know it can't last forever. I'll talk to Megan tonight."

"I think that's a good idea," Wade said, chuckling.

"What's so funny?"

"I wish you could have seen your face," Wade replied, enjoying another hearty laugh.

Reed grinned at his boss and left the Sheriff's office. Most of the team had returned from lunch and were waiting for their next assignment.

"Sheriff Adams suggested that we bring in Garret Dillingham and Janet Lozano at the same time. We'll want to keep them separated, so we'll need two vehicles. I'd want Lindsey and Lodge to pick up Dillingham. Farrington and Logsdon will pick up Lozano. I'll interrogate the suspects, and Sheriff Adams will be in the observation room. The rest of you will verify statements and keep things calm out here."

"One more thing," Wade began. "We don't want Dillingham and Lozano to talk with Hallmark and Sims before we finish all four interrogations. The same teams will return the first two suspects and pick up the next two."

"If there aren't any questions?" Mints paused. "Let's get to work."

Both teams left the Sheriff's office at the same time. Lindsey and Lodge went in first. Farrington and Logsdon were to wait until Dillingham was escorted out of the building to pick up Lozano.

"We need to speak with Mr. Dillingham," Lindsey said when he reached the president's office.

Dillingham was leaning over a desk, looking at a set of documents. He stood up and said, "I'm Garrett Dillingham. What can I do for you?"

"I'm Texas Ranger Collin Lindsey, and this is Deputy Lodge. We'd like you to come with us, Sir."

The color drained from Dillingham's face. "Am...am I under...arrest?"

"No, Sir," Lindsey replied. "We need to ask you some questions at the Sheriff's office."

"Can't it wait? We're in the middle of an audit."

"No, Sir. We have a vehicle outside," Lindsey said, leaving no room for debate. "We'll bring you back afterward."

"It seems I have no choice. Janet, refer my calls to Hallmark until I get back," Dillingham said. "Make my apologies and explain the situation to Mr. Thiele."

"Yes, Sir," Janet replied wide-eyed.

Mitchell Hallmark and Addie Sims watched as the officers escorted Garrett Dillingham outside. Their surprise doubled when Farrington and Logsdon approached Janet Lozano.

"Janet Lozano?" asked Farrington.

"Yes?"

"I'm Texas Ranger Cassidy Farrington, and this is Deputy Logsdon. We'd like you to come with us, Ma'am."

"But you just took my boss," Janet replied, afraid. "I have to stay here until he gets back."

"I'm sure someone else can handle things until your return," said Farrington. "We'll bring you back afterward."

Janet looked helplessly at her coworkers and took her purse from a desk drawer.

"Don't worry, Janet," Hallmark said. "We'll take care of things here. Everything will be all right."

Lindsey and Lodge had already gone when Janet Lozano was escorted from the bank. They took their time getting the suspect to the Sheriff's office, so Lozano wouldn't have an opportunity to speak with Dillingham.

Dillingham was seated in the interrogation room when Farrington and Logsdon escorted Lozano to the waiting room. Mints nodded at the young woman as he passed with a folder tucked under his arm.

"Mr. Dillingham," Mints said when he opened the door. "I'm Texas Ranger Dale Mints."

Mints sat down and laid the folder on the table, "I want to talk with you about your wife's car."

"My wife's car? What about it?"

"Do you happen to know where it is at this moment?"

"It's parked in our garage," Dillingham answered, confused.

"When did you last see the car?"

"The day my wife left to take care of her mother," Dillingham replied.

"When was that?"

"Two, no three weeks ago."

"You haven't been in your garage for three weeks?" Mints asked doubtfully.

"No, it's a one-car garage," replied Dillingham. "I park under the carport beside it."

"You've had no reason to go into the garage for the past three weeks?"

"No, I keep my tools in the shed out back. The garage is where my wife keeps her craft and sewing supplies."

"What would you say if I told you that your wife's car is sitting in the Sheriff's department garage as evidence in two, and possibly three murders?"

"No!" Dillingham replied, surprised. "That's impossible."

Mints opened the folder he'd carried in and removed photographs of the Silver Nissan Sentra. He placed them side by side on the table in front of Dillingham.

"Is that your wife's car?"

"Yes, but I don't understand. What happened to it?"

"We found it abandoned on farm-to-market road 1811 yesterday afternoon. We found blood on the front, matching that of a hit-and-run victim. Do you want to know what we found inside?"

Dillingham swallowed hard and said, "I'm afraid to ask."

"We found Tiffany Pruitt's blood and cell phone in the trunk,"

Mints said and sat back, waiting for Dillingham to process the information.

"That can't be," Dillingham said. "My wife has been out of town for weeks. She couldn't have done this."

"What makes you think it was your wife?" Mints probed.

Dillingham hesitated a second too long before answering, "Who else could have done it? The car was in our locked garage, and she has the keys."

"Why would she want to kill Tiffany Pruitt?" Mints asked, watching every move Dillingham made.

"I don't know that she would," Dillingham said, backtracking.

Beads of sweat began to form on Dillingham's forehead. He clasped his hands on the table, but Mints could see them trembling.

"This is what we know," Mints began. "We know your wife hasn't left her mother's side for more than a few hours. That wouldn't be enough time for her to fly to Dallas, drive to Vernon, and get back to the hospital in Orlando, Florida. We also know that you have another key to that car."

"I misplaced my keys the weekend after Lynda left," said Dillingham. "I searched for them all weekend. My bank keys were on the same ring. I had to report the loss the following Monday. All the door locks and secure file locks had to be replaced."

"I assume that can be verified," Mints said.

"Yes," said Dillingham. "I had to have the locks changed at my house too."

"Did you have the lock to the garage changed?"

Dillingham looked at Mints with a shocked expression. "No, it didn't occur to me. Do you think someone took my keys and stole my wife's car?"

"That's a possibility," said Mints. "Back to your wife and Tiffany Pruitt. Why would your wife want to kill Tiffany?"

Neither man said anything for a full sixty seconds. Dillingham finally broke the silence.

"I had a brief affair with Tiffany Pruitt," Dillingham reluctantly admitted. "It ended when my wife found out."

"When did you last see Tiffany?" Mints asked.

"The middle of September, I think. We had a standing date every Thursday. I told my wife I was playing poker with the guys."

"And the last time you spoke with Tiffany?"

"A couple of days after my wife left," said Dillingham. "She was angry that I didn't meet her as planned. I promised we'd meet the following week."

"But you didn't."

"No."

"Did Ms. Pruitt have a pet name for you?"

"Yes, it's rather embarrassing," replied Dillingham. "It was Snuggles. We used pet names and cheap phones so no one would know our identities if our phones were discovered."

"Where were you the night Miss Pruitt died?"

"I was home alone."

"Where were you the evening of October seventeenth?"

"I had dinner at the steakhouse and then went home to call my wife."

"Can anyone verify that?"

"The waitress at the restaurant and my wife," replied Dillingham.

"And where were on the afternoon of the twenty-second?"

"I spent the day with my daughter and son-in-law. We had brunch and watched the Dallas Cowboys."

"I'll need your daughter's name and contact information," said Mints.

Lindsey opened the door and handed Mints a legal pad and pencil. Mints passed them to Dillingham.

"Write down the names and contact information for anyone who can verify your statements," Mints ordered.

Dillingham began to write.

"When you've finished, I'll need your fingerprints."

The suspect stopped and asked, "Why?"

"We found prints at the crime scene," said Mints. "We'll compare your prints with those. If you weren't there, you have nothing to worry about?"

"What happens if I refuse?"

"We can arrest you for suspicion of murder. You won't have a choice about being fingerprinted."

Dillingham finished writing and passed the pad and pencil back to Mints. Mints left the room and closed the door behind him. He handed the information to Lindsey, and the team began verifying Dillingham's statements.

"We have some bad news," Lodge told Mints. "We can't use the fingerprint scanner. The bulb is out. It'll take a week to get a new one."

"Sounds like we'll have to do it the old-fashioned way," Mints replied. "How long will it take to compare and get results back?"

"A couple of hours to a couple of days," said Lodge. "It depends on the quality of the prints."

"Who's the best at obtaining prints?"

"Maddie's the best, but she trained Baker and me."

"One of you will get Dillingham's prints while the rest check his alibi."

"I'll set up the equipment and get started," Lodge said and hurried to his task.

Mints went into the observation booth to speak with Wade. "What do you think?"

"Dillingham is nervous," answered Wade. "He was nervous the first time I spoke with him about Drew's disappearance."

"Do you think he had something to do with it? He says he can account for his whereabouts for two of the three murders."

"I've been thinking about that," said Wade. "There was no evidence of a second person at the Foust crime scene or his house. That part of my theory could be wrong."

"So you think he could have been part of Pruitt's murder and leaving Clifton behind."

"Dillingham is hiding something," Wade said. "It could be Tiffany's murderer or something else."

"He told me about the affair," Mints pointed out.

"His wife already knows. It wasn't a risk."

"Good point."

Lindsey opened the door to the observation room and said, "Dillingham's alibis check out.

"Has Lodge printed him yet?"

"No! Dillingham refused. He wants a lawyer."

"All right," Mints said with a sigh. "Put Dillingham in one of the offices," said Mints. "It's time to talk with Lozano."

Farrington led Janet Lozano into the interrogation room. Wade watched her fidget and bite her nails until Mints entered the room.

Mints introduced himself, sat across from Lozano, and said, "Miss Lozano, I want to ask you a few questions."

"Okay," replied Lozano.

"I understand you were a nursing student at the local college. Is that correct?"

"Yes."

"And part of that training took place at the local hospital, yes?"

"Yes, Sir."

"Were you trained in one hospital department or all of them?"

"All of them."

"Did you graduate?"

"Yes, I'm a registered nurse."

"Why are you working at a bank?"

"I worked at a hospital in Wichita Falls for a year. I realized that it wasn't for me," admitted Lozano. "I couldn't stand seeing people sick and in pain."

"When was the last time you were at this hospital?"

"A few months ago," said Lozano. "My grandmother was ill."

"Where were you on the afternoon of the twenty-second?"

"I was home, watching a movie."

"What movie?"

"It was on the Hallmark channel. I don't remember the name, but it was a mystery."

"Can anyone verify that?"

"No, I was alone."

"Did you know that Mr. Dillingham recently misplaced his keys?" Mints asked

"Yes, I helped him search his office for them," Lozano replied. "I made the call to have the locks replaced."

"What do you think happened to those keys?"

"I don't know," Lozano began. "Mr. Dillingham misplaces things often, but that was the first time he'd lost his keys."

"Did you know Tiffany Pruitt?"

"I don't think so," said Lozano. "We may have met in the past, but I didn't know her."

"Where were you on the night of October twelfth and the morning of October thirteenth?"

"I was home in bed with a virus or the flu," replied Lozano. "I was sick for days."

"Can anyone verify that?"

"No."

"Did you see a doctor?"

"No."

"Where were you the evening of the seventeenth?"

"I was home alone, reading a book," said Lozano annoyed. "No one can verify that either."

"I have a theory about these murders," said Mints. "Would you like to hear it?"

Lozano didn't respond.

"I think you found Dillingham's keys. You took those keys, went to his house, and stole his wife's car. Maybe you took it joyriding, or maybe you had a specific destination. It doesn't matter. Are you with me so far?"

Lozano remained silent.

"You drove past The Watering Hole and saw Tiffany Pruitt staggering across the parking lot. You decided to stop and give her a ride home. But she wasn't the only one needing a ride. You offered a ride to Andrew Clifton as well."

Lozano glared at Mints.

"You drove Pruitt home and followed her inside. The two of you got into an argument. She turned her back on you. You picked up a paperweight and hit her with it. She fell, and you realized she was dead. You panicked and called someone to help you. Who did you call Janet?"

"I didn't call anyone because I wasn't there," Lozano answered, trying to control her temper. "I think I'd like to call my attorney."

"That's your right," said Mints. "You haven't been charged with anything yet."

"I'd still like to call my attorney."

"Would you consent to be fingerprinted?"

"No! Not without my lawyer."

"If we arrest you for suspicion of murder, you'll be fingerprinted anyway."

"I want to call my lawyer," Lozano demanded.

"I'll see what I can do," said Mints as he stood and left the room.

Mints went into the observation room to watch Lozano and talk with Wade.

"Does she fit your profile, Adams?"

"Lozano's smart, and she has a temper," said Wade. "If she's a mystery fanatic, she could know enough to clean up a crime scene."

"She was cool as a cucumber until she lawyered up," said Mints.

"She was nervous before you went in. What do you want to do?"

"We don't have enough evidence to hold either of them,"

admitted Mints. "I'd like to have their prints, but we'll have to arrest them first."

Wade kept quiet while Mints weighed the options.

"We'll let them go and bring in the other two," said Mints. "Maybe one of them will confess."

# CHAPTER TWENTY-SIX

LINDSEY AND LODGE escorted Garrett Dillingham into the bank. Mitchell Hallmark watched Dillingham enter his office and close the door, obviously shaken.

"Mitchell Hallmark, we'd like you to come with us," said Lindsey.

Hallmark didn't argue. He turned to Addie and said, "Take a message if anyone calls. Garrett doesn't look up to talking."

Addie stood and moved toward Dillingham's office. She stopped when she saw Farrington and Logsdon bringing Janet Lozano back.

"Janet, what's going on?" Addie asked.

"Addie Sims, we'd like you to come with us," said Farrington.

"Why? What's happening?"

"We'll discuss it at the Sheriff's office," said Farrington.

Addie glanced at Janet. She stared into space with her hands over her mouth.

"Janet? Are you okay?"

Janet Lozano didn't respond.

"This way, please, Miss Sims," Farrington ordered.

Reluctantly, Addie Sims followed the officers outside. No one spoke during the ride to the sheriff's office.

Farrington escorted Sims to the waiting area and offered the suspect a beverage.

"May I have a coke, please?" Sims asked, her voice quivering.

Mints and Wade watched Hallmark from the observation room. His previous easygoing attitude had been replaced with anxiety.

"I don't see any point in asking for prints, do you?" Mints asked.

"You can ask, but we haven't had any luck with that so far," answered Wade.

"I guess it never hurts to try," said Mints. "Time to find out what Hallmark has to tell us."

Mints opened the door to the interrogation room. He looked at the suspect for a moment before he began. He said nothing until he was comfortable across the table from Mitchell Hallmark.

"Mr. Hallmark, I'm Ranger Dale Mints. I understand you had a disagreement with Andrew Clifton before his disappearance."

"We never had a disagreement," said Hallmark.

"Not even a heated discussion?" Mints probed.

"No."

"I understand the bank is being audited. Is it a standard audit?"

"No, it's a surprise audit," replied Hallmark.

"You didn't know the auditor was coming?"

"We knew, but not when or why?"

"I imagine the bank employees aren't happy about it."

"Audits aren't pleasant," replied Hallmark. " We have nothing to hide, but it's inconvenient and nerve-wracking."

"I'm confused," said Mints. "One of the bank employees over-heard part of an argument between you and Clifton. The employee thought it was about the audit. Could it have been about something else?"

Hallmark didn't respond right away. He seemed to be trying to remember the incident.

"I think I know what that was about," he said. "One of Drew's customers had called to complain about a loan payment that wasn't showing up on his account. We were trying to figure out what had happened. We may have gotten a little loud."

"I see," said Mints. "Where were you when Andrew Clifton was killed?"

"I had my daughter for the weekend," Hallmark replied. "We had lunch, and I drove her back to her mother's."

"And where was that?"

"She lives east of Dallas in Rockwall."

"Were you acquainted with Tiffany Pruitt?"

"I think I met her a few times. She used to come to the bank to see Addie Sims."

"When was the last time you saw Ms. Pruitt?"

"It's been a while, months. I think she and Addie had a falling out."

"Why do you say that?"

"She didn't call to talk with Addie or stop by, so I assumed they had a disagreement."

"Did you ever see Ms. Pruitt outside the bank?"

"Do you mean socially?"

"Yes."

"We may have run into each other, but I can't recall," said Hallmark.

"Where were you the night of the twelfth and the morning of the thirteenth?"

"That was two weeks ago! I don't remember what I was doing yesterday."

"Think about it," said Mints. "It was a Thursday night. The night that Clifton disappeared."

"Oh, right. I can't believe I forgot that," said Hallmark. "I believe I was home trying to repair a leaky faucet. It took most of the night. I remember being exhausted when we heard about Drew."

"Can anyone verify that?"

"No, I live alone."

"Where were you on the evening of the seventeenth?"

"Home, alone. That may have been the night my neighbor and I repaired the fence between us. His dog broke through some rotted pickets and got into my yard."

"Don't you like dogs?"

"Yes, but on other people's property."

"Write down your neighbor's name and address," asked Mints, moving a legal pad toward the suspect and handing him a pen. "I'll also need your ex-wife's information."

Hallmark scribbled the details on the pad and returned the pen to Mints.

"Mr. Hallmark, would you consent to be fingerprinted?"

"Why do you need my prints?"

"We found prints at one of the crime scenes. We can't eliminate you as a suspect without them?"

"One of the crime scenes? How many are there?"

"Four," Mints replied. "Three murders and one attempted murder."

"What? I thought this was about Drew's death."

"Mr. Clifton's murder is one of them," said Mints. "Would you like to hear my theory?"

"Sure, why not?"

"Ms. Pruitt was picked up at a local bar and driven home by someone she thought was a friend. That friend also picked up Andrew Clifton. The friend followed Ms. Pruitt inside. I assume they had an argument, and the friend killed Ms. Pruitt. This friend panicked and called someone for help. Would you happen to be that someone, Mr. Hallmark?"

"I think I should call my attorney," said Hallmark, scowling. "I'll pass on the fingerprints."

"Ranger Lindsey will be here in a moment to escort you to

another room," said Mints. "We'll verify your statements before we return you to the bank."

Mints left Hallmark alone, and Wade watched from the observation room. As soon as the door closed, Hallmark took a deep breath and massaged his forehead. He bounced his leg so quickly that the table began to vibrate.

"Well?" asked Mints when he joined Wade.

"You rattled him," said Wade. "The table would move across the floor if it wasn't bolted down."

"There's Lindsey," Mints observed. "Maybe Sims will be the one to crack."

"Logsdon was in here earlier. She said Sims is out there."

"Out where?"

"Out there, as in strange," said Wade. "Joyner said she was too flaky for him."

"That says something about her," said Mints. "I can't imagine Joyner rejecting any woman."

Farrington opened the door to the interrogation room, and Addie Sims floated inside.

"This is going to be interesting," Mints said, rolling his eyes.

Wade grinned at the Ranger and said, "Good luck!"

Mints closed the door behind him and entered the room next door. "Miss Sims, I'm Ranger Mints. I want to ask you some questions."

"I like questions," said Sims, smiling. "Especially twenty questions. Are we going to play that game?"

"No, but it's similar to twenty questions," Mints said, trying to be patient.

"Ok, what are the rules?"

"There are only two rules. I'll ask the questions, and you'll answer them truthfully."

"Okay, this is going to be fun."

"Were you friends with Tiffany Pruitt?"

"Yes."

"Are you still friends with Ms. Pruitt?"

"No, she's dead."

Mints gritted his teeth and asked, "Were you friends the week before she died?"

"No."

"Why not?"

"She wasn't a nice person," said Sims.

"What did she do?"

"Tiffany started going out with a man that I was seeing."

"Who was that man?"

"It was Allen Joyner, but it doesn't matter anymore."

"Why not?"

"Because Tiffany's dead."

Mints took a deep breath. He was about to try another approach when Lindsey opened the door. He handed Mints a note from Wade.

Mints nodded, put the note in his pocket, and said, "I'll get right to the point. Do you like stories?"

"I love stories," Sims replied, clapping her hands.

"Once upon a time, a girl named Addie saw her friend, Tiffany, in a bar parking lot. She offered Tiffany a ride home. She also offered her coworker Andrew Clifton a ride."

"I like this story," said Sims.

"Addie took Tiffany home. She followed Tiffany into the house. They began to argue. Then Addie grabbed a paperweight and hit Tiffany on the head, killing her."

"I don't think I like this story anymore," said Sims.

"Where were you the night Tiffany Pruitt was killed?" Mints demanded.

Addie's demeanor changed, and Wade could see the anger in her eyes.

"I was out with friends," she replied.

"Can you prove that?"

"I don't have to prove anything," said Sims. "You have to prove that I wasn't."

"Where were you on the seventeenth of this month?"

"At home with my cat."

"Where were you when Drew Clifton was murdered?"

"I went for a drive by myself."

"Were you driving Mrs. Dillingham's car?"

Sims crossed her arms in front of her and raised her chin. "I'm done talking now."

Mints stood and opened the door. "Farrington, would you come in here, please?"

Farrington hurried to the interrogation room and waited for instructions.

"Addie Sims, I'm placing you under arrest for the murders of Tiffany Pruitt, Andrew Clifton, and David Foust. You have the right to remain silent..."

Farrington cuffed Sims while Mints read her rights. She escorted Sims to a holding cell and went to the conference room. Lindsey and Lodge had already taken Hallmark back to the bank.

"Do we have enough to hold her?" asked Farrington.

"No, she was playing us," said Mints. "Adams said I should get tough."

"Well, you certainly did that," said Farrington.

"Adams, what made you think she was acting?" Mints inquired.

"I interviewed her at the bank after Drew disappeared. She was odd, but today was over the top. She reminded me of a movie character."

"She knew we weren't buying her act when I started that story," said Mints. "She stopped the charade and clammed up."

"What's our next move?" asked Lindsey.

"I'd like to talk with Thiele," said Mints. "He may have found the answer for us."

"Could Clifton have been the target all along?" asked Farrington.

"What's on your mind?" asked Mints.

"Suppose Clifton knew more about the issues at the bank than he shared," Farrington began. "He may have known who was responsible and how the transactions were made. But he couldn't prove it. That's why he called Thiele."

"That's logical," said Wade.

"The embezzler hears about Thiele's visit and gets nervous. This person realizes that Clifton knows. He sees Clifton coming out of the bar and decides to take matters into his own hands. Tiffany Pruitt sees him first and gets in the car."

"Okay, keep going," said Mints.

"The embezzler tries to convince Pruitt to help discredit or dispose of Clifton. She refused and ended up dead. Embezzler calls the friend or partner to help dispose of Pruitt's body and discredit Clifton. They left Clifton at the Handley house, believing he'd call for help when he found the body. His prints would be the only ones found. He was seen with Pruitt in the bar. He'd be arrested for the murder, and no one would believe his embezzlement story."

"They might even think he was the embezzler trying to cover his tracks," said Lindsey.

"But Foust came along and ruined the plan," continued Farrington. "He removed Clifton from the scene and tried to blackmail the embezzler. Foust and Clifton were killed because they could identify the embezzler."

"That's a sound theory," said Mints. "Both theories are sound, but pieces are missing. Why was Foust watching Pruitt? Why did he go to the Handleys' house?"

Wade's cell phone rang, interrupting the discussion. He answered and listened before saying, "Lodge will let you in."

Lodge left the meeting and opened the main door. Walker Thiele followed him to the conference room.

"Mr. Thiele, we were just talking about you," said Mints. "Join us, please."

"I'm here for two reasons," Thiele began. "I believe I'll accept your offer of protection, Sheriff. The mood of some of the bank employees is problematic. And I've found the discrepancies Mr. Clifton mentioned, plus several more. Someone is trying to hide the initial activity with sheer volume."

"Do you know who is responsible?" Mints asked.

"Not yet," said Thiele. "I'm going to need assistance from a team of auditors to get to the bottom of this. It could mean disaster for the bank."

"Where are you staying, Mr. Thiele," asked Wade.

"At a hotel near Highway 287 and Highway 70."

"That's where we're staying," said Mints. "The three of us will be happy to protect you at the hotel if the Sheriff will provide protection during the day."

"That can be arranged," said Wade. "What time do you need to be at the bank, Mr. Thiele?"

"The lobby opens at nine and closes at three. I prefer to stay later if someone with a key will stay."

"We'll make sure you get to the bank safely," said Mints.

"One of my deputies will be there and escort you back to your hotel," Wade offered.

"I'll take the watch," volunteered Wagner. "I need to get out of this office."

"Thank you, Wagner," replied Wade.

"Farrington, do you think Miss Sims is ready to talk?" Mints inquired.

"I'll find out," said Farrington and stood to leave.

"I didn't get around to asking about her hospital experience. See if you can get her to discuss that with you."

"Yes, Sir."

Farrington made her way to the holding cell and looked through the door's window. Sims rocked back and forth on her bunk with her arms crossed as if hugging herself.

Farrington opened the door and asked, "How are you doing? Would you like to talk?"

"No! I want a lawyer. Don't I get one phone call?"

"Yes, you do. Would you like to make that call now?"

"Absolutely!"

"I'll be right back," Farrington said, closing the cell door.

"She's not talking and wants to make her phone call," Farrington said when she returned to the conference room.

"It was worth a try," replied Mints. "All right, let Sims make the call."

"Use this," said Wade, handing her a cell phone. "It's handy for situations like this."

Farrington took the phone and went back to the cell. She opened the door and handed the cell phone to Sims.

"You get one call, period. Make it count," Farrington told her.

Sims nodded and began punching numbers. Farrington stood near the door listening.

"Hi, it's me. I've been arrested, and I need a lawyer. I'm at the Wilbarger County Jail. Okay, I'll see you soon."

The call ended, and Farrington retrieved the cell phone. She relocked the cell door and returned to the conference room.

"Who did she call?" asked Mints.

"It wasn't a lawyer," Farrington replied.

"May I see that phone," asked Wade.

Farrington handed him the phone, and Wade looked at the call log.

"Baker, find out who this number belongs to," Wade said and read the number aloud.

Baker went to his computer and returned a few minutes later. "You're not going to believe this. She called Dillingham."

"Do you think he'll get her a lawyer?" asked Lodge.

"We'll have to wait and see," said Mints.

The Texas Ranger escorted Walker Thiele to his hotel. Wade and Reed waited for the attorney that Sims requested. Wade sent Reed home when the night shift arrived, then waited another hour before he left the office and drove to the inn.

The dinner party was in full swing when Wade opened the back door. He went inside and opened the microwave.

He smiled when he saw the meal Lizzie had saved for him. He closed the door and pressed the reheat button. Two minutes later, he took the plate and a bottle of water to the office to eat.

He turned on the television and devoured the food while watching ESPN. He finished his meal and returned the plate to the kitchen. He was about to go back to the office when someone called his name.

"Sheriff Adams! How could you have allowed such a thing?" said an angry woman.

"Pardon me."

"How could you have allowed the bank officers to be hauled away like common criminals? And in front of the customers."

"Who are you?" Wade asked as politely as he could.

"I work at that bank, and I've never been so embarrassed in my life."

"I'm sorry, Ma'am, but I'm not at liberty to discuss an open case," Wade replied. "Especially in my home."

"Well, we want to discuss it!" the woman said and stormed out of the room.

Wade heard Lizzie's voice coming through the hallway. "Mrs. McCardell, there you are. Did you take a wrong turn?"

"I certainly did. Sheriff Adams is in there acting as though nothing happened today."

"The Sheriff is here? Where?" said another woman's voice.

"I'd like to talk to him." said a man's voice.

"Psst, Wade," came a voice from the pantry. "You'd better duck in here."

"Grace? What are you doing?"

"Apparently, something happened at the bank today that those people aren't happy about," Grace replied. "Now that they know you're here, you'd better make yourself scarce."

"This dinner party was for the bank?"

"Not for the bank, but half of them work at the bank."

"Wade? What's going on?" Lizzie asked from their bedroom door.

"Why didn't you tell me this party was for the bank?"

"I didn't know," Lizzie replied. "I booked a dinner party for the McCardells. I had no idea the guest list included bank employees. Besides, it wasn't an issue when I booked the party."

"I'm going back to town," Wade growled. "I can't discuss the case, and I don't want to deal with those people right now."

"Can't you stay in our room?" Lizzie asked.

"With that mob? They'll tear this place apart. I'm out of here."

Wade stormed out of the house and jumped in his truck. He sped away, leaving Lizzie, her guests, and the inn behind. He drove into town without thinking about where he would stay.

*I should have called Lodge. No, he'd want to talk about the case. I'll go to a hotel. But not the one where the Rangers are staying.*

Wade parked in front of a small but reputable hotel. He went inside and asked for the quietest room available.

"Are you in trouble with the wife?" joked the desk clerk.

"Probably, but I'm here because I need a quiet place to think undisturbed. There's too much going on at home."

"Being a weekday, you can take your pick," said the clerk. "If quiet is what you need, I have one on the second floor in the corner right above us."

"How much for tonight?"

"I'll make you a deal," said the clerk. "You can have it for fifty dollars if you send people my way."

"You know my wife runs the Paradise Creek Inn, right?"

"All I'm saying is send the overflow from those big to-do's my way."

"You've got a deal," said Wade.

# CHAPTER TWENTY-SEVEN

WADE WALKED up the stairs and unlocked the door. The room was small but clean, and the bed looked comfortable.

He stretched out on the bed and put his hands behind his head. He closed his eyes and tried to push the incident at the inn out of his mind.

His cell phone rang. He looked at the caller id and declined the call. It wasn't a familiar number, and he was in no mood for telemarketers or complaints.

Focusing on the sound of the heater fan, he tried to clear his mind. Something had been nagging at him all day. Every time it came close to the surface, something happened, and he lost it.

He was in that place between wakefulness and sleep when visions of Lizzie passed through his mind. He knew he should go home or at least call her.

Exhaustion and stubborn pride kept him where he was. He knew if he waited long enough, she'd call him. Pushing thoughts of Lizzie from his mind, he focused again on the heater fan.

At one forty-five in the morning, Wade bolted out of bed. He stood still and listened.

*Was that real or a dream?*

He looked around the room and remembered where he was and why he was there. Realizing he'd been dreaming, he stretched out on the bed again and tried to go back to sleep.

But sleep wouldn't come. That nagging feeling kept him awake.

*The evidence. I need to look at the evidence.*

Wade got up and showered. He wished he had a change of clothes, but these would have to do. He left the room key on the dresser and went downstairs.

"Sheriff? What are you doing here?" asked Odom.

"I can't sleep," said Wade. "This case is giving me nightmares. I thought I'd go through the evidence while there aren't so many distractions."

"Do you want help?" asked Gonzalez.

Wade grinned at his deputies and asked, "Are you bored?"

"Yes," they said in unison.

"This is what I have in mind," Wade began. "I want to look at every piece of evidence from the beginning until now."

"I'll pull up the files," said Odom.

"I'll make a fresh pot of coffee," volunteered Gonzalez.

By the time the day shift arrived, Wade, Odom, and Gonzalez had sifted through every piece of evidence and gone over every statement made concerning the case.

"It looks like somebody's been burning the midnight oil," said Mints when he entered the office.

"Odom and Gonzalez have been a big help," said Wade. "I have an idea we need to discuss."

"The whole team or the two of us?"

"I think the whole team needs to hear this, but we can discuss it alone if you'd prefer."

"All right. We'll gather in the conference room when everyone is here. Wagner will have to hear it later."

Odom and Gonzalez set up the conference room so the evidence photos could be projected onto a screen. Wade finally felt in control of the situation and was ready to start.

"Please take a seat," said Wade. "We have a lot to cover."

The team sat down and gave Wade their attention.

"I've had a feeling that we've missed something for a couple of days," Wade began. "Last night, I couldn't sleep because of it. I decided to go through the evidence again, so I came back to the office. For clarity, we'll use Suspect A and Suspect B again."

"Gonzalez and I helped the sheriff sift through all of the evidence and organize it into three separate categories," said Odom.

"We found one piece of significant evidence at every crime scene," added Gonzalez. "That was the lack of fingerprints except those we were supposed to find."

"That made me realize that the print on the paperweight may be important. It may have been left accidentally or intentionally," said Wade.

"We decided to compare the partial print from the paperweight with those found in Tiffany Pruitt's bedroom," said Odom. "It didn't match."

"However, it did match those found in her son's room," said Gonzalez.

"Are you saying the little boy killed his mother?" asked Logsdon.

"No, we're saying it was left there accidentally," said Wade. "The suspects washed and wiped the entire surface except for that little spot. They missed it and the trace of blood on the paper label."

"Getting fingerprints from the suspects is useless," said Odom. "None of them will match the partial found on the paperweight."

"Next, we went through the tire tracks," said Gonzalez. "We accounted for all of the ones found at the scenes. They either belonged to cars driven by the Handleys or Foust or the Nissan Sentra that belongs to Lynda Dillingham."

"The only thing the tire tracks tell us is which cars were at each scene," said Wade. "The one exception being the hospital."

"Weren't there security cameras on the hospital parking lot?" asked Logsdon.

"There were, but our suspect never appeared on camera," Baker replied.

"There was one type of evidence that we focused on at the beginning of the Pruitt case," Wade continued. "It's the only evidence we can use to tie Suspect A and Suspect B to the crime."

"The shoe prints," said Mints.

"Yes," said Wade. "It isn't an exact science, but it could be enough for an arrest."

"That may help us solve the Pruitt case, but how will it help with the others?" asked Lodge.

"Whoever killed Tiffany Pruitt had to have been responsible for the deaths of Foust and Clifton," said Wade. "There was the possibility that the men could identify at least one of the suspects. Otherwise, there'd be no reason to kill them."

"What about Clifton and the audit?" asked Mints.

"That's what has been bothering me," Wade admitted. "I couldn't figure out why the suspects left Drew in that house rather than killing him."

"That's been bothering me too," said Baker.

"What did you come up with," asked Farrington.

"I think Tiffany's murder could have been an accident or a heat-of-the-moment action," said Wade. "The suspects weren't murderers. They didn't have the stomach to kill someone who was a friend. Incriminate, yes. Get him out of the way, certainly. But kill him, no."

"Then who murdered David Foust and Andrew Clifton?" asked Lindsey.

"Suspects A, B, or both," Wade replied. "They didn't murder anyone until they were afraid they'd be identified. They knew Clifton had seen at least one of them. Foust may have seen both."

"What about the woman on the hospital security video?" asked Reed.

"I believe that was Suspect A," said Wade. "But we don't know that she killed Pruitt or Foust. And we don't know that she shot Drew. It could have been the woman each time, but it also could have been the man."

"And you think this clears things up," said Lodge sarcastically.

"There's one other piece of evidence we haven't found," said Wade. "Where are the keys to the Nissan Sentra?"

"They weren't in or beside the car when we found it," said Baker.

"It's possible whoever stole the car discarded the keys like that gold towel Baker found in the alley," said Wade. "It's also possible one of the suspects has the keys hoping to plant them where we'll find them and incriminate another person."

"They may have already planted those keys," said Mints.

"That's true," said Wade. "But if we use the evidence of the shoe prints and the keys, we should be able to find the truth."

"I'd still like to know why Foust was watching Pruitt," said Lodge.

"So would I, but that information may not be useful," Wade replied. "We need to use what we have to narrow the suspect list and make an arrest."

"I agree with Sheriff Adams," said Mints. "We have to keep after our suspects until we find out what really happened that night. How do you suggest we proceed, Sheriff?"

"We need search warrants giving us access to the suspects' homes, cars, and workplaces," said Wade. "We'll collect all the shoes and look for those keys."

"Who do I need to call for the search warrants?" Mints asked.

"I have the name and number in my office," Wade replied.

With search warrants in hand, the Texas Rangers and the Wilbarger County Sheriff's department went into action. They searched the property of all six suspects before moving to the workplaces.

Rather than taking the shoes from the suspects' feet, the officers used an ink roller and blank paper to get the shoe prints. The search at the bank was the most beneficial.

"Deputy, I need to speak to the Sheriff immediately," Thiele whispered to Wagner.

"He's at the office," Wagner replied. "Would you like to go now?"

"Yes, please."

Wagner escorted Thiele to his truck and drove to the sheriff's office. They went inside and walked directly to Wade's office.

"Mr. Thiele? What can I do for you?"

"I've found something most interesting," said Thiele. "I'm not supposed to remove files from the bank, but considering we're dealing with a criminal offense, I thought it best."

Thiele pulled a stack of papers from his briefcase. Several of the pages were marked with paperclips. Thiele pulled the first page off the stack and showed it to Wade.

"Do you see these alphanumeric codes?" Thiele asked, pointing to a column.

"Yes, are they important?"

"Yes, it turns out they're essential. This particular bank uses alphanumeric codes to identify the users in the system."

"Couldn't someone steal these like passwords are stolen?" asked Wade.

"These codes are assigned to specific computers," explained Thiele. "I doubt anyone knows the code for every computer in the bank."

"So, the code is registered whenever someone uses a computer."

"Yes, what's odd about this is that the highlighted code is assigned to Mr. Clifton's computer."

"Are you saying that Clifton was embezzling?"

"I thought so at first, but then I noticed increased activity from his computer after hours."

"Do you mean after the bank closed or everyone went home?"

"You can see here that no one else was on the computers, and the time stamps show that it was well after everyone had gone home."

"I'm not following," said Wade.

"Mr. Clifton contacted me on this date," Thiele said, pointing to one of the pages. "The after-hours activity began after that."

"Either it was Clifton, or someone wanted it to look like Clifton had been there," said Wade.

"Yes," said Thiele. "What was the date of Mr. Clifton's disappearance?"

"October twelfth."

"I thought so," said Thiele, "I wanted to be sure before showing you this."

Thiele pointed to codes from Drew's computer on October thirteenth.

"Someone used his computer after he went missing," said Wade.

"It stopped that day," said Thiele. "The culprit may have learned of Mr. Clifton's disappearance and stopped using that computer."

"Is this the computer in Mr. Clifton's office?"

"Yes, here it gives a room number so the machine can be located."

"Thank you, Mr. Thiele. This computer person may be our murderer. You may have helped solve the case."

"I should be getting back now," said Thiele.

Wagner shook Thiele's hand and helped him put the stack of papers back in his briefcase.

"Wagner, Mr. Thiele is ready to go back to the bank."

"Yes, Sir."

"And give the team a heads up to dust Drew's office and especially his computer for prints."

"Are you saying fingerprints may be useful after all?"

"Unless somebody wiped that down too."

Wade locked the office door after Wagner and Thiele left. It was a lonely place when everyone else was out on assignment.

He contemplated calling Lizzie until his cell phone rang.

"Adams"

"Sheriff, we found the keys to the Sentra," said Baker.

"Did one of the suspects have them?"

"No, Sir, they were in a big vase beside the teller windows."

"Was anything else in there?"

"Some kind of fake fern thing," replied Baker.

"Bring it all in for processing," said Wade.

"Yes, Sir."

"It's past the lunch hour," Wade said. "Tell everyone I'll have pizza waiting for you."

"That sounds good to me, Sir," said Baker. "I'll tell them."

Wade swallowed his pride and dialed Lizzie's cell phone.

"Hi," Lizzie said. "I was beginning to wonder if I'd hear from you today."

"I'm sorry it took me so long, and I'm sorry about last night," Wade said. "I ended up at the office working most of the night."

"Did you make any progress?"

"Those people from the bank will be even madder today."

"About last night," Lizzie began.

"Honey, I don't want to argue right now," said Wade. "Can we talk about it when I get home?"

"Are you coming home?"

"Of course, I'm coming home. Why wouldn't I?"

"Lately, it seems like it's the last place you want to be," Lizzie replied.

"Lizzie, I love you, and I want to be where ever you are," Wade told her. "Last night was a little overwhelming. I left because I didn't think those people would leave me alone, and I didn't want to disrupt the event more than I already had."

"That wasn't your fault," said Lizzie. "I think Mrs. McCardell was looking for you."

"Well, she found me," said Wade. "Why was Grace hiding in the pantry?"

Lizzie giggled and said, "She wasn't hiding. She was getting more breadsticks for the salad bar."

"Thank her for saving me," Wade said, chuckling.

"Aunt Grace and I were talking, and we think we've come up with a solution."

"Honey, I have to go. We'll talk when I get home. I promise."

The call ended, and Wade helped the team carry the evidence into the building. Boxes labeled with names and addresses were filled with shoes.

"This might take a while," said Wade. "What kind of pizza, and how many should I order?"

"Order one of everything," said Reed. "Large. We're starving."

"You've got it," Wade replied and went to his office to place the order.

"Did you remember to feed Sims?" asked Farrington.

"I did, and she refused it," Wade replied. "She isn't happy that her attorney hasn't been here yet."

"I'll be surprised if one shows up," said Farrington. "Dillingham is about to crumble."

"That's interesting," Wade replied.

"I think the pressure of the audit, the questioning, and the search is too much for him," Farrington continued. "Finding his keys at the bank almost sent him over the edge. Calling a lawyer for Sims isn't on his priority list."

The team had a system in place when the pizza arrived. They compared the shoes to the shape of the shoeprints found. Those that didn't match were returned to the correct box. Those that did went to the lab for size analysis. By late afternoon, three pairs of shoes were identified as matches.

"These match the shoe prints at the Handley house," said Mints holding up two pairs of shoes. "And this pair matches the shoe prints at the Foust scene and the scene at his house."

"Do you think it's enough for a warrant?" asked Wade.

"I don't know," admitted Mints. "It depends on the judge, but I'd like to have more before we make an arrest. Has Baker finished with those keys yet?"

"Not yet," said Wade. "He was helping with the shoe analysis. It shouldn't take him long to find out if there are any prints on them."

Farrington joined the men and said, "Sims is asking questions about a lawyer. What should I tell her?"

"Tell her the truth," said Mints. "We haven't heard from an attorney. Suggest that we can have a public defender assigned to her, but since it's the weekend, it might be Monday before she gets one."

"She's not going to like that," said Farrington. "She's been mellowing, but this might get her going again."

"There's nothing we can do," said Mints.

"I'll try to break it to her gently," said Farrington as she left the room.

Wade's cell phone rang.

"Adams."

Sheriff, the lab tech had a suggestion to give our shoe evidence more weight," said Baker. "Lodge and I would like to go to the scenes to collect soil samples. The tech can compare those with residue on the shoes."

"That sounds like a good idea to me," Wade replied. "Any luck with those keys?"

"There were no prints, but some small fibers were caught in the ring," said Baker. "We might be able to match it to a piece of clothing."

"We may need to use that before we're done," Wade said and ended the call.

"Baker says Dillingham's keys won't help us, but they're going back to the crime scenes."

"Why?" asked Mints.

Wade repeated the information, and Mints agreed that it couldn't hurt.

"Thiele found something interesting," Wade said and told Mints about the meeting.

"You know, I can't figure out if our suspects are really smart or really stupid," said Mints. "The results have been the same either way, but still."

"What do you mean?" Wade asked.

"Pruitt is killed. They wrap her head in a towel and put her in the trunk of a car. Then they clean up the house, take her miles away, and put her in a tanning bed. Why not leave the towel on her or dump it there? Instead, they take it back to her house and toss it away in an alley."

"I see your point," said Wade.

"Then the deal with Foust," Mints continued. "Why give him the money or some of it and then run him over? Why not kill him and be done with it? And where did they get the money for the blackmail?"

"We don't know how much Foust wanted," said Wade. "They might have stolen it or…"

"Or embezzled it!" Mints said, finishing Wade's sentence. "Then the deal with shooting Clifton. Why take off after one shot? Why not make sure he was dead and finish the whole thing."

"I think those are the things that have kept us running from one clue to the next, like a dog looking for a scent," said Lindsey. "By the way, you two have been spending way too much time together."

"Why do you say that?" Mints said with irritation.

"You're starting to finish the Sheriff's sentences."

The men roared with laughter.

"I think we'll wait until the samples Baker and Lodge collect are analyzed before we try to get arrest warrants," said Mints. "We need all we can get for a conviction."

"In that case," Wade began. "I'm going home. I have some apologizing to do. I'll see y'all in the morning.

# CHAPTER TWENTY-EIGHT

WADE DROVE to the flower shop and bought a dozen yellow roses for Lizzie. This apology needed to be special.

He went to the inn rehearsing what he wanted to say and hoped she'd forgive him. He knew he'd been an ass. It wasn't her fault the McCardell woman sought him out.

He parked in his usual spot and got out of the truck. He carried the roses behind his back and walked through the back door.

Granny and Grace were putting away the dinner party decorations while Lizzie and Dan decorated for the anniversary party.

"Wade! Your home!" Lizzie cried and ran to him.

"I brought you something," he said and handed her the bouquet.

"They're beautiful, thank you."

"Can we talk?" asked Wade. "Privately."

"We can take a hint," said Granny. "Come on. We'll see if we missed anything in the event room."

Granny led the way with Grace and Dan close behind.

"Thank you!" Wade called to them as they left the room.

"Lizzie, I'm so sorry about last night. I know it wasn't your fault. I'm sorry about the way I reacted."

"It wasn't entirely your fault either," Lizzie began. "Your reaction was abrupt, but that woman caused it all. I should have kept a better watch on her. She was agitated when she got here. I'm sorry."

"Did you tell him yet?" Granny called from the next room.

"I was about to!" Lizzie shouted back, grinning. "Are we good?"

"We're good," Wade replied. "What are you supposed to tell me?"

"Remember I told you on the phone that we may have a solution to this problem?"

"I'm all ears."

"Can we come in yet!" shouted Granny.

"Yes, come in!"

Granny, Grace, and Dan returned to the dining room.

"Did you tell him?"

"Give me a chance," Lizzie teased.

"Somebody tell me," Wade said, grinning.

"It was Aunt Grace's idea," said Lizzie. "I'll let her tell you."

"There's a hidden room in the cellar," Grace began. "I stayed there last year until you decided to put me in protective custody. Did you ever see it?"

"No, but I remember talking about it. I didn't want to know where it was so I wouldn't have to lie," Wade answered. "What does that have to do with me?"

"We cleaned it up for you," Lizzie said excitedly.

"You'll have a space that's all yours," said Granny. "You can go down there, and no one will ever know."

"I like that idea," said Wade.

"Do you want to see it?" asked Lizzie.

"Yea!"

The small room had been there since before Lois was born. It was so well camouflaged that only those who knew of its existence could find it. They didn't know what its original purpose had been.

Wade looked at the room, amazed. He had no idea the space existed.

"We moved most of this stuff in here last year," Granny told him. "Lizzie added the mini fridge and electronics for you."

A sofa from the cellar sat against one wall with a side table and lamp beside it. A small dresser sat opposite the sofa with a television and blue-ray player on top. A fully stocked mini fridge sat in the corner.

"We can use the alarm system we set up for Grace to let you know when all the guests have gone," said Lizzie.

"How do you like your new man cave?" asked Grace.

"This is awesome!" Wade exclaimed. "I can't believe you did this."

"We should have thought of it sooner," said Granny. "We used this space for storage until last year."

"I know it's small, and it may not be good for every event," said Lizzie. "But do you think this will give you the privacy you need?"

"It's perfect!" said Wade.

"I'll run a cable down here from the satellite," said Dan. "You'll be able to watch tv."

"Thank you," Wade said. "All of you."

"I'm going to talk to Deanna about a man cave when we get married," Dan said.

"Don't do that until you've been married awhile," Granny replied. "She might not appreciate it."

"How is your case going, Wade?" asked Dan.

"We're getting close," Wade replied. "We know who we're after, but we don't have enough evidence yet."

"I heard you made an arrest," said Dan, curious.

"We did, but we haven't filed formal charges. Our evidence is circumstantial and won't hold up."

"What are your options?" asked Lizzie.

"We're combing through evidence and looking for more," said Wade. "There isn't anything else we can do at the moment."

"That's enough shop talk," said Granny. "My stomach is growling. It must be time to eat."

"That sounds good to me," Wade said, rubbing his stomach. "I haven't eaten much since last night."

"I could eat," said Dan.

"We'd better get inside and feed y'all," Grace said.

Lizzie made dinner while Granny and Grace cleared the dining table. Wade and Dan stored the boxes of décor in the cellar and admired the man cave while there.

When dinner was ready, the family sat at the table and enjoyed a hearty meal. They laughed, talked, and teased each other until it was time for dessert.

"This is nice," said Granny. "I love having the family together. All we're missing are James and Ellen."

"When are they supposed to be back?" Wade asked, unsure of the details.

"I'm supposed to meet them at the airport Sunday afternoon," said Grace. "I'll fly to Vegas, and they'll drive the car back."

"I wish you could stay longer," said Granny. "You've hardly seen James and Ellen."

"Well, now that you mention it," Grace began. "I'd like to stay and help with the Halloween parties. I haven't had the time to see any of the local real estate yet."

"That would be wonderful," said Granny. "But don't you need to get back?"

"I don't have anything scheduled, and I can write here," said Grace. "I'd love to stay if that's all right with everybody."

"You can stay here in your old room," said Lizzie.

"I'd like that," Grace replied. "Do you think James and Ellen will mind?"

"Not at all," said Granny. "Have you ever known James to turn down extra help?"

The room filled with laughter. The family enjoyed being together until it was time to say goodnight. They had a busy day ahead of them.

* * *

Wade went to work the next morning feeling better than he had in days. The issues at home had been solved beautifully by Lizzie and her family. Life would be back to normal if they could solve the murders and send the Texas Rangers back to Austin.

He liked all three of the Rangers. They were excellent investigators, and he'd call on them again if needed. Unfortunately, they were beginning to feel like party guests who had overstayed their welcome.

Wade parked his truck and got out. He was about to open the office door when a car with Kansas license plates pulled up. A woman got out and approached him.

"May I help you?" asked Wade.

"I'm Patty Starnes," she replied. "David Foust was my brother."

"We've been expecting you," Wade replied. "I'm Sheriff Adams. We can talk inside."

Wade opened the door for her and followed her into the office. He led her to the conference room and offered her some coffee.

"Yes, coffee would be nice," said Starnes. "With sugar, please."

Mints entered the office as Wade returned with the coffee. He followed Wade into the conference room.

"Mrs. Starnes, this is Texas Ranger Dale Mints," Wade said, handing her the coffee cup and two sugar packets. "He's the lead investigator in your brother's case."

"It's nice to meet you," said Starnes.

"It's a pleasure to meet you as well," said Mints. "I wish it could be under different circumstances."

"So do I," she replied.

"What can you tell us about Mr. Foust," asked Wade. "Any information you can share may help us solve the case."

"I haven't seen him since our mother passed away," Starnes began. "We talked on the phone once or twice a month. He told me he was driving a truck and traveled all the time. I understand that wasn't true."

"No, Ma'am," said Mints. "We haven't found a record of recent employment."

"I can't say I'm surprised," she said. "David didn't like doing things the normal way, or what most people think of as normal. He wanted to get rich quick and dabbled in every scheme imaginable. We took turns tending to mother until she had to go into the nursing home. We agreed that David should get her house when she passed."

"Did Mr. Foust have any friends we can talk with?" asked Mints.

"David was a man of few words," Starnes said, chuckling. "He didn't say anything that wasn't necessary. Our phone conversations seldom lasted more than five minutes. He never mentioned anyone."

"There's some paperwork to do to claim your brother's body," said Wade. "You'll need to identify him first."

Starnes nodded and said, "I'd like to get that part over with if you don't mind."

"We understand," said Mints.

Wade went to the office and called the morgue attendant. He asked for Foust's body to be moved into the viewing area. The attendant notified him when the task was done.

After Patty Starnes identified her brother, Wade led her back to the conference room to complete the paperwork. She completed the forms and waited for her copies.

"I almost forgot," Starnes said, digging in her bag. "This was in my mailbox when I got home. I thought it might be useful."

Wade took the envelope and read its contents. A key was taped to a sheet of paper with a handwritten note.

"What is it?" asked Mints.

"It's a key," Wade replied. "The note gives directions in case something happens to him."

"He must have put something in mother's safe," said Starnes.

"Will you show us that safe?" asked Mints.

"Yes, I want to know what this is about."

"We'll take my truck," said Wade.

Mints explained to Mrs. Starnes that the house was a crime scene and the circumstances that led to that designation. Crime scene tape fluttered in the breeze when they arrived.

Wade opened the door and let Mrs. Starnes go inside first. She wandered through the house, reliving memories in each room.

"Mother kept a safe in her closet," she said, leading them to one of the bedrooms.

Mints opened the closet but saw nothing inside. "Are you sure?"

"David got his secretive nature from our mother. If you'll look in the corner, the carpet is loose. Pull it back."

Mints followed her directions. He pulled the carpet back and found a small trap door beneath. He lifted the door and saw a floor safe.

"Would you like to open it?" he asked Starnes.

"No," she replied. "We emptied it when mother died. Anything you'll find in there belongs to David."

Wade held a pair of rubber gloves and the key for Mints. Taking the gloves, Mints put them on before unlocking the safe. He reached inside and took out a shoe box.

"Let's have a look," Mints said as he moved from the closet to the bed.

He opened the box and found a flash drive and a three-inch by five-inch spiral notebook. Mints flipped the notebook open.

"This is it," Mints exclaimed. "This is what we need to close the case."

"Time to get those warrants?" Wade asked, grinning.

"Mrs. Starnes," said Mints. "Thank you. That shoebox contains the missing pieces to our investigation. Your family and two others will have justice now."

They left Oklaunion and drove back to the Sheriff's office. Patty Starnes left the team to their work, and she had lunch with an old friend.

"What do you think we'll find on this flash drive?" asked Mints.

"More evidence if we're lucky," said Wade.

"Sheriff, the report on the shoes came in," said Baker. "The particles from the men's shoes and the women's high-heeled shoes match the samples from the Handley house. Those from the women's athletic shoes match the samples from the barn where Foust was killed and Foust's home."

"This keeps getting better and better," said Mints.

"Any word on the prints taken from Drew's computer," asked Wade.

"There were prints," Baker replied. "We're trying to determine which were Drew's and which were someone else's."

"We're about to find out what's on this flash drive," said Mints. "You're better at technology. Why don't you get it started?"

Baker took the flash drive and plugged it into his computer. He opened the files, and a video of Tiffany Pruitt's house filled the screen.

"Can you zoom in a little," Wade asked.

Baker obliged, and they could see Tiffany Pruitt and a woman standing in front of the large window. They were obviously arguing. Both women walked away in opposite directions.

Pruitt entered the frame again. She appeared to be shouting and pointing her finger at someone and the door. She moved away when the second woman entered the frame. The suspect threw an object in Pruitt's direction, then disappeared from view.

Pruitt wasn't seen again, but the suspect moved in and out of view. A man arrived and entered the house. The two could be seen moving in and out of the frame. The video ended after several minutes of inactivity.

"That's our proof," said Mints.

"Here's another video," said Baker. "There are photos here too."

"Pull up the video first," Wade requested.

Baker started the video, and they watched the Silver Nissan Sentra leaving the Handley house. The footage showed Foust entering the house and recording each room. Drew slept on the twin bed, and Tiffany's body lay in the tanning bed. The video ended when Foust left the house.

"The video and the pictures have time and date stamps," said Baker.

"What does Foust have to say in that notebook," Wade asked Mints.

Mints flipped the notebook open and gave them the highlights.

"Foust was hired to follow Garrett Dillingham. His wife believed He was having an affair with Pruitt. He lost track of Dillingham and decided to wait to see if he turned up at Pruitt's house."

"Did he?" asked Baker.

"Hold on," Mints replied, reading the pages. "Foust's hand-writing is hard to decipher. Are there pictures of any other men there?"

"No, Sir. Just the suspect," Baker answered.

"He doesn't mention seeing the man he was following," Mints continued. "The next entry is about what we saw in the video. It says it was too quiet, and he wanted a closer look. Then it says the suspects left while he was trying to see into the house. By the time he returned to his car, he'd lost them and decided to go home. He happened upon the car at the Handley house on his way."

"Is there anything about Drew?" asked Wade.

"He talks about his plans to claim a reward or blackmail," said

Mints. "Right here, he says he's found the names of the suspects and plans to approach the woman. Later he says he made contact. She agreed to pay him five hundred thousand dollars in exchange for his silence and Clifton's location."

"We have enough," said Wade. "We shouldn't have any trouble getting the arrest warrants."

"I'll make the call," said Mints. "We'll need copies of this notebook and maybe a transcription."

"I'll take care of that," said Baker. "How many copies should I make?"

"Make a dozen," said Wade. "We can always shred those we don't need later."

"I have an idea," Wade said. "We may be able to use the police department's fingerprint scanner if I ask nicely. It would speed up the booking process."

"Good idea," said Mints. "You know we still don't have enough evidence. We can't prove Suspect A killed Clifton."

"I know," Wade replied. "I want another look at the security video. Baker, can we see the hospital video and Foust's video side by side?"

"I can put them on the big screen in the conference room," Baker suggested. "They'll be easier to compare."

Baker typed in the commands and said, "It's ready to go."

The three men went into the conference room. Baker ran the controls while Wade and Mints gave directions.

"Baker, zoom in on the woman getting on the elevator," said Mints. "That's good right there. Now, zoom in on the woman standing in Pruitt's window."

"It looks like the same woman," said Wade. "The height and build are the same, but I think we need to see her face in the hospital video to get a conviction."

"Okay, Baker. Try zooming in when she's getting off the elevator," said Mints.

Baker zoomed in, and they stared at the image.

"Ohhhh," said Wade, a broad grin spreading across his face.

"What's wrong?" Mints asked.

"Nothing," Wade replied. "I'll be right back. I have to check on something."

Wade left the office without looking back or explaining. Mints and Baker looked at each other confused.

"What did he see?" asked Mints. "Do you see anything?"

"I don't see anything," said Baker.

Wade drove to the flower shop and went inside. The store owner greeted him and asked, "Are you still in trouble?"

"Yes, and no," Wade replied. "My wife speaks to me again, but I still need to apologize to her grandmother."

"What are her favorite flowers?"

"She prefers something that will last," lied Wade. "I want to get her a nice big plant. I saw one yesterday that I think she'd like."

"Which one do you have in mind?"

Wade turned and made a show of looking at all the plants. He snapped a picture of one before he said, "This is it. But before I buy it, I want to make sure that none of her friends have the same plant. You know how it is with older ladies."

"Well, you're in luck," said the store owner. "There is only one other pot like that one. I sold it last week."

"Would you mind telling me who bought the other one?" asked Wade. "I'll never hear the end of it if she sees it at her friend's house."

"Certainly, I can pull up the sale on my computer," said the woman, typing on the keyboard. "It was purchased by a young woman on Friday the twentieth."

"I think I'm safe then," said Wade. "How long do you keep those files on your computer?"

"I keep them here for up to a year and then move them to the cloud. It makes reorders easier."

The phone rang, and the owner said, "I'm sorry I have to answer that. I have a grandbaby due any minute."

"Take your time," Wade replied. "I'm in no rush."

The woman moved away from the computer, leaving the previous sales record on the screen. Wade leaned over and snapped a picture with his cell phone.

"No grandbaby yet," said the store owner when she returned.

Wade paid for his purchase and smiled all the way back to his office.

# CHAPTER TWENTY-NINE

WADE CARRIED the plant he'd purchased into the office, wearing a huge grin. He set it on the desk in front of Mints and waited.

"What's this for?" Mints asked.

Wade moved to a nearby desk and sat down. He propped his feet on the desk and put both hands behind his head. "Evidence," he said at last.

"Evidence?"

"Well, not the plant itself," Wade said. "That pot is exactly like the one our suspect delivered to the hospital. She bought it two days before killing Drew. That pot and this one are the only two in town."

Mints grinned and leaned back. He propped his feet on the desk and mimicked Wade. "Evidence!"

"Sheriff," Lodge said, entering the room. He stared at the two men reclining at the desks and grinning like idiots.

"What can we do for you, Lodge?" asked Wade.

"The warrants are ready. Do you want me to pick them up?"

"Who do we want to talk to first?" asked Mints.

"I think Suspect B should go first," Wade replied. "He might turn on Suspect A and give us more to use."

"That's an excellent idea," said Mints. "Lindsey and I will get him. We'll pick up the warrants on the way."

"The lab called," said Baker. "They've isolated the prints from Clifton's computer. All we need are prints to compare them with."

"Do you want to print him before you bring him in or after?" Wade asked.

"I think before would be best," Mints replied. "I'd rather not move him after he's charged."

"I'll let Fleeks know you're coming," said Wade.

Mints and Lindsey escorted Suspect B into the interrogation room an hour later. They let him sit there alone for a while before questioning him.

Wade manned the observation room again and watched. The suspect appeared to be subdued and resigned. He knew he'd been caught.

Mints entered the room with a folder filled with copies of Foust's photos and notes. Lindsey stood in the corner watching with his arms crossed.

Mints sat down and looked at the man across the table. He opened the folder and spread the pictures so the suspect could see them.

"Tell us what happened the night Tiffany Pruitt died."

Mitchell Hallmark looked at the photographs and hung his head. "I was home asleep when I got a phone call. She was crying, screaming, and begging me to help her. She told me where she was, and I got in my truck and drove over. I never expected to see..."

"What did you see?" asked Mints.

"Tiffany was on the floor. Her hair was bloody, and she wasn't moving. I knew she was dead."

"Then what happened?"

"I must have been in shock," said Hallmark. "I followed orders.

We wrapped Tiffany's head with a towel and put her in the trunk of the car in the driveway. Then we drove out to a house somewhere near Oklaunion. I used the tire iron to open the back door, and we carried Tiffany inside. We undressed her and put her in the tanning bed."

"What about Andrew Clifton?" Mints inquired.

"I didn't know he was in the car until we were outside the city limits," Hallmark replied. "He started snoring in the backseat and scared me half to death. I guess he woke up while we were inside the house. He was trying to get out of the car. I got there in time to keep him from face-planting in the dirt. We drug him inside and put him on a bed until we finished."

"What happened next?"

"I rigged the timer on the tanning bed. I could hear doors opening and closing while I worked. Drew snored so loud I thought the whole county would hear him. Then we left and went back to Tiffany's house to clean up. We didn't want to drag Drew back to the car, so we left him there. We planned to go back for him when we'd finished."

"Why didn't you?"

"We thought he might have woken up and found Tiffany by then. We knew he'd call the Sheriff. We didn't want to be caught there."

"What happened the night of October seventeenth?"

"I don't know," said Hallmark. "You asked me about that last time."

"That's when David Foust was killed," said Mints. "His body was found near the Oklaunion water tower."

"What? I swear I had nothing to do with that. I didn't even know the man."

"That's interesting," said Mints. "The car you drove from Tiffany Pruitt's house to Oklaunion was used to run down and kill David Foust."

"Oh, no, no, no," said Hallmark.

"We believe it was also used when Andrew Clifton was shot."

"I can't believe she'd do something like this. She said Tiffany's death was an accident, but Foust and Clifton couldn't have been accidents. Could they?"

"No, they weren't accidents," said Mints. "Right now, you're facing an accessory to murder charge. That can mean a long jail sentence. If you cooperate, the judge might take that into consideration."

Someone tapped on the door, and Lindsey stepped into the hall. He returned with a note that he handed to Mints. After reading it, Mints slipped it into the folder that contained the photographs.

"Why would this woman call you for help?" Mints asked.

"We've been dating for the past few months," said Hallmark. "I met someone else and broke it off, but she wouldn't let it go. I felt bad about the situation, so I drove over when she needed my help."

"Who were you seeing?"

Hallmark looked at Mints and sighed before he said, "Tiffany Pruitt. We'd only be out a couple of times. She was seeing someone else, but it wasn't going well."

Mints pointed to the suspect's picture and asked, "Is it possible that this woman knew you'd been embezzling and used that information to her advantage?"

Hallmark gaped at Mints before he confessed. "Yes, she caught me on Drew's computer one afternoon when he was out. When Drew started digging, she figured out it was me. She's been holding it over my head ever since."

"I believe that's all we need," said Mints. "For the record, who is the woman in the pictures? The woman you helped move a body and tamper with a crime scene."

"Janet Lozano."

"Thank you, Mr. Hamilton," said Mints. "You'll be escorted to your cell now. I understand you've been read your rights."

Hamilton nodded, and Lindsey escorted him from the room. Mints stepped next door and spoke with Wade.

"I'm surprised he didn't ask for his lawyer this time," Wade said.

"I was, too," said Mints. "I don't think we'll be so lucky with Lozano."

"I sent Logsdon and Farrington to bring her in," Wade said. "I was afraid she'd find out we had Hamilton and disappear."

"That was a good call," said Mints. "It sounds like they're bringing her in now."

"Get your hands off me! I'm not saying anything without my lawyer!"

Mints closed the door to the observation room. The two men watched through the two-way mirror.

"We'll be happy to call your attorney for you," Farrington replied calmly. "Once you're comfortable, I'll need his name and number."

"Her name and number!"

Farrington led Lozano to a chair and wrote down the name and number of her attorney. She closed the door when she left, leaving Lozano alone.

"How are you going to handle her?" Wade asked. "She isn't likely to talk before her lawyer gets here."

"I'm going to let her sit there until the attorney shows up," said Mints. "Then I'll stoke the fire on that temper of hers. Do you need a break?"

"Yea, I could stretch my legs," Wade replied. "I thought I'd call Maddie and give her the news."

"Good idea," Mints replied. "Ask Farrington to release Miss Sims. I'll keep an eye on our guest."

It was half an hour before Lozano's attorney arrived. The isolation did nothing to calm the suspect's temper. Wade and Mints watched while the two conversed in hushed tones.

Mints looked at his watch and said, "If we're going to finish before dinnertime, I'd better get started. Are you ready?"

"Ready when you are," Wade replied.

Mints and Lindsey entered the interrogation room and took their usual places. The elder ranger said nothing as he placed the photographs on the table in front of Lozano and her attorney.

"Tell me what happened that night," Mints said, tapping a photo from the night Tiffany Pruitt died.

"I don't know what you're talking about," Lozano replied.

"Isn't that you in this picture?" Mints prodded.

"It kind of looks like me, but it isn't. I wasn't there."

Mints said nothing while he placed photos of the car in front of Lozano, "We know this car belongs to Mrs. Dillingham. We also know that you drove that car on at least four occasions. How did you get the keys?"

"I didn't," said Lozano, "I've never seen that car in my life."

Next, Mints placed photos from the hospital security feed in front of her. "Why did you kill Andrew Clifton?"

"I didn't," said Lozano. "That's not me."

"Do you remember that theory I told you about the last time we talked?" asked Mints.

Lozano glared at him but said nothing.

"That theory has improved since then. It's leaning heavily toward fact now. Let me share what we've learned."

Mints laid out the whole story for Lozano and her attorney. The attorney kept looking from Mints to Lozano and at the photos while he spoke. Lozano remained silent when he finished.

"All right," said Mints. "It's your right to remain silent. We have everything we need to convict you for all three murders. I wanted to hear your side of the story. I guess we're done here."

"You can't possibly have enough evidence," Lozano sneered.

"Why do you say that?" Mints asked.

"Because I didn't do anything!" Lozano shouted, furious.

"I have proof that you did," said Mints. "Your boyfriend's statement was the icing on the cake."

"What boyfriend?" Lozano said warily.

"We arrested Mitchell Hallmark earlier today," said Mints. "He told us everything."

"That's impossible!" Lozano shouted.

"He confessed to helping you move Pruitt's body and cleaning up the crime scene," Mints poked. "He told us how you met with David Foust and ran over him. He also told us about your plans to get into the hospital to kill Andrew Clifton."

"He's a liar. He wasn't there!" Lozano shouted. "I knew I shouldn't have trusted that idiot!"

"Why don't you tell me what happened?" Mints said. "Start with the car keys."

"Miss Lozano, as your attorney, I advise you not to say anything more."

"Oh, shut up!" Lozano spat. "If I'm going down, I'm taking other people down with me!"

The attorney raised her hands as if to say have it your way and sat back to listen.

"Dillingham would lose his head if it wasn't attached!" Lozano said. "It was always Janet, help me find this or Janet, help me find that. He dropped his keys on the way out one day. He forgot to lock his door at home, so he didn't notice. His wife hired a detective because she thinks he's sleeping with Tiffany Pruitt, but he's moved on to Addie Sims."

"Why didn't you give them back?" Mints prodded.

"My car was in the shop, and I knew his wife was out of town," Lozano said. "When he went to see Addie on Thursday, I went to his house and borrowed the car."

"Then what happened?"

"On my way home, I saw Drew Clifton leaving the bar," said Lozano. "I could tell he was too drunk to drive, so I pulled in to offer him a ride home. Tiffany saw the car and got in. She thought I was Dillingham. Drew got in, and I drove to Tiffany's house."

"Why did you go inside?" Mints asked.

"I knew Mitchell had asked her out. I wanted to reason with her and explain that Mitchell and I had an exclusive relationship. She laughed at me. She laughed at me!"

"And you lost control?" asked Mints.

Lozano nodded and said, "We screamed at each other. Tiffany said she'd see Mitchell whenever she wanted, and there was nothing I could do about it. Then she started poking at me with that long bony, manicured finger and ordered me out of the house. She started to walk away, and I picked up something round and heavy. I threw it, never expecting it to hit her."

"And?"

Lozano was wide-eyed as though she were seeing it all again. "She fell. There was blood on the ball, and her head was bleeding. I checked to see if she was breathing and for a pulse, but she was gone. I knew I couldn't revive her when I saw her head. I panicked and started trying to clean up the blood. I called Mitchell to help. He didn't want to, but I convinced him he should."

"You threatened to expose him for embezzlement, didn't you?"

"How did you know that?" Lozano asked.

"He confessed," Mints said.

"What a moron!" Lozano said. "All he had to do was keep his mouth shut, but nooo!"

"Why did you kill Foust?" Mint asked, bringing her back to the topic.

"He saw what happened and wanted money to keep quiet. I had to take money from the vault. I had no intention of letting him keep it. I wanted the proof he said he had. He laughed when I asked him for it at the drop. He laughed!"

"So, you ran over him and retrieved the money," Mints said.

"Yes."

"Why did you shoot Clifton?"

"I found out where Foust lived and decided to see if he'd left the proof in his house. I didn't expect to find anyone there," said Lozano. "I looked through the window and saw someone looking back at me. I panicked and shot. He fell, and I got out of there. I didn't realize it was Drew until I heard he was in the hospital."

"Then you decided to kill him so he couldn't identify you." Mints concluded.

"Yes," Lozano said. "I liked Drew. I didn't want to kill him. But I had no choice."

"Tell me how you planned it." Mints urged.

"I went to the hospital when I heard he was there. I wanted to see him, to find out if he recognized me. But I couldn't get close. A deputy stood guard at his door. I almost got in during the shift change on Saturday morning. Drew started shouting, and the guard went in to check on him. I knew I could get in if I looked like a hospital employee. I put on my old scrubs and carried a plant with me. I hid in an empty patient room until I saw my opportunity. Drew was weak, but he was awake when I went in. He looked at me, and I knew that he recognized me. I took the pillow from under his head and…and…"

"You smothered your friend," Mints said.

Lozano nodded and began to cry.

"Miss Lozano, Ranger Farrington will escort you to your cell now," Mints told her.

# CHAPTER THIRTY

THE ANNIVERSARY PARTY at the inn was underway when Wade got home. He took advantage of the opportunity to try out his new mancave.

He opened the cellar door and went down the stairs closing the door behind him. Light came through the partially open entrance to his hideaway.

He went inside to find that Lizzie had added a microwave to his domain. Opening the mini fridge, he found she'd also left him a plate of food. He warmed the food in the microwave and cracked open a can of cold beer.

*I could get used to this!*

* * *

On Sunday morning, the Texas Rangers packed their belongings at the hotel and returned to the Sheriff's office once more. They gathered their things and cleared their temporary desks.

"Adams, it's been a pleasure," Mints said, shaking Wade's hand.

"If you ever decide to look into becoming a Texas Ranger, give me a call. We could use a good man like you."

"Thank you," Wade said. "I'm satisfied where I am."

Farrington and Lindsey said their goodbyes and the Rangers were on their way. Lodge managed to get Farrington's phone number before she left.

"Lodge, you look like you have something on your mind," Wade said.

"I have two things on my mind," said Lodge. "Cassidy Farrington and long-distance relationships. Austin is a long way."

Wade laughed and slapped Lodge on the back before he went inside. Life was normal again.

It was a mild sunny day when Andrew Clifton was laid to rest. His family and friends said farewell with a moving tribute that fit his personality.

Brody stood quietly with tears in his eyes. He watched as people filed past, giving their condolences to Maddie and the family.

"Maddie, we're so sorry about Drew," said Ellen Fletcher. "Please call us if you need anything."

"I will, Mrs. Fletcher, thank you."

Baker approached and said, "I'm sorry. I know I can't go back and change what happened. I would if I could."

"You kept your promise," Maddie said. "And helped catch the person who killed Drew. That's enough."

The two deputies hugged before Baker moved away. Wade and Lizzie were next in line.

"Maddie, we're a phone call away if you need us," said Lizzie.

"Thank you, Lizzie," Maddie replied. "You've already done so much."

"Are you going to take some time off?" Wade asked. "You have vacation time coming."

"No, not right now," Maddie replied. "Brody and I need to get back to a daily routine. It'll be different than we're used to, but I think it'll be best for both of us."

\* \* \*

The Halloween parties were a success. Guests wanted to book parties for the following year. James Fletcher's collection of animatronic creatures, ghosts, and goblins had grown to the point that Dan and Lizzie had only one costume change.

The family sat together at the dining table and discussed past and future events. The Halloween parties and Dan's upcoming wedding were at the top of the list.

"I have a suggestion about Halloween," said Grace. "There are so many people wanting to have a party. Why don't you have one big annual event and charge admission? Anyone could come."

"I could buy more creatures," said James with a twinkle in his eye.

"It has the potential to make more money for the inn," said Grace. "You wouldn't have to decorate and redecorate for multiple parties."

"We could run the program once instead of three or four times," added Lizzie.

"I think that's something we should look into," said Dan. "We could have a maze and make it a daylong event."

The family chatted about the idea for several minutes. The subject soon changed to Dan and Deanna's wedding.

"In a few short days, you'll be a married man," Lizzie teased.

"I'm looking forward to it," Dan said.

"I seem to remember you asking me something. Now, what was it?" Wade joked. "Oh yes, have you thought about your honeymoon?"

"Yes," Dan replied, laughing. "Unlike you, I haven't taken care of everything. Deanna wants to stay close enough that we can get back in case her dad's condition declines. We'll go to Dallas and decide what we want to do when we get there."

"Are you nervous? Wade was on his wedding day," James teased.

"Maybe a little," Dan admitted. "I'm sure this marriage will turn out better than the last one."

"On that note, I think it's time to change the subject," said Granny. "Grace has some news."

"I found some land I want to buy," Grace began. "I want to build a house on it for Lizzie and Wade."

"Are you kidding?" Lizzie asked.

"That's too much!" said Wade.

"No, I'm serious," Grace replied. "I've been here long enough to see that living at the inn isn't healthy for newlyweds. The man cave is a temporary fix. It won't help in the warmer months during outdoor events. So I have a proposal. If you don't like it, we'll do something else."

"But Aunt Grace, we don't want you to spend your money on us?" Lizzie protested.

"I think you should hear what she has to say," said James.

"Thank you, Little Brother," Grace said with a smirk.

"All right, we're listening," Wade said.

"I want to move back home," Grace began. "I don't need much space and want to be close to y'all. The two of you need more privacy and space for future additions to the family. The land I'm considering is across the road. Lizzie will be close enough to walk to work. Wade's commute won't change much, but his truck could be parked in a garage shielding it from view."

"That sounds interesting," Wade replied.

"I'll move into the inn and take care of overnight guests," Grace continued. "Lizzie will still be in charge. I'll be the night manager or whatever you want to call me. I can write during the day or when the inn is empty. If it doesn't work out, we can trade living spaces. What do you think?"

"Won't that wipe out your savings?" Lizzie asked.

"I've been wondering about that myself," said James. "How can you afford to do that?"

"I have a feeling there's something that Grace hasn't told us," said Wade.

"You've always been able to see through me, haven't you," Grace said, shaking a finger at him.

"What is it, Grace," Granny demanded.

"It's nothing bad, I promise," Grace replied. "I don't know how you'll feel about this. I'm still not sure how I feel about it."

"Grace, stop stalling."

"Do you remember Jody Ratliff?"

"She was the FBI agent who was killed here last year," Wade answered.

"Yes, she left everything she had to her uncle, Todd Anthony. Her pension, her life insurance, and her father's estate."

"What does that have to do with you?" asked Lizzie.

"If you'll remember, Todd and I were close. He left everything to me," Grace replied. "His pension, life insurance, and the inheritance from his niece."

"What!" everyone said at once.

Grace waited for the news to sink in before she continued. "I hadn't told you before because I wanted to be sure there weren't any other legal claims."

"Are there?" asked Wade.

"There are no other living relatives, stipulations, or legal issues. If Todd had passed away first, Jody's money would have gone to the FBI. Jody and I were both Todd's beneficiaries. Because she passed before Todd, I'm the sole beneficiary."

"What will you do with it all?" asked Ellen.

"I'm planning to donate the property that belonged to Jody's family to an organization that cares for disabled children. I'll keep the money and enjoy my retirement.

"How much money are you talking about?" Granny asked.

"Enough to last a long time."

\* \* \*

Dan stood in his best suit, waiting for his bride to join him under the arch decorated with fall foliage. His dad stood beside him as his best man.

Flameless candles and fall foliage lined the banisters. Deanna walked down the stairs and joined her father. Using a cane for support, Mr. Garnett walked his daughter the rest of the way to the altar. Mrs. Garnett waited for her daughter as matron of honor.

Mrs. Hayes and Mr. Garnett sat with the Fletcher family as they witnessed the marriage. Reverend Stevenson officiated the ceremony.

"Do you, Dan take this woman to be your lawful wedded wife?"

"I do!"

"Do you, Deanna take this man to be your lawful wedded husband?"

"I do!"

"I now pronounce you husband and wife. You may kiss the bride."

The celebration followed immediately after the ceremony with dinner, cake, and champagne. The happy couple drove away in Dan's truck for their brief honeymoon.

\* \* \*

On Monday morning, Reed asked his coworkers to gather in the conference room. He had something he wanted to say.

"Are you sure you want to do this?" Wade asked with a raised brow.

"Yea, it's time," said Reed. "They're going to find out sooner or later anyway. I'd rather get it over with."

"Okay, the floor is yours."

Reed stood and said, "May I have your attention? I have something that I need to tell y'all. Please, hold your comments until I've finished. I won't get through this otherwise."

"Is this going to be a long speech?" Lodge teased.

"No, not long, unexpected," Reed said.

"Are you leaving us?" asked Baker, grinning.

"No, but I'm thinking about it now," Reed retorted. "I've already discussed this with Odom and Wade. Now, it's time the rest of you knew."

"Get on with it before you faint," said Lodge.

"All right, here it is," Reed began. "Megan Ford and I have been dating for a while now. It's going well, and I don't expect anything to change. There I said it!"

"Is that all?" asked Lodge, smirking. "We've known that for a couple of months."

"You have?" Reed asked, astonished.

"Megan isn't exactly what you'd call subtle," said Baker. "Besides, I saw you two together in Wichita Falls."

"Why didn't you say anything?"

"To be honest, we didn't expect it to last long," said Odom. "My sister can be...unpredictable."

"You're telling me we've been sneaking around and hiding our relationship for nothing?" Reed asked, annoyed.

"Pretty much, yea," said Wagner. "Who won the pool?"

"You had a pool!" Reed shouted.

"I won," said Maddie, grinning.

Wade couldn't control himself any longer. He howled with laughter, and the entire team joined in.

The End

Sign up for Dianne's newsletter at diannesmithwick-braden.com for the latest news and announcements about upcoming books. (use the QR code below for a direct link)

If you've enjoyed *Murderous Opportunities,* follow Wade Adams and Lizzie Fletcher in the fall of 2023 with Book Six of the Wilbarger County Series, *Quiet Revenge*

# PREVIEW OF QUIET REVENGE

## Chapter 1

Hulsey and Genavive Gray toddled to their car dressed in their Sunday best. It was a beautiful morning in early March.

"Good morning!" called a passerby from the sidewalk.

Startled, the elderly couple jumped before they turned and replied, "Good morning!"

"I've never noticed anyone jogging around here before," said Hulsey. "Did you see who it was?"

"No, I didn't," replied Genavive, following the jogger with her gaze. "They were too bundled up. It isn't cold enough for a sweat-suit and gloves, let alone a ski mask."

"It might have been colder when they started," said Hulsey. "It's probably a high school kid training for the track team."

"It could be one of our neighbors," Genavive observed, still watching the stranger move down the street.

"Are we going to church, or do you want to stand here gawking all morning?"

Genavive glared at her husband and got into the car without a word. Hulsey got into the driver's seat and carefully backed out of the driveway.

The jogger turned onto the adjoining street and slowed to a walk. At the end of the alley, the runner stretched and waited until the Grays' Ford Focus drove past. The couple would be away for at least an hour. That was more than enough time.

*It was stupid to draw attention to myself like that. I shouldn't have said anything.*

The runner moved down the alley, located the back gate to the Grays' property, and slipped into the backyard. Striding across the lawn to the back door, the intruder found the spare key under an empty planter. Upon entering the house, the aroma of Sunday lunch roasting in the oven made the trespasser's mouth water.

The intruder went to the pantry and opened the door. There were three pint-sized jars of mushrooms lined up front to back on the middle shelf.

Taking a syringe from the sweatshirt pocket, the intruder laid it on the shelf. *Hulsey and Genavive don't deserve this. I wish there were another way. But there are no other possible test subjects.*

Pushing the reservations away, the intruder twisted the band off the front jar and pried the lid up enough to insert the end of the needle. The syringe contents were squeezed into the jar, and the band was replaced.

The intruder left everything as it had been and continued jogging through the neighborhood. *All I have to do now is wait. No one will suspect the truth until it's too late.*

\* \* \*

Brooding in front of the television on Tuesday evening, the jogger was growing anxious. *They ought to be seriously ill by now. What if they're already dead or die in their sleep? How long will it take someone to discover their bodies? What if it wasn't enough? What if it didn't work?*

*Genavive Gray makes beef stroganoff with mushrooms every Monday for dinner. There was enough toxin in the syringe to kill them both. The mushrooms are sure to be blamed.*

The returns for the 2018 primary elections were starting to come in. The jogger tried to focus on the television screen.

Davis Grantham was already leading the race by forty-five percentage points. But it was still early. One percent of the vote had been counted.

Everything hinged on the test results and the election. The best-case scenario would be for the test to be successful and for Grantham to lose. That would allow more time and involve fewer risks.

A win for Grantham meant working quickly and taking more chances. Everything would have to happen at the right time and the right place. Another accidental poisoning will be harder to accomplish while he's campaigning.

The sound of an approaching siren eclipsed the volume of the television. Flashing lights danced through the sheer curtains. The jogger went to the window, stood at the edge, and held the curtain back to see down the street. An ambulance stopped in front of the Grays' house.

*Finally!*

The jogger closed the curtain with an evil smirk and returned to the chair in front of the television.

\* \* \*

Wilbarger County Sheriff Wade Adams drove home with a sense of satisfaction. He and Deputy Gordan Reed had worked out the best possible schedule for the weekend event at the inn.

The Paradise Creek Inn was located on the Fletcher farm in the western part of Wilbarger County, Texas. It was a family business that they all depended on.

As the managing partner, Lizzie's education and experience made the inn successful. James, Ellen, and Lois Fletcher lived a short distance from the inn. They helped with events and routine maintenance.

The inn had been Wade's home since he'd married Lizzie Fletcher eighteen months earlier. The couple decided it was best to begin their life together there.

Wade didn't work late unless he was on a case. But Lizzie often worked long hours and needed to be on-site for overnight guests.

It hadn't been an ideal situation. Issues arose due to the lack of privacy, especially when Wade was in the middle of an investigation.

Wade parked his truck behind the inn and went inside. He opened the door to find Lizzie sitting at the bar, staring into space. The look on his wife's face concerned him.

"What's wrong?" Wade asked.

"I just got off the phone with Mrs. Grantham," Lizzie replied, massaging her temples. "This event is becoming a much bigger headache than we anticipated."

"What do you mean?"

"The guest list for Saturday has doubled and may get even bigger," Lizzie said wide-eyed.

"Isn't that good?" Wade asked, confused. "It could mean new clients and more revenue. Besides, I thought you had everything ready."

"I thought so, too," Lizzie replied. "I've already spent the deposit on food and supplies for a hundred people. I don't have the funds to buy more."

"Oh!" Wade replied, understanding her concern. "What did your folks say?"

"I haven't told them yet," answered Lizzie. "I'd better call them now. We need to talk about how we're going to handle this."

Lizzie picked up her cell phone, and Wade took his phone from his pocket. The security plan would have to be revised. He walked into the bedroom and tapped Reed's number into his phone.

"Reed, our security plan isn't going to cut it," Wade said when his deputy answered. "There may be over two hundred people here Saturday night."

"The two of us can't handle that many!" Reed exclaimed. "We'll need more staff."

"I know," replied Wade. "We may have to ask for volunteers or make it mandatory shifts. Think it over tonight. We'll discuss it in the morning."

The call ended, and Wade returned to the kitchen.

"They'll be here when Daddy comes in from the field," Lizzie told him. "It might be a long night."

"What do you want to do about dinner?"

"I'll make sandwiches or something," Lizzie said, shrugging.

"Why don't you call and order pizza for all of us," Wade suggested. "It should be ready by the time I get back to town."

Lizzie smiled, got up, and walked toward him. Standing on tiptoe, she wrapped her arms around his neck.

"I don't know what I'd do without you, Wade Adams," she said, looking into his green eyes and playing with the dark blonde curls around his collar.

Wade brushed a lock of her red hair from her face with his fingertips and kissed her.

When the kiss ended, he said, "You'd better make that call, and I'd better get moving. Your family could be here any minute."

Lizzie's vivid blue eyes sparkled with mischief. "Are you saying you don't want them to catch us in an embarrassing situation?"

"I'm saying this conversation should be continued in private when we have more time," Wade replied, kissing her passionately, leaving her knees weak.

When he released her, she said breathlessly, "I think you're right. Some things are best discussed without an audience."

Wade grinned and pointed at the cell phone on the bar where Lizzie had left it. "Order the pizza!"

Lizzie obeyed as Wade headed toward the door.

Wade returned to the inn as his in-laws arrived. James helped carry the food and a twelve-pack inside.

"Pizza and beer?" James observed. "This must be serious."

"It is, Daddy," Lizzie replied. "We need to talk."

"Can we eat while we talk?" asked Wade, rubbing his growling belly.

"That's a good idea," James replied. "I'm starved."

"You're always starved," Ellen joked.

"I can't help it," James answered, patting his stomach. "I'm still growing...out."

Everyone laughed as they moved to the dining room.

Wade placed the food and drinks in the center of the table, and everyone made themselves comfortable. They filled their plates and ate a few bites before starting the discussion.

"What's going on?" Ellen asked.

"It's the Grantham event," Lizzie began. "Lesley Grantham has called four times today, making changes and demands."

"What does she want to change?" Lois inquired.

"The original plan was fifty to a hundred guests from Wilbarger County," Lizzie replied. "Now, they're inviting more than two hundred people from the entire thirteenth congressional district."

"We've hosted large events in the past," said James. "This one is a little different, but nothing we can't handle."

"The size of the event isn't my only concern," said Lizzie.

"What else are you worried about?" asked Ellen.

"I usually have weeks to prepare for a big event," Lizzie began. "We have three days to put this together. Three days!"

"It won't be easy, but we can handle it," said James.

"I have a feeling there's more," Ellen observed.

"In addition to increasing the guest list," Lizzie continued. "She now wants a sit-down dinner instead of hors d'oeuvres and cocktails. I spent the deposit last week, and we won't be able to use the food I bought."

"Did you explain that to her?" asked James.

Lizzie nodded and said, "She said to put everything on their tab. She's also booked all the guest rooms."

"We'll have to start from the beginning," said Ellen, feeling Lizzie's stress. "Cooking dinner for at least two hundred people and meals for overnight guests is a huge undertaking on such short notice."

Lizzie nodded and added, "It won't be easy finding wait staff at this late date."

"Does Lesley Grantham realize how much work is involved?" asked Lois.

"I don't think she cares," Lizzie replied. "She's without a doubt the most difficult person I've ever dealt with."

"This situation leaves us open to all sorts of problems," mused James, helping himself to a slice of pizza.

"I know, Daddy," Lizzie answered. "I don't like doing business last minute. There's too much to do in a short time. Something is bound to go wrong."

"Why don't you cancel it?" asked Wade.

"We can't cancel!" Ellen exclaimed. "Lesley Grantham would destroy our reputation in a matter of days."

"Canceling now wouldn't give them time to find another venue," said Lois. "That would be bad for business."

"We'd have to refund their money, too," said James. "We're finally beginning to recover from the fire. Another financial setback could be the end of the Paradise Creek Inn."

"This celebratory fundraiser for Grantham is the most prestigious gathering we've ever hosted," explained Lizzie. "The wealthiest and most influential people in the area have been invited. It could increase awareness and bookings."

"The planning committee meeting on St. Patrick's Day weekend will involve some of the same people," added Lois. "They'll be staying in the guest rooms and using the large event space."

"We don't have to do business with them in the future," James pointed out. "But we committed to this event. We need to make sure it goes well. Bad blood with the Granthams and that group of people could ruin us."

The family nodded and contemplated the consequences while they ate. Everything they'd worked for over the past seven years depended on the success of this event.

Wade took advantage of the conversational lull to lighten the mood. "Your worries will be over if Grantham loses tonight."

"That would solve everything," said James, smiling. "Let's turn on the news and see where he stands."

Lizzie found the remote and turned on the big-screen TV in the dining area. The crawler at the bottom of the screen showed Davis Grantham had a fifty-two percent lead.

"I heard he's favored to win three to one over his nearest opponent," said James.

"It sounds like Grantham will win," said Ellen. "What do we need to do first?"

"I'll have to buy more food, but that will put us over budget," said Lizzie. "I can use the business credit card. That could put us in a financial bind if the Granthams don't pay on time."

"Can you use anything you bought?" asked James concerned.

Lizzie shook her head. "I may be able to return the nonperishable items. I could freeze the rest and use it for the meeting on St. Patrick's Day weekend."

"Unless Mrs. Grantham changes the menu for that, too," Lois grumbled.

"Do we have everything you need for the decorations?" Ellen asked.

"For the most part," said Lizzie. "We'll use the entire inn now. I may have to buy a few more items to decorate the extra space."

"How much food will you need to buy?"

"I'll decide what to return tonight," Lizzie replied. "I'd like to get an early start in the morning. We can start preparing tomorrow afternoon if we finish the shopping before lunch."

"None of that will matter if the menu or guest list is changed again," said James. "I think you should use our credit card. We can make monthly payments if needed."

"May I make a suggestion?" asked Wade.

"We're all ears," said Ellen.

"If Grantham wins, call and finalize the plans before buying anything else. Explain that there isn't time for further changes if she wants the event to be a success."

"That's a good idea, Wade," said Ellen. "That would eliminate the guesswork and relieve some of Lizzie's stress."

"What time is the event supposed to start?" asked Lois.

"At six on Saturday evening," Lizzie replied. "That gives us three full days and most of Saturday."

"In the meantime, we need a plan of attack," said Lois. "I'll stay here tomorrow and answer the phones."

"I'll go with Lizzie to do the shopping," said Ellen. "Two can gather everything faster than one."

"Dan and I will start setting up the stage and moving tables into the large event room. We can help hang decorations, too."

"Don't forget you're supposed to pick up Grace from the airport tomorrow morning," Lois reminded him.

"Oh! That's right," said James. "I'll help Dan when we get back. I may put Grace to work, too."

"Where is Grace staying until she gets settled?" asked Wade.

"She's planning to stay here until her apartment is ready," said Lizzie. "That could be a couple of weeks. She'll have to stay somewhere else this weekend."

"We can make room for her," Ellen replied.

The family finished their meal while they discussed the upcoming event and Grace's arrival. They were cleaning up when the office phone rang.

"I hope that isn't Lesley Grantham again," Lizzie said as she left the room.

She returned a moment later and said, "It's for you, Granny."

"For me? Why would anyone call me here at this hour?"

Lois went to the office perplexed. She returned a short time later with tears in her eyes.

"What's wrong, Mom?" James asked, alarmed.

"That was the hospital. Genavive is seriously ill, and Hulsey passed away."

"I'm so sorry, Granny," Lizzie said.

"What happened?" asked Ellen.

"The nurse I spoke with didn't know," Lois answered, crying. "They came by ambulance and were both admitted. Genavive is stable, but they couldn't save Hulsey."

"Who are Genavive and Hulsey?" Wade asked.

"Hulsey is Mom's cousin," said James. "Their mothers were sisters. Genavive is his wife."

"Were they in bad health?" asked Wade, concerned.

"I don't think so," replied Lois. "They're a few years older than I am and don't get out much. They've started running tests on Genavive."

"Is there anything we can do?" asked Lizzie.

"You have enough to deal with," Lois answered. "But I need to go see her tomorrow."

"You go with Lizzie in the morning. I'll stay and answer the phones," Ellen suggested.

"Granny, I'll handle the shopping," said Lizzie. "You can stay with Genavive."

"Won't you need help to finish by noon?"

"I'll come get you if I do," Lizzie promised.

"We have a lot of work ahead of us," Ellen began. "And Lizzie needs to make her list."

"We'll be here by eight," Lois said, hugging her granddaughter goodnight.

"See you in the morning," Lizzie said.

After the family had gone, Wade cleared his throat and said, "I think we should table our earlier discussion under the circumstances."

Lizzie moved toward Wade and snuggled against his chest. "I do have a lot of work to do before morning. Is it wrong to hope that Davis Grantham loses tonight?"

"Not considering the circumstances," said Wade. "Good night, Sweetheart."

"Goodnight," Lizzie replied, kissing her husband.

After Wade went to bed, Lizzie went to the office and sat at her desk. She opened a spreadsheet on the computer and added the requested menu items to the shopping list.

*I should be able to get all of this in Vernon. If not, I'll make a quick trip to Wichita Falls.*

Lizzie worked until midnight. She made her new shopping list and decided what decorations needed to be changed. Satisfied, she crawled under the covers beside Wade and drifted off.

At four, Lizzie sat up in bed and screamed, jolting Wade from a sound sleep.

"Lizzie, what's wrong?" he asked, confused.

He wrapped her in his arms and gently rocked her. She sobbed in his embrace. Tears ran down her face and dripped onto his bare chest.

"It's okay, Honey," he soothed. "It was just a bad dream."

"It was horrible!" Lizzie cried.

"Shhh, it was a bad dream," Wade assured her, his heart still racing. "Everything's fine. There's nothing to worry about. Try to go back to sleep."

"I have a terrible feeling," said Lizzie between sobs. "Something awful is about to happen."

To continue reading *Quiet Revenge*, scan the QR code below.

# ABOUT THE AUTHOR

Dianne Smithwick-Braden is an avid reader of fiction but mysteries are by far her favorite genre. It seemed only natural that her own novels would be mysteries.

The Wilbarger County Series is set near Dianne's home town of Vernon, Texas. She was raised on the family farm in the western part of Wilbarger County. She graduated from Vernon High School in 1979.

Dianne currently lives in Amarillo, Texas with her husband, Richard.

Please take a few moments to rate and/or review this book. Dianne would love to know what you think.

Subscribe to Dianne's monthly newsletter at www.diannesmith-wick-braden.com.

# ALSO BY DIANNE SMITHWICK-BRADEN

*Coded for Murder*

## The Wilbarger County Series

*Death on Paradise Creek (Book One)*

*Death under a Full Moon (Book Two)*

*Flames of Wilbarger County (Book Three)*

*Gambling with Murder (Book Four)*

*Murderous Opportunities (Book Five)*

*Quiet Revenge (Book Six)*

**Subscribe to Dianne's newsletter at:**

www.diannesmithwick-braden.com

**Follow Dianne at:**

www.facebook.com/smithwickbraden

www.instagram.com/smithwickbraden

twitter.com/smithwickbraden

www.pinterest.com/smithwickbraden

www.goodreads.com

bookbub.com

www.ingramcontent.com/pod-product-compliance
Lightning Source LLC
Chambersburg PA
CBHW070403260626
47161CB00001B/256